tomorrow's lies

tomorrow's lies

S. R. GREY

This is a work of fiction. Names, characters, places, and incidents are products of the author's imagination or are used fictitiously and are not considered to be real. Any resemblance to actual events, locales, organizations, or persons, living or dead, is entirely coincidental.

Tomorrow's Lies
Copyright © 2015 by S.R. Grey

All rights reserved. No part of this book may be used or reproduced in any manner whatsoever without written permission, except in the case of brief quotations embodied in critical articles and reviews.

ISBN-10: 098615654X (e-book version)
ISBN-13: 978-0-9861565-4-0 (e-book version)

ISBN-10: 0986156558 (print version)
ISBN-13: 978-0-9861565-5-7 (print version)

Editing: Hot Tree Editing
Cover Design: ©Hang Le
Formatting: E.M. Tippetts Book Designs

E.M. TIPPETTS BOOK DESIGNS

emtippettsbookdesigns.com

Other Books By
S.R. GREY

Judge Me Not series
I Stand Before You
Never Doubt Me
Just Let Me Love You

Inevitability duology
Inevitable Detour
Inevitable Circumstances

A Harbour Falls Mystery trilogy
Harbour Falls
Willow Point
Wickingham Way

Laid Bare novella series
Exposed: Laid Bare 1
Unveiled: Laid Bare 2
Spellbound: Laid Bare 3

Author's Note

Thank you for taking this journey with me. Flynn and Jaynie's story is fictional, but there are all too many real stories of abuse in the foster care system. Thank you to those individuals I spoke with, who shared their own experiences so readily. This story is for you and for all the children who have no voice.

Prologue

Jaynie
(Present Day ~ October)

"Jump," Flynn says.

I stare down at the swiftly moving river. "I can't, I can't," I cry.

"You have to, Jaynie."

From where we stand, on the edge of a cliff made of sandstone streaked with iron and copper, the water, black as night, scares me. Ink swirling in a bottomless well and I'm supposed to jump in?

I toss a glance back to the forest, and Flynn sighs. He knows what I'm thinking. "There's no going back, Jaynie," he says softly. "The only choice now is to move forward."

The cliff, the water, jumping in. He *is* right. Still… "I'm scared," I confess.

Flynn blows out a breath. "I know, sweetheart."

Soft, understanding, Flynn always gets me.

Tomorrow's Lies

Regrets, the likes of which I've never known, wash over me, and I want nothing more than to turn back the hands of time and start this day over. The girl I was this morning, she is no more. That frightens me. Scarier still is who I may become if I leave Flynn. A lump forms in my throat at the thought.

"I changed my mind," I declare, shaking my head. "We shouldn't separate, Flynn." I tug on his arm, urging him to retreat with me as I take two steps away from the edge.

It's a move born of desperation, a last ditch attempt to pretend we're not in the situation we're in. But my delusion is short-lived. Flynn's expression tells me all I need to know. Going back, at least for me, is no longer an option.

"What if I never see you again?" I whisper.

"You'll see me soon enough." He doesn't sound so certain, and that scares the hell out of me.

"I'm out of here," I say.

When I start to walk away, Flynn grabs my arm. "Where do you plan to go, Jaynie?"

"With you, of course. Back to the house."

His grip tightens. "Uh, I don't think so."

He's right, but still, I try to slip away. My resistance is futile. One tug and Flynn has me snuggled in close to him. "Flynn…"

This is good, this is home, and I can't help but relax against him. I'd like to stay this way all night, my back pressed to Flynn's firm chest, my heart brimming full with his love.

Leaning down to whisper in my ear, Flynn gently nudges me back to reality when he says, "No changing the plan. You're leaving this place, today, now. This is me, Jaynie, making sure you're never in danger again."

And that's it for me. My walls crumble and I start to cry. "Please, no. Don't make me go. I don't think I'll make it without you."

Flynn's warm breaths, soft caresses on the back of my neck, send shivers down my spine, especially when he chants my name, like a prayer. "Jaynie, Jaynie." And then, "You're stronger than you think. You can do anything you put your mind to."

I let out a derisive snort. "You believe in me *way* too much, Flynn."

"Nah, you don't believe in yourself enough. You never have, babe. You keep forgetting who you were when you first got here."

"I remember." *How could I forget?*

"Then you know how far you've come."

"Until tonight, Flynn. Tonight I screwed everything up." My voice cracks as I continue. "I failed myself. I couldn't hold it together, and I ended up failing *us*."

"Shh..." He walks me forward till we're back at the cliff's edge.

"The abyss," I murmur, looking down. *Still inky, still black, still scary as hell.* "You can't make me jump into that nothingness, Flynn."

"No, I can't make you. But you will jump."

I let out a scoffing noise, and press back into him.

His hands tightening at my waist, he says, "You want to know why I'm so sure you'll go?"

"Yes. Why?"

"Because, Jaynie." I feel his chin against my head as he nods to the water. "It's not 'nothingness' down there. That river is your way out."

I almost jump, right there and then, but panic overcomes me. I spin away from Flynn's grasp and come dangerously close to falling over the edge in the process. "Jaynie, Jesus," I hear Flynn say.

Shaken up, I move away from him, insisting the whole while, "I'm good, I'm good."

Yeah, right. I'm not anywhere near being okay.

As I back farther away from the cliff's edge, my heels digging into the soft earth, I try reasoning. With myself, with Flynn, I don't know. I guess with us both.

"I don't think I can go, Flynn. I really don't think I can."

He sighs, and I can tell he's gearing up to get me back to where I was. "Jaynie, come on."

Dirt cooled by the shortened days of fall squishes up between my toes, reminding me how rushed we were tonight. Suddenly, I have the most brilliant idea.

With a flourish of my hands, gesturing to my bare feet, I say as evenly as I can, "I forgot to put on my shoes before we left. I can't go without shoes, Flynn."

Flynn steps toward me, carefully, the way someone might approach a spooked animal.

"Shoes would just weigh you down, Jaynie. Better you left them behind. Swimming will actually be a whole lot easier this way."

I shake my head, the gravity of the situation we're in fully catching up to me. "I don't know, Flynn." I cover my face with my hands. "I don't know, I don't know. I don't know anything anymore."

But I do. The problem is I know too much. And that's what's killing me. This is the end—the end of my time with Flynn in this place, the end of easy smiles on warm summer days, the end of the family I cobbled together. But hardest of all to accept is this is the end of Flynn loving me. No one has ever loved me the way he has.

My heart breaks and I can almost see the shards of what's left of me falling away in the darkness.

"How can you let me go?" I sob.

Flynn yanks me to him, and I struggle to break free. But in the end, he wins. Holding me to him tightly, he buries his face against my neck.

Suddenly, I am angrier with him than I've ever been in the past. I try to shove him away—to no avail.

"How can you let *us* go?" I want to know, breathless and panting.

When he doesn't reply, I try to step back so he'll have no choice but to look me in the eye.

Flynn is far stronger, though, and easily holds me in place.

"Please…just…stop," he whispers, voice cracking.

I stop struggling. This is hard on Flynn, too.

He squeezes my hip gently. "Be strong for both of us," he whispers. "The past is behind you. Your future is away from here." He finally lifts his head, eyes glistening with unshed tears as he nods to the river. "This is your chance to get away from all this bad."

But it's also me getting away from all that was good, I long to say. Instead, I simply ask, "What about you?"

"I told you before I'll be fine. I always am."

"I love you, Flynn."

A whir of wind kicks up and I fear my words are lost. Flynn hears me, as he always does. "I love you, too," he replies.

Sliding his hands up from my hips—carefully, so as to avoid the areas where I've been bruised—he murmurs wistfully, "You always look so beautiful in this dress."

"Even tonight?"

"Especially tonight."

Strong hands trail over white cotton worn to sheer in some spots. Those are the places I feel Flynn's warmth the best.

After a minute, he wraps his arms around me and we rock together. A slow back and forth, a final dance of sorts, one intended to soothe our broken souls.

Lips brushing over my ear, Flynn whispers, "Jaynie-bird. You'll always be my Jaynie-bird."

I smile. Flynn called me Jaynie-bird only once before. We were getting to know one another, and, ironically, we were standing in the same spot as we are now. I had told him if I had one wish it would be to fly away. *Away from this place, away from the pain*. Flynn promised me then that someday it would happen—I would fly away. But he was always supposed to go with me. This, this leaving without him was never an option, never a consideration. Not for me, at least. Doesn't he realize I can't do *this*—leave and possibly go live my life without him?

"I don't think I can live without you, Flynn," I confess, cramming all my fears into nine little words.

"You have to, baby, at least for a little while."

"No, Flynn. I don't like this one bit. What if things go wrong?"

"Just follow the original plan. Stop in the next town. Get yourself set up. Wait for me, okay? I'll be along when I can. You'll see. We'll be back together in no time."

"Yeah, that's the plan," I state flatly.

Disheartened doesn't even begin to cover the way I feel. Plans are great and all, but Flynn and I both know the truth. He may never make it out of here. Not with what occurred earlier tonight.

I choke back a sob, and he reminds me, "There's no other way, Jaynie. Not after—"

I press a finger to his lips. "Don't say it, Flynn. Don't say anything more."

He doesn't.

Eventually we join hands. Peering down at our solidarity, I am amazed that even in the black heart of a black night the bloodstains on our hands are still visible. Blood doesn't wash off so easily, and the night doesn't hide it so well. Maybe it shouldn't.

I shudder. No, I can't think about how those bloodstains led us here. So, instead, I focus on Flynn. Tall and strong, sandy brown hair as messy as ever, eyes as gray as the stormy day I met him.

"Jaynie," Flynn says when he sees me drifting off to a past we can no longer dwell on. "It's time to go. We can't stay here forever."

"I know."

"One of us *has* to make it out of here. If not, everything that happened earlier will have been in vain."

My heart constricts. "These things we've done and can't undo."

"Jaynie, don't."

I throw my arms around him and hold onto the love of my life one final time. I sob a good-bye I can't fully articulate, but he gets it. When we rock back on our heels, Flynn wraps a long strand of my hair around his hand. Raising the auburn tress to his nose, he takes a whiff and closes his eyes.

Smiling around a sniffle, I ask, "What in the world are you doing?"

"Breathing you in," he replies. "I'm making you a part of the air in my lungs."

He's also trying to lighten the mood to make this easier on me.

"There." He lets go of my hair. "I think you're in there pretty good now."

"Stop," I mutter.

Our eyes meet and smiles falter. We then literally fall into each other, sharing an embrace tinged with the desperation of knowing this will be our last night *ever* in this forest.

These woods have offered us refuge so many times in the past. This was a place to get away from all the bad down at the house. I'll miss these woods where Flynn and I shared so much. Naked and bare, in more ways than one, nestled in the bosom of the land, secrets were spilled like blood across the forest floor. We've loved and healed up here, away from prying eyes. Secrets remain safe here. We could share what we did tonight, and the forest would never tell a soul.

We say nothing, though. There will be no confessions, not on this night.

What was it my mother, whom I haven't seen in four years, used to say? *The times they are a-changin', Jaynie.*

A shiver runs through me, and Flynn leans back so he can see my face. "What are you thinking about?" he asks.

"I'm thinking again that maybe I should stay."

"No." His voice is firm now. He's tiring of this back-and-forth. "We agreed if it ever came down to only one of us getting out, it would be you. We agreed to save *you*, Jaynie."

"But we never imagined—"

"No, we didn't."

"So—"

"Jaynie, *no*. No more stalling, no more putting off the inevitable."

Flynn moves farther away, giving himself more space. Still, it's not enough and he can't stop touching me.

Placing a calloused finger to my lips, he says, "We're out of time, babe."

I grab his hand and slide it up to my cheek. Memories of how Flynn's fingers feel pressed to other places on my body come to mind. And then I am reminded it's all about to end. "No," I whisper.

With care, Flynn lifts a strand of my hair and tucks it behind my ear.

My heart aches at the reminder of how I was first touched by him. It seems so long ago. "Flynn—"

"Jaynie, go. Please. Just leave."

I stare at him, taking him in one final time. Full lips, straight nose, the little crescent-shaped scar below one eye. I memorize it all. Placing my hands on his wide shoulders, I look up at a boy who became a man before my very eyes. Taller and stronger than the day I first met him, muscles more corded and defined, Flynn is formidable to someone like me. Next to him, I am a waif. And I am all too happy to break beneath him. I do so now, as I've done so many times before.

"I thought you were beautiful the day I met you," I confess. "But you're so much more than that." I tap his chest. "Your most beautiful places are in here." I choke back a sob. "You've helped me so much. Flynn. I was such a mess."

Tucking another strand of unruly hair behind my ear, he smiles sadly. "Quit thinking about the past. No more looking back, okay?"

"What if I don't make it, Flynn? I mean the fall, the water."

Tears form in his eyes. "You will," he whispers, like saying the words will make them come true.

I nod, because what else can I do? We don't think the fall will kill me, but you never know. In case we're wrong, I drink him in. His cheekbones are too sharp from not getting enough to eat—*never enough food, never enough of anything*—and the fine sprinkling of freckles across his nose are barely visible now that he's practically a man.

"What are you doing, Jaynie?" he asks, smiling.

I lift my hand and trace his lips with tentative fingers. "I'm trying to memorize everything about you. I don't want to forget a single thing."

Flynn snorts, "Fuck that."

His lips crash into mine, and I realize this is what I've wanted all along, to get lost, to forget everything. Losing myself with Flynn is always easy, especially when his lips are on mine. Hell, he sure doesn't kiss like an eighteen-year-old guy. He kisses like a fully grown man, lips and tongue moving with a skill far beyond his years.

When he finally drops back, I grab hold of his shirt. "Promise me you'll be all right. Swear to me this will all turn out okay."

Tears flow down my cheeks unchecked, hot and burning. Not he, nor I, can stop them. Not tonight.

"I promise," he says.

"Swear to me we'll meet where we said we would, as soon as you can get away."

"I swear."

"Don't you dare go and forget about me, Flynn O'Neill."

"Like that would ever be possible," he says, chuckling. But then he, too, is choking back tears. "I promise you, Jaynie Cumberland, I will *never* forget about you. You are burned in my soul."

"Mine, too," I say.

"We'll meet, like we planned, as soon as things settle down. I promise you, a thousand times, okay?"

"Today's promises are nothing but tomorrow's lies. Isn't that what you once told me?"

He looks stunned. "I didn't mean for it to ever apply to us, Jaynie."

"But it could. We can't predict the future."

"Stop it."

His voice is a plea, and I back off.

"You'll find me, then?"

"Yes, of course."

"Say it again."

"Jaynie, enough."

Scrubbing his hands down his face, he tilts back his head and stares up at the starless night. His eyes are wet and glistening. Flynn is breaking right along with me. One last time, he tangles his hand in my hair, pulling and grasping, yanking me to him. This letting go is killing him, too.

"Nothing will *ever* keep me from you," he hisses, forehead pressed to mine.

"But what about what I've done?"

He steps back, eyes flashing. "Don't say it like that. It's what *we've* done, not just you."

"No, Flynn. I did it. It was all me."

Sighing, he says, "It doesn't matter. It was justice for what we lost."

Something squeezes my heart, making me choke out, "Oh, Flynn—"

"Don't think about it, Jaynie. Just go."

He turns me to the water. There is no going back, not this time.

I close my eyes.

Then I jump.

...And I am falling...

　...falling...

　　...falling...

　　　...falling...

Chapter One

Flynn
(Five years earlier)

"Flynn O'Neill!" a deep voice bellows.

My dad, waking me from a dead sleep—a routine that sadly has become more common than not.

"You get your no-good ass out to this living room right now," he continues. "And bring that little shit of a brother with you."

The walls are thin in this, our latest apartment, and I can hear, clear as a bell, the *whish* of a belt being drawn through pant loops.

Shit, Dad's been drinking . . . again.

My little brother doesn't miss the ominous sound and he cowers closer to me on the mattress we share. "No, no, no," he cries. "Flynn, what are we going to do?"

I wish I knew. This shit with our father started shortly after our mom was killed in a car accident last year. What should I tell Galen tonight? *Learn to live with the fear, kid, there's no end in sight?* Um, yeah, no, I don't think so.

"We'll be okay," I say to my kid brother.

Out in the living room, Dad strikes the belt against a piece of furniture—the fake leather sofa. "I don't think we'll be okay," Galen says.

Another strike, such a sickly sound, kind of slick and dark, like what it is—a promise of the pain to come when Dad's belt meets all-too-real skin.

Galen jumps up from our bed and inadvertently throws his ratty blanket in my face. I swat it away as he bolts to a closet in the corner of the room, screaming the whole way, "Flynn, hide me! Tell Dad I ran away or something. Anything, please. Just make him go away."

I sit up, watching as Galen wedges his tiny seven-year-old body beneath the hanging clothes. In this house, the monsters are not *in* the closet. They exist outside of it.

"Where are you little fuckers?" Dad yells, fists pounding on the closed and locked bedroom door. "If I have to break this door down to get to you two, it ain't gonna be pretty."

Galen hisses in a terrified breath, and I assure him, "Don't worry. I got this covered, little dude."

I take the beatings for my brother when I can. Dad sometimes grabs hold of Galen, despite my best efforts to prevent that from happening. Our father is surprisingly fast when he's drunk. But before he can get more than a few licks in on my brother, I'm always quick to blurt out a smartass retort that turns the heat back on me.

I'll do anything to save Galen from pain.

Setting my brother's faded blue blanket aside, I stand and tug my T-shirt up over my head. It's the usual drill. One time, I was careless and left a shirt on. After Dad was through with me that thing was nothing but a bloodied and ruined rag. I don't have too many clothes, so bare on top is the only way to go. Underwear can stay. Dad doesn't generally hit below the belt.

Galen continues to cower in the closet, staring out at me, watching fearfully. Two dark saucers meet my gaze. His eyes are the same color as mine, gray, but tonight they are dilated in terror, making them appear as black as the night.

"You're still hurt, Flynn," Galen says, worried. He points to three purplish welts, two on my right shoulder and one on my chest. "Don't go out there, okay?"

"I'm fine," I assure him, sounding far more confident than I feel. "I can handle a few more bumps and bruises."

I have to. It's me or the kid.

Galen sniffles, eyeing me warily. He knows I'm bullshitting him. He's young, but he's well-aware a twelve-year-old kid shouldn't have oozing welts, especially not ones doled out by his own father.

My little brother suddenly squeezes his eyes shut and shoves his thumb in his mouth. Fucking Dad has his youngest reverting back to toddler behavior.

I walk over to the closet and kneel down on the worn wooden floor in front of Galen. "Hey, I'll be okay," I tell him. "Dad sounds like he's pretty drunk tonight. He'll probably hit like a pussy."

Galen shakes his head. "No. He never goes easy on us, Flynn. He hits even harder when he's drunk. And if he's smoking, you'll get this."

My baby brother holds out his arm for me to see what I already know is there.

The sight of my failure kills me. The cigarette burn our father bestowed on Galen two nights ago glares up at me like an angry, accusing eye. *You didn't protect your brother that night, now did you?*

I will not fail Galen tonight, I vow. He's staying in this room no matter what the cost to me. I'll take extra hits, burns, whatever the hell Dad can mete out in his drunken rage.

Speaking of which, another shout rings out, piercing and sharp. "You have one minute, you little pieces of shit, to get the fuck out here."

"Uh-oh," little brother says.

I'm about to tell Galen not to worry *too* much when Dad breaks the lock on the door and bursts in the room. Galen starts wailing like a banshee, and I feel a hand grabbing hold of my hair.

As I am dragged toward the living room with my scalp screaming in protest, Galen cries harder.

"Shut the fuck up," my father screams at my brother.

Galen quiets immediately. One lone whimper escapes, though, as he peers down at his lower half. It's then I notice piss running down his legs.

That's it. I am done with this shit. Someone has to take a stand.

Wrenching away from my father's grasp, I stumble out into the living room of my own volition. When I spin to face my dickhead dad, he cocks his head and gives me a look that dares: *What are you going to do?*

That's when I take a swing.

My fist makes contact with his jaw, which is good. I pray to hear a satisfying cracking sound. That motherfucker deserves it.

Sadly, my punch is too weak to inflict much damage. No broken jaw for Dad, but I do leave one hell of an angry red mark.

My father's eyes dance wildly, but he remains oddly calm. This is something I've never witnessed before, and it sure as hell can't be good.

Dad winds back his arm, like in slow motion, while making a fist that looks like a small ham.

And then it comes. I am hit over and over, again and again and again. Those ham-fists may as well be rocks. My father is that fucking strong.

I am chased around the room, temporarily blinded at one point. I stop and blink, but everything remains black. Then Dad hits me in the temple, and everything turns to a blinding white. I don't know which is worse. I only know that, through it all, my head never stops ringing.

"Stop," I'm finally able to blurt out at one point. "Please, Dad, enough."

My pleas fall on deaf ears. And when I raise my hands to protect myself, I am hit even harder. The blows stop only when I crumple to the floor.

"Get up!" my drunken father slurs from above me. "Get up, or I'll make it so you can't walk for a week, son."

I try to get up—oh, do I try—but my legs fail me time and time again. The best I can do is rise to my knees.

And that's when the belt is put to use.

Dad whacks me across the back, over the shoulders, and on the side of my already-pounding head. My skin passes stinging and goes straight to numb.

"I—I can't stay up," I rasp as I collapse back down to the floor.

"Fine," Dad says. "Take your punishment down there. Doesn't matter to me."

I am hit only once, but it's a bad one. Dad swings his belt, leather whishing across my face as the buckle hits me below my right eye. A new flash of pain registers, sharp and deep. Shit, my face is cut. And I can tell this one will scar.

"You fucking listen to me next time I tell you to come out of that room," my father screams.

When I don't respond, he gets down on the floor and breathes whiskey-tainted breath all over my face. "You don't make me drag you out next time and it won't be so bad. It was worse for you because you pulled that stunt. Locking the door," he scoffs. "Don't defy me like that ever again. You got that, son?"

"Yes," I croak out as I curl up in a fetal position. "I understand."

"Your momma ruined you," my father goes on. "She never could tell you no, made it so you got too used to getting your own way. Well, let me tell you one thing. That fucking charm don't work on me, boy."

He stands, and delivers a sharp kick to my already aching ribs. Just Dad, backing up his words.

My father thinks I have it too easy because of this so-called "charm." Teachers, who tried to get me to run for student council back when Mom was alive, used the word *charisma*. Maybe I got it, maybe I don't. I guess I've sort of seen it in action, especially when girls try to get my attention and then fall all over me. But, really, here's the deal—I'd throw away all the charisma in the world if it meant my father would stop hating me.

A few more kicks to my balled-up body tell me that will never happen.

Everything hurts when the blows finally stop coming. I am left a mess. Blood seeps from the cuts on my chest, my arms, my back. The worst by far, though, is the cut on my face, the one from the belt buckle. Fuck, does that one sting.

Blinking, I stare up at the water-marked ceiling, watching as the brown stains zoom in and out of focus. I try to speak, but nothing comes out. Dad huffs and turns away, but not before telling me, "You're pathetic, Flynn."

He stomps off, and all I can think is *thank God it's over*.

Silence descends and I close my eyes. Just a short rest, that's all I need. Then I'll drag myself back to the bedroom and tell Galen it's safe to come back to bed.

My rest is short-lived. Within minutes, I hear the worst blood-curdling screams I've ever heard in my life.

Galen...no!

"Please, Daddy," a little voice rings out. "Daddy, no, I wanna stay in here. Please, don't make me come out."

Stay in the closet, I mentally try to convey to Galen. I have to help him, but when I sit up too quickly, the whole room tilts. Still, I swear if my father hurts my brother, I will kill him.

Rising to my knees, I almost hurl. I make myself go on. Crawling across the floor, I head to the bedroom. Crawling is the best I can do. Even then I feel like I might pass out. With the movement, blood flows down my cheek to my lips. I lick it away. Disgusting, I know, but the sharp, coppery taste keeps me from losing consciousness.

Galen starts screaming uncontrollably, and I know Dad's got him. The first blow falls. Fuck, it sounds like a full-on punch. Dad's strong as an ox, and a seven-year-old kid can't take that kind of hit.

Again, I try to stand. And again, I fall to my knees.

More blows, more crying, and then a hard cracking sound.

Silence descends, an ear-splitting quiet that is worse than the screams. It cuts me to the bone, and I crawl faster.

When I reach the bedroom door, hanging by a hinge, I collapse at the sight before me. "No, no, no, no, no."

My father is weeping. He's on the floor, sitting in front of the closet. And Galen, my brother, Galen…*Oh, God, if you're up there, why?* Galen lies limp in my father's arms.

My dad looks over at me and bites back a sob. "Call 9-1-1, son. Your brother might be dying."

I see all too clearly what he can't, or won't, acknowledge. It's too late for help. Galen is already dead.

Chapter Two

Flynn
(*As the next four years go by*)

They say you don't know what you've got till it's gone. In the months—and then the years—following Galen's death, I discover what they say is fucking true. I also learn you never really heal. There's something inside you that remains broken when you've suffered a loss like the one I suffered.

Eventually, you get used to living with the pain. The empty hole in your heart, the one that makes your chest hurt on the nights you can't sleep, becomes a constant companion.

My dad is arrested for killing Galen. He's tried and convicted, sent away to rot in prison.

I wouldn't have it any other way. Even when it means I become an orphan, a ward of the state.

Whatever, man. My dad wasn't doing such a great job, anyway.

The state can call me anything they want, but the truth is I am one of the unwanted, the discarded. Another kid in the system, another cog in a broken wheel.

At first, I live in a group home—a prison unto itself. Then, I am sent to one temporary home after another. Some families are okay, but I unfortunately soon discover many are in it for the money. In any case, I am bounced all around. Even the decent families send me on my way. No one wants to adopt a troubled teen boy.

After a bunch of new moms and a few new dads—not a single one of them really interested in becoming a real parent to me—I take off.

I run for a while, discovering soon enough that the streets aren't kind to a runaway kid. I end up trying drugs to ease my loneliness. That shit does nothing but make me feel lonelier, so I replace drugs with sex.

At fifteen, I hook up with a seventeen-year-old girl, a runaway, like me. We have tons of sex, and she let's me try everything a teen boy can think of. All we engage in is safe sex, of course. The last thing either of us wants is a disease, or, God forbid, we produce a kid who'll be stuck out on the streets with us.

Runaway Girl is pretty cool, and she teaches me a thing or two when it comes to pleasing a woman. We practice a lot, and I get damn good at everything she shows me. Probably why she sticks around for a while. Eventually though, like everything else in life, our relationship ends and we go our separate ways.

Not long after, I am caught stealing some shit from a store and get my ass sent to juvie. When I finish my stint, I am thrust back in the foster system. *What a cluster-fuck.* I move through a carousel of homes, switching houses instead of merry-go-round horses. Spinning around, moving through different rooms. Some are shared and some I have all to myself. A few foster moms buy me clothes, but most don't bother. The one constant is I'm never in the same place for long.

Round and round I go. Where I'll stop, nobody knows.

Then, one dreary October day, I get word I've received a permanent placement for my final two years in the system.

"Mrs. Lowry promises to keep you until you're eighteen," my overworked, underpaid social worker tells me in a monotone voice.

"Great," I reply, just as enthusiastically.

It's my sixteenth birthday. *Happy fucking birthday to me.*

Part One
Present Day

Chapter Three

Jaynie

"You're lucky to be getting this placement, Jaynie. Mrs. Lowry is quite selective of the kids she chooses to come live with her."

Saundra, my social worker, relays this tidbit to me in a way that conveys I should be thanking my lucky stars. What does she want? Does she expect me to drop to my knees on the candy- and gum-wrapper-strewn floorboard of the little rust-bucket car we're in and praise Jesus?

Yeah, like that's going to happen.

I have nothing to be thankful for, certainly not this placement. Besides, the ability to feel real gratitude is something I lost a while ago, along with a lot of other things.

Saundra turns at a faded green sign that indicates we're entering the city limits of *Forsaken, West Virginia*. I suppress a laugh. Seems I may have found an appropriate home after all.

Saundra nods to the sign as we pass. "Don't let the name fool you,

Jaynie. This town is actually a solid community. A bit rundown," she adds when we start driving by cars on blocks, dotting the front yards of dilapidated homes. "But Forsaken is still a good place."

Sure it is, I think. I keep my mouth shut, though. One thing I've learned during the past three years in the state foster system is that keeping quiet is the best way to stay out of trouble.

Leaning my head against the side window, I sit quietly and take in my new town.

Wow, what a shithole. Cracked sidewalks, boarded-up buildings, and houses marred by broken windows inspire little confidence that Forsaken is a good place, like Saundra claims. A dirty curtain sticking out of the second-floor window of one home, pink and felt-like, reminds me of a dog's tongue hanging out of his mouth on a hot summer's day. But not in a cute, happy way. This is more like a dog left out with no water.

We pass one particular house that garners my attention. It's more a shack than a solid structure, really. A young girl of about six is standing out in the middle of the muddy yard. She's crying—wailing, really—but no one comes to her aid.

Between this and my thirsty-dog imaginings, I conclude this town is really living up to its name. Thunder rumbles and I hope for rain. Maybe Forsaken and all its misery will be mercifully washed away. But, of course, that doesn't happen.

A smattering of raindrops peppers the windshield, fat droplets that look like oversized tears. I think of the girl crying in the yard and feel like crying right along with her. Crying wouldn't help. Nothing can wash away the sadness in my soul.

Saundra flips on the wipers, fiddles with the controls, and finally settles on delay. Sweeping a swath of curly brown hair over her shoulder, she tells me, "It won't be long now. We're almost there."

We make a sharp turn at an abandoned paper mill and start a climb up a narrow gravel road that hugs the side of a heavily forested mountain. A scary ascent ensues, and I focus on the woods instead of the far side of the road, which appears to drop off to absolutely nothing.

Yeah, so the trees, let's think about the trees, and not the possibility of accidental death.

The trees really are quite pretty. The branches are tipped in springtime buds, painting the forest in a filmy cast, like a light green veil has been thrown over everything.

When we slow to a crawl, I notice whole sections of the road have been washed down the mountain, forever lost. I shudder. It seems the closer we creep to my new home, the worse things become.

"I think we should turn around," I blurt out. "Is it too late for me to go back to the group home?"

Saundra snorts. "Yes, I should think so."

"Why?"

Aggravated, she replies, "Because it just is, Jaynie."

"I think I might want to go back, though."

Saundra stops the car right in the middle of the road. Doesn't matter, no one is around.

"Listen," she says as she twists in her seat to face me. "I am not driving you all the way back to Clarksburg. You'll just change your mind again once we get there. I know it."

"I don't think that will happen," I mumble.

"Oh, Jaynie…"

Saundra shakes her head and slips off her tortoise-shell glasses to rub her eyes. I've clearly annoyed her. "You have no idea what you're saying. You spent one month in group. One month. That's nothing. You think living in a group home until you're eighteen is going to be better than living with Mrs. Lowry up on this beautiful mountain?"

"Maybe." I shrug. "Group wasn't *that* bad."

She ignores me, puts on her glasses, and starts driving again.

I'm stuck.

Maybe she's right. Group wasn't completely terrible, but it certainly wasn't great. The kids stayed away from me. Rumors abounded that I was weird. Okay, true, I don't talk too much. And I wear way too many layers of clothing. But the biggest impediment to my fitting in anywhere is the one thing I'm trying like hell to overcome—I lose my shit if I'm touched by a guy. I'm not always great with women, either. That's the reason for all the clothes. Leggings under skirts and big, bulky sweaters over long-sleeved tees offer a layer of protection if someone accidentally bumps into me, or brushes by.

I don't want to live my life this way, and I don't plan on staying screwed up forever. I want nothing more than to be normal, like I used to be. I was once a happy and fun girl. Touchy and feely, even. I hugged people all the time. But not anymore. The girl I used to be was ruined by one man.

I clench my fists, hoping Saundra doesn't notice.

I refuse to give up on getting back to the real me, the one buried under the fear. I've been fighting every day to heal, and I've made some progress. Last week, my therapist was able to touch me. Just on the shoulder. And she's a female. But still, it's progress. I just need the right environment to take me all the way.

A few other things need to change, too. Like the flashbacks. They need to go away.

Lift up your nightgown, Jaynie.

Touch me where I put your hand.

Quit clenching your legs together, bitch.

If you scream again, I'll fucking punch those pretty white teeth out of your mouth.

"Okay," I whisper. "No more screaming, I promise."

I start to shake. *Don't lose it here.* Frantically, I smooth and smooth and smooth the long, black skirt I'm wearing over my gray wool leggings. I still feel overexposed. I can almost feel *his* hands on me, wrenching my thighs apart with one hand, while reaching for a condom with the other.

No, no, no.

Tugging my sweatshirt over my head, I place it over my lap. *Another line of defense to my most secret place.* "Try to touch me now, motherfucker," I mutter.

See, I'm fighting to be strong.

Saundra glances over, concern in her eyes. She's trying to keep her focus on the road, but how can she when the crazy girl next to her is having a meltdown.

"I'm fine," I say, voice shaky. My eyes dart her way, then back to my lap. "I promise I'll be all right. Just give me a second."

"Jaynie," she sighs. "I am so sorry we missed what was happening to you in your last home. It's just that it was so good there for so long." Her lamenting tone makes it sound like what happened at my last home hurt her more than it hurt me. "Who would have known, right?"

"Right."

She either doesn't hear, or ignores, my sarcastic tone.

"I should have been checking in on you more often," she says, more to herself than to me. "I'm just so overworked, and I never thought something like that would ever happen in Mrs. Giessen's house. She's such a great lady. And her son wasn't due out of prison for another year. Soon as I heard he was released early,"—she peers over at me meaningfully—"I started the paperwork to get you out."

"Yeah, you did."

I don't add that it took her six weeks to get me out of that place. It wasn't Saundra's fault, though. The system is broken. And now, so am I.

Unfortunately, while the paperwork was tied up in processing, I remained stuck in Mrs. Giessen's house. There was no immediate rush to pull me out. After all, I was told, Mrs. Giessen's son (I refuse to let his first name cross my thoughts or my lips, ever) may have been an ex-con, but he wasn't a sex offender…until he was. And, lucky me, I got to be his first victim.

Trust me when I tell you a lot of harm can be done in a month and a half, especially to a seventeen-year-old girl with no way to protect herself. I was at the mercy of a monster, a foul man who kept the things he did to me at night, when his mother was fast asleep, a horrid secret. A secret he told me over and over must be kept between us. God, the things he did to me as he told me that. And the worse things he promised if I did tell.

I squeeze my legs together as tightly as I can. The physical pain he inflicted on me has long passed, but the wounds on my psyche are far worse than the ones he ever inflicted on my body.

"He hurt me, he hurt me," I chant.

When I start rocking back and forth, Saundra slams on the brakes. "Jaynie, calm down. Rog—"

"Don't say his name!"

"Okay, okay. I was just going to say he's not here. You're all right, you're safe."

I nod. I'm glad we're out of the town, past the ramshackle houses. I don't need rumors starting up within the first ten minutes of arriving in this new place.

"Jaynie," Saundra continues when the rocking slows, but doesn't stop. "It's okay. Everything is okay. I told you you're safe now."

We'll see.

Finally, I stop rocking and cautiously, so cautiously, Saundra reaches over to comfort me…

…and that's when I involuntarily jerk away.

Pressing my body to the passenger door, I whisper, "Please, don't. I'm all right, I swear. Just don't touch me. Not now, okay?"

"Okay, Jaynie, okay." Saundra slumps back in her seat. "I'm sorry. I shouldn't have reached for you like that. I know better, I do."

I feel rotten. "No, I'm the one who should be apologizing. I know you're only trying to help." I scrub my hands down my face, wishing I could disappear. "I don't know what's wrong with me today."

"It's understandable you don't want to be touched. It's only been a little over a month since I got you out."

"Yeah, but…" I lower my head. Saundra defending me only makes me feel worse.

After a few seconds, I try to explain. "It's usually not this bad with women. I guess I'm just extra stressed with all the new stuff going on."

She smiles over at me. "It's okay, honey. Really, it is. There've been a lot of changes in your life recently. This is to be expected."

"Yeah, but still…I'm sorry."

She puts the car in gear, starts to drive again. "The system, Jaynie…it just sucks."

That it does.

As we travel higher up the side of the mountain it's like my meltdown never happened. There's no more talk of returning to group; I am going to my new home.

And then we arrive.

At the top of the mountain, I cast a sweeping gaze over acres and acres of open land. It's a striking landscape, like some bucolic painting that's too good to be true. And maybe I am right about that assessment. The high gates at the front of the property, not unlike those found at a fortress, don't exactly inspire confidence that this place will be a haven.

"This is it?" I ask warily.

Saundra nods as we creep closer and closer to the imposing entrance.

"Why such high gates?" I inquire.

Without missing a beat, Saundra says, "Those are there to keep bad elements out."

"I thought you said the town was good?"

"It is." She waves her hand, dismissing my concern like a pesky bug. "It's just a precaution, Jaynie."

Is that guilt I hear in her tone? What does she know that she's not sharing?

"Listen, Jaynie," she says, a little too quickly, a little too shrill. "Mrs. Lowry is very protective of the kids up here. She'll keep you safe from everything. Focus on the good. There's a lot of structure in her home, and you need that now more than ever. This is going to be such a good experience for you. There's home-schooling to keep you busy and lots of voluntary work projects. And the home itself is quite lovely. Doesn't that sound exciting?"

"Yeah, sure," I lie.

"And don't forget, you won't be alone. There are four other foster kids living up here."

I have to laugh. Saundra thinks more kids in the house will somehow ensure my safety. At the last home—which also happened to be my first, and only, placement after my mom took off, leaving me an orphan—I was the only kid. It was lonely sometimes, sure, but it was also kind of nice living with a lady in her late fifties who treated me kindly. If only things had stayed the same. I could have made it through the foster system unscathed. But my luck ran out when Mrs. Giessen's thirty-year-old, ex-con son came home. His sentence ended and mine began.

Maybe this place *will* be a good home. I sure hope so. I was given a little background before I left group. Mrs. Lowry has only one daughter. No sons and no husband. Thank God for small favors. Anyway, she owns what used to be a dairy farm. The cows are long gone, but she still runs a business—a successful crafting enterprise. Well-known regionally and growing rapidly, Mrs. Lowry calls herself "Crafty Lo." And, oh, how she is loved and adored in these parts. She's the ex-school teacher, who reinvented her life when her husband died ten years ago and she inherited the family farm.

Mrs. Lowry's twenty-one-year-old daughter, Allison, lives with her. She supposedly helps out with the family business. Although I heard rumors in group that it's the homeless children Mrs. Lowry fosters who do all the work. Crafty Lo has a reputation for being this great benefactor of unwanted children, but the behind-the-scenes word is she works you hard for what little you receive.

Oh well, I'd rather work my ass off making useless crafts than be forced to do things no teenage girl should ever have to do.

When we reach the high gates, the rain comes to a sudden stop. I glance around. In addition to the fortress-like entrance, there is tall wire fencing sprouting from the heavy brush to my left and to my right. Though I can't see the top, it looks as though the fence wraps around the full front of the property.

Huh. Is Mrs. Lowry really just trying to keep bad elements out? I don't know, but it sure looks to me like she's trying to keep something *in*. Like maybe the kids who live up here?

Carefully, I ask, "So, you mentioned four other foster kids. Do you know their names?"

The gates open slowly, like a yawning mouth, as Saundra says, "I'm not sure of their names, but I know there's a set of twins, a cute little boy and girl."

"Oh, how cool. How old are they?"

"Eight."

We drive on, the heavy gates closing behind us, locking us in.

"What about the other two kids?"

"Well," Saundra says, "the other two fosters are not exactly kids. Both are seventeen"—she smiles over at me—"like you."

"Two girls?" I ask, hopeful.

"No. One guy and a girl."

Great, we'll see how well this goes. I hope the guy keeps his distance.

We proceed down a long driveway and eventually come to a stop in front of a spacious, red-brick colonial. The house looks a little too picture-perfect to me. The flagstone walkway leading to the porch is lined with tulips and daffodils, all in full bloom and evenly spaced. To the left of the walkway stands a large maple tree, the tips of its limbs covered in soft shades of pink. Pretty and welcoming, yes, but usually when something appears too good to be true, it is.

I scan around to uncover the "real" feel of this place. When my gaze lands on a large pole barn, constructed of steel, located across from the house and down a slight incline, I suspect I've found it.

"That's the craft workshop," Saundra says as she dips her head to follow my gaze. "Mrs. Lowry erected the barn not all that long ago in order to provide a nice, clean work environment. All her crafts are made in there."

I might as well find out now if all the rumors I heard at group were true. "So, Mrs. Lowry and her daughter make all the crafts in that barn?" I say, baiting Saundra.

"Um…" She peers down at her hands, which are still grasping the steering wheel, even though we're parked. "They do, but the kids help out a lot."

"Wait, she has, like, no actual employees?" This could be worse than I thought.

Saundra shakes her head. "No."

I stare at the barn. It doesn't look like a sweatshop, but I'm suspicious.

"That's enough shop talk," Saundra says brightly as she pops open the driver's door. "Let's go introduce you to Mrs. Lowry. She'll get you settled in and you can ask her more about the business then."

"Whatever," I murmur.

I make no effort to exit the car. Instead, I twist in my seat to peer out at all the rolling fields where I suppose the cattle used to roam. There's another barn way off in the distance, a ramshackle structure of brown lumber that looks dark and wet. Beyond the fields there appears to be nothing but endless acres of thick forest.

Tomorrow's Lies

A chill runs up my spine. Not from fright, but from worry. Forget the high entrance gates and the wire fencing. This place is a natural fortress. The high-up-on-the-hill location plus the miles of wooded land practically guarantees there will be no easy way out.

It's all a little too claustrophobic, and I tell Saundra, "I don't think I'm ready to go in the house just yet."

I'd feel better if I could see the other kids. This place feels too disconnected from the town below. Not that Forsaken is much better, but there's more than one way in. And more than one way out.

"No problem." Saundra reaches over to pat my knee, but then thinks better of it. "Stay in the car as long as you like. I'll go on ahead and talk with Lo… I mean Mrs. Lowry. Come on in whenever you're ready. Or, if you prefer, I can come back out for you?"

"That's okay. I'll come in on my own when I'm ready."

"Okay, honey."

After she's gone, I return to my perusal of what will be home for the next seven months. Again, it doesn't look bad aesthetically, but I keep reminding myself appearances can be deceiving.

"Eighteen," I murmur. "Eighteen and you are so out of here."

From the corner of my eye, I suddenly detect movement over at the pole barn. The doors are sliding open, I suppose since the rain has stopped. Opening doors mean one thing, someone is inside. *One or more of my new foster siblings?* Probably.

A mix of fear and hope leaves me shaky. Too many raindrops have gathered on the tinted passenger window, casting my view in blurry tones of surreal blue. I roll it down. I need for this to be straight-up real.

It's bright inside the pole barn, a contrast to the dreary day. There are long rows of tables that seem to extend all the way to the back. Most of the surfaces, at least the ones I can see, appear to be covered in crafts and craft materials. Two kids, a little boy and little girl, both quite pale and very similar in appearance—the twins, I assume—are working diligently at a table right by the entrance.

As I continue to watch, another person comes into view. The older girl, the one who's my age. She leans over the table to help the twins with something. The girl looks a bit like me, auburn hair, fair skin, but even bent over as she is I can tell she's taller than me. And, whoa, definitely way skinnier.

So here they are, three of my four new foster siblings, smack dab in front of me. I watch them closely, looking for signs of friendliness. God, I hope they accept me. There seems to be closeness among them which calls to my need to connect with someone. I'm tired of feeling so alone all the time. Watching the interactions of the girl and the twins, even viewed from afar, I get the sense they care for one another.

The little boy—skinny as can be and with a mess of black hair in dire need of a trim—peers up at the older girl with affection when she begins to help him with a craft. Auburn-haired Girl hands the little boy a seashell that's as big as his hand. He sets it down on the table—awkwardly since it's so large for his hands—and mouths a *thank you*. He then proceeds to paint something on the side of the shell, using a long, slender brush. When the older girl pats him on his shoulder approvingly, he beams up at her.

The girl twin then starts to tug on the older girl's jade green sweater. Little Girl looks so much like her twin. She is tiny and slender, and has the same raven-colored hair as her brother.

I have a good feeling about these three, but I'm still apprehensive. *Where is the fourth foster kid, the guy my age? He must be around here somewhere.*

Just then, like serendipity is at work, a plume of wispy-white smoke trails from around the far side of the barn. Maybe the foster kid I've yet to see is remaining hidden on purpose, since he's clearly catching a smoke.

I scoot up in my seat and lean my head out the window to have

Tomorrow's Lies

a better view. But the car is angled in a way that I can't see shit on the side of the structure I'm curious about.

"Damn," I mutter as I flop back in the seat.

I'm going to have to get out of the car if I really want to see the mystery kid. I'm hesitant, but curiosity wins out in the end. Cautiously, I push open the car door.

When I stand, my ankle boots squish down in the mud immediately. I take a tentative step to drier land, which happens to be in the direction of the barn. The air feels thick and wet up here, but oddly inviting. My earlier fears are quelled. Maybe this new home and this new family of broken kids is the place for me, after all. I don't know, but I have an overwhelming sense I might find the girl I once was while I'm here.

Encouraged by a once-familiar, but currently rarely felt, confidence, I walk toward the barn with purpose. I may as well introduce myself to everyone, right? If I'm going to fit in, I should start off on the right foot.

Unfortunately, the older girl and the twins are no longer working in the front of the barn. I may be putting on a courageous front, but it's not enough for me to waltz in and search these people out.

Quickly, I change direction and head for the side of the barn instead. The elusive fourth foster kid might be easier to meet, just a simple one-on-one hello. Plus, I can get a vibe on whether he's a pervert or not, and then plan accordingly.

When the kid comes into view, I skid to a stop. "Oh," I breathe out. "Wow." The guy is gorgeous.

Despite my limitations in the getting-physical-with-a-guy department, I can still fully appreciate a fine male specimen. And this guy is that, and more. Tall, and with a body hard and lean, he's quite the hottie.

The guy is wearing faded blue jeans and a T-shirt the color of steel. His hair is sandy-brown and disheveled as all get out, like some lucky girl might have been running her fingers through it.

"Too bad that will never be you, freak," I chastise myself.

This guy is so far out of my league, even if I were normal, that it's not even funny. With a face as fine as his body, he is nothing short of perfection. Damn, he is far too good-looking to be an orphan. But here he is, in this place like me, so he must be just as unwanted.

Gorgeous takes a drag from his smoke, and then leans back and rests his head against the side of the barn. It's like he has not a care in the world. Yeah, right. I know it's just a façade. You don't end up in the foster system if you've led an easy life. But you sure posture like you have.

He lifts the cigarette to his full lips and takes another drag, blowing another wispy trail of smoke up in the thick air, where it lingers for a beat. Gorgeous watches the smoke dissipate around the barn, and then he flicks the spent butt to the wet grass.

Oh, smooth.

This guy oozes confidence. Hell, you'd think he owned the place. And then it hits me—he *does* own this place, in a foster-world kind of way. He's in charge around here, at least among the kids.

Suddenly, like he's just realized someone has been watching him the whole time, he glances my way. Even from afar, his curious gaze is piercing. Or maybe it's just me, seeing him that way. In any case, his stare is too intense and I can't maintain eye contact.

With my focus moving to the ground I'm standing on, I decide to wait him out. Surely, this good-looking guy will get bored with the strange girl staring at her shoes and go on about his business.

He does no such thing. *Oh, hell.* I hear his shoes squishing in the wet grass as he heads toward me. And in less than a minute there's a shadow darkening my view.

He clears his throat, but I don't look up. "You lose something down there?" he asks as he points a sneakered toe to the spot where I'm staring.

"Maybe," I reply.

When he takes a step closer, his maleness becomes overwhelmingly palpable, thick and loamy, like the air.

Do I run? Do I stay?

Something in me snaps, not unlike those little firecrackers that make a surprisingly loud bang. I feel ripped down the center, torn in two, conflicted. Part of me wants to flee from the gorgeous guy and the confusing way he's making me feel. But a bigger part of me wants to stay.

So, I stay.

Frustrated by my warring emotions, and the confusion they're causing, I promptly lash out. "Smoking is a fucking disgusting habit, you know."

The guy laughs and volleys back, "Nice language."

"Fuck you, smart ass."

"Ooh, feisty. I like you already."

He's playing along, even if he is somewhat confrontational. What the hell, I started it. Maybe he's not so bad. I'm definitely not getting a pervert-vibe or anything.

A smile threatens to bloom, and I say, "You're a bastard, you know that?"

"Nah," he replies, matter-of-factly. "I have a dad. A real piece of shit, but a father, nonetheless."

That gets me to look up at him. Bad move. This guy is even better-looking up close.

Eyes back on the ground, I ask, "So, where is he, then? Your dad, that is."

I hear him sigh. "Prison."

"Oh."

I ask nothing more. You don't go digging around in another person's wounds.

"I don't disagree, by the way," he says, after a long beat of silence.

I kick at a bug crawling over a blade of grass, and it skitters away. "What are you talking about?"

"The smoking, what you were saying about it. You're right. It *is* disgusting."

Oh, what the hell. I take a chance and glance up at him again. I'm going to have to live with him, and I can't always be looking away.

He's peering at me curiously, with eyes that are the coolest shade of gray. Like something soft and woolen, a place you could curl up in and find comfort. This is a bit much for me, though, so I stare past him, to the side of the barn.

"So, why do it?" I murmur. "Why smoke?"

"Eh." He shrugs. "Why not?"

"Great answer." I glance at him briefly and make a face.

"Hey, it's the best answer I got, so take it or leave it."

I grow serious. "You really should quit, though."

"Maybe I'm trying," he says. "Ever consider that possibility before spouting off, Miss the-truth-dot-com?"

I ignore his smartass retort. "Good." I nod. "Otherwise, it'll probably kill you."

I expect him to say something along the lines of *you really are an anti-smoking commercial come to life*, but instead he utters a soft, "Dying young might not be so bad."

"What?"

His eyes—clear and sincere—meet mine. "It's nothing, never mind." He looks away. "I was just making a bad joke."

"Okay, whatever you say."

He squares up his shoulders defiantly. I know then his past is stormy and turbulent, like mine. As he stares at some faraway point up in the fields, I have a chance to check him out without being blatantly obvious about it.

He's younger looking up-close, more so than when he was leaning up against the barn. I guess that's because of the faint smattering of freckles across the bridge of his nose. But, still, far away or up close, there's no denying this guy is beautiful.

Still, he is not without flaws. There's a tiny scar marring his cheek, located just below his right eye. A little crescent of fish-belly white, shaped like a comma. I wonder how he got a scar like that. In any case, he's not perfect, after all, and I'm glad. It makes him more appealing, more real.

He catches me staring and clears his throat.

I say the first thing that comes to my mind to save face. "It's not just the dying thing, you know. Smoking will ruin your good looks, too."

Shit. That just made things worse. Now he knows I think he's hot.

Smiling kindly, he says, "Hey, can I let you in on a secret?"

I shrug. "Yeah, sure, go for it."

"I'm not really a smoker. I can take it or leave it. And what I said before was true. I *am* trying to quit, like, permanently. I wasn't lying to you about that."

"Yeah, I noticed." I nod to the side of the barn where he was smoking. "Seems like that commitment to quit is really working out well for you."

My attempt at smart-assery does not go over well, and I feel like a fool. *Great way to make friends, Jaynie.*

In a tired voice beyond his years, he says, "Whatever. Go ahead and make a joke. Sad to say, but sometimes catching a smoke is the only way to get a break around this goddamn place." Cryptically, he adds, "You'll see."

His bitter tone isn't lost on me, and I know then and there I was right about this new home—it will be no haven. Not a big surprise there. *Eighteen,* I remind myself. *Eighteen and I am out from under the state's care.*

"Hey, I didn't mean to upset you," he says when he notices my bereft expression.

"No, no." I wave my hand around, dismissing his concern. "It's not you. It's just…never mind. You know what, I should go." I gesture to the brick house. "My social worker is inside, and I told her I'd be in."

"Ahh," he drawls. "I figured you were the new girl. Jaynie Cumberland, right?"

"Yes." I smile.

"Hey, it's good to meet you. If you have any questions about anything, ask away." He extends his hand. "I'm Flynn, by the way. Flynn O'Neill."

I stare down at his waiting hand. Panic I thought I had under control bubbles to the surface. Dammit. I was doing so well. My heart pounds frantically as I go through my limited options.

Do I *try* to shake his hand? Or do I ignore him? I really want to come off as normal, and shaking his hand would be the way.

What the hell, I'm going to go for it.

I want so badly to get over my issues, so, taking a deep breath, I extend my right hand.

But just as our fingers are about to touch…I have to back out.

"I can't," I whisper, jerking my hand away.

I physically *can't* touch him or I know I'll lose it.

Dropping my arm to my side, I say, "I'm sorry, Flynn. I, uh, I… Just forget it."

His reaction is not what I expect. There's no mocking, no laughing. No walking away from the damaged girl. Instead, in a soft and understanding tone, Flynn says. "Hey, don't worry about it." He raises the hand he was holding out to me and rubs the tiniest bit of scruff on his jaw, like that's what he intended to do all along.

I try to muster a smile, but fail. "Sorry," I whisper.

"You don't have to keep apologizing." His eyes fill with sadness and knowledge, telling me that he, too, has seen too much. "I get it, Jaynie, I do."

Tomorrow's Lies

In that moment, something indefinable is born between us, some feeling that rocks me to the core. You know how sometimes you meet a person and you have this overwhelming sense they're going to play an important role in your life? Well, that's the feeling I get with Flynn.

I know, I just know from somewhere in the deep recesses of my damaged soul that this guy will be the one to help me heal. I sense he has the power to break through my walls, help me find *me*. Hell, he broke through one wall today. I mean, I couldn't touch him, true, but I'm not running away from him, now am I?

No, I am not. And the best part is I don't *want* to run away, not from Flynn O'Neill.

Chapter Four

Jaynie

The next several days are a jumble of things to learn, most of which are rules, lots and lots of rules, not many allowances.

Saundra was told work was voluntary. Ha, not even close to the truth.

My social worker's little car was barely halfway down the driveway when Mrs. Lowry spun toward me on the front porch, teetering on her too-high heels. "You're to be showered and dressed by seven-thirty every day." She ticked off her points, manicured nails flashing red. "Monday through Saturday, at eight o'clock sharp, homeschooling commences in the pole barn. You'll find a small classroom set up in the back. Sunday is for chores and finishing up projects not completed during the week. Lunch is always at noon. On work days, you work in the barn until six or seven in the evening. Got it?"

"Yes," I replied. My stomach growled like it knew what was coming. "What about breakfast and dinner?"

Mrs. Lowry harrumphed. "You'll receive a nutrition bar daily for breakfast. As for dinner, it's only served if you make your work quotas. The quantities and types of meals vary, but hot dogs are on the menu a couple times a week."

She smiled wickedly, like hot dogs constituted a gourmet meal.

Turns out, they do. And that conversation should have been a clue. Eight days have passed so far, and we've had dinner only three of those days. Hot dogs each time, and one per person, no seconds. As a result, I've lost weight already. My leggings, skirts, and sweaters hang on my frame. I'll be far too thin soon enough, like everyone else in this wretched place.

Alas, there is nothing I can do about it. Except count the days till I'm eighteen—211.

Sighing, I scan the barn for the boy who makes me smile every day, despite everything. Flynn is quickly becoming my bright star, one that manages to be seen even on the cloudiest of nights.

My star, however, is nowhere to be seen on this day. And frankly, I'm a little worried. It's lunchtime, and missing lunch is nuts. It's the only sure meal of the day, not counting the dried-out nutrition bars we receive for breakfast.

I can't think of food, not now. I am far too hungry. So, I return to thinking of Flynn and where he might be. He doesn't always attend classes. I have no idea how he gets away with that. But because this deviation from routine is permissible for him, Flynn missing this morning's lesson seemed like no big deal. Work hours are fast approaching, though, and as Mrs. Lowry made clear to me on day one, laboring on crafts is absolutely mandatory.

As I take a bite of a limp apple slice—we are allotted one per lunch, along with a small half-sandwich, a pint of milk, and sometimes, if we're lucky, a tiny bag of chips—I stare at the empty chair across from me. That's where Flynn always sits.

We don't interact much during school hours since there's too much work to cram in, but yesterday I did glance over at him at one point and he winked at me. I'd been surreptitiously tearing the wrapper away from the extra nutrition bar I had nabbed at breakfast. Flynn showed me that little trick one morning last week—how to palm two bars instead of one. Mrs. Lowry always stands guard over the box on the counter, but she never really pays much attention when we walk by and grab our breakfast before heading out to the barn. Palming two bars instead of one isn't all that difficult.

When we walked outside that morning, Flynn gave both his breakfast bars to the twins. I wanted to be as magnanimous when I grabbed two bars the next day, but I was far too hungry to share.

Finishing with my apple slice, I glance over at the girl my age, the one with the matching auburn hair. Her name is Mandy, and she sits next to me during class. I notice she hasn't touched her food yet today. Though it's only because she's been too busy helping one of the twins—the boy, whose name is Cody—with a number of tasks. Cody sits across the table from me, next to where Flynn should be. Cody has thrown several glances to Flynn's chair—maybe even as many as I have—but at the moment he is preoccupied with struggling to open his bag of chips.

Mandy swoops in to help him.

Cody seems to have trouble every day with something, especially schoolwork. It's clear he has a learning disability. Yesterday, he couldn't even complete his printing lesson. Flynn had to take him aside to show him how to make his letters right-side up and also not backwards.

And now Cody can't open his bag of chips. His sister, Callie, seated next to Mandy, two seats away from me, rips open her bag with ease.

As Callie *crunch-crunch-crunches* away, I realize something. The atmosphere in the barn feels different with no Flynn around. The space is too big, too empty, and far too quiet. Flynn is always making conversation with everyone during lunch and often telling silly jokes that never fail to get everyone laughing, especially the twins.

He's such a good guy, and I like him a lot as a person. I'm surprisingly at ease around him, too. It's like our conversation the day I arrived broke the ice. Still, Flynn doesn't try to touch me, not after the failed attempt at a handshake on day one. He gives me my space, and as a result, my feelings for him grow and grow. I guess Flynn is quickly becoming my first official crush.

You know what, though? It feels really good knowing there's something still normal about me. A crush gives me hope that there may be a regular 'ole teenage girl buried beneath all the fucked-up stuff.

"I hope so," I mutter to myself.

Mandy glances over at me. "What's that, Jaynie?" she asks.

"Oh, it's nothing. I was just talking to myself."

She chuckles. "Sometimes it feels good to hear your own voice, right?"

"Right." I agree.

I know Mandy would like if I talked more in general, interact with everyone more than I do. And I'm trying, I really am. I want to get along, especially since I feel like I kind of fit in around here. I like that I can be myself around Mandy. My weirdness seems to be okay with her. She's been nice to me since day one, thank God. My first night, I was a mess. Up in the small bedroom we share with Callie on the third floor of the main house, Mandy was the one who calmed me down. She showed me which bed—nothing but a twin mattress on the floor actually, pushed up against a wall—was mine. And since my mattress was bare, she searched around till she found a sheet set and two pillows buried in the closet. She was also kind enough to give me a blanket from her own bed, which is a full-size mattress situated about four feet from mine. Her bed is in the center of the room, with Callie's twin bed on the opposite wall from mine.

The placement is fitting; Mandy is there for both of us.

Mandy also went over the third-floor rules that first night. 1) Once you're in the room at night, you can only leave for a bathroom run. 2) Cameras in the hall ensure you don't take too long or deviate from your course. 3) There are no detours allowed, meaning no boys in the girls' room and no girls in the boys'.

Thinking of the boys reminds me again of Flynn, and that gets me back to thinking about his absence today. I glance over at the open barn doors, like I expect him to saunter in any minute, all confident, like he always seems to be.

When I sigh, Mandy, who misses nothing, says softly, "If you're wondering when Flynn is coming in, don't bother. He won't be working with us in the barn today."

I begin to flounder. I'm embarrassed I've been so easily read. "Oh, uh, he's not working with us this afternoon, huh? Okay." I try to appear nonchalant. "I wasn't really thinking about him," I fib, "but that's good to know."

The too-high lilt in my voice gives me away, and, as established, Mandy *is* perceptive.

With a knowing grin, she says, "It's okay if you like him, Jaynie. Flynn *is* really cute. And he's a sweetheart, too."

I don't want to step on any toes, so I carefully inquire, "You and Flynn aren't, like, together or anything, right?"

Mandy laughs out loud. Waving her half sandwich in the air, she says, "Oh, God, no. He's too much like a real brother to me. And besides"—she blushes—"I have someone special waiting for me. When I get out of this place, I plan to meet up with him."

I'm curious to learn more about Mandy's mystery man, but my interest as to why Flynn is missing supersedes everything.

"So, where *is* Flynn?" I go ahead and straight-out ask.

Mandy takes a huge bite of her sandwich—we're always ravenous around here—and then starts to say, "He—"

And that's when Cody leans across the table and interrupts her.

Tomorrow's Lies

Tugging on the sleeve of Mandy's threadbare blouse, he sheepishly whispers, "Cody can't open this, either." His little-kid voice is squeaky and high as he awkwardly holds out a tiny red and white milk carton. "Mandy help me?"

"Of course, honey. Let me get that for you." Mandy slips the carton from Cody's outstretched hand, squeezes the little flap open, and hands it back to him.

Cody sits back down and takes a huge drink. Mandy meanwhile reaches across the table and gently combs hair as dark as night back from Cody's forehead.

It's then that I notice Cody's twin, Callie, is watching the whole exchange with great interest. Much like her brother, her large brown eyes are obscured by the tips of her too-long bangs. She pushes the wayward strands from her face, mimicking how Mandy tamed Cody's hair. When she's done, Callie's gaze slides over to me.

I smile, but it feels forced. I am so not a natural with kids. Since Callie barely knows me, I half-expect her to have a negative response. To my complete surprise, she presents me with a wide, genuine grin, one that warms my cautious heart.

The five of us spend every day together, almost every hour, but this is the first either of the twins has made a real effort to interact with me. Up until today, I've been invisible.

That's your own damn fault, I think. And then I realize deep inside that I want to connect with these kids, just like I've connected with Flynn and Mandy.

I glance over at Mandy. She's busy again with Cody. He's leaning across the table, whispering that he has to go to the bathroom. I discovered on day one that the bathroom is just an old outhouse in the back of the barn. We're not allowed back in the house till the work day is over, not even for necessary bodily functions.

Outhouse runs with Cody are usually a task handled by Flynn, but he's obviously not available to help. And I still have no idea why.

Holding up two fingers like a peace symbol, Mandy says, "I'll be back in two, Jaynie."

Cody has gotten up and is tugging away at her arm. His other hand is clutching the crotch of his pants. "Gotta go-o-o *now*," he desperately proclaims.

"Okay, okay." Turning to me, Mandy cups her mouth and whispers, "We'll finish our talk as soon as I'm back."

"Okay," I reply. "Sure."

Mandy stands up and asks Callie, "Hey, can you do me a favor?"

"Yes." She straightens in her seat like a star pupil. Callie clearly views herself as Mandy's little helper and she takes that job seriously. It's actually really cute.

Mandy says to her, "Can you keep Jaynie company while I take your brother out to the bathroom? Maybe talk with her a little, make her feel all warm and welcome."

Callie peers down at the table and puffs out her lower lip. She's contemplating, and I am left on pins and needles, waiting for this little girl to say *no way* does she want to sit with the odd girl—me.

When she looks up, to my delight, her little head bobs up and down in assent. "Yes, I'll stay with Jaynie. I like her, she's nice, and I think she should feel super-duper welcome. She's part of our family now, right?"

"She sure is, sweetie." Mandy smiles encouragingly at me as she walks away. "See?" she mouths.

Mandy has been insisting for days that the twins like me. I guess I just found it hard to believe. Stupid me, I should have trusted Mandy. She seems to know everything when it comes to this place. Flynn may be the ultimate decision-maker in this makeshift family, but Mandy is the one who knows stuff. She makes sure things get done. I guess you could say she's like a mother hen to everyone. Seems it's time to accept that now includes me.

That thought makes me happy. I could use a friend, and Mandy has an easy way about her, kind of like Flynn. I know already I'll be sad when she turns eighteen in late July. I'm sure that's when she'll leave to meet up with the guy who is waiting for her.

I exhale loudly, resigned that everything in life is temporary.

Callie, eyeing me curiously, asks, "What's wrong, Jaynie? Why are you blowing air out of your mouth? Mandy does that when she's sad. Are you sad?"

Whoa, I am not used to young kids and their direct questions. However, I don't want to upset Callie with talk of Mandy's inevitable departure, so I stick with, "I was just thinking about how nice Mandy is and how much I like her."

Callie's face lights up. "Mandy *is* nice, Jaynie. She's the bestest-best almost-Mommy Cody and I could ever have."

"She is pretty awesome," I agree.

"I don't just like Mandy, though," Callie goes on, her voice a cheerful sing-song. "I love, love, love her. And Cody loves, loves, loves her, too."

"I can see why," I say, laughing.

Callie just about breaks my heart then, when she grows somber and says, "Did you know our real mommy didn't want us?"

I shake my head. "No, honey, I didn't know that." Sadly, I am not surprised. There's a reason the twins are in foster care, after all.

"She left us a long, long time ago." Callie blinks back tears and whispers, "And I don't think she's ever coming back to get us."

My heart hurts hearing the pain in Callie's tone. And then there is this…

"Hey," Callie exclaims, like something just clicked in her head. "Do you know my real mommy?"

I sigh. Kids see the world as so small. I'm an adult to Callie, and that makes her think I might just know her mother. Of course, I don't.

"No, honey," I say as gently as I can. "I don't know your real mommy."

"Okay." Her bottom lip quivers, and I expect her to cry. But the little girl pulled it together a minute ago, and she does so again now.

"It doesn't matter, anyway," she says. "Do you want to know why?"

"Okay," I reply. "Why."

"I'll tell you." Callie lowers her voice to a whisper. "But it's a secret, okay?"

"Okay."

She kneels on her chair, leans over Mandy's seat.

Cupping her mouth, Callie says softly, "Our real mommy doesn't matter because Mandy is going to be my real mom. Cody's, too, like, for real, for real."

"Yeah?" I'm confused, but I play along. "That's good."

"It is," she says. "We're going to live with Mandy someday when she gets her own place. She'll adopt us, and we'll all be a family."

Oh, God, if you're up there, please make that happen. Mandy would be a better mom to these kids than any of the foster parents I've ever heard about or come across.

"That'd be amazing, Callie," I reply. "I hope it really happens."

"It will," she says confidently as she slides back down in her chair.

Silence descends, and while my thoughts drift, I distractedly scoop what chips remain in my small foil bag. I notice Callie's eyes zooming in on my food like a laser, hunger naked in her gaze. I am freaking starving, but I now understand what compelled Flynn to give his nutrition bars away. I can't say no to this sweet little kid who has gotten such a raw deal in life.

Holding my last handful of chips out to her, I say, "You can have the rest if you want."

Callie's eyes widen in disbelief. "But they're yours. Aren't you hungry?"

I *am* famished, but I tell Callie, "I'm actually pretty full." I hold out the chips and say encouragingly, "Here, take them. I want you to have them."

"Thank you, Jaynie," she whispers.

Callie is careful not to touch me as I drop the chips in her hand. Word has clearly gotten out that I have a problem with touching. Thing is, I'm fine with children. To prove that point, I reach over and ruffle Callie's hair with my non-greasy hand. Her brown eyes widen and she stares at me like I've grown an extra head. "Mrs. Lowry told us not to ever, ever touch you," she says. "She told us it upsets you. Is that true?"

I resist the urge to roll my eyes. *Thanks, Crafty Lo, for broadcasting my issues to everyone in the house. And double thanks for getting the facts wrong.*

I tell Callie, "No. You and Cody can touch me anytime you want, okay? And Mandy is probably fine, too."

"Whaf about Fhlynn?" Callie asks from around a mouthful of chips.

Hmm, what about Flynn?

"Good question," I murmur.

I've been wondering the same thing lately myself. The thought of Flynn touching me certainly doesn't disgust me. Still, I've got a long way to go. Imagining something is far different than experiencing it.

Shrugging, I add, "I don't know, Callie. Maybe someday."

Under the table, I cross my fingers and hope there may indeed come a day where I'll be okay with Flynn touching me. Nothing crazy; just a hug would be nice.

Cody and Mandy come back in the barn just as Callie is finishing the last of the chips from me.

Mandy, noticing the empty foil bag I'm folding, sits down, and says, "That was sweet of you, Jaynie."

"It was nothing." I wave my hand dismissively, not wanting my gesture to be turned into a big deal. We all help each other around here, I see that now.

Mandy lets it drop and returns to our original subject. "So," she says, smiling conspiratorially, "back to Flynn."

"Yes, back to Flynn. He's not sick, is he?"

"No." Mandy's eyes, a paler green than mine, fill with irritation.

Concerned, I ask, "What's wrong, Mandy?"

She sighs. "The reason Flynn isn't working with us today is because he was assigned to spring cleaning duty up at the house."

"Spring cleaning?" I frown, confused. "But Sunday is for chores. Plus, we have so much to do right here. The house didn't look dirty to me," I continue. "And won't Flynn have twice as much work tomorrow to make up for missing today?"

"Yep, he sure will. But, according to Allison"—Mandy rolls her eyes—"Flynn was *desperately* needed at the house."

"Ugh, poor Flynn. I don't think I like Allison very much."

"Watch out for her, Jaynie." Mandy's tone is grim when she adds, "She's a dangerous, jealous bitch."

I suspected as much. Mrs. Lowry is the stern taskmaster who hides behind a false bubbly persona, but for as bad as she is, I sense her daughter, Allison, is worse. Mrs. Lowry is all about maximizing profits; her working us hard isn't personal. Allison, on the other hand, has a gleam in her eyes, the kind that warns you to watch out for her. She's that seemingly harmless dog you reach out to pet and end up with your hand ripped off.

"I'll be careful," I promise, shuddering at the vivid imagery in my head.

"Be careful what you say and do around her," Mandy continues. "Especially with Flynn in the picture."

"What do you mean, exactly?"

Mandy glances over at Callie and Cody, like she doesn't want to say too much with them within earshot. The twins are preoccupied, however, busy taking their empty milk cartons apart so they can make shapes and pretend they are toys.

Mandy and I share a sad smile when we turn back from Cody

and Callie.

"Anyway," she begins, "the problem with Allison is she wants Flynn, like, bad."

Mandy chuckles, and I ask, "What's funny about that?"

"It's funny 'cause Flynn can't stand the bitch."

"So, how'd she get so fixated on him?"

Mandy snorts, "Have you ever looked at him?" *I sure have.* "Dude is hot." *He sure is.* "But it's not just that." Mandy sighs. "Allison got obsessed with Flynn after she started giving him cigarettes and smoking with him." *So that's where he gets them.* "He's trying to give them up now. He doesn't want to owe her anything, you know?"

I feel sick.

"What does she want from him?" I force myself to ask.

Mandy lowers her voice to an almost-whisper so the twins don't accidentally overhear. "Sex, of course," she says. "Allison wants Flynn in her bed. What'd I say before, Jaynie? That body, those muscles. Allison is like a bitch in heat. She wants Flynn *bad*."

"He hasn't, uh, done anything with her, has he?" *Please say no, please say no.* For some reason, it's important to me.

"Hell, no." I breathe a sigh of relief, and Mandy continues. "Trust me, Jaynie. Flynn doesn't plan on doing anything with her. I told you he despises her. And he sure as hell doesn't trust Allison at all."

I'm relieved, but I find it hard to believe Flynn isn't the tiniest bit attracted to Allison Lowry. Sure, she may be an epic bitch, but she is extraordinarily pretty—shoulder-length platinum hair, blue eyes, and long legs. She's a younger version of her mom. And Allison is crafty, too, just like Mrs. Lowry, but not in the literal way. She's crafty in a slick, oily way. She's sneaky and shady, like a snake.

I don't like thinking about her, and I'm glad she's mostly ignored me this past week. But all I can picture after hearing of her lusting for Flynn is the two of them together.

Ugh.

When Mrs. Lowry struts in the barn, wearing one of her signature woolen business suits, I'm actually relieved to see her. I need a distraction.

"Time to get to work, boys and girls," Crafty Lo announces with a flourish of her slender hands.

"She is a fucking nut," Mandy mutters under her breath.

I can't disagree. Mrs. Lowry sure looks crazy as she pats her tight bun of blonde hair and giggles like a little girl.

"Have fun, darlings, and remember to work smart, not hard. There are hot dogs for dinner later. That is," she qualifies, "if you make your quotas."

"Naturally," Mandy says sarcastically under her breath.

And then our benefactor is gone. Don't for a minute think Crafty Lo lifts a perfectly manicured nail to actually work on any of the crafts bearing her name. *Dream on.*

An hour later, Allison still hasn't made an appearance in the barn, which is unsettling. She often looks in throughout the day to make sure we're not goofing off. Her continued absence leaves me feeling nauseated. I can't help but imagine her in the house, trying her best to seduce Flynn.

The projects help to distract me some. In fact, we are all kept busy with the crafts. There's wood to be cut for various projects, print screening to be prepped for T-shirts bearing the Crafty Lo logo, and a final big project for the day—a jewelry project involving intricate sets of beads with many tiny pieces that need assembling.

With the project underway, and the day waning, the twins grow tired and weary. They begin to struggle with the little beads and thin wires, both of which are difficult to work with even when fully focused.

Cody appears close to a meltdown after failing for a fourth time to thread a bead onto a wire. Callie, who has better dexterity than her brother, though not at the moment, tries to help him.

"I can't, I can't," he cries out, his plaintive wails full of frustration and anger as the bead drops to the floor for the umpteenth time.

When Callie leans down to retrieve the rolling ball, Cody loses his shit. He knocks the whole plastic container of beads to the floor, scattering shiny orbs of pink, red, and orange. Bouncing and rolling balls that look like wayward BBs go everywhere.

Mandy and I drop to our knees to clean the mess quickly. "If Mrs. Lowry or Allison comes in and sees this," Mandy says, frantic, "Flynn won't be the only one assigned twice as much work tomorrow."

Callie joins the effort, and the three of us are eventually able to capture most of the bouncing beads.

Cody remains seated at the table, arms crossed. "I want Flynn!" he yells out. "Where he go? Why he not here? Flynnie always helps me. He shows me how to do stupid beading stuff so it no drops on the floor."

Flynn does take care of Cody. He treats him like he really is his little brother.

"These kids should be outside, playing," Mandy hisses as she smacks a bouncing bead down on the floor. "They shouldn't be stuck in this barn for hours and hours. They need a goddamn break once in a while. It's not normal, keeping little kids cooped up all day, working, working, always fucking working."

She wipes away a tear.

Mandy is usually so calm and collected. I'm surprised by her reaction, but understand it completely. I feel the same way. Every part of this set-up feels so very, very wrong. Mandy and Flynn essentially run the home-schooling, supervise the craft projects, and are in charge of making sure we're locked in our respective bedrooms every night. Yet we have no privileges or rights. Instead, we contend with things like portioned-out food, loads of work assignments, cameras in the upstairs hallway, high gates at the entrance, and wire fencing.

"This place is sort of like a prison," I murmur.

Mandy looks over at me and shakes her head. Her eyes are watery, filled with more tears. "You're just figuring that out?"

"No, but I guess it's finally really settling in."

"Just make sure *you* don't get settled in," she says. There's a note of warning in her tone. "Don't ever get too comfortable here, Jaynie. Make sure you always have an out."

I can't help but wonder what she means.

But I'm not entirely sure I want to find out.

Chapter Five

Flynn

I don't sleep well, haven't since I was twelve years old. I toss and turn most nights, and when I do drift off, my rest is fitful. Old wounds, on my psyche and in my soul, haunt me when it's dark.

So this night, same as most, sleep is elusive.

I stare up at the slanted ceiling of the third floor bedroom I share with a kid who reminds me of the brother I lost. A heavy rain is pouring down outside, pelting the window, washing away another fucked-up day, courtesy of Allison Lowry.

Pulling me from a day of work in the craft barn was Allison's not-so-veiled attempt to have me around while her mother went into town this afternoon. The cleaning projects she had me wasting my time on were ridiculous. Dusting the living room, mopping the kitchen floor, all things already completed on chore day. At the end of the day, Allison had me helping her load the washer and dryer, and then we smoked a cigarette in the back of the house.

Shit, she sure was pissed when she offered me the rest of the pack and I declined. Truth is I've been meaning to quit smoking anyway. Plus, Jaynie's words have been ringing in my head since the day I met her. I don't care much about the smoking-will-kill-you part—we all have to die from something, right?—but I can't deny it is a pretty gross habit.

So, I'm in the process of quitting, really quitting. It isn't easy, though. Like, I sure could use a smoke right about now. If I'd accepted that pack from Allison, I'd be pushing open the window by my bed, hopping up on the window sill, and kicking back while I exhaled plumes of white out into the rainy night. If Cody were awake, he'd be bugging me to make smoke rings for him. He likes shit like that.

Turning to my side, away from the window, I punch the pillow. "Fuck."

I did the right thing, I know I did. I don't like living a life beholden to Allison Lowry, and she was my cigarette lifeline. One less connection to her is a good thing, especially since her advances have become more insistent. This afternoon when she called me up to the second-floor bathroom, where she was taking an all-too-convenient middle-of-the-day shower, she pushed back the curtain *all the way* and asked me to hand her a bath towel.

Yeah, I saw everything. But then I walked away. Good body or not, I have no interest in that conniving bitch.

Thunder rumbles in the background, like a warning. I have a bad feeling this thing with Allison won't end well. I used to find her harmless, just another girl who liked the way I look. Hey, I don't see it, but I seem to get hit on everywhere I live. Not that I haven't indulged—some hot chicks have offered to do some very hot things, and I *am* a guy—but I'm kind of past that stage in my life.

Another aversion I have to Mrs. Lowry's daughter is that my past hook-ups have always been with girls my age, and usually girls in the system. I've never screwed around with any actual family members of my foster families, especially not one four years older.

Tomorrow's Lies

A second low growl of thunder shakes the house, and then a bright flash of lightning crackles and illuminates the room. Cody stirs in the bed across from mine.

When he starts to whimper, I say in a low, soothing voice, "Everything's okay, little man. It's just a storm brewing."

He's not awake, but sometimes if I whisper soothing words to calm him, he stays asleep. Keeping his terrible nightmares at bay is my mission, especially with the new girl in the house. The last thing any of us needs is for Cody to have one of his night terror episodes.

When the nightmares come, and surely they will again, there's only one thing that calms Cody—falling back to sleep next to his twin. Problem is Callie sleeps in the girls' bedroom down the hall. It doesn't sound like a problem till you factor in we're not allowed to wander the halls at night. Cameras make sure the only place we dare venture is to the bathroom located between the two rooms.

Cody mumbles something incoherent and kicks his blankets to the foot of the bed. "Shit," I mutter.

It's going to happen, I know it is. A whole week and a couple of days without a nightmare is a record. The Good Dreams gods were blessing us, but our luck is about to run out. I sense it in the storm-electrified air.

Luckily, Mandy and I devised a system not long after I arrived. Mandy was already here, taking care of the twins. I replaced a kid who wanted nothing more than to get out. He used to let Cody scream and scream throughout his bad nights.

What happened to the guy I replaced, who knows? And who cares? He never reported the poor conditions here. Or maybe he did, and Mrs. Lowry paid off any interested parties.

Mrs. Lowry works the system best as she can. She takes advantage of underpaid social workers to make sure they leave her alone. She likes to foster four kids at any one time to make sure quotas are met. Jaynie has been brought in to replace Mandy for when she turns eighteen in July and leaves.

I like Jaynie, but she'll have to be made aware of this Cody situation soon enough. Maybe Mandy has already filled her in on the fact that when Cody has a nightmare he and I go to their room to stay the night. I don't know how Jaynie is going to react to me sleeping in there with her, but the system is the system. I sleep on the floor till the cameras are shut off at dawn, then I slip back to our room with Cody in tow. In case Mrs. Lowry does an early morning walk-through. Unlikely, but why take a chance?

Damn. Jaynie sure has a lot to learn while she's here. She seems so quiet and unsure, another girl broken by the system. I'm happy Mandy has helped ease her in. I'd like to help, too. There's something about Jaynie that appeals to my protective nature. Not to mention, I find her attractive, despite her love of multi-layered clothing. Too bad for me she clearly has an issue with guys.

That's another reason I worry she'll freak when Cody and I show up in their bedroom. Probably tonight by the way Cody is thrashing.

Just then, a thunderbolt of lightning flashes across the sky, followed by an ear-piercing crack.

And that's when Cody begins screaming.

Chapter Six

Jaynie

"So, you're telling me we're *never* allowed off the property by ourselves?" I am positively incredulous.

"No, never," Mandy confirms.

"What if we want to take a walk down the mountain, maybe head into town for an hour or two?"

"Yeah, good luck with that," Mandy snorts. "It's never going to happen."

Callie is sleeping in the bed next to Mandy's and she stirs at the sound of our conversation. We're all up in our bedroom. Mandy and I are discussing life at the house. Tired as I am from the long work day, my hunger for information is keeping me alert. I want more than the bull I was handed when I first arrived.

Callie makes another noise, and Mandy and I peer over at her at the same time. "She's still sleeping," I whisper. "We didn't wake her."

"Still," Mandy says in a hushed tone. "I should come over to your bed if we're going to talk more."

"Sure." I scoot over and adjust the bulky sweatshirt I'm wearing over my flannel pajama top.

Mandy tiptoes over to my bed and sits down carefully on the edge. "Is this okay?" she asks.

"Yes." I wave my hand. "You're fine."

Like I mentioned to Callie at lunchtime, I should be fine with Mandy. At least, I hope I am. As if she knows what I'm thinking, she gives me an encouraging smile. And then we continue our discussion.

"Anyway," Mandy says, "we're only allowed in town if Mrs. Lowry or Allison accompanies us. And that rarely, if ever, happens."

I pick at a tear in the arm of my sweatshirt. "Yeah, but how can they really stop us?"

Mandy laughs, but it's a bitter sound. "Go ahead and hike around the property, Jaynie. Walking around up here, at least, is permitted. Go as far as you can, in all directions. Check out the property lines. You'll have no trouble finding them. There's high fencing around the entire perimeter, with barbed wire on top."

"Barbed wire?"

"Yep."

"I hadn't noticed," I reply dismally.

Mandy continues, "The only open area is way up in the deep part of the woods, north of the house. But even that area ends at the edge of a cliff overlooking a river. It'd be a damn steep drop to the water." Her eyes meet mine. "It's doable…but dangerous."

Not sure I heard her correctly, I say, "What? Jumping off the cliff? That seems a bit extreme, Mandy."

She shrugs and stares down at the covers. "Just remember, it's an out."

God, she's serious. Could things ever really get *that* bad?

"Listen, Jaynie," Mandy says. "It's like what we talked about earlier in the craft barn. The bottom line is we're all trapped up here."

I nod slowly as I envision the fortress-like gates at the entrance to the property and the wire fence in the front. Guess it extends everywhere. God, I really am a prisoner in this place, more so than I thought. We all are.

"Mrs. Lowry tells us all these measures are to keep us safe from possible intruders." Mandy rolls her eyes. "Don't believe her crap. Every inch of fencing and every locked gate are nothing but devices to keep us from running away."

"Don't the townspeople question what's going on up here?" I'm still trying to come to grips with how trapped I really am. "They must find it odd to never see any of us around town."

Mandy laughs. "Don't be naïve. Those people have their own problems down there. You drove through the town on the way here, right?" I nod. "Then I'm sure it was clear most of those people have no jobs and no money. They're as desperate as we are."

I think of the boarded-up buildings, the cars on blocks in the yards, and the young girl crying in the middle of a muddy mess. I sigh. "I see what you're saying."

"There's more, too, Jaynie."

"I think I'm afraid to hear anything else," I mutter.

But Mandy goes on. "Mrs. Lowry gives the small handful of influential people in Forsaken a lot of money to leave her alone. End result, no one cares what goes on here. It works out well for all those involved. We kids stay out of sight, and the people in town pretend we don't exist. Bu the way, don't think that doesn't include our social workers. You'll see."

I'm quick to retort, "Saundra said she'd stop in and check on me from time to time."

"Did she check on you at your last home?"

I swallow the lump that forms in my throat. "No."

"Then don't count on things being any different now that you're here, especially with Crafty Lo calling the shots."

I know she's right, and it makes me ill.

"So, what are we supposed to do?" I ask. "Just count the days till we turn eighteen?"

"Yeah, pretty much."

I glance over at Callie, resting peacefully. She's as much of a prisoner as we are. And she's only eight.

"What about the twins?" I ask. "After we're gone are Callie and Cody going to end up being stuck here for ten more years?" I shudder. "What kind of life would that be for them? Working all the time, never being allowed to play?"

"It's already like that," Mandy reminds me. "And it *is* a terrible life for them." Her voice cracks and she looks away, swiping at her eyes discreetly. She loves those kids, no doubt about it.

"We should do something once we're out," I whisper.

"What would we do, Jaynie? Report the fabulous Crafty Lo? No one will ever believe us. Everyone around here loves that lady. There were kids here before us, you know. They turned eighteen, left, and never looked back. Sometimes it's easier just to not make waves."

It sounds harsh, but I have to ask, "Is that what you plan to do? Leave at the end of July and never look back?"

"No fucking way." She shakes her head. "I have a place to go, and I'm going to work my ass off to change the things I can."

She doesn't appear to be joking, but I have to ask, "How can you change anything? You just said it was impossible."

Mandy bites her bottom lip and stares over at the sole window in the room. It's raining like crazy and sheets of water are beating against the glass.

I'm waiting to hear Mandy's grand plan, but she doesn't say a thing.

"What?" I say, puffing up the pillows behind me to sit up straighter. "Are you afraid I'll blab your plan to someone? I'd never say a word to anyone, if that's what you're worried about."

Mandy sighs, her eyes remaining on the window as a flash of

Tomorrow's Lies

lightning brightens the room to a silvery-blue. "Yeah, I guess not," she says, at last.

She's still quiet, so I try to prod her along. "So, where are you planning to go when you leave?"

"As soon as I get out of here, I'm heading straight to Morgantown."

"Why Morgantown?"

"Before I was sent here, that's where I was living."

"That's in a different county, though."

"Yeah," Mandy replies as her gaze finally returns to me. "I wasn't in foster care at the time. I had run away from the home I'd been placed in. It sucked, and I wanted out. I'd always heard you could make money in Morgantown, enough to get by on your own."

"You got a job in Morgantown?" I ask.

Mandy laughs. "No, Jaynie, not money from a real job. I'm talking about panhandling for cash. I was too young to work, and I was a runaway from the system. Begging for money was my only real option."

I nod knowingly. It's never come to that for me, but it could.

"Anyway," Mandy says, "the students up there were surprisingly generous. It seemed the ones I ran into had a lot of empathy for my situation." She shrugs. "Or I don't know, maybe they were just glad they weren't in my shoes."

"How old were you at the time?" I ask softly.

"Fifteen," she says.

"Oh, wow. I can't even imagine."

"It wasn't that bad, not really. I wasn't above begging. And panhandling was definitely better than the alternative."

"What was the alternative?" I ask, even though I suspect I already know the answer.

"Prostitution," Mandy says, confirming my suspicion.

"Damn, Mandy."

She pauses for a beat, looks away. In a soft voice she tells me, "I have to be honest, Jaynie. I thought about it more than once."

"Hooking?"

She nods. "Yeah. There were times when I was so hungry I couldn't sleep. Those nights, hooking didn't sound so bad." She takes a breath, while I hold mine, imagining a fifteen-year-old Mandy contemplating selling her body.

"I always came to my senses, though," Mandy says. "I'd remind myself how there's always a pimp who shows up and takes a cut of the money you earn lying on your back. Then, if you refuse to work for him,"—she makes a fist and punches the air—"you get your ass handed to you. Hell, even if you *do* agree to work for the dickhead, he still lays you out from time to time. So, yeah, hooking was out."

"That's crazy," is all I can think to say.

Mandy has clearly lived much more than me. Sure, horrific things have happened in my life, but there are far worse things that could still occur. I sure as hell don't want to end up selling my body to untold numbers of men. One man taking what he wanted damaged me enough. But the worst could still lie ahead. Living in the world of the unwanted is like living on thin ice. It could crack open at any time, and God help you if you fall in.

I feel the blood draining from my face, and Mandy asks, "Jesus, are you okay?"

Shakily, I reply, "Yeah, I'm good."

Clearly, I am not, and Mandy stares at me like she'd like to ask more. I know she's curious to hear my full story, but I'm not ready to get into what I went through. Still, my reticence to speak about myself doesn't mean I'm not curious about how Mandy ended up where she is. Like, how'd she land in foster care in the first place?

I don't have the courage to ask, not now, so I focus on the story at hand.

"So," I begin, "what great thing happened in Morgantown that has you so set on returning when you get out of here?"

Mandy lights up, and not from the fresh flash of lightning illuminating the room. "I met this guy when I was there," she says softly.

"Ahh, it's always a guy."

She smiles. "Seems that way, huh?"

I can't believe it, but the unflappable Mandy is flustered. "Are you blushing?" I ask.

I feel so normal all of the sudden. I mean, here we are in a crappy situation, but we can still smile and blush over a boy. Emboldened, I take a chance and nudge Mandy with my knee. I wait for the panic to set in, but everything is fine. I feel good. Maybe there's hope for me yet.

Mandy glances down at my knee, then back up at me. I know she's surprised I made contact with her, but, to my relief, she says nothing. Instead, she treats me like I'm normal, nonchalantly smacking me with the edge of the top sheet.

"Shut up," she says. "I am *not* blushing." She ponders for a few seconds, and then qualifies, "Though I have to admit that Josh is certainly a blush-inducing kind of guy."

"Josh, huh?"

"Yeah," she sighs. "Josh."

Mandy clearly cares for this "blush-inducing" guy. I mean, hell, he's her reason to return to Morgantown, so I feel confident in asking, "Is Josh the special someone you told me about in the work barn?" She nods, and I add excitedly, "Well, tell me more about him."

We both hunker down in the covers. I scoot lower on my pillows and she moves an inch closer.

"Okay," she says. "I may be biased, but I have to say Josh is really super cute."

"Go on," I prompt.

Smiling, she tells me, "He has wavy blond hair and the bluest eyes you've ever seen. And, Jaynie, he is freaking *built*."

I nod approvingly. "Nice."

"*Very* nice," she agrees with a waggle of her eyebrows.

We laugh for a minute, but then things turn serious when she says, "More important than all those things, though, is that Josh is a great guy. He's a good soul, Jaynie. Like Flynn." She smiles at me, and I smile back. "He really helped me a lot. I don't think I ever would have made it for so long without him. He was a runaway, too, at the time, but he'd been out on his own for a lot longer than I had. He knew things, like which fast food restaurants didn't lock their dumpsters at night and who dumped the most food. He also knew the best places to panhandle, and where it was safe to sleep."

"He sounds amazing," I say. "Was he fifteen at the time, too?"

"No, he was seventeen when I met him, almost eighteen."

Mandy stares at the wall behind me, and I know she's lost in a memory. Maybe she's thinking about what Josh might be doing right now, maybe she's wondering if he still thinks of her, the way she's thinking of him on a stormy April night.

Mandy clears her throat. "Oh, I should tell you something else about Josh. Something that kind of makes him…well, him. He's a really talented musician."

"Wow, that's pretty cool."

"Yeah, it is. He used to play gigs around town, mostly in coffee shops. He sang a capella, at first, since he had no money for an instrument. But once he earned enough cash, he bought himself a pawned guitar. He was really catching on about the time I got picked up."

"Picked up? What'd you do?"

"Something stupid." Mandy makes a face. "I got arrested for shoplifting a donut and was thrown back in the system."

"Ugh, that sucks."

"Yeah, it sucked big time. Josh had been saving money at the time. We were hoping to get ourselves an apartment. There's this state

Tomorrow's Lies

program Josh knew of where you can apply for subsidized housing."

I perk up. "Wow, really? I might be interested in that. After I get out, that is."

"We'll keep in touch," Mandy says. "Once I hook up with Josh, I'll get the details for you."

I like the idea, and I ask, "Do you think Josh has his own place by now?"

"He may, Jaynie. I sure hope so. But if not, we'll find one together."

Curious, I ask, "How do you plan to get in touch with him?"

Mandy smiles a *we got that covered* grin. "We worked out a plan ages ago. After I get to Morgantown I'm supposed to wait at our secret spot every evening at sunset. He'll find me. He knows I'll be there shortly after my birthday."

"Secret spot, huh?" I can't help but smile. "That sounds romantic."

Mandy snickers softly. "Yeah, I guess it does. We had a little home set up under an overpass, right along the river. Josh used to play guitar at night and sing me to sleep. That's where we plan to meet."

"He sounds really sweet."

"He is, Jaynie, he really is. And we're going to have the life we want together. I figure if I get a job right away, and Josh is earning money from working *and* playing music, we can apply to be foster parents. That's my real plan, Jaynie, to foster the twins. I just want to get them out of here. And eventually I hope to adopt Cody and Callie. I want to officially become their mom."

"The twins do love you," I say. "I think it's a great idea."

Mandy's plan *is* amazing. Callie already told me she wants nothing more than for Mandy to become her mom, and I'm sure Cody feels the same way. Silently, I send up a prayer for everything to work out for Mandy and Josh, and for Cody and Callie, especially. I send up a quick prayer for Flynn, too, just in case he has a plan, as well.

Mandy glances over her shoulder at Callie, then back at me. "Do you want to hear the twins' story?" she asks. "I can tell you how they ended up in foster care, if you want to know."

"Of course I want to know," I reply. And I do. I want to learn as much about my new family as possible.

"Well," Mandy says. "I should start by telling you the twins have been in the system since they were four."

"How'd they end up orphaned at such a young age?" I ask.

Mandy glances over at Callie once more, to make sure she's asleep. When she turns back, she says, "Their mom was an addict. And they ended up in the system when she tried to sell them to her dealer to pay off a meth debt."

"Jesus."

"I know. It's awful, right?"

"I can't even…"

"It could've been worse," Mandy says. "Lucky for the twins the dealer had a brother with a conscience. He dropped the kids off at Child Protective Services."

I think of Callie mentioning how her mommy didn't want them. But then she asked if I knew her mom. It kills me to think some part of that little girl still wants her mommy, despite everything.

"The things people do to their own children," I say, disgusted. "It sickens me."

"I know, Jaynie. I feel the same way." Mandy rubs a hand down her face. "Ugh. Let's talk about something else, okay?"

"Fine with me."

Silence descends for a minute as we listen to the rain. And then I clear my throat and ask, "Do you know when Flynn turns eighteen?"

"Yeah." Mandy nods. "October."

"Does he know about your plan to foster the twins?"

"Yeah, he knows everything. And he thinks it's a great idea, too."

"Okay, I have to ask…" I trail off.

Mandy waits for me to continue, and when I don't, she says, "Come on already. What?

I blurt out, "Does Flynn have any sort of plan for when he turns eighteen?"

Mandy laughs. "Yeah, his plan is to get the hell out of here."

"That's it?"

"More or less," Mandy says. "Flynn's not much of a planner. But, still, I'm sure once he gets settled, he'll want to come up and visit the twins." She contemplates, and then adds, "Maybe Flynn will stay up in Morgantown with us for a while. I know he loves Cody dearly. I think it's because he reminds him of Galen."

"Who is Galen?" I inquire.

Mandy lowers her voice to a barely audible whisper. "He was Flynn's little brother."

"Was?"

"Yeah, Jaynie…*was*." She looks at me for a beat, then peers down at the bunched-up covers.

I know the answer has to be bad, but I can't help but ask, "Flynn's brother is dead, then? What the hell happened?"

Mandy closes her eyes and shakes her head sharply. "Flynn should be the one to tell you the story. It's not my place. But, yeah, his little brother is dead."

Suddenly, lightning lights up the sky outside our window more brightly than ever. The blinding flash is accompanied by a vicious boom of thunder. The next crack is so loud, kind of like a whip cutting through the air, that both Mandy and I jump out of bed.

"Shit, that was loud," Mandy says. She places her hand over her heart as she steadies herself.

"I know, right."

Callie is awake now, too. She's sitting up, rubbing her eyes. "Where's Cody?" she asks drowsily.

What an odd question, seeing as Cody is down the hall in the room he shares with Flynn. Maybe Callie dreamt her brother was here with us in our room.

I try to sound consoling when I reply, "I'm sure Cody is fine. He's safe in his room with Flynn."

"Yeah," Callie agrees as she yawns and stretches. "He's always safe with Flynn, but they'll still be here soon enough."

I look to Mandy, questioning, and she says, "Uh, there's something I need to tell you."

Chapter Seven

Flynn

Here's how it works...

I know how to sneak around the watchful red eyes of the cameras in the hall, so I lead Cody down the short hall. He follows, stepping in my exact footsteps. He's an accurate little guy, as he knows one mistake and we are fucked.

The camera outside the girls' bedroom door is tilted up, only the top half of the hallway is visible within its intrusive view. That means we can outsmart it. Hopefully, Mrs. Lowry will never get around to re-adjusting the damn thing.

"Okay." I turn to Cody and drop down to my knees, putting me at about his height. With forced cheerfulness, I say, "Ready to do some covert crawling, little dude?"

"Uh-huh." Cody nods and gets down on his knees, mimicking me. When he looks my way, waiting for the signal to go, I notice his eyes are so red-rimmed from crying that it gives me pause.

How long can this shit go on? The kid needs professional help for these bad dreams and night terrors. Tonight's nightmare has left him visibly shaken. It was worse than the others, and it took me a full ten minutes to calm him down.

Despite my efforts, snot still pours from Cody's nose. I sigh and peel off my white T-shirt, leaving me in dark blue boxers and nothing else.

Placing my balled-up tee under his nose, I wipe away the goo and ask, "Is that better?"

"Yeah," Cody says, throat thick with phlegm. "Thank you, Flynnie."

Damn, I know the kid loves me. And God help me, I love him, too. Leaving when I turn eighteen is going to be hard. I hope Mandy's plan to foster the twins actually comes to fruition.

Cody tilts his head and asks, "What wrong now?"

I reach over and tousle his dark hair. "Nothing, bud. Let's go."

When we reach the girls' room, I knock once on the door, down low, out of camera range. After a few seconds, Mandy opens the door. She must have been awake; she looks alert. She doesn't acknowledge us in any way, as that would blow our cover. Instead, she glances down the hall to the bathroom, like she's not sure if she has to go or not. It's all part of our ruse.

While Mandy mock-contemplates, Cody and I crawl past her legs and into the room. That's when Mandy does her final act for the camera, sighing and pretending she's changed her mind.

After Mandy closes the door, the cameras are no longer a concern. Cody and I stand. And while I brush away fibers from the carpet from my knees, Cody is throwing his little arms around Mandy's legs.

Kneeling down, she encircles him in a hug and assures him, "You're safe, sweetie. Everything is okay."

"I had bad dream, Mandy, with monsters. Scary monsters chase me all over the place." Cody clings to Mandy tightly. "It was scary, so scary."

"I know, sweetie, I know." She kisses his cheek. "But nothing bad can get you now. We're all together. Me, you, Flynn, Callie—"

"Callie," he calls out frantically, his gaze sweeping the room for his sister. "Where are you?"

"I'm here, silly." Callie slips from her bed, rubbing her eyes, and Cody runs to his twin.

I'm still standing by the door. While I shove hair out of my field of vision—I really need a damn haircut—I say quietly to Mandy, "It was really bad tonight for him. I don't know how much longer this can go on. The kid needs to sleep in order to function."

"Yeah, but what can we do, Flynn?" Mandy's face is pained. This situation is killing her too. Our helplessness, our inability to do more for Cody, is wearing us down.

I sigh, and out of the corner of my eye, I notice Jaynie, sitting up on her mattress, leaned forward with bunched-up pillows behind her. She starts tugging at the cuffs of the bulky sweatshirt she's wearing. The strain on her face is evident. I know it has to be uncomfortable for her to have a guy standing in her room, at night, wearing only boxers. I don't know Jaynie's story, but I'm smart enough to have figured out she was assaulted in some way. Fuck, I feel like an ass. I should have left the stupid T-shirt on.

I suddenly realize I'm still holding the snot-filled, balled-up cotton tee. *Gross.* I turn and toss it in the direction of the laundry basket in the corner. When I turn back around, Jaynie is watching me curiously.

I smile at the girl in what I hope is a reassuring way, and not some pervert grin. Shit, maybe it comes off as shady, seeing as Jaynie quickly averts her gaze to where Mandy has gone to the twins. She's getting them settled on her full-size mattress in the middle of the room.

I wonder then if Mandy has given Jaynie the full details of how this kind of night usually unfolds. Mandy always gives her bed to

Callie and Cody so they can sleep in a bed with lots of room. Mandy then sleeps in Callie's bed. And that leaves me. I usually sleep on the floor where Jaynie's mattress now resides.

Shit.

Going back to my room is not an option. There's too much risk of getting caught if the door keeps opening and closing. I shift from one foot to the other as I watch Mandy crawl under the covers in Callie's empty bed. She looks over at me and says, "Flynn, you better get some sleep. It's almost three AM."

"Yeah, you're right." I yawn at the reminder. "Morning will be here soon enough."

"Yep," she says. "And then it's back to work for all of us. Oh, yay," she sarcastically adds.

"That reminds me." I cross my arms over my chest. "I damn well better be assigned back to work in the barn. I don't think I can take another day with Allison."

While I head toward the space on the floor between the twins and Mandy, Mandy says, "I hope you're back, too. We didn't make quota today."

"No wonder Cody had a nightmare," I grumble. "His dreams are always bad when he's really hungry."

"Do you think you can steal a few extra bars tomorrow at breakfast?" Mandy looks to me, hope in her eyes. "Like, maybe more than two?"

"I can try." I tell her.

I then attempt to lie down on the floor between Mandy and the twins, but the space between the mattresses is far too narrow.

"We pushed them closer to give Jaynie more space," Mandy whispers to me when she sees my dilemma. "Sorry."

"Eh, it's okay," I say.

But it's kind of a problem. The only other open space would be on the floor next to Jaynie. *Great.*

Mandy, her gaze following mine, says, "Just sleep over there. I think she'll be fine for one night. We can move the beds back the way they were tomorrow."

"Uh, okay." I feel less confident than I sound. But what choice do I have?

I tiptoe over to the space between Jaynie's bed and the twins. The kids are fast asleep already, but Jaynie sure as hell isn't. She has the covers pulled up to her chin, and her wide eyes are watching my every move.

"I'm not going to hurt you," I tell her.

"I know," she snaps.

I can see she's trying hard to be brave, but it's not working out too well for her. Which is a shame 'cause we've been getting along so well. What the hell happened to this girl to set her back so far? All I know is we were informed on her first day here not to touch her, like, ever. If she was sexually assaulted, as I suspect, it must have happened not all that long ago. Her wounds—the ones in her psyche, the kind that stick—seem fresh.

I hardly know Jaynie, but from what I've seen she seems like a sweet, kind girl. I feel a sudden surge of anger. I have no tolerance for men who inflict pain on someone weaker. And, yeah, I know why.

Damn, I'd like to get my hands on the motherfucker who made Jaynie this way. I can tell she was once fiery. That was evident the day I met her. Her witty retorts amused me, and I liked the spark in her pretty emerald eyes.

Gesturing to the floor, I ask, "Do you mind if I sleep here?"

"No," she whispers. "That's fine."

"I promise I don't snore," I tease as I lower myself to the floor. "At least, not too loudly." Maybe I can relax her with my dumbass humor.

And hey, wouldn't you know it, it works. She cracks a smile.

I try to get comfortable on the hardwood floor, but it's tough, especially since I'm trying not to make a bunch of noise as I roll from one side to the other. When I settle on a position facing Jaynie, I think everything is cool. But then she scoots away. As she presses her back to the wall behind her, I hear her swallowing hard.

"Hey." I lift my head. "I can face the other way if that'd be better for you."

She bites her lip, like she's surmounting a huge obstacle.

"No," she says at last, her tone determined. "You're good like that."

She's trying hard to be accommodating, but I can't in good conscience sleep this way if it makes her that uncomfortable.

I roll to my other side and whisper over my shoulder, "Actually, I sleep better on this side."

"Okay, Flynn."

She sounds completely unconvinced, and I hear her sigh. Then there's some rustling of covers. I guess she's trying to get comfortable.

It's chilly on the cold floor without my T-shirt, so I curl up to keep warm. Eventually, despite the cold, I start to drift off. But before I am completely out, I feel the soft texture of a blanket as it's draped over me.

"'Night, Flynn," Jaynie whispers.

"Good night, Jaynie," I whisper back, smiling as I fall asleep.

Chapter Eight

Jaynie

The next week flies by. The week after passes quickly, too, and before I know it I've lived in my new home for over a month.

I make a lot of progress, which fills me with pride. I'm comfortable with my new foster siblings, in a way that helps me heal. Every day, I draw a little closer to the girl I once was.

How do I know I'm getting better? One indication is when I feel comfortable enough to abandon my multi-layered attire. Hell, the weather alone sets me on that path. May is far too warm for wool leggings and sweaters. I throw longing glances daily at Mandy's shorts, tees, and light summer dresses, wondering if she notices.

Well, she sure notices one Sunday morning when she walks into our bedroom—armed with a basket of freshly laundered clothes—and catches me holding up one of her dresses, admiring it wishfully. A simple cotton number, white as snow, with cute spaghetti straps and a scalloped hem, I love it.

I'm supposed to be dusting and cleaning, though, not gawking at

Mandy's apparel.

I stammer to explain. "Oh, uh, I'm sorry." I swiftly lay the dress on Mandy's bed. "I didn't mean to be messing with your stuff. I just thought that particular dress was pretty."

Setting the laundry basket on the floor and stretching out her back, Mandy says casually, "You can have it if you want. It's too short on me, anyway." She scans me from head to toe. "On you, though, I think it'd fit perfectly."

I know I'd be far cooler in Mandy's white dress than in the jeans and long-sleeved tees I've been wearing lately. Still, I am hesitant to accept her offer.

"I don't know." I rub my forehead. "I don't want to take your clothes. None of us have all that much to begin with. I think I'll be fine with my jeans and stuff."

Mandy is folding Callie's clothes and placing them in a drawer. She stops what she's doing and comes over to where I'm standing. Picking up the dress, she holds it out in front of me.

"Look at the length, Jaynie. Like I said, it'd be perfect on you. No more discussion. The dress is yours."

Before I can argue, she drapes the lightweight material over my arm.

"It is pretty," I muse quietly as I peer down at the dress, not knowing whether I'll ever be brave enough to put it on. "I just don't want to take something of yours that I might never end up wearing."

"You'll wear it," Mandy replies with a smile. "But until you do"— she turns to the dresser—"I have some other clothes you can have, too."

I follow her, but before she can fully open a drawer, I place my hand on the edge to stop her.

"Wait, Mandy. I really shouldn't take any more of your clothes. The dress is enough."

She opens the drawer all the way, ignoring my hand as it moves along with it. So much for stopping this determined girl.

"Don't be ridiculous, Jaynie. I have way more clothes than you, especially summery things. And do you think I want to have to lug a bunch of clothes up with me to Morgantown?"

"Guess not," I murmur, acquiescing.

"You'll actually be doing me a favor," she goes on.

"If you say so, Mandy."

In the next few minutes, I become the proud new owner of two pairs of shorts, another dress, and four lightweight cotton tees.

"There, all set," Mandy declares. Her hand brushes mine accidentally as she hands me the last article of clothing.

"Oh," I blurt out, surprised at the direct skin-to-skin contact. But when I feel nothing but calm, I happily add, "Hey that was okay. I'm fine."

Mandy pats my hand, and I remain fine. "See," she says softly. "You're getting better every day."

And I am. It's not just wishful thinking.

My progress is never more apparent than when more middle-of-the-night visits from the boys occur. I not only become more comfortable with their presence, I actually begin to look forward to the nights when all five of us are sleeping in one room. It's like we're the Waltons or some other famous TV family…in a twisted, mixed-up sort of way. One glaring difference is I sure don't think of Flynn as a brother.

Speaking of Flynn, he sleeps on the floor next to my mattress all the time. And I always give him a blanket. Even when the nights become too warm for covers, he still takes it. Those nights he uses the blanket as a pillow.

When I can't sleep, which is often, I watch Flynn. He remains careful around me, always sleeping on his back, or rolling away so he's not facing me. Though he doesn't come out and say it, I know he wants me to be as at ease as possible when he's in our bedroom.

He needn't worry so much. Not anymore. I see Flynn in a new light with each passing day. My initial crush on him has blossomed to genuine affection. And there's something more, something I never thought possible, not after what I went through. But there it is, I can't deny it. I am insanely attracted to Flynn.

His wide chest and muscular legs don't bother me anymore. In fact, I secretly enjoy looking at him in just his boxers. I'm especially happy when he abandons the tees completely and sleeps sans shirt. Flynn's half-bare body is amazing—so male and all strong and lean. While he sleeps I like to stare at his flat stomach, or admire how the muscles in his back move and bunch in the shadowy night when he stretches.

"Flynn," I whisper one night when I feel a particularly strong urge to touch him. Just once, to know he's real.

When he doesn't respond, and I am sure he's asleep, I reach down till I'm actually touching him.

Oh, God.

I'm committed now—and not having a meltdown—so I take a chance and trail my index finger, ever so slowly and softly, across his firm stomach.

Holy shit.

My newfound courage comes to a screeching halt, however, when I reach the fine trail of hair that disappears under the band of his boxers.

What in the hell am I doing?

With a start, I jerk my hand away. Not from an impending panic attack, but more due to all the confusing emotions overwhelming me.

My body wants things I know Flynn could give me. That's the normal seventeen-year-old girl part of me talking. But the damaged part fears Flynn's touch and what it might trigger.

A panic, the likes of which I haven't felt in a long while, rises to the surface. Wincing, I scoot back until I am pressed up against the wall as tightly as I can be. Thankfully, Flynn remains asleep.

Oh, no. What if when I *am* finally ready to be touched by a man, I'm reminded of the abuse I suffered? I tell myself over and over that Flynn is not Mrs. Giessen's son. He's not a predator like that horrible man. Flynn is just a boy my age that cares for me. I shouldn't allow myself to even associate the two. What was done to me was an act of violence. And what I crave from Flynn is affection.

I know this, I really do. So, why do I still feel culpable, like I should have somehow stopped Mrs. Giessen's son? I mean, really, what good am I when I failed to protect myself?

Turning away from Flynn, I curl up against the wall and cry myself to sleep.

One week to the day from when Mandy gives me clothes I have yet to wear, an amazing thing happens. Mrs. Lowry and Allison leave for the day. Equally amazing is that we are given no chores, no Sunday tasks.

I soon find out this means we have a rare day off!

I can't believe it, even as Mandy and I stand on the porch and watch Mrs. Lowry and Allison drive away in a sleek BMW, a car bought with our sweat and tears.

Turning to Mandy, I say, "You know what? We deserve a day off."

Mandy laughs. "We sure as hell do."

Curious, I ask, "How often does this happen?"

"Not often. I think the last time we had a day off was"—Mandy counts swiftly on her hand—"five months ago. It was sometime around Christmas, I remember that."

"Wow. That's sad."

"It is," she says. "And who knows when the next one will come. That's why we need to make sure we enjoy this one."

I nod vigorously, agreeing. And then I ask, "Where are they heading to, anyway? How long do we have to ourselves?"

"They're going shopping," Mandy replies. "I overheard Allison mention something about outlets in Pennsylvania."

I am cautiously optimistic. "That means we may have hours, then. Wow. Are you sure you heard her correctly? You're definitely positive Allison said they were driving all the way up to Pennsylvania?"

"Yes, Jaynie," Mandy says, laughing at my skepticism. "I'm sure."

Mandy is happier than I've ever seen her, which makes me happy. When Flynn steps outside with the kids, he doesn't miss our grins.

"What's going on?" he asks, leaning his jean-clad butt against the rail.

Flynn looks exceptionally good today, especially when he crosses his arms across his chest and the muscles in his arms bulge.

I mentally smack myself to get back on track so Mandy and I can get him up to speed. When we're finished relaying the facts, Flynn frowns. Even wary and scowling, the guy is hot.

"Are you absolutely sure Allison said they're driving all the way up to PA?" he asks, oblivious to my perusal of his body.

"Yes, yes." Mandy nods emphatically, and then rolls her eyes. "God, you sound exactly like Jaynie."

He smiles over at me and my heart flip-flops. Thankfully, he turns away quickly to address the twins, giving me time to put my nonchalant face back on.

"Hey, think you guys are up for having some fun today?" Flynn asks Cody and Callie.

"What kind of fun?" Callie is wary. "Today is Sunday. We have chores to do."

"There are no chores today," Flynn announces. "And as for your other question, you can have any kind of fun you want today."

"Yay, yay, yay," Cody starts yelling. Jumping up and down, he adds, "I want have fun, I want have fun."

Tomorrow's Lies

Callie's little brow creases. "We can stay outside all day if we want?"

Flynn tugs her long ponytail lightly. "Yes, you sure can. In fact, that's *my* plan, little miss."

That makes Callie laugh.

So, outside all day it is. Sure, we're relegated to the grounds, but it sure beats working.

"Let's go play, Cody," Callie says to her brother as she grabs his hand.

He's all in agreement. But then the twins get no farther than the base of the porch steps before they are turning back to us. "Where we go play, Flynnie?" Cody asks, perplexed.

Callie gazes up at us, waiting for an answer right along with her brother.

"Anywhere you want," Flynn tells them.

Callie's brown eyes widen. "*Any*where?"

"Well, anywhere on the property," Mandy interjects.

"Like there's a choice in that matter," I mutter.

No one hears me, and no one cares. The twins are simply glad to have some freedom for at least a day.

Callie suddenly says, "Hey, I have an idea." She leans over and whispers to Cody, and then they're off, running and shouting gleefully, in a way that should be allowed more than once every five months.

We allow the kids to play alone for a while. Flynn and Mandy sit on the top porch step, and I take a seat a couple of steps below. We talk about nothing important, just mundane shit, and when it gets too warm we head to the pump behind the craft barn and take turns drinking water. Finally, we decide to join the twins up in the expansive grassy fields. We find them near the old barn, playing close to the tree line.

Callie, spotting us first, runs over and asks if we want in on her and Cody's game of Tag.

"We sure do," Flynn tells her, feigning great excitement for her benefit.

The game commences, but it doesn't take long for Cody to tag me out. Who knew the kid was so darn fast?

Ready for a break anyway, I head over to our designated sideline and plop down on the grass. But after a few minutes under the blazing sun, I am burning up. I start to wave my hand around, fanning myself.

"Ugh," I grumble like a little old lady. "This heat is killing me."

I'm wearing black leggings that feel as if they've been soaking up every single drop of sun. The black tee I pulled over my head this morning probably wasn't the greatest idea, but since it has short sleeves, my top half feels relatively cool. The problem is definitely my covered legs. I really need to start wearing the shorts Mandy gave me.

I decide to head down to the house soon as the game is done. Leaning back on my elbows, I prop myself up and watch everyone running around.

Callie is on Flynn's butt, and he slows down purposely so she can tag him out. The little girl is elated. "I got Flynn, I got Flynn," she calls out.

I can't help but smile at Flynn's continued thoughtfulness and generosity. When he sees me hanging out in the grass, he jogs over to me.

Nodding immediately to my covered-up legs, he says, "Shit, Jaynie. All black. You have to be dying out here in those clothes."

"Yeah." I blow out a breath and pluck moist hair from my cheek. "I wasn't planning on spending the whole day outside."

"None of us were," he says, dragging a hand through his own sweaty hair. "But it sure is a welcome development."

"Sure is," I agree. None of us can argue that.

As Flynn shifts from one foot to the other, I shade my eyes and peer up at him. The sun, behind where he's standing, bathes him in a golden glow, making him look like an angel. Damn, I must be overheating.

Back to fanning myself, I say, "I think I need to put on some shorts."

"Me, too," Flynn replies.

I nod to his denim-covered legs. "Yeah, why are you wearing jeans?"

"Same reason as you. I never dreamed we'd be outside all day." He points down to the house. "Let's go change."

"Sounds like a plan," I say, standing.

"Cool."

Gesturing to Mandy and the twins, who are still running around having fun, I say, "Should we tell them we're going down to the house?"

"No." Flynn shakes his head. "We'll only be gone a few minutes. They won't miss us."

Flynn breaks into a light jog, until I protest. "Hey, no more running, okay? Not till I lose these leggings."

Flynn slows to a walk, and from there we stroll leisurely. Still, by the time we reach the front porch it's like the temperature has shot up another ten degrees.

"Blech, it must be closing in on ninety," I gripe as I lean next to the front door and mop my brow.

"I think it is ninety," Flynn agrees, tugging on the handle of the screen door.

When the light screen swings back, I use my hip to keep it propped open so Flynn can open the front door without this one falling back on him.

"I think I'll wash up a bit while we're in there," I muse to myself as I make the door bounce with my hip.

Flynn pauses, chuckles at my amusement. "No problem. I'll wait for you."

Pushing back a clump of moistened hair from my forehead, I make a face and add, "I feel so totally gross right now."

Flynn gives me the 'ole once-over, and I cringe at how I must look to him.

To my surprise—and let's face it, absolute delight—he says, "I don't know what you're talking about. You look really pretty, Jaynie, as always."

He turns back to the door.

Wow, wow, wow. I almost faint on the spot. "Thank you," I whisper.

I feel like we may have just had a little moment, but that warm and fuzzy feeling dissipates rapidly when a breeze blows and I detect what feels suspiciously like the little legs of a bug on my cheek.

"Oh, God, what's on me, Flynn?" I smack at my face. Lightly, since I sure as hell don't want to get stung.

"Is it a bee?" I freeze and ask.

Flynn looks at me and starts to laugh. "It's not a bee," he assures me.

I go back to swishing my hands around my face, while the screen door smacks against my butt. "What is it, then?" I ask. "Something is definitely still there."

"Hold on a minute." Flynn's still smiling, shaking his head. "Would you stop waving your hands around everywhere?"

"Okay, sure." I lower my arms and stand completely still.

"It's not a bee or a bug," he reiterates, nodding reassuringly. "It's just a long strand of your hair that's stuck on your cheek. It's kind of poking you, uh, right about…*here.*"

He starts to reach out—I'm sure to push away the wayward, feels-like-a-bug strand—but then he remembers my issues.

"Anyway…" He drops his hand to his side, sighing. "The hair's stuck to your cheek. The breeze was making it move. That's why it felt like a bug."

Reaching up to my face, I ask. "Where is it, exactly? I can't feel anything now." I touch different places on my face and ask, "Here? Here?"

Flynn tries to point to the spot. "A little lower and to the right," he says.

"Um…"

"Ah, fuck it."

He reaches out, and I drop my hands to my sides. *I can do this, I can do this.*

Then again, maybe I can't.

Just as Flynn's hand is about to make contact with my cheek, I involuntarily flinch.

He freezes, hand suspended in the air. "Jaynie…?"

It's a question. Should he stop, or do I want him to keep going?

Our eyes meet, and all the things Flynn doesn't outright state are in those depths of gray. He wants to try again. He's just waiting for permission.

Taking a deep breath, I give it to him. "Go ahead, Flynn. Touch me. I'll be okay."

I don't know if what I'm so bravely stating will bear out to be true, but I sure as heck plan to try. I refuse to allow the monster who made me this way to win.

Quietly, he asks, "Are you absolutely sure?"

"Yes."

And that's all he needs to hear. Flynn brushes over with my cheek with his finger, lightly, just to see how I handle it.

Not great, as it turns out.

I gasp, and he jerks away.

I don't feel the usual panic, though. This feels different. Flynn's warm skin pressed to my own, even if only for a brief second, felt electric. Maybe it did for him, too. He appears a little flustered, which is not like Flynn.

"Try it again," I whisper.

He raises a brow. "Yeah?"

I nod. "Uh-huh."

His fingers brush across my cheek once more, this time more slowly. I close my eyes, acclimating myself to his touch. *I am okay.* I feel his fingertips, warm and appealingly rough, as he lifts the elusive strand of hair from my damp skin. So carefully, so gently. Wow, this is what it feels like to be cared for. I need this. Oh, how I need this.

Without opening my eyes, I lean into Flynn's lingering touch. He tucks more wayward hair behind my ear, pieces that weren't even stuck to my cheek. He just wants to touch me. "Is this all right?" he whispers.

"Yes."

I open my eyes, and he smiles at me. I smile back at him. He's as excited by this development as I am. And, damn, it feels *good*. A million unsaid things are expressed as we gaze into each other's eyes. Maybe not a million, but many, and all of them point to two things—I like Flynn, and he likes me. We are more than friends, more than pretend siblings.

Time freezes, and I revel in the magic of the moment. But alas, when he moves his fingers away from my face, the moment is lost.

"We should go in," Flynn says, clearing his throat.

"Yeah, we should."

In the house, neither of us mentions a word about what happened out on the porch. There's no need for discussion; we both know this is huge. Flynn—a guy—touched me, and I didn't have a meltdown.

Maybe there *is* hope for me, after all. Like real hope that I can have a normal relationship. I feel more like myself now than I have in a long time. So maybe this is the family I needed all along to help me reach this point.

And then there are my feelings for Flynn. Maybe Flynn is more than just the here and now. Maybe he's my future.

Chapter Nine

Flynn

Jaynie and I change into shorts, but before we head back out, I check to see if the lock on the door to the kitchen is unlatched. Sometimes Mrs. Lowry forgets to lock it when she goes out for a full day. There's never much food to raid, but the nutrition bars are always there.

Today, unfortunately for us, the kitchen is locked. "That fucking bitch," I mumble.

Jaynie flicks the padlock. "Looks like Crafty Lo remembered this time."

I shake my head. "Nah, this is Allison's doing."

Jaynie bites her lip and eyes me curiously. "Why do you think it was her?"

I am not about to fill her in on how many of Allison's advances I've dodged this past month, nor how jealous Allison has become of Jaynie. She wants me more than ever these days. It's her underhanded way to stick it to the pretty, new waif-like girl. It's fairly obvious to everyone in this house that Jaynie likes me. And that's cool. I kind of like her, too.

Okay, I have to be honest—I really like Jaynie. And if I ever needed confirmation, I got that out there on the porch. Something happened out there, a breakthrough for Jaynie. And something more, something between us. Shit, I am in so deep with her now.

Like I wasn't before? Yeah, right. Quit lying to yourself, Flynn.

My feelings for the new girl stopped me from getting a blow job the other day, and that's saying a lot. Allison, bypassing her usual innuendo, flat-out offered. And hell, I'd be lying if I didn't admit I seriously considered it. See, Allison has these big, pillowy lips, and a part of me would have liked nothing more than to have that mean whore down on her knees, sucking me off.

I couldn't do it, though. If I had it would have felt like a betrayal to Jaynie. See, in deep. Eh, who cares? Jaynie is amazing, and beautiful, and witty, and her soul is more than good.

Speaking of which, as the object of my affection waits for an answer to her question, I stand at the padlocked door, grinning like a fool. She must think I'm crazy.

Shrugging, I play it off. "Never mind, it's not important. Let's go back outside."

She lets it drop with an, "Okay, Flynn."

The girl is easy-going like that. For all her issues, she's far from high-maintenance.

Back in the fields we catch up to Mandy and the twins. As soon as Cody sees me, he runs over and hops up in my arms.

"Whoa, little man. You're getting too big to jump up on me like that."

I'm totally teasing. Truth is Cody is below normal height and weight for a boy his age, side effects of a lack of proper nutrition.

Placing his thumb in his mouth—and reminding me far too much of Galen—he puts his head on my shoulder. "Sorry," he mumbles.

Tomorrow's Lies

I pat him on the back. "Aww, you're good, buddy. I was just joking."

He leans back, his big eyes meeting mine. "Where you go, Flynnie?" he asks.

"Jaynie and I went inside to change into shorts. What are you guys doing out here? You come up with any new games?"

Excited, he replies, "Yeah, we did. We play Hide and Go Seek now. Wanna play?"

"Sure."

Cody peers over my shoulder to where Jaynie is standing. "Jaynie play, too?" he asks quietly.

Spinning around with Cody in my arms, I face Jaynie. "I don't know, bud. Let's ask her."

Turns out, Jaynie is up for playing Hide and Go Seek. For the next half an hour the five of us have a blast. We hide behind hay bales and crawl under bushes. The old barn up in the fields makes a great hideout, too. As time wears on, the game moves beyond the old barn and up into the dense forest.

When it's Jaynie's turn to try and find us she covers her eyes and counts to sixty. Four of us run amok, each trying to claim the best hiding place. Cody chooses a massive boulder, not far from the thick-trunked tree I've chosen to utilize as cover. Out of the corner of my eye I catch sight of Mandy ducking into a thicket of green. And then I spy Callie crouching down by an old wood pile. She wraps her oversized pink tee over her pale, skinny legs, like that's going to help hide her.

My laughing at Callie gives me away, and Jaynie finds me first.

"Really, Flynn, hiding behind a tree is the best you can do?" She tsks. "I expected more from you."

"Oh, I'll give you more," I playfully retort. "You just say the word."

At first, I worry I've gone too far, especially when Jaynie dips her chin and stares at the ground. But then she whispers, "Oh, stop," with no conviction at all.

Damn. The girl is flirting right back at me. Talk about progress.

Encouraged, I keep this playfulness going. "Yeah, okay, whatever you say." I lean back and stretch, knowing my tee will lift and expose my abs.

When I catch Jaynie sneaking a peek, I can't help but smile. My ploy worked.

I don't want to push too far, though, so I lose the grin and say, "Do you want some hints on where the others are hidden?"

"Flynn!" She feigns indignation. "That's cheating."

"Okay, I won't say a word." I make a show of pretending to zip my lips.

Jaynie glances around. There are no signs of anyone. "I guess one little hint wouldn't hurt," she says softly.

"I knew you'd cave," I say.

She huffs. "Just shut up and tell me."

Chuckling, I nod to the thicket where I know Mandy is hiding. "Try over there," I whisper.

Jaynie thanks me for the tip, then creeps off. But before she can reach Mandy, Cody gives himself away when he springs up from behind the boulder he's hidden behind and yells, "Hey guys, help, help! I see snake, I see snake."

All of us converge on Cody—to hell with the game—to make sure he's okay. "Which way did it go, little man?" I ask as I crouch down to his height. "You didn't get bit, did you?"

"No, I okay." Pointing to the boulder, he says, "Snake slithered under *there*."

I suspect what Cody saw was a garter snake, based on the tiny space beneath the boulder where it supposedly slithered in to.

"Hmm," I begin. "If the snake is under that rock, Cody, I think he's probably staying there for a while. Believe it or not, we're scarier to him than he is to us."

Cody looks wary. "No. Snaked scared of me? He was big, Flynnie, real big."

Fighting back a smile, I ask in a somber tone, "How big, bud?"

Cody holds his arms *way* apart. "This big!"

I give him a look like *for real?* And he quickly narrows the space between his hands to about six inches.

"That's more like it," I say. "So, think about how much bigger you are than that little guy."

Cody is far from reassured. He wants to go back. "I like playing close to house better," he tells me.

I tousle his hair. "No problem, kiddo."

With the decision made to abandon our game in the woods, Mandy gestures for Cody and Callie to follow her back to the trail that leads down to the open fields. Just as I'm about to fall in line behind them I feel a tug at the back of my T-shirt.

When I turn around, Jaynie takes a step back. "What's up?" I ask.

Hesitantly, she says, "Would it be all right if you and I stayed in the woods a while longer? It's just so pretty up here. And…" She glances around at all the flora around us, everything thick and green. "I really like this place."

I raise a brow. "Even with snakes lurking all about?"

"Pfft…" She waves her hand dismissively. "Snakes are the least of my worries, Flynn."

Her eyes—green as the foliage around us, but troubled—tell me Jaynie has had to worry about far worse things than little snakes.

"No problem," I tell her. "We can stay. Just wait here a sec."

I run ahead to catch up with the others. Once I have Mandy's attention I tell her Jaynie and I are going to stay in the woods a while longer.

Mandy narrows her eyes and gives me an *I know what you're up to* look. She's protective of Jaynie, but she needn't worry. I am, too.

"It's nothing like that," I assure her, rolling my eyes.

"Not yet," she says in a sing-song-y voice. "But I can see it coming."

I push her shoulder. "God, get out of here. Now, I'm not sure if you'll kick my ass if something happens…or if something doesn't."

"I like to keep you on your toes, Flynn," she says as she starts to jog away to catch up with the twins, who've run way ahead on the trail.

"Having you around is as bad as having a real sister," I call out.

Yelling over her shoulder, Mandy gets in the last word. "I have every intention of remaining like a real sister, Flynn. For as long as I'm here. And I guarantee you're going to miss all this sisterly concern when I'm gone."

Shit, that part is probably true. Mandy leaving is definitely going to suck. Apart from missing her friendship, it will be up to me and Jaynie to take care of the kids. That won't be easy since the twins rely so much on Mandy.

When I return to Jaynie, she watches me curiously as I rake my hand through my hair.

"What's bothering you, Flynn?" she asks.

We begin to walk, and I think about how I usually deflect questions of that nature. Today, though, I feel like I could use someone to talk to.

"I was just thinking how hard it's going to be when Mandy leaves."

"Yeah, it'll suck. The twins are going to be a mess."

"That's an understatement," I scoff.

Jaynie stops. She reaches out to touch my arm, but then it's like she realizes what she's doing.

"Oh." Her arm drops back to her side. "Anyway, we'll still be here for the twins."

"Yeah, we will."

We start walking again, heading deeper into the woods. The trail narrows for a while and we have no choice but to walk single file. When it widens, we walk side-by-side.

"Hey, Flynn," Jaynie says with a sigh. "Can I ask you a question?"

"Sure."

"What is Mandy's story? How'd she end up in the system?"

I motion to a huge old oak. "Here, let's sit for a minute."

We use the thick roots protruding from the ground as seats, and after we're settled, I say, "Mandy never had a real home, like ever."

Jaynie looks over at me, brow furrowing. "What do you mean?"

"She's been in the system since birth."

"Oh, Flynn." Jaynie appears absolutely stricken. "That's awful."

"Yeah, but it is what it is. Mandy's mother was a foster kid who got pregnant at fifteen. She was in a group home at the time."

"Mandy was born in a group home?"

I nod. "She was. And she was taken away immediately because her mom had psych problems."

"Wow. Where'd they place Mandy?"

"She was sent to live with a family who wanted to foster an infant."

Jaynie picks up a stick and starts tracing the grooves in the tree roots. I can tell the story unsettles her. Hell, what foster story is soothing?

"Did those people adopt Mandy?" Jaynie asks.

"They were in the process, supposedly. But, uh, something bad happened."

Jaynie stops tracing and looks over at me. "What happened?"

I blow out a breath. "They were killed in a boating accident, and Mandy was thrown back in the system."

"Damn, Flynn. That's…I don't know. Just…talk about bad luck."

"I know, Jaynie, I know."

Things are turning too dour. I want this day of freedom to stay positive, since we have so few.

"Hey," I say, tone upbeat. "Enough of all this sad talk, okay?"

Jaynie tosses her tracing stick off to the side and stands up. "Sounds good to me. Let's keep walking."

"Yeah." I jump up and point to where the trail continues. "You up for seeing a place up here that's really cool? It's actually my favorite spot to go when shit down at the house gets to be too much."

Nodding enthusiastically, Jaynie says, "I'd love to see it, Flynn."

We wind our way through the forest, diverging away from the trail. Jaynie doesn't know it yet, but we are close to the edge of the mountaintop, the only part of the property that's not fenced off.

Finally, we arrive at the spot that's my sanctuary—a thick copse of pines growing in a perfect circle. The trees soar high into the air, seemingly to the heavens. Their long limbs provide a heavy canopy of green that stretches all the way to the edge of the cliff. The cliff itself juts out over a swiftly flowing river.

"I can't wait to share this with you," I say to Jaynie, wishing I could take her hand. I nod to a break in the pines that lead into the circle, but Jaynie walks instead over to the edge of the cliff.

"Mind I see the view from the edge, first?" she looks back and asks.

I shrug. "Sure." She seems pretty focused, so whatever.

At the cliff's edge Jaynie is peering across the forested valley. She then looks down to the water, flowing hundreds of feet below. "Where does the river go, Flynn?" she wants to know.

I walk over so I can stand beside her. "Downstream," I say. "There's a little town named Lawrence not far from here. After that, I'm sure the water keeps going. I guess this river eventually dumps out into an even bigger river."

"Oh."

Jaynie sounds distant and lost in thought, so it's with care I inquire, "What are you thinking about?"

Jaynie turns to me, eyes sparkling and bright. She looks so alive and happy right now, and I almost tell her how I think her eye color is a perfect match to the boughs of the pines above us. I ultimately decide to save that observation for another day.

"I was thinking that I wish I were a bird," she replies, at last.

Her answer catches me off-guard. "Why in the hell would you want to be a bird?"

She faces the water again and throws her head back. Spreading her arms, like wings, she says, "Because then I could fly away."

I step closer to her, until her hand is near my face. I expect her to curl her fingers away. But she doesn't. She leans toward me, allowing her fingertips to brush over my cheek. "Flynn," she sighs.

We stay like that for a while, her barely touching me, but touching me nonetheless. I want to hold this moment for as long as we can, so I don't move an inch. My heart sure races, though.

Quietly, just loud enough to be heard over the rushing rapids, I say, "If someday you fly away, Jaynie-bird, can I go with you?"

She opens her eyes and peers over at me. When she lowers her arms, I can't help but sigh at the loss of feeling her touch.

With her attention returning to the water, she asks, "Would you go with me? Like, for real? If we could leave this place, Flynn, would you go?"

Answering that question is easy. "Yes."

Chapter Ten

Jaynie

"We could really go," Flynn tells me. "If things ever get to be… you know, too much."

"What?" I gesture to the river, so far below us. "You really think we could jump into the water from up *here*?"

He sounds like Mandy. What do they know that I don't? It's not that horrible here…yet.

"Yeah," he says, dead serious. "You can swim, can't you?"

"Well, yeah." I peer down at the dark rapids, trying to calculate the distance and just how dangerous a jump like that would be. And, crap…

"Wouldn't the fall kill us?"

Flynn chuckles. "No, we'd be fine. The water is deep in this part of the river, and there are no rocks down there to hit your head on. The fast-moving current keeps debris from settling."

"So, how would it work?"

"Simple. We'd jump, land in the water, float to the surface within a few seconds, and then let the current do its work to help us swim away."

I eye him curiously, this guy who keeps more secrets than I, apparently. "Hmm, sounds like you've put a lot of thought into this, Flynn."

"I have," he murmurs.

His expression, so serious, makes him look far wiser than a seventeen-year-old guy. But then again Flynn is well-acquainted with sorrow. He knows life is not all sunshine and rainbows.

Softly, he says, "You should always have a plan, Jaynie. You never know when things may go to hell. You need to be ready to roll if that happens."

He's right, of course, like someone else I know. "You sound like Mandy," I say with a small smile.

Flynn levels me with a curious stare as his hair falls over one eye. "Oh, yeah? What'd she say?"

"She told me not to get too settled, especially here at Mrs. Lowry's house. She said I should always have an out."

He nods approvingly. "She's right."

"Does she know about this place?" I nod to the river. "Is this her out, too?"

Flynn chuckles. "Yeah, Mandy knows about this place, but she's not going anywhere. She's playing it cool till July. She's got less than three months now, and she's not about to jeopardize anything."

Flynn knows about her plans to foster and eventually adopt the twins, and I assume that's what he means by her not jeopardizing anything.

Back to his plan, I ask, "So, what would we do if we jumped? Swim to the next town? What did you say it was called? Lawrence? How far away is that? Like, miles and miles?"

When I look over Flynn is staring at me like he can't believe I may actually be onboard with his idea. But I am. Quite solidly, in fact. If I'd had an escape plan at my last home I wouldn't have ended up a victim.

One thing for sure, *that* will never happen again.

Flynn watches my face changing, surely expressing all the emotions conjured by the memories that still haunt me. And I know then that he knows. It doesn't take a genius to figure out what happened to me.

Quietly, he says, "Swimming wouldn't be hard. Like I said, we'd have the current helping us. And Lawrence isn't that far away."

"Well, then." I turn to him, rubbing my palms on the hem of my tee and down the sides of my long shorts. "We should make a pact."

Flynn steps closer. "Okay, it's a deal. If things ever get too bad, this"—his eyes move to the cliff's edge—"is our way out."

"Deal."

Flynn extends his hand, same as he did the first day we met. He wants to seal our pact with a handshake, and I do, too. But when I make an attempt, I end up jerking my hand back.

"Come on," Flynn urges. "You can do this, Jaynie. It's no different than before."

But it is. Him brushing hair from my face, and me barely touching his cheek with my fingertips, those were fleeting encounters. A handshake requires grasping, squeezing, prolonged contact. "I don't know, Flynn."

"You can do it," he encourages.

Tentatively, I extend my hand to meet his. And…I do it. We seal our pact with a quick shake.

"See, not so bad," he teases when I quickly slide my hand from his.

"Not bad at all," I agree, rubbing my hand. "I think I'm getting used to us touching each other."

We both turn red at the unintended innuendo in my remark. When I start stammering, trying to explain, Flynn smoothly diffuses

Tomorrow's Lies

the tension.

"Hey, come on." He motions for me to follow. "Let me show you the best spot up here."

I follow him to the thick clumping of tall pines, the same trees I bolted past to rush to the cliff's edge. "So, this is your favorite place up here, yeah?"

"It sure is," he says as he holds up a branch. We slip under and into the circle of pines.

Sunlight is filtering through the tops of the trees, creating a crisscross pattern of light and dark on a thick bed of pine needles covering the ground.

"Are they soft?" I ask, gesturing to the needles.

"Very," Flynn replies. "Here, follow me."

I trail behind him to the middle of the circle. Flynn flops down on the ground, smack dab on an especially thick mound of pine needles. I suppose to prove his point that they are indeed soft.

"Comfy?" I ask.

"Quite." He raises a brow. "You should come down here and join me. See for yourself."

I dig one sneakered toe into a nearby mound of needles. "Maybe. I'll think about it."

"Guess I'll have to amuse myself while you decide." Flynn starts moving his hands and legs in scissor-like fashion.

I ask him around a laugh, "What in the hell are you doing?"

Without stopping, he glances up at me. "Isn't it obvious?"

"No," I shake my head. "Can't say that it is."

He snorts, "I'm making a snow angel, silly. Only this is more of a pine-needle angel."

"You're ridiculous," I tell him, but the whole thing is rather amusing.

"Hey," he retorts, slowing his movements to an almost halt. "Sometimes, dear Jaynie, you have to work with what you're given in this life."

"Is that kind of like making the best of things?"

"It's exactly like that," he assures me.

We share a look.

Sitting up, Flynn pats the spot next to him, and says softly, "Come on. Sit next to me."

I acquiesce and plop down beside him.

The first thing out of my mouth is, "Ooh, the needles *are* soft."

"I told you," he says smugly. "And when summer comes the softest, greenest grass you've ever seen grows in here. Comes right up between the needles."

"Seriously?" I stare up at the high treetops, blotting out so much of the sun. "How does that work? Grass growing without enough light?"

"Life finds a way," Flynn says quietly.

With one knee bent, he lies back on the needles. I follow suit. We stare up at the sky. The high boughs of deep green create a pattern in the air once you've stared at them long enough. The robin-egg blue sky appears segmented, like puzzle pieces. This place *is* beautiful and tranquil, and I fully understand why Flynn comes here to escape.

Flynn shifts a little and our bodies seem closer than ever. Close enough that I can feel his warmth. I like it, but there's nothing I can do with it. Not with how I am. Closing my eyes, I imagine a different world, a different time and place, one where Flynn and I are just a normal boy and girl, lying on a bed of pine needles, under a springtime sky.

My heart quickens. Not with fear, but with possibility. I want a normal life so badly I can taste it. My hand twitches next to Flynn's arm. It would be so easy to reach down and take hold of his hand. But then what…?

In this different world, Flynn might lean over my body, block out everything but him. Would he lower his lips to mine? Would he kiss me?

"Oh," I gasp out at the thought, my eyes fluttering open.

Flynn glances over at me, concerned. "Something wrong, Jaynie?"

I can't look at him.

Shaking my head, I say, "No, no, nothing is wrong at all. I was just thinking how cool this place is."

"It is pretty cool," he agrees, grinning as he closes his eyes. He probably suspects I was thinking of him in some romantic way.

I look over at him, this beautiful almost-a-man boy. He looks as if he's falling asleep. He really is stunning, but there's so much more to him than his looks. He's a good person with a kind and caring heart. He deserves peace. And he obviously finds it here. This is the most relaxed I've ever seen Flynn. Here, he can be young and without care. He can rest at ease.

Silence descends, apart from the rushing water and the occasional bird song. I soon nod off, as well.

When I wake up, I sit up with a start. I have no idea how long I was out. The sun's shifted in the sky, but it's not anywhere near dark.

We're still good, but I know our time here will come to a close soon enough.

I glance down at Flynn. He is awake now, too.

Sitting up next to me, he stretches and yawns. "Should we head back?" he asks.

"I don't know. Are you okay with staying a while longer?"

Truth is, I'm not ready to return to the real world. Up here in this secret place, it's just me and Flynn. Anything feels possible.

"Sure," he says. "It's still early. No Lowry women are returning from a shopping trip this soon."

I chuckle. And then, after a long beat of silence, I ask, "Do you ever think about why things are the way they are? Do you wonder why we were given *these* lives?"

"All the time," Flynn says, sighing.

"Like, for me," I continue, wanting—no, needing—to share something to seal this closeness I feel with Flynn. "I wonder how things would have turned out differently if even just one variable was changed. Like, if my mom had never left…or if I'd known my dad."

"You never met your father?" Curiosity turns Flynn's eyes to a deeper shade of gray.

"No, I never met him," I reply dryly.

"Does your mom know who he is?"

I shrug. "She says so, but who really knows?"

Flynn blows out a breath. "That's kind of fucked-up."

"Sure is."

We both fall silent, until I say, "So, what variable would you change?"

Flynn bursts out laughing. "You want the short list…or the long, extended version?"

I shake my head. "No, no long list. Pick one thing."

Flopping down on his back, he covers his eyes with one arm and says, "I wish my little brother had lived."

The little brother Mandy told me about. "Galen?" I ask.

Flynn moves his arm and looks over at me, surprised. "Mandy told you what happened?"

I shake my head. "No. She only said you had a brother, and that he died."

Flynn's arm goes back over his eyes. "Yep, that's the long and the short of it." He sounds bitter.

Sighing heavily, I debate how much further I should dig. There's an unwritten rule in the foster world that you don't go prying into other people's business. If someone wants to tell you something, they will. But here, out in the forest, with only the trees listening in, things feels different.

Still, it's with caution that I say, "Can I ask what happened to Galen?"

"My father killed him," Flynn whispers. "Gave me this that night, too." He lifts his arm and points to the crescent-shaped scar under his right eye. "It's a constant reminder."

"Oh, my God, Flynn, I am so sorry."

Now I know why his dad is in prison. I should have never asked.

But he continues speaking, his arm going back over his eyes, his voice strained. "Yeah, sometimes I can't believe it myself. But it's true. Galen was beaten to death by my drunk and flipped-out Dad. Nice story, huh?"

I never expected this horrible tale, and I hastily say, "We don't have to talk about this, Flynn."

"No, I want to."

Lowering his arm from his face, his eyes, wet with unshed tears, implore me to let him talk.

"Okay," I tell him. "I'm here."

"Jaynie," he says, voice cracking. "It was so…fucking…bad. I never talk to anyone about this, and I only told Mandy the bare minimum. But for, like, the first fucking time, I want to talk about it. With *you*. I feel like if I tell you this shit in my head you'll understand me better."

I nod solemnly. "You can tell me anything, Flynn. And I want to know you better."

"Maybe it's the forest," he says, glancing at the pines.

"Yeah, maybe it is." I offer an understanding smile to the boy whose heart clearly still hurts from the loss he's endured.

We both know it's not the forest—no matter how special and magical this place may be—that has led us to this subject. It is us, Flynn and I together, that make sharing secrets feel right.

Flynn blinks, and a single tear escapes, a fugitive of sorrow trailing down his cheek. And then he tells me how he lost his mom in a car accident a year before losing Galen. He talks about how bad it became at home, how his father started drinking, and how, eventually, he ended up hitting him and Galen.

"He was never like that before," Flynn says, sitting up. "Although I remember one time overhearing my mom talking to her friend. She was in the kitchen having coffee with this lady. I guess this lady's husband was a bad drinker, and a worse drunk. She was thinking of leaving him." Flynn clears his throat. "Christ, I wish I had a cigarette right now."

I know he quit, but under these circumstances, I tell him, "If I had one to give you, I would."

He smiles at me, and I smile back.

"Thanks, Jaynie. But it's probably better you don't have any. I haven't smoked for weeks, and I think I really kicked it this time."

"That's good," I say.

"Yeah, it is." He scrubs his hands down his face. "Anyway, so Mom started telling this lady how back when she and my dad were first married, Dad used to drink heavily. I guess he hit her a few times when he was drunk. When she got pregnant with me she told him if he didn't get help, she'd leave his ass."

"He got help?"

"Yeah, apparently he did. Up until the day when I overheard my mom, I always wondered why Dad didn't allow alcohol in the house. This one time a friend of his from work came over. It was around the holidays, and this guy had a fifth of whiskey with him. He'd obviously been drinking already; the bottle was half-empty. Anyway, he held that thing up and said he and my dad were going to drink to the New Year. He kept going on and on about how it was high time my dad loosened up and got his drink on. Those were his exact words."

"What a douche," I remark.

"Yeah, he was a tool. But Dad set him straight." Flynn shakes his head. "He yanked that bottle out of his buddy's hands. The guy was protesting the whole time, but my dad ignored him. Went straight to the sink and dumped the whiskey down the drain."

"Wow."

"Yeah, and then he kicked the guy out of the house and told him to never come back. He said if he ever offered him alcohol again, he'd lay his ass out. It was harsh, but I knew why after I overheard my mom's story. I knew then she was the one keeping him sober." Flynn pauses for a minute, reflects, and then continues. "After Mom died, Dad started drinking again." He sighs. "And, well, things got worse than ever."

Tentatively, I brush my hand over his. I wish I could give him a hug, or hold him close in a comforting way, but the barely-there brush is the best I can do…for now. "I'm sorry, Flynn," I say.

He looks down to where my hand brushed over his. "It's not your fault, Jaynie."

I know then that he means something other than what we're talking about. He means my issues are not my fault.

My eyes meet his—steely gray, cloudy, wet. Like the sky after a storm.

In a whisper, I say, "I wasn't always fucked-up like this."

"Hey, hey,"—his brow creases—"don't say that. You're fine."

I let out a *yeah-right* cough. And then I nod my chin to where my hand rests near his, to where I can't do more than offer a light brush for comfort. "More like pathetic, you mean."

"The touching thing?" he says. I nod, and he adds, "That doesn't make you fucked-up. You just need time to work through, uh, whatever it is that happened."

He looks away, and I cringe. This is not his fault, it's mine. I'm tired of feeling this self-inflicted shame. Flynn has shared with me; it's time to share with him.

There's no easy way to phrase what happened to me, so I end up blurting out, "I was raped at my last foster home."

There's a long silence…and then Flynn blows out a breath. "Yeah, I figured as much."

His eyes remain averted, but I need him to look at me, now more than ever. I need him to show me he doesn't see me any differently now that he knows for sure.

Look at me, Flynn, I want to scream.

Instead, when he doesn't, I rise to my knees. "I was also sodomized." My voice is as loud as a gunshot piercing the forest.

"Jesus, Jaynie."

Flynn sure is looking at me now, wide-eyed, and with no clue of how to handle what appears to be an impending meltdown of the girl next to him.

"He never even kissed me," I go on.

It's like I can't stop now that I started. I have to get this out. "I was *that* disgusting to him. He'd lift my nightgown, Flynn. Just enough to get what he wanted. He treated me like a whore."

I gasp for breath, spitting out words like I'm spitting out my rapist. Maybe I am. "No, worse than a whore," I grind out. "At least whores get paid to fuck and take it up the ass."

"Jaynie—"

Cutting him off, I throw my head back and shout up at the pines surrounding us, "What's the going rate for fucking a virgin, anyway? What's the cost of stealing away someone's innocence, their first time?"

I twist to face Flynn, and say quietly, "He never gave me a choice, Flynn. I was forced to do those disgusting things."

Flynn tries to console me with words. "It's not your fault, Jaynie. You were a victim."

I am lost in myself now, though, and not fully hearing him. Swallowing gasps of air that can't come quickly enough, I cry and rock back and forth. I dig my fingers so deeply into the pine needles that the dirt beneath grinds up under my nails.

Flynn starts to reach for me, but then he remembers. I sob harder.

If Flynn had any sense at all, he'd run from the freak that has just lost her shit.

But no, he stays and lets me cry it out.

His hand remains close, in case I need it. Solid, that's what this guy is. Flynn is a guy who'll stay by your side, no matter what.

"Jaynie, what happened to you, it never—"

I cut him off with a wave of my hand. "I can't talk about it anymore, okay?"

He nods as I get a hold of myself. "Okay, Jaynie."

After a minute, he asks, "Do you want to leave?"

I shake my head. Despite my breakdown—or maybe because of it—I feel better, like a burden has been lifted. Plus, I know we have more time before it gets dark and Mrs. Lowry and Allison return.

"I'd like to stay," I say. "That is, if you're good with staying. This has been such a good day, Flynn. Well, until I ruined it."

"You didn't ruin anything," he tells me. "And of course I want to stay. You just needed to get that out." He takes a deep breath, exhales. "And, wow, you sure did."

I suppress a laugh. It's not funny, but sometimes it's better to laugh than cry. I'm done crying, damn it, at least for today.

"I didn't mean to take it out on you, Flynn. I'm sorry, I really am. Once I got going, though..." I make a waving motion with my hand. "I guess I needed to really vent. And you were here to bear the brunt of it."

"Hey, don't apologize." He squares his shoulders. "I'm tough, I can take it."

I look at him, this guy who has no idea how amazing he is. His wide shoulders carry so much of his own pain, but he's willing to carry mine, too. And beneath that hard chest lies a good heart. Maybe someday I'll find the courage to lean my head on him. I've found comfort in confiding in Flynn, but I suspect far more comfort would be found in his arms.

A wave of warmth washes over me as I think about what it might have been like had someone like Flynn been my first. What would that act feel like when done for the right reasons? I know sex can be beautiful. What was perpetrated upon me wasn't the model of what I should build upon; it was nothing but pure violence. And the monster won't win. I will never allow what happened to me to define my life. I'm willing to be touched again, in *every* way, and by a man like Flynn. Shit, maybe it *should* be Flynn.

Shaking my head, I struggle to clear my mind before I start blushing and Flynn figures out what I'm thinking about. He's going to think I'm crazy for mixing two such divergent thoughts. But the horrors of life are not always wrapped up in neat little packages. The bad things get intermixed with the good things sometimes, because it's the good *and* the bad that makes us who we are.

Suddenly, I have to stand to put a little distance between me and Flynn.

He peers up at me, curious, his hand shading his eyes against the waning sunlight filtering through the lowest branches of the trees. "I thought we were staying a while longer?" he says.

"We are," I reply. "But no more sad stuff. We need to find something to do to forget about this crap."

"Sure," he says. "What did you have in mind?"

Shooting him an *are you up for it* grin, I say, "Let's play a game."

Chapter Eleven

Flynn

I learn quickly that Jaynie is way better at Hide and Go Seek than she let on earlier in the day. She must have been going easy on us to give the twins a chance. Here in the deep forest, however, with only me searching for her, it's a far different story.

"Jaynie," I call out as I trudge through crunchy, dried-up leaves left over from last fall. "You know I'm going to find you. May as well give up now, save us both some time."

No response.

Jaynie knows she has me stumped. *Clever girl.*

"Where could she be?" I mutter to myself just as I spy a bunch of boulders, one of which would provide a perfect hiding spot for a petite girl like her.

Switching to ninja-mode, I head to the largest of the rocks with sure and stealthy steps. When I reach the massive boulder, I jump up on it and say, "Gotcha!"

When I look down, no one is there. Shit, I always find my Hide and Go Seek adversaries, no matter how well-hidden they think they are.

I am at a loss and blow out a long breath. Turning slowly, I re-scan the area. It's getting dark, and Jaynie is so small she could be hiding behind any number of thick-trunked trees. She may have even climbed up in one.

Tilting my head back, I stare up at the foliage filling in for summer. Lots of buds and green leaves, but there's no one hiding in their midst.

I hear something then, a barely audible rustle. Not originating from up in the trees, but from behind a tall clump of dense lilac bushes, which happen to be in full bloom.

Aha!

Quietly, I make my way to the fragrant bushes, the sweet aroma filling my nose. I love spring, and I wish Jaynie and I could spend every day up here in the woods. The forest is resplendent with life, a perfect place—and a perfect time of the year—to focus on healing, renewal, and sorely deserved second chances.

Someone suppresses a sneeze from behind the bushes, confirming my suspicion that Jaynie is hidden in the brush. There is a break in the bushes, but it is much too narrow for me to climb through. It's Jaynie-sized, though, for sure.

When I crouch and peer through the leaves, a lilac sprig brushes against my face. When I push it away, I spy Jaynie.

She is turned away, watching a different area of the bushes for my approach. Long, auburn hair shimmers in the setting sun, her features soft in profile. God, she is gorgeous and doesn't even realize it. I could watch her for the next hour, but the sun will be down soon.

Softly, I call out, "Boo."

Jaynie jumps and awkwardly spins to face me. "Damn it, Flynn." Her hand goes to her heart. "You're supposed to find me, not give me a freaking heart attack. I thought you'd given up."

"Never," I say.

She crosses her arms. "I think you may have gone over the time limit for finding your opponent."

"What?" I pretend to be offended. "We never discussed time limits."

Jaynie Cumberland clearly does not like to lose, but it's good to see a competitive streak in her.

I can't help but smile, and she gives me a sour look in return. "You're just pissed I won," I say.

"Okay, maybe a little," she admits.

I step back to give her room to step through the branches without having to brush by me. "Get on out here, sore loser."

"Shut up," she mumbles, though in a good-natured manner, as she climbs through the opening.

Once she's out she brushes debris from her shirt and shorts. "How'd you find me, anyway?" she asks.

"I heard you moving around in there. Plus, I heard you almost sneeze."

"Hmm, you must have, like, superior hearing."

I shrug. "I don't know about that."

I'm feeling the tiniest bit self-conscious, but in a good way. Jaynie has the ability to make me feel like I'm some kind of superman. Maybe to her, I am.

Before we leave, Jaynie breathes in all the purple blooms. "I love lilacs," she says.

"They do smell good," I agree. And then I'm struck with an idea. Maybe it's stupid, but I take a chance and say, "Let me pick you a bouquet to take back."

Truth is, I want to be *that* guy—the boy who gives the pretty girl flowers. I can't go to a store and buy a bouquet for Jaynie, but maybe this is better.

Jaynie must think so, too. She dips her head and whispers, "I'd like that, Flynn."

I proceed to pick Jaynie the best damn bouquet, one filled with the fullest and most robust blooms. I add in a few leaves for greenery, and find two daisies nearby to add to the mix.

"You're really putting a lot into this," Jaynie remarks as she follows me up and down the line of bushes.

"You deserve it," I tell her.

When I turn and present her with my creation there are tears in her eyes. Not tears of sadness, but tears of joy. "You're the first boy to ever give me flowers," she says.

"I feel honored," I reply, and it's true.

She raises the bouquet to her nose. "Thank you, Flynn. These really are amazing."

"I wish I could give you more," I tell her.

She knows I mean much more. I wish I could take away her pain and give her the peace she seeks.

"Flynn..." She looks up at the sky, blinking back tears. I don't know if these new ones are tears of sadness or happiness, but I do sense they're tinged with regret.

"We should go," she says, quietly. "It'll be dark soon."

We don't say much on the way back to the house, but Jaynie does sniff her lilacs a number of times. At one point, she looks over at me and mouths, "Thank you, Flynn."

"You're welcome," I say.

"I mean for everything, for this whole day."

I nudge her shoulder, ever so lightly. She doesn't flinch or shift away. This truly *is* turning out to be an incredible day.

When the house comes into view, Jaynie clears her throat. "Ugh, back to the grind tomorrow."

"Yeah." I sigh.

She slows to a stop. "Hold up a sec."

I turn to her. "What is it?"

Tomorrow's Lies

She breathes in deeply. Her eyes dart to me, but then skitter away.

"It's just… What I said before is true. *You* made this day special. And not just because of the flowers you gave me." She holds up the bouquet. "I don't know how to say what I'm trying to get across."

She sounds frustrated, but I understand. "I know what you mean, Jaynie. Playing with the kids, having fun under the sun, our talk in the woods." Our eyes meet on that one. "Anyway, every part of this day was amazing. And we don't get too much amazing around here."

"That's for sure."

We start to walk again. "Yeah, it *was* a good day, Flynn. A really good day."

Yeah, Jaynie Cumberland, it was the best.

Chapter Twelve

Jaynie

The really good day screeches to a grinding halt when Flynn and I return to the house.

Mrs. Lowry and Allison are waiting for us and they are none too happy. Mrs. Lowry meets us at the front door and ushers us into the kitchen. Allison is seated at the table, surrounded by fast food wrappers.

Allison immediately snarks, "We brought food back for dinner, but you and Flynn missed it."

"When I give a day off," Mrs. Lowry chimes in, "it is not to be taken advantage of." She walks to a sink full of soapy water and dishes, tsking, "Shame, shame. You two should never have stayed out this late. It's dark outside."

Allison glares at me, but smiles when she makes eye contact with Flynn. She's wearing a tight dress, low-cut and so incredibly short that when she crosses her long legs, her lacy thong is exposed. It's pink, like her glossed lips and the painted nails she's tapping on the table.

Flicking a spent burger wrapper onto the floor, she purrs, "So, Flynn, I was just about to head out back." She stands and adjusts her dress. "Come have a smoke with me."

Mrs. Lowry says half-heartedly, "I told you I don't like you smoking, young lady."

Allison ignores her, so she shrugs and resumes washing dishes.

"I quit smoking," Flynn says. "You know that."

"So you did." Allison spins a little case in her hand, which I assume holds her cigarettes. "I swear, though," she goes on, "it seems more than that. You are just no fun anymore, Flynn O'Neill."

"Flynn, we should go upstairs," I interject.

Allison's eyes snap to me. "Did I say you were dismissed?"

"Allison," Mrs. Lowry admonishes from the sink. She does nothing to stop her daughter, however. Just continues with the dishes.

Allison steps over to where we're standing. "I think your newly adopted shitty attitude, Flynn, may be due to little Jaynie here. She's clearly a bad influence."

I open my mouth to defend myself, but when I see Allison's face, just waiting for me to dare speak up, I think better of it. I fear what kind of punishment she may come up with if I dare defy her. All five of us are ultimately at her mercy, and I don't wish for the others to be punished because of me.

Allison backs off when I remain silent.

Without turning around, Mrs. Lowry says, "Go get some sleep, you two. There's lots of work on the agenda for tomorrow."

I turn to go, but Flynn doesn't move.

Clearing his throat, he says in the nicest of tones, "Um, Mrs. Lowry, is there any food left for me and Jaynie? If not, even a nutrition bar would be great. We're both kind of hungry."

He's downplaying the truth. We've eaten nothing since morning and are freaking starving.

Mrs. Lowry finally turns to face us. "Well, I don't know." She dries her hands with a dish towel.

"Don't give them anything, Mom," Allison interjects, smirking.

"Hmm." Mrs. Lowry appears to think it over. "On this one, I tend to agree with my daughter. If you were so concerned with food, you would've made more of an effort to get back to the house before dark. I think it's for the best if you go to bed hungry tonight. That way, you'll have ample opportunity to ponder the consequences of your actions for the future."

I can't believe she's serious. Not even a nutrition bar.

"Please, please, Mrs. Lowr—" I start to say, but Flynn cuts me off by bumping my hip with his.

When I glance over at him questioningly, he shakes his head, as if to say *don't beg these people.*

I shut my mouth.

Mrs. Lowry's cell phone rings, and she goes to another room to talk. Flynn and I then turn to go.

But Allison stops us.

Or rather, she stops me. "Hold up a minute, Jaynie."

I am so damn tired and hungry that I want nothing more than to go up to my room and fall asleep.

Flynn, noticing my crestfallen expression, whispers, "You want me to stay with you?"

I shake my head. "No. Go get some rest. I'll see you tomorrow in the craft barn."

"Okay." He smiles sadly. "'Night, Jaynie."

When I turn around, Allison is smiling at me. It's an act; there is venom in her grin.

"What do you want?" I ask weakly. I am so tired I can barely stand on my feet.

Zoning in on the bouquet of lilacs I almost forgot I was holding, Allison says, "I want you to stay put for a sec so I can give you a vase to put those pretty flowers in."

I don't trust her, or her pretense of good intentions. "Um, thanks, but that's okay. I was planning on putting them in a cup of water up in our bathroom."

Allison walks toward me. "Don't be silly, Jaynie. You definitely need a vase. But you look so tired. Maybe it'd be best if you leave your flowers with me. I'll put them in something, something nice, for you, okay?"

"Uh…" I absolutely do not want to do that.

"Jaynie, earth to Jaynie, are you listening to me?"

"Yes, I hear you."

Allison laughs. "I bet Flynn picked those flowers for you. Am I right?"

I don't answer, and she comes closer, stopping mere inches from me. A stir of panic threatens to bloom, especially when she hisses, "Did you hear my question, Jaynie?"

"Um, yes, yes." I nod like crazy. "Flynn picked them for me."

"Uh-huh. I thought so."

There's a flash of something like hatred in her eyes, and I take a step back. "I'm going to go upstairs now, okay?"

"Not yet, Jaynie." Allison's tone is firm, and I know better than to move. "Since Flynn gave you those pretty lilacs, I'm sure they're very important to you. Surely, you wouldn't want to stick them in some old, crusty paper cup up in a bathroom." Allison mock-shudders. "No, no, we can't have that. Give me your flowers and I'll put them in a vase. I'll even place them nicely on the home-schooling table later tonight. That way your flowers will be there for you tomorrow morning. You and the others can enjoy the lovely aroma of lilacs all day. How nice will that be?"

She wants an answer; this is her game. Playing along, albeit reluctantly, I say, "Sure, that sounds really nice."

"Of course it does. Because it is nice, *I* am nice, Jaynie."

Yeah, right.

With a wolfish grin, she reaches for my flowers. I have no choice but to relinquish them.

And just like that, Allison takes away what Flynn has given me.

Chapter Thirteen

Flynn

When I arrive upstairs, I stop in my room briefly to retrieve two nutrition bars I've been saving for an emergency. Cody is fast asleep, exhausted from the day of play. I'm glad the twins and Mandy got dinner, but it still irritates me that Cody and Callie don't have normal days like this more often.

After placing a blanket Cody had kicked off back on him, I use the system for getting into the girls' bedroom undetected to drop off the nutrition bars for Jaynie.

When Mandy lets me in I fill her in on what went down in the kitchen after Jaynie and I returned from the forest.

Mandy is outraged. "I can't believe those bitches didn't give you guys *any* dinner."

"Nope, nothing," I place the nutrition bars on Jaynie's pillow.

"Did you have anything at all to eat today?" she asks.

I shake my head. "Nothing since breakfast. But I'm good."

Mandy lifts one end of her mattress up off the floor. She reaches under and pulls out a candy bar in a faded wrapper.

"It's kind of old." She checks the expiration date. "Still good, though." Holding the chocolate bar out to me, she urges, "Go ahead and take it, Flynn. I know you want Jaynie to have both nutrition bars, but you need to eat something, too."

"Thank, Mandy." Accepting the candy bar, I tear the wrapper off and take a bite. "Best candy bar ever," I say around a mouthful of chewy chocolate-covered caramel.

Mandy smiles smugly. "What makes it even better is that I stole it out from under Allison's nose a couple of months ago. She left it on one of the work tables. Dumbass kept looking around for it later that day, like she knew she'd left it somewhere, but couldn't remember where."

I chuckle as I finish the chocolate bar. Little victories mean a lot when you're tired, hungry, and your life is dictated by the whims of others.

Licking my fingers, I nod to where Callie is sleeping, wrapped up in a cocoon of blankets. "At least both kids had a full meal."

Mandy rolls her eyes. "Burgers and fries. How nutritious."

We both know it's still better than nothing, and the subject is dropped.

Mandy shifts from one bare foot to the other. "Where did you and Jaynie go anyway? How far did you take her?"

"I took her all the way up to the cliff's edge."

"Oh." Mandy's appears surprised. "You took her there."

"She can be trusted, Mandy."

"I know. I already mentioned the cliff to her before." She sighs. "I guess I just can't envision Jaynie ever jumping."

Mandy and I have discussed the same escape plan I shared with Jaynie. However, like I told Jaynie, there's no chance of Mandy leaving before she turns eighteen. She's not about to jeopardize her good record of late. Mandy is really committed to fostering, and eventually adopting, Cody and Callie.

Though that doesn't mean she's averse to helping me.

"I think she would jump if she needed to," I say. "She's stronger than you think, Mandy."

Mandy eyes me curiously. "You like her, Flynn, don't you? Like, *really* like her."

"I do," I confess in a soft tone.

Exhaling resignedly, Mandy says, "Guess that means you want me to provide clothes for Jaynie, along with the stuff for you?"

Since Mandy is out of here at the end of July, the plan has always been for her to stash a backpack containing a change of clothes for me at a public park that's by the river's edge down in Lawrence. The contingency plan, if I ever have to run, involves exactly what Jaynie and I discussed—jumping into the water from up on the cliff's edge.

There are lockers in the park in Lawrence, for when the weather's good and people go there to swim in the river. Mandy knows the area well, and she has a good hiding place in which to place the key. Up in the branches of a hundred-year-old oak is a carved-out nook, perfect for a small item, like a locker key.

"Yes," I reply. "If you could throw some clothes in the backpack for Jaynie, that'd be great."

"Consider it done. Once I'm out of here, I'll get those things set up for both of you. Did you tell Jaynie about the guy I know, Bill Delmont?"

"We didn't really get that far," I tell Mandy. "But I'll get Jaynie up to speed."

According to Mandy, her friend, Bill, is a good, trustworthy dude. He was once homeless, but turned his life around big-time. He now runs a sandwich shop in Lawrence and can set me up with a job if I ever need to run.

"I'll check in with Bill before I head to Morgantown," Mandy says. "I'll make sure he knows to give Jaynie a job, too."

"I don't want to get too far ahead of ourselves." I run my hand through my hair. "It may never come down to running."

Mandy gives me a look like the likelihood in this life of it coming down to running is far higher than if we were normal kids.

At last, she says, "Hey, even if you just leave at eighteen, go look Bill up. Remember, his place is called Delmont Deli. You're going to need a job, Flynn. Jaynie, too, since it's looking like she may end up with you no matter what."

Mandy is smiling like she has some great insight. Is it that obvious that I'm falling hard for Jaynie?

In a serious tone, I say, "I'd be okay with Jaynie and me ending up in the same city."

"Of course you would." Mandy smacks my arm. "Jesus, dude, you need to lighten up. It's cool that you two like each other."

I give her a wary look. "Other people in this house might not have the same warm, fuzzy feelings as you."

"Don't let Allison stand in the way of your happiness, Flynn. She already takes too much from us."

"Ain't that the truth," I reply.

Callie mutters something indecipherable in her sleep, halting my conversation with Mandy. When Callie rolls to her back, her face appears angelic in the moonlit room.

Mandy and I smile at each other. "It'll all work out," she says.

"I hope so, Mandy."

I turn to leave, but she grabs my arm. "Hey, do you want to go get Cody? You can stay in our room tonight, if you want."

Since I have no idea what kind of shit Allison is down in the kitchen doling out to Jaynie—she may need me tonight—I am quick to agree. "Yeah, that's not a bad idea."

Twenty minutes later, when Jaynie comes into the room, she seems relieved to see me on the floor next to her bed.

"Is this okay?" I ask in a light whisper, since the little ones are fast asleep, and Mandy is snoring lightly.

Jaynie nods as she steps over me to climb into her bed. Lying down in the same clothes she's worn all day, she places her arm over her eyes.

"You plan on sleeping in those grimy clothes?" I ask, trying to get her to laugh.

I'm in my usual boxers and nothing else. It's gotten warm up here on the third floor with the evolving season. Soon it will be stifling in the rooms. Jaynie's modesty has taken a back seat to comfort when nighttime rolls around. She sleeps in boy shorts and tees these days, though she keeps her covers up to her neck most nights so no one can see.

"I'll cover my eyes if you want to change," I tell her when she fails to crack a smile.

With her arm still covering her eyes, she mutters, "I'm fine like this."

She stifles a sob, and I know then just who caused her pain.

Sitting up swiftly, I place an elbow on the edge of the bed. "What happened down there? What did that bitch say to you?"

"She didn't say anything I couldn't handle," Jaynie whispers in the night. "But she did take my lilacs, Flynn."

Inside, I rage. I wish I could break something. I am so sick and tired of feeling helpless. Going off, I mutter a litany of choice words, things I'd like to say to Allison's nasty face.

"Getting mad won't help," Jaynie sniffles. "Just let it go. I have."

I wish I could believe her, but her soft cries as she turns to face the wall make me think otherwise. I want so badly to crawl under the covers and comfort her. Nothing sexual, I just want to hold Jaynie, let her cry on my chest. Maybe someday that can happen.

Jaynie eventually falls to sleep. But I remain awake. I have a sick, nagging feeling this is just the beginning of Allison's vendetta against Jaynie. She has singled her out, partly because of me, but also because

Jaynie is vulnerable.

As I close my eyes, waiting for sleep to come, I am consumed with the feeling that having an escape plan just became more important than ever.

Chapter Fourteen

Jaynie

I never see my lilac bouquet from Flynn again.

"Those flowers died," Allison tells me the next morning, smirking.

We are minutes from the start of home-schooling, and the smug look on her made-up face makes me want to puke.

"I had to throw them away," she continues, rubbing salt in the wounds. "But really, what did you expect from a bunch of weeds."

"They weren't weeds," I grind out between clenched teeth.

"Sure they were, Jaynie."

She spins away from me to address the others, effectively dismissing me. "So, anyway, I have an announcement from my mother—"

I am not done. "You're a liar," I snap.

Allison blinks, surprised. "Did you say something, Miss Cumberland?"

Mandy kicks me under the table. "It's not worth it, Jaynie," she whispers. "Don't give her the satisfaction."

Mandy is right, of course. Allison can take away my lilacs, but she can never erase the fact Flynn was the one who gave them to me. And that's what she hates. She wants to steal away the way his sweet gesture made me feel. Too bad for her, that bitch can't touch what's in my head and my heart.

"No," I say, like I have no clue what she's referring to. "I was just clearing my throat."

"That better be all you were doing," Allison warns as she turns away, smoothing the fabric of her skimpy baby-doll dress.

"As I was about to announce, before I was so rudely interrupted"— she sneers at me—"my mother is planning on attending a number of business conferences this summer. She's looking for investors for her business. As you know, the Crafty Lo enterprise has been growing by leaps and bounds. Orders are up all over the country. Mom wants to bring in more money to expand internationally and really maximize profits."

More child labor must be at the top of that list. Wonder if she'll apply to foster more kids. I shudder at the thought.

"Anyway," Allison goes on, "she's putting me in charge during her absences. And, as luck would have it, she left early this morning for trip number one. So, boys and girls"—another sickly, phony-sweet grin that makes me want to vomit is sent my way—"my stint as boss begins today."

Flynn groans, but Allison ignores him.

"First off," she continues, "*I* will be setting the quotas for today. There will be none of that slacky shit my mom lets you off with. Everything is doubled. You don't leave tonight till *all* the work is done."

No one groans this time, at least not outwardly. In fact, it's like we bind together. The resulting collective silence is deafening. Not a single one of us wants Allison Lowry in charge. A bad situation is about to get worse, and we all know it. Even the twins sit quietly, heads down, their little hands clasped tightly in desperation. Mandy is staring straight ahead, her lips set in a straight line. And when I look over at Flynn, I catch him rubbing his hands down his troubled face.

Allison huffs. She wants a reaction. She slams a folding chair beneath the table and the metal leg hits my own soft limb, hard.

"Oops, sorry, didn't mean to hit you," Allison says to me. Her eyes tell a different story. Not a single thing she does is ever an accident.

I bite my tongue to remain quiet. Reaching down, I gingerly rub my ringing kneecap. I'm glad I wore jeans today, or I'd probably have a cut and be bleeding all over the floor.

Allison sniffs. "I really *didn't* see your leg there, Jaynie." She's baiting me.

Flynn makes a scoffing noise, and under the table I nudge his foot. "No," I whisper.

Like Mandy just reminded me, engaging Allison is not worth the grief. And that's exactly what we'll all be wallowing in if we fall into her trap.

No one says a word, and when Allison leaves we start with home-schooling. Home-schooling now involves teaching only the twins. Flynn, Mandy, and I finished our final exams last week. We all passed and are officially high school graduates.

There was no celebration, of course, no fanfare of any kind. Mrs. Lowry told us our diplomas would be sent to the county and placed in our files. I don't know how much a high school education will benefit me, seeing as I'm already behind the eight ball. But the twins need a decent education, and it's up to the three of us to make sure they stay on track.

So, I put on a happy face and get to work, alongside Mandy and Flynn.

The first lesson of the day is math. Cody is so far behind his sister he can't even master basic addition. He really should be in a special class to address his needs. Callie is the complete opposite. The lessons are too easy for her. She should be in a special class, as well, something more advanced, as she needs more challenging work.

But it is what it is. There is nothing three teenagers, no matter how good their intentions, can change.

When Callie becomes frustrated with Cody's slow learning pace, we have to separate the two.

"You're stupid," Callie says to her brother as we place her two seats away.

"Am not, dumb face," Cody jabs back.

"Hey, hey, that's enough name-calling." Flynn sits down in the chair between the two siblings, who look ready to come to blows.

"Listen up." The kids respect Flynn and give him their full attention as he looks from one to the other. "First of all, Callie... No one here is stupid, okay? Everyone learns at a pace that works for them."

"But he can't do *anything*," she protests.

"At least I no have a dumb face," Cody retorts.

Callie's lip quivers and she starts to cry.

Flynn attempts to smooth over her hurt feelings, and Mandy soon joins him. Taking a seat on the other side of Callie, Mandy touches Callie's forearm and says, "Don't cry, sweetie. Your brother is just frustrated."

"That's right," Flynn adds, and then he says to Cody, "You don't really think your sister has a dumb face, right?"

When he hesitates, Flynn reminds him, "You do realize you're twins, right? That means she has the same face as you, little man."

That makes Cody reconsider.

He reaches for Callie and Flynn scoots back to accommodate him. "I sorry, Callie," he says. And then he crawls over Flynn and gives his sister a hug she reluctantly accepts.

Once all is forgiven, we resume teaching. Flynn and I take Cody, and Mandy works with Callie.

After we review simple addition with Cody, we give him a worksheet to complete. He stares down at it, face scrunched up, and pencil in hand.

"Two plus two…equals…"

I prompt, "What did we say earlier two plus two equals, Cody? Think about it for a minute."

He shrugs his little shoulders. "I dunno," he mumbles. "Five?"

"Close," I say encouragingly.

Cody puts his pencil down and closes his eyes. "I can't do it," he whispers. "I *am* stupid."

"You are not stupid," Flynn interjects, his tone firm. "You *can* learn this." To me, Flynn says, "I have an idea."

"Okay."

I watch as Flynn heads to the front of the barn. He stops at one of our work stations and returns with a handful of wooden dowels in varying colors and sizes. The dowels are supposed to be used in one of the craft projects, one which involves assembling stick-figure reindeer and stick-trees for Crafty Lo's Country Christmas line. But right now the wooden sticks are about to be used to teach Cody addition. What a much better purpose.

I smile as Flynn places the dowels on the table. "Great idea," I say with a smile.

He smiles back. "Thanks."

Cody picks up two wooden sticks and starts drumming on the table. "Hey," Flynn whispers to me. "The kid's got rhythm."

I laugh. "Maybe music is more in his wheelhouse."

"Maybe," Flynn agrees. "But he has to get his addition down, regardless."

"True."

Cody is making a racket, but it does sound kind of good.

"I make drumming," he says to Flynn, giggling. "I good at that, right, Flynnie?"

Flynn slips the sticks from his hands. "Yeah, you're good, buddy. But let's save it for later. We need to use these sticks for some learning first. Is that all right with you?"

"I guess," Cody mutters. He's clearly displeased and scrunches up his face accordingly.

"Only Flynn could get away with that," Mandy whispers as she leans over to me, her lesson with Callie interrupted by the drumming.

Callie, addressing her twin, admonishes, "Be good, Cody. Listen to Flynn. He's going to help you learn how to add."

"Okay," Cody mumbles. "Flynnie help teach me."

"You got it, buddy." Flynn hands me a bunch of the dowels. "Jaynie's going to help, too."

Wide eyes fall on me. "You help me learn to with sticks?"

"Yes, sweetie." I nod. "And learning to add is really not that hard. Flynn and I are going to try to make it super easy for you."

"Okay, I ready," Cody says. He folds his hands in front of him on the table, making him look like a perfect student.

We spend the next hour using the colored dowels to teach Cody basic addition, and progress is made.

At one point, Flynn hands Cody two green dowels. "How many green sticks do you have there, buddy?" he asks.

"Two," Cody says.

I hold two blue dowels out to Cody. "Take them," Flynn urges.

Cody carefully slides the dowels from my grasp.

"Now how many do you have?" Flynn prompts our student.

"Two blue sticks and two green sticks!" Cody holds his bounty aloft proudly.

"Yes," Flynn goes on. "And how many sticks do you have if you add them all together, Cody?"

Cody's rosebud mouth moves silently as he counts. And then he says out loud, "One, two…three…four."

Excitedly, Cody looks from Flynn to me, then back to Flynn. "Four. I have four sticks."

Flynn is beaming as his eyes meet mine. "Yep, you sure do have four sticks, little man."

We both lean in from either side of Cody to give him a hug. My arm brushes Flynn's, and it feels like the most natural thing in the world. Cody is not the only one overcoming obstacles.

The lesson continues, and, with the continued help of visual aids, Cody starts to master addition. "Subtraction is up next," Flynn announces.

Cody groans, but you can see he's actually excited. If anyone can succeed in teaching Cody math, Flynn can. I'm beginning to think Flynn can do most anything.

After a few more minutes of watching Flynn and Cody interact, observing how infinitely patient Flynn is with the boy, and how completely committed he is, I know then that, without a doubt, Flynn is as beautiful inside as he is on the outside.

The burgeoning hold he has on my heart tightens. Despite all the odds against us, I have surpassed mere attraction and gone beyond friendship.

I never thought I'd say it, let alone *feel* it, but I think I'm falling in love with Flynn O'Neill.

Chapter Fifteen

Flynn

A surprising thing occurs as summer begins. I actually feel happy. I know it's because I have Jaynie in my life. She makes even the bad days bearable.

But there aren't too many bad days.

Allison is in charge most of the time, but, shock upon shock, it's not entirely awful. Sure, there are higher work quotas with which to contend, and the bitch never has a kind word to say to anyone, but the good thing is she's easily bored with her role of supervisor. She's young herself and wants to enjoy the summer. As a result, she begins to leave us alone more days than not. She takes off early for town—or wherever she goes—most mornings, leaving us alone for hours and hours.

"Something sure is keeping her preoccupied," Mandy muses one late afternoon when Allison fails to come home at all.

Since Allison has almost completely stopped hitting on me, I suspect she's found a boyfriend. Mandy agrees.

Tomorrow's Lies

Jaynie does, too, when I mention my suspicions to her, only she adds in a heartfelt, "Thank God."

So, most days when the work is done, our time is our own. After we log our numbers in a ledger Allison insists we keep up-to-date, we are done for the day. Allison fills the refrigerator with packages of wieners and an assortment of cold cuts for lunch sandwiches. She puts Mandy in charge of meals since she can't be bothered to care. With the kitchen unlocked at all times, we can eat as much as we please. There's not a wide selection, and we're careful not to overindulge and deplete what's available, but for the first time in a long time none of us feel hungry.

The twins thrive. They feel energized and want to play all the time. So, after work and dinner, Mandy, Jaynie, and I take them outside. We play Tag, Hide and Go Seek, and whatever else the twins want to do. By evening they're usually worn out from fun times, which is much better than seeing them tired from too little food and too much work.

Once Mandy takes the kids in the house, my time is spent with Jaynie. We take long walks through the woods and talk until we've run out of words. Most of our free time is spent in our secret place at the cliff's edge. We hang out under the ancient pines that have probably watched a thousand boys and girls fall in love.

And that's what I think I'm doing—falling in love with Jaynie.

I can't help but smile when I consider how much she has healed since that rainy April day when she first arrived. Jaynie is better in many, many ways. And really, all of us are. The five of us mesh well.

Hell, there are days I fear this is the calm before the proverbial storm, but that's okay with me. I'm grabbing my bit of happiness by the balls while I can and running with it.

One warm, sultry evening, the type of night where the humidity soaks straight through your clothes to leave a sticky coating on your skin, I find Jaynie out by the water pump near the barn. She's bent over, splashing water on her face. And she has on a dress. I've never seen Jaynie in a dress. And, God, she is gorgeous in this snowy white number with skinny straps at the shoulders.

One strap slips down Jaynie's arm, and I suddenly want her. We are so far from anything like that, but my body doesn't know. Parts begin to stir. Well, one part in particular.

I clear my throat to alert her to my presence.

"Oh," she spins to me and hastily shoves the strap back into place. "Flynn. I didn't see you there."

"I didn't mean to startle you." I can't keep my eyes off her as I tentatively step toward her. "I would've said something sooner, but you caught me off-guard. I've never seen you in a dress."

"Oh." She swishes her hand in the air. "This old thing isn't even mine. It belongs to Mandy. Well, it did. She gave it to me, so I guess it technically belongs to me now."

Jaynie seems nervous, so I stop a few feet away from her.

Crossing her arms across her chest, she says, "I look silly, don't I?"

"Are you serious?" I can't even believe she'd think such a thing. "You look beautiful, Jaynie."

Slowly, she lowers her arms to her side. "Thank you, Flynn," she murmurs.

"Hey, I actually came out here looking for you to see if you wanted to go up to our spot."

Holding out her hand, she says, "Let's go."

I stare down at her hand like a fool. She wiggles her fingers. "Flynn, take my hand."

"But—"

She shushes me. "Don't make a big deal," she says. "It feels right."

"It does," I agree, my hand moving closer to hers.

Our fingers touch, and she says, "So, do it."

I don't need any more convincing. I take Jaynie's hand in mine, so warm and small, and we're off. Up across the fields and into our woods, holding hands the whole way. I feel closer to Jaynie on this day than all the others combined. I've been falling for her since the day she arrived, and I am in deeper than ever now. I think about her all the time, even when I'm not around her, which isn't often. When it's just the two of is I ask her questions. I thirst for knowledge of everything about her.

And then there's the reaction I had minutes ago. There's no way around the fact that I long to touch Jaynie. Like, *really* touch her. I want to hold her close to me, and not just her hand. I want to feel her whole body pressed to mine. I want to love her and kiss her. Jaynie has never been kissed, and I want to be her first. Not because of some misplaced male bravado. I just think at least one of Jaynie's "firsts" should be done right. She deserves to be given a memory involving intimate contact that is positive. And, not to sound smug, but kissing—doing it in a way I know every girl loves—is something I have mastered.

"What are you thinking about, Flynn?" Jaynie asks, eyeing me curiously as we reach the tall pines.

I wipe the grin off my face and gaze up at the tops of the trees. I sure as hell don't plan on sharing those thoughts with Jaynie, so I change the subject.

"I'm glad you wanted to come up here," I say as I walk to the center of the circle of pines.

Plopping down on the soft needles and the lush, green grass that has grown in—just like I told Jaynie it would—I motion for her to join me.

With a smile, she says, "Of course I was up for coming here. I love this place."

"You do, don't you?"

"As much as you do, Flynn."

I nod to the spot next to me. "So, come sit with me."

When she sits down next to me, she sighs. "This is becoming *our* place, isn't it?"

"It sure is," I agree.

And it is. Jaynie and I have found much-needed peace and solitude up here, something that's usually impossible to find down at the house. Here, though, everything is good. It's a different world, *our* world. I'm so glad I get to share this place with Jaynie.

I glance over at her auburn hair as it glints red under the sunlight slanting in. When she looks at me, questioningly, I see what I once noticed before—Jaynie's green eyes match the color of the pines. I was reticent to share my observation with her in the past, but not anymore.

"Did you know your eyes are the same color as the pines?"

Cocking her head, she peers upward and says, "Really? You think so?"

I nod. "Yeah, they are."

Jaynie tucks her chin and draws her knees up to her chest. Her dress rides *way* up in the process, exposing her creamy thighs. *Kill me now.* All too quickly for my tastes, she covers her exposed skin with the scalloped hem.

Laughing nervously, she says, "Sorry. Guess I'm not used to wearing a dress."

"I'm not complaining," I mutter.

She looks away, but I can see she's smiling.

It's a moment, and that's how moments are. Not necessarily defined by an earth-shattering event. It's usually the almost missed split seconds that offer insight to where something is heading. And in that instant, under the pines, I know our futures are destined to be intertwined.

Clearing my throat, I say, "Things have been really good lately, haven't they?"

I mean with her, with how far she's come, but she misunderstands and thinks I mean things have been good down at the house, which is also true, so I roll with it.

"Yeah," she says. "I hope Mrs. Lowry keeps taking those business trips. Allison's not as bad as I thought she'd be. I expected her to come at me hard, but she barely even notices me lately."

I screw up my face. I don't want Jaynie to get too comfortable. "Stay wary, Jaynie," I warn. "Things could change in an instant. Allison running the show is bound to turn miserable at some point. She's been distracted lately, that's all."

Jaynie rests her cheek on her raised knees and peers over at me. "Do you think she has a boyfriend in town? Mandy thinks so for sure. She said that's why Allison has been leaving us alone so much lately."

Chuckling, I flick away a long blade of grass that's stuck to my jean-clad leg. "Yeah, I think Allison has a piece of action going in town. She's probably pulled the wool over some poor sap's eyes."

Jaynie lifts her head from her knees. "So…she's still not hitting on you?"

"Nope, not at all."

Jaynie blows out a breath, clearly relieved. "I'm so glad," she says. "I hate the idea of her and you."

"There is no her and me," I say. "And there never will be."

"I know. I just want it to stay that way."

"It will," I assure her. "I would never do anything with Allison."

"Good, 'cause she's a fucking nasty wench."

Wow. I'm a little surprised and a whole lot thrilled by Jaynie's blatant jealousy. My face warms, while red creeps up Jaynie's neck. To avoid further discomfort on either of our parts, I change the subject to something less volatile.

"Hey, what about Cody's progress lately? He's been doing great with addition *and* subtraction."

Jaynie nods enthusiastically. She's as excited as I am, and damn, is that cool.

"Yeah, he is. In fact, I think we can probably start him on multiplication soon."

I let out a laugh. "Oh, that should be an adventure."

"Yeah, but we can do it, Flynn."

She is so certain of the power of us that I nod and say, "We can do it…and we will." I scoot closer and nudge her shoulder with mine. "We make a good team, yeah?"

Quietly, she agrees. "We make the best team."

Pleased with ourselves and how well we work together, we talk more about the best methods to teach Cody more mathematics.

Jaynie makes a face at one point, prompting me to say, "What?"

"I was thinking Cody could probably see his worksheets better if we got some of that hair out of his face."

Thinking of Cody's mop of dark hair, I laugh. "He does need a haircut, no doubt."

Reaching over and flicking a piece of *my* hair out of my face, Jaynie says, "You could use a haircut, too, you know."

I don't disagree. But I do put up a fuss when she flips her auburn tresses over her shoulder and threatens, "Maybe I'll chop off some of my own. Go with something short and simple for the summer."

I am aghast. "No way. Don't you dare."

She shoots me a satisfied grin. "Hmm, I didn't think it mattered so much to you, Flynn."

"Well, it does."

"Oh, really?"

Suddenly, I find the laces of my shoes infinitely fascinating.

"Well," Jaynie says softly. "I kind of like my hair the way it is, so don't worry. There's no haircut in my future. At least, nothing drastic."

Flopping to my back, I throw an arm over my face and mutter, "Glad you came to your senses."

It was literally hurting me to imagine Jaynie's thick tresses lying lopped off on the floor.

Tomorrow's Lies

Jaynie stretches out next to me, and I close my eyes. I'm so relaxed I could fall asleep, but Jaynie's restless flipping and flopping from side to side keep me awake.

I open one eye. "What's up?" I ask.

She rolls to her stomach and peers up at me. "I was just wondering something."

There's a mischievous glint in her eyes that gets my attention. Now I am fully awake. "Yes?"

Biting her lip, she says, "What would you have done to me if I *had* decided to chop off my hair? After all, you used the words, and I quote, 'Don't you dare.'"

"Uh, I don't know." I sit up. "I hadn't really thought it through."

Smiling up at me, she says, "Well, assuming you *had* thought it through, Flynn. What would you do if you had to convince me to see things your way?"

I raise a brow. This is an interesting development—Jaynie Cumberland is blatantly flirting with me, innuendo and all.

Playing along, I tell her, "I would've tickled you, maybe."

Rolling to her back, she stares up at the trees and says, "Until I relented?"

"Sure, if that's what it took."

"Well, I am reconsidering," she says slowly. "Now that I think of it, a crew cut might be the way to go. Easy care,"—she lifts slightly to fan her long hair out from under her head—"and think how much cooler I'd be."

I lower myself to my stomach and scoot up to her. "No way would you go through with something so drastic," I challenge in a low and husky voice.

Arching her back—which has me suppressing a groan—she says, "Maybe I *will* go through with it. Convince me not to, Flynn, or I may really do it."

The air crackles with sexual tension. We're playing a dangerous game. "Jaynie…" I let out a sigh. "I don't know how much will be too much."

She closes her eyes. "Just try, Flynn. Please, for once, treat me like I'm normal."

I swallow hard. Her desire for this validation outweighs any need to take things slowly. Jaynie is still a woman with urges and desires. And she wants me to do something.

I maneuver my body till I'm hovering above her. Placing my hands on either side of her head, I lock my arms till they're straight and tense. *Oh, God, please don't arch up now. I am only so strong.*

Slowly, I place one hand on her side, my fingers grazing over the soft, worn fabric of her dress.

Jaynie gasps, sucking in a startled breath, and I jerk away.

She grabs my hand, her fingers interlocking with mine. "Don't stop," she says, squeezing.

When she opens her eyes, our gazes meet. "It's okay," she tells me. "Keep touching me, Flynn. Please, I need this. I need to know I can be normal."

This is no longer about tickling, or haircuts, or convincing anyone of anything. This is so much more. This is the next step in her healing.

Guiding my hand back to her waist, Jaynie lets go, leaving the next part up to me.

Taking a deep breath, I flatten my hand against her. And then, gently, cautiously, I move my hand so I can *feel* Jaynie. She's small beneath me, fragile. I slide my hand from her slight waist to her hipbone, waiting for a reaction. When she remains calm, her breathing shallow but steady, I move my hand to just up under her breasts.

Her mouth parts in a little *o*, and I feel her every heartbeat beneath my palm. Jaynie pumps life into me, and I am renewed.

Lowering my face to hers, we share breaths more heated than the hot air surrounding us. There is nothing else in the world right now, only she and I. Forgetting my fear of moving too fast, I go with what feels right. In the recesses of my soul, in the core of my being, I know kissing Jaynie—right here, right now—is what we both need.

I lower my mouth to hers, and as if we've done this a million times before, Jaynie lifts up until our lips touch. Dewy soft, warm and full, Jaynie's lips are perfection pressed to mine.

Slanting my head, I close my mouth over her lower lip and suck it into my mouth. She lets out a barely audible groan, and taking that as a good sign, I move to her upper lip and do the same thing. Soon, we begin kissing in earnest. And when she starts kissing me back as hungrily as I'm kissing her, God, there are no words.

Jaynie shoves her hands in my hair, while her body rocks against mine. My instinct is to move my hand up under her dress, to feel the thighs she flashed me earlier. I'd then move up to her softest, warmest spot.

But no, this isn't about sex.

Trailing kisses down her neck, I press my lips to her collarbone and say softly, "We should probably quit while we're ahead."

She's showing no signs of losing it, but I don't know how far might be too far. What's occurring between us is amazing, but I don't want to go teenage-boy crazy and fuck it all up.

"Okay, yeah," she says, voice quivering.

As I lift my body up and away from her, I glance down…and damn. There are tears staining Jaynie's cheeks.

"Shit, Jaynie." I scoot all the way off her. "That was too much, wasn't it?"

"No, no." She shakes her head. "It's not that."

I sit back and, rising my knees, I discreetly adjust myself. I feel guilty as hell for remaining turned on while Jaynie is obviously in distress.

"It's not you," she chokes out.

Swiftly, she sits up and covers her face with her hands. "I loved the way you kissed me, Flynn. It was my first kiss, and it was better than anything I ever expected. I thought I'd lose it, but I didn't. I'm okay with you, Flynn. When you touch me, I feel good and normal and…"

"Jaynie, that's a good thing," I interject.

"Yeah, it is," she agrees. "The problem was when we stopped."

"I'm confused. What do you mean?"

"When we stopped kissing, *things* started coming back to me. As long as I was caught up in the moment, I was okay, I thought only of you. But the second we stopped…" She fights back tears. "Flynn, I don't want *him* in my head after I'm with you. I don't want to think of him before, after, or *ever*."

She breaks down completely, and I gather her in my arms. "Shh, shh, it's okay. This was your first taste of intimacy, you know, after…"

"It's not okay," she cries onto my shoulder. "I am not okay. I am damaged and ruined."

"No, you're not."

"Yes, I am. Do you know what I'm thinking right now?"

"What?" I cautiously inquire.

She pulls away, knees up, guarded as she tells me, "I'm so messed up that a part of me wants you to take me right now. I want you to have sex with me and erase the horror of what *he* did to me in every way you can. And I know it would work, throughout the 'during' part." Her eyes meet mine, sad and watery. "I'm terrified of the afterward. Will it all come back to me, always? I'm worried I'll never be able to be with you and not think of *him* when we stop. And Flynn," she sobs, "I can't do that to you. You deserve so much more than the broken girl I am."

Wrapping my arms around her, I whisper, "Jaynie, Jaynie, can't you see I want the broken girl you are." I hold onto her more tightly. "You think *I'm* not damaged?" I laugh humorlessly. "We just need to take this thing one day at a time. No one ever said it would be easy."

"And that's okay with you?" she mumbles against my shoulder.

I lean back so she can see how serious I am. "Yes, of course it's okay."

"You're really sure you're up for dealing with me and all my issues?"

"Hey." I nudge her chin. "I'd be lucky to have you any way I can. And who knows? Maybe someday you'll even agree to be my girlfriend."

Her eyes widen. "You'd really want *me* for a girlfriend?"

It breaks my heart to see so much doubt in her eyes. "Are you kidding? I'd be the luckiest guy on the planet if you'd agree."

Jaynie sits for a moment, pondering, I suppose, until she opens her mouth and says, "I agree."

"To which part?" I am cautious; I don't want to misunderstand.

There's no mistaking her intentions, though, when she says, "I want to be your girlfriend, Flynn."

"You do?"

She nods. "Yes."

And then I think, *to hell with it.*

With my arms around my new girlfriend, I kiss her again and again.

Chapter Sixteen

Jaynie

The following evening finds me tromping through the summer-thick woods with my first-ever boyfriend, Flynn. We are heading back up to our spot.

Under the pines, we can't keep our hands off one another. We become singular in purpose, drawn to each other like moths to a flame. We kiss until our lips are swollen and we taste of each other.

Flynn has his hands all over me this night, and I love that there are no stirrings of panic. However, I am troubled by more confusing thoughts.

Still torn between lust and fear, I want more of Flynn. But I'm frightened of the potential aftermath. I have no desire to be tortured by images of the violence inflicted on me once we stop. *So, maybe we should keep going?*

On this night, I remain oblivious as long as Flynn is trailing kisses down my neck. And when he stops at the v of my top, he flicks his tongue out, tasting the salt on my skin. I am left aflame, but in the

Tomorrow's Lies

best sort of way.

As he works his way back up my neck, I watch as the muscles bunch up in his arms. Flynn holds himself above me, straining triceps and biceps in full view as he tenses to keep his own lust at bay.

When a light moan escapes me, Flynn's lips crash into mine, hot and wet and urgent.

I am losing control, dizzy with lust and uncertainty. I don't know if we should keep going, so I push at Flynn's chest. "Wait. I need a break."

He pulls away from me quickly, a blur of hotness as he rocks back on his heels.

"Shit." He rakes his hand through his sandy-toned hair, his chest rising and falling as he collapses onto his back. "I'm sorry, Jaynie. I just got caught up in the moment. I wasn't thinking clearly—"

Sitting up, I place a hand on his forearm. "No, Flynn, you were fine. I was just as caught up as you. But I'm still confused."

Peering up at me, he laments, "I should have slowed up sooner."

I lie down on my side next to him. "I'm good, I swear. I just need a minute."

Cautiously, he asks, "How do you feel now that we stopped? It's not the same as yesterday, is it?"

I think about it, facing my fears straight-on. When I purposely think of Mrs. Giessen's son, he's there. But images of him aren't popping up in my head unexpectedly like yesterday. As long as I keep him pushed away, I seem all right.

"There's nothing really bad right now," I tell Flynn. "Nothing I can't deal with, at least. It's not like yesterday."

Blowing out a relieved breath, he says, "Maybe yesterday was bad because it was the first intense physical experience since it happened."

"Yeah, maybe." My tone is cautious, and I share my underlying concern with Flynn. "Every time might not be like this, though. You were right when you said none of this will be easy."

Flynn chuckles. "Hey, nothing worthwhile ever is."

This boy is too good to be true. "I don't deserve you," I whisper.

He admonishes me with a stern, but kind, "Stop saying that."

I curl up in his strong arms. "I wish we could sleep here all night."

"Yeah, me, too. But we can't."

He's right. Nightfall is near and we'll have to return to the house soon, in case Allison comes back from town early. We've been pushing it lately, but our luck could run out at any time. Still, I beg to stay a little longer.

"Sure," Flynn says. "We can start back in a few."

I snuggle in closer, breathing in Flynn's distinctly boy scent. "Let's talk about something, okay? It's too quiet up here."

Most of the animals and birds have gone to bed. The only noise is that of the water rushing far below the nearby cliff.

Depositing a light kiss on the top of my head, Flynn says, "So, what do you want to talk about?"

"Hmm, I don't know. Anything, really."

"Well, okay." He ponders for a minute, and then says, "Why don't you tell me more about you. Like how your life was when you were little. You never talk about your childhood, or your life before you got in the system."

I suppress a bitter laugh. "That's because there isn't much to tell. Nothing I care to talk about, that is."

I sense Flynn's gaze, and I look up to find he's frowning. He thinks he's upset me. But the truth is I'm fine. To satisfy his curiosity, though, I rack my brain for at least one positive story from my days with my mother. It's not easy, but I finally come up with one nice tale.

"I thought of a story I can share with you," I say. "One that's sort of happy."

Flynn squeezes my shoulder. "You don't have to tell me any stories if you don't want to." His tone is kind. "I'm cool with talking about something else."

Tomorrow's Lies

"No," I reassure him. "This is a good story. I don't mind sharing this one."

"Okay," he says.

And I begin…

"So, no surprise, since I am where I am, but my mom rarely had time for me when I was a little girl. She wasn't blatantly mean, she was more neglectful. My mom was too busy with men. She was always chasing men, worrying about men, trying to get one to stick around. You know the type, right?"

Flynn nods. The neglectful mom may not be part of his story, but it's a common story, nonetheless, in the foster care world.

"Anyway," I go on, "this one day, out of the blue, my mom comes into my room and tells me we're going on a day trip." I smile, despite myself. "I was so excited, Flynn. We *never* did things like that. So, we struck out on the road, and the whole time she kept telling me we were embarking on a real adventure."

"That sounds fun," he interjects.

"It was one of her good days," I say, nodding. "Anyway, we drove to this huge state park." I pause, remembering how in awe I was. "It was so beautiful there. It *was* an adventure. To me, the place didn't even seem real. There were all these funky rock formations, I remember that. They were huge and looming and seemed to be bursting from the ground. It was overwhelming, especially to a ten-year-old girl who'd never been anywhere. I thought my mom had taken us someplace magical. And the forest, Flynn, wow. There were trees everywhere"—I motion to our forest-y surroundings—"even more than there are up here."

"Nice," Flynn murmurs.

"Yeah, it really was. But the best part for me was that my mom was happy that day. That was unusual for her. Usually, she was completely miserable around me. She told me one time that having me had made her feel like her youth had been ripped away."

"Jaynie, that's an awful thing to say to a kid."

Flynn shakes his head, but I brush it off. "She was like that all the time, Flynn. That's why the day at the park was so special. For the first time, like, ever, she was happy just hanging out with me." I smile up at him sadly. "I was never enough. But that day, I was."

"Jaynie," he sighs.

I can tell from his tone he thinks my mom was awful, and really, she kind of was. Still, I feel this crazy need to explain her to him, to give him my theories as to why she was the way she was back then, and probably still is today. It's like with Callie still wanting to know about her mom. Our mothers can do so much wrong to us, and we still strive to absolve them.

"See," I begin, resting my chin on Flynn's chest, "my mom was… is… I don't know. I guess she has mental issues. She's a complicated person is all I know."

"Aren't we all?" Flynn retorts.

"Yeah, I guess so."

I think back, recalling my mother in a way I haven't in a long while. "One of my therapists told me she's probably a narcissist, prone to histrionics."

"What does that mean?" he asks.

"Basically, that she only thinks of herself and her needs. And that she always comes first. My mother's problems were *always* larger than life. Or," I amend, tapping my temple, "she wanted you to *think* they were."

"I've known some people like that," Flynn muses.

"She was always trying to 'find' herself, I remember that. She used those words a lot. I guess I always kind of knew I'd end up getting in her way. It became clear as time passed, and I grew more aware, that her search for whatever kind of inner peace she was seeking would always come at my expense."

Flynn shakes his head. "That was totally not fair to you, Jaynie."

Tomorrow's Lies

"I know." I sigh. "But what can you do. The hard part was she promised me so many things. She promised to always protect me. She swore she'd never leave me. On and on, she'd commit to a lot of things. But she never backed anything up. She never came through. When I think about it, my mother broke *every* damn promise she ever made to me."

Flynn, knowing disappointment all too well, says, "I know how you feel, Jaynie. Most of today's promises are nothing but tomorrow's lies."

"Is that a quote or something?" I ask.

"No, it's the truth."

"That's for sure." I exhale a long, resigned breath. After a minute of reflection, I say, "You want to know the worst part?"

"What's that?"

"The one truth she told was the day before she left. She came into my room the night before and told me she had to leave. I thought she meant just for the night. But then she told me the real reason."

I stop to swallow the lump forming in my throat, and Flynn asks tightly, "What did she say, Jaynie?"

"She said there was no space for me in her life anymore. And, weird as it sounds, I sort of understood. Her issues had become so big that I had to be pushed aside to make room for them. She couldn't grow and breathe with me *and* her issues in her life. But my mom and her issues were one. That's why she couldn't take me with her. I was in the way, and I could be discarded."

I look up at Flynn and his eyes flash with irritation. He's angry at the woman who hurt me, my own mother, convincing me I was in the way.

"You don't believe that bullshit, do you?"

I sit up and shrug, but it comes off more like a flinch. Some wounds cut so deeply they never stop hurting and bleeding, even when you think you have them cauterized.

Flynn sits up and pulls me onto his lap. As he cradles me, I lean into him, needing the comfort now more than ever. "I feel so alone sometimes, Flynn."

"I know, sweetheart, I know. I do, too."

Only Flynn can truly understand my pain.

"But there is one thing, Jaynie," he says. "Something I need for you to do for me now."

"What's that?"

"Promise me one thing. Can you do that?"

"Yes."

"Stop thinking your mother's leaving had anything to do with you. She was selfish, Jaynie. Every person on this planet has issues and problems. Shit, we're all trying to find ourselves in one way or another. She could have sought out help. Your mom leaving you is unforgivable. She's your mother and *you* should have come before anything else."

I know every word Flynn is spilling out is true, and I choke back a sob. Taking my hand, he holds it to his heart until I stop crying.

Under the pines Flynn tells me are the same color as my eyes, we hold onto what we have here, today, and in this moment—each other.

Chapter Seventeen

Flynn

Hair cut time arrives. It's the same drill as every time before, only now Jaynie is in on it.

The plan is put into action, and it is smooth sailing…at first.

Stealing a large pair of scissors from the craft barn during the course of the work day isn't all that difficult. Sneaking them into the house becomes a challenge, though, when damn Allison corners me as I'm on my way to the porch at the end of a long day.

"Flynn-n-n," she whines annoyingly from the top step. She shifts her lithe body, clad in tiny lime-green shorts and a matching tank, effectively blocking my way.

"Have you been avoiding me?" she asks distractedly as she tugs her too-short shorts down a millimeter. "It seems since you quit smoking, we never talk anymore. And, well, I miss you, Flynn."

She flutters her eyelashes, and I glance beyond her to see if everyone is in the house. The twins are through the door, but Mandy and Jaynie are waiting for me on the porch. Shit.

Jaynie is watching my interaction with Allison, worry creasing her brow. Mandy just rolls her eyes at Allison's antics. She is well-aware I am capable of handling myself.

Grabbing Jaynie's hand, Mandy mouths to me from behind Allison's back, "You got this?"

I nod discreetly. Meanwhile, Allison continues to whine about how much she misses me. She misses our smoke breaks, and why don't I talk to her more. I swear the girl's a broken record.

I entertain a brief fantasy of pulling the scissors out from where they're hidden—tucked in my sock under the leg of my jeans—and brandishing them in front of me like a sword. "*En garde*, bitch. Out of my way or blood shall be shed."

I let out a chuckle. That'd get her moving, no doubt. But it's only a fantasy. I need to stay calm and play the bimbo, as usual.

Folding my arms across my chest, knowing it will accentuate my pecs and arm muscles in the snug black tee I'm wearing, I smile at her. I am bigger and stronger than even a month ago, a benefit of the more-than-sufficient sustenance as of late, and it shows. Allison sure as hell takes note.

Playing right into my hands, she licks her lips. "Wow, Flynn, you look amazing. Have you secretly been lifting weights?"

I almost burst out laughing. Like all the manual labor I do—hauling and sawing large pieces of wood so we can make the crafts, lifting the shit that's too heavy for the twins or the girls—isn't enough.

I have Allison on the line. I just need to reel her in.

First, I make damn sure Jaynie and Mandy have gone in the house, especially Jaynie. After confirming the coast is clear, I turn my attention to Allison.

In a low, filled-with-the-promise-of-sex voice, I say, "Seems to me you're the one who's gone all the time these days. I've been right here, every day, same as always."

Jutting out her hip, Allison pretends to pout. Please. It's not working, but she sure thinks it is.

"Would you like for me to be home more often?" she coos. "If you want that, Flynn, I can make it happen. Just say the word."

Hell, no. Allison spending this much time away from the house has been the best thing to happen around here in a long time.

Time to tread carefully, as Allison has just placed a mine field before me.

"I doubt your boyfriend would like that." I try to sound disappointed, yet accepting.

Allison leans in closer. "Can I tell you a secret, Flynn?"

I take a deep breath, let it out slowly. "Uh, sure."

In a breathy whisper, she says, "Just because I have a boyfriend doesn't mean I can't have some fun on the side. Who would need to know?" She shrugs. "With my mom away, you could come down to my room any night you want. And Flynn, I'd definitely make it worth your while."

Playing along to gain more info, I ask, "What about the cameras?"

She straightens and sniffs with self-importance. Examining her nails, which match her outfit, she snips, "What about the cameras? They're not a problem. I actually turned them off days ago, if you must know. I don't have time to keep an eye on a hallway that's empty except for when you guys go take a piss. But here's the deal..." Her eyes scan up and down my body suggestively. "I'll *keep* those cameras off indefinitely if you think you might actually come down to my room some night to visit me."

She raises a questioning brow, and though there is no way in hell there will ever be a visit from me to Allison's bedroom, I need her to believe it's a possibility. Those fucking cameras must remain off. No watchful red eyes make life easier for all of us, particularly Cody. We'll be able to sleep in the girls' room all the time now. The twins remaining together at night means no more nightmares for the little man. He deserves a shot at some restful sleep. Leading Allison on is a small price to pay to make that happen.

Leaning toward a girl I want nothing more than to run the fuck away from, I whisper seductively in her ear, "Keep the cameras off and maybe"—I run my hand up her arm, and she lets out a little gasp—"just maybe, I'll surprise you one night."

I let my lips touch her neck, and she purrs, "Oh, Flynn. Please do."

She's so discombobulated that I'm able to slip past her, leaving her on the steps, no doubt wet and wanting for a night that will never come.

a few hours later, in the girls' bedroom, Cody is getting his much-needed haircut.

"Mandy, Mandy, I can see now," he marvels when Mandy's done.

She snips a single straggler by his brow. "I bet you can, bud," she says, laughing.

Jaynie and I are seated side-by-side on the edge of her bed, watching Mandy work her magic. Cody is perched on a stool in the middle of the room, his dark hair scattered on the floor beneath his dangling feet. Callie is seated on the floor in front of the stool.

She peers up at Cody with keen interest, and says, "Cody, you don't look like me anymore. You look like *you*."

Cody, uncertain fingers tugging at his new short-do, puffs out his lower lip. "I no want to not look like Callie."

Mandy assures him, "You still look like your twin, sweetie. But now you look more like the boy you are."

That makes him happy. "I *am* a boy," he says proudly.

Callie rolls her eyes. "Yeah, yeah, you're a boy. And I'm a girl. Big deal. Doesn't change the fact that being a girl is still better."

"Is not," Cody counters.

"Is, too."

Tomorrow's Lies

"Okay, okay," Mandy interjects. "Everyone is great—boy, girl, or space alien."

"Who's space alien?" Cody peers at the rest of us suspiciously.

"Nobody is an space alien, stupid," Callie says.

And that's when I jump in and diffuse a potentially volatile situation. "Hey, hey, what did we agree on about name-calling?"

"That it's not nice," Callie says.

"Exactly. So, tell your brother you're sorry."

"Sorry, Cody."

Cody appears unaffected. He's still fixated on the possibility that one of us may be an alien from another planet.

Mandy leans down, and I hear her whisper to Cody, "No one is an alien, okay?"

Cody nods. "Okay, good."

She squeezes his shoulder as he jumps down from the stool. Then, brandishing the long-bladed metal scissors, Mandy says, "Who's my next victim?"

Cody runs over to me. "Flynnie, Flynnie!" He pulls at my hand. "Flynnie next victim. He need a haircut, too."

I'm hesitant, since, well, Mandy and sharp scissors, I don't know. But the truth is that I like my hair a little long and on the scruffy side.

But when Jaynie leans toward me and says, "You *could* use a little trim," I allow Cody to drag me off the bed and to the stool of doom.

"Not too much," I warn Mandy as I reach back and protectively pat the strands of hair poking at the neckline of my tee.

Mandy smacks my hand away. "Give it a rest, Flynn. Getting your hair cut won't kill you. Who do you think you are, anyway? Samson?"

"Who is Samson?" Cody immediately asks. "Space alien?"

"God help us," I hear a too-cynical-for-her-years Callie mumble. She has moved to the space next to Jaynie on the bed, my vacated seat.

Cody is in his sister's former spot in front of the stool. Peering down at him, I answer his question. "Samson wasn't a space alien, little man."

"There are no such things as aliens," Callie chimes in, loudly, from over on the bed. "Quit asking about them, all right? You're giving me a splitting headache." *Kids.*

Cody ignores his sister's rumblings and asks me again, "Who is Samson?"

"Nobody, bud," I reply. I'm worried the story might upset him in some way, especially the haircut aspect.

But Mandy goes right ahead and tells him. *I give up.*

"Samson is a character from an old Bible story," she says. "He was super strong,"—Cody's eyes widen—"and his hair was the source of all his mighty strength."

"What happen to him?" Cody asks.

Mandy sighs. She tilts my head forward. "Well, his girlfriend, this chick named Delilah, betrayed him. She allowed a bunch of bad guys to sneak in, and they chopped his hair off so they could get the jump on him."

Cody swallows with an audible gulp. "Was he okay?"

"He was fine," I interject.

Mandy smacks my arm. "Quit re-writing the tale, Flynn. Cody is old enough to hear the truth."

"I want the truth, I want the truth," Cody chants.

"I can't fight you both," I say, sighing.

As Mandy combs through the ends of my hair, she says, "Samson wasn't fine, Cody. All his strength was gone, right along with his hair."

Like a flash, Cody is up on his feet in an instant. Tugging my hand, he begs, "No get your hair cut, Flynn. You not be strong anymore."

"See what you did," I mutter under my breath to Mandy. "Told you to edit the story."

Mandy crouches down next to Cody. "Sweetie, Flynn will be fine. It's just an old Bible story."

I chime in for good measure, "Yeah, it's more like a fable, little man. Remember when we read the stories where each one had a lesson?"

"Like the one about the rabbit and the turtle?" Cody asks.

"Exactly like that one," I say.

Cody is content with my explanation, but Callie, inquisitive girl that she is, can't let it go. "What's the moral of the Samson and Delilah story?"

"Don't trust women," I murmur facetiously.

Mandy smacks me across the head with a towel. "Don't push it, Flynn. I have scissors in my hand, you know."

She's kidding, but I lean away, just in case. "It was a joke," I insist.

"Ass," she murmurs.

While Mandy and I continue to spar verbally, I overhear Jaynie telling Callie the moral of Samson's story is to remember who you are and to not trust the wrong people for the wrong reasons. I don't know if she has it right, but it sounds good to me.

When Mandy gets back to work on my hair, I relax. I feel cooler and better as clumps of light brown locks drift down to the floor.

"All done," Mandy declares when she's finished. She pushes me off the stool. "Off you go."

"Okay, okay."

Cody immediately has me flex, just to make sure I'm not any weaker. And then I have to pick him up and walk around the room with him perched on my shoulders. "See," I say when I put him down. "All's good."

Cody nods. "Yep. Flynnie still strong."

A few hours later, following haircut-time, and after I decide Cody and I may as well stay in the girls' bedroom tonight since there are no cameras to worry about, I am lying on the floor, raking a hand through hair that hasn't been this short in ages. Mandy did a great job, and I sure feel a lot better. Still, it's an adjustment.

Suddenly, from up on the mattress, I hear Jaynie ask. "Flynn, are you still awake?"

I prop up on one elbow. "Yeah, I'm up. I thought you were sleeping, though."

Resting her chin on the edge of the bed, she stares down at me. "I was," she says. "Well, kind of."

She stifles a laugh, and I ask, "What's so funny?"

"You," she replies, pointing. "Your hair is sticking up all over the top of your head in just about every direction. Were you messing with it?"

I nod, and she adds, "I want to feel it, Flynn, now that it's so much shorter."

I may not be Samson, but just like him, there is a woman in my life who's definitely my weakness. Her name is Jaynie, though, not Delilah. Still, like Delilah, what Jaynie wants, Jaynie gets.

I sit up and lean my back against the bed. "Have at it," I say over my shoulder.

"Not like that, Flynn." I hear her scooting back toward the wall. "Come up here on the bed with me."

Whoa. I twist around until our eyes meet in the darkness. "What are you saying?" I ask.

"Just come up here and lay down next to me." Her tone is matter-of-fact. "I want you to sleep in the bed with me tonight."

I pause. "Do you really think that's a good idea?"

She shrugs. "I don't know. We lay next to each other all the time out in the woods. What's the difference?"

She has a point. But this *is* different. Sleeping in the same bed with Jaynie changes a lot of things. I mean, shit, her mattress is *really* narrow. Limbs are bound to touch and become entwined. I sleep in nothing but boxers, and Jaynie's tiny tee and boy shorts may as well be nothing.

What it comes down to is this: Do I *want* to sleep with Jaynie, even if we do just sleep?

Answer: *Hell, yeah.*

But then there's my conscience saying: *Should* I sleep in the same bed as Jaynie?

It's probably not the best idea in the world, considering, well, everything.

Since my resistance is for shit, when she presses the issue a second time, I give in and crawl up on the bed.

A minute later I'm pressed against her warm, soft body. Damn, this is so not a good idea. This is Jaynie going from baby steps to giant leaps. And, sure enough, once those little hands are in my hair, stroking and caressing, we both start breathing harder.

"How does it feel?" I ask huskily.

"What?" Her lips graze over mine, and I let out a groan. "How does what feel?" she asks again.

"My hair," I whisper, breaths ragged.

Raking her fingers through my hair, she hitches one leg over one of mine. Not a big deal, till she scoots up higher. Then it becomes huge, the deal *and* me.

I groan. *So much for trying to hide how hard she makes me.*

She seems okay with what she has to be feeling against the inside of her thigh. Still, I worry the moment will come when we push things too far.

I really need to get a grip for the both of us.

Unfortunately, I am a seventeen-year-old guy, and I can't make myself move away. I want nothing more than to keep feeling her body pressed to mine. And maybe she wants the same thing. Seeing as she's rubbing all up against me. *God, that feels good.*

And when she suddenly says, "You feel *amazing*, Flynn," I sure as hell know she doesn't mean my hair.

Chapter Eighteen

Jaynie

Flynn feels good, really good, and I don't mean his new shorter hair—though that feels great, too.

Draped as I am, basically all over him, I can easily feel *all* of him. I have to admit it thrills me to no end to know he wants me so damn much. That's why it's with much regret that I lift my body off his and lie next to him instead. It's the smart thing to do, to not push myself. For as much as I like feeling Flynn, I do feel apprehensive.

"Is this better?" I ask.

He shifts so he can roll to his side and face me. "I can't say this is better, necessarily."

"Flynn!" I can't help but smile, despite my pretend chastisement.

He touches my face lovingly, and I ask, "Are you going to stay with me? Do you think you can sleep up here?" He raises a brow, and I clarify, "I mean with us all smooshed together like this. Do you think we'll get too warm?"

I mean a little more than that and he knows it. Still, he assures me, "I'm good if you are."

I nestle into him. "I'm better than good, Flynn. I like having you so close to me. I feel safe for maybe the first time in my life."

He tugs me in closer and whispers a contented, "Jaynie."

From that point on, whenever Flynn stays in our room, he sleeps in my bed with me. No more hard and uncomfortable floor for him, no more tossing and turning for me.

Mandy raises a brow the next night as she watches Flynn nonchalantly climb into bed with me. "What?" I say.

"Nothing," she replies. And then I hear her murmuring to herself, "Guess it was bound to happen."

She doesn't sound mad, and I know then Mandy is happy I've reached this pivotal point. A guy in bed with me? Who would have thought such a crazy thing would ever be possible?

The twins aren't fazed one bit by Flynn sleeping with me. They know we care for each other, and it's not like we're messing around in front of them or anything. Besides holding me close to him, the only indication Flynn is more than a friend is when he kisses me good-night.

So, yeah, we maintain restraint at night, but let me tell you, the mornings are a whole different story. The second Mandy leaves the room with the twins, following the alarm clock that wakes us all, Flynn and I are all over each other. Soft kissing turns to full-on making out in no time at all. From there, we begin to engage in cautious exploration, in the form of wandering hands and tentative mouths.

And a funny thing happens as time progresses. As I give more and more of my heart to Flynn, his touch triggers nothing but feelings of love and acceptance. What we build together becomes strong enough to blot out the monster—before, during, *and* after. Still, I know recovery isn't a straight line. I expect to have setbacks, especially as we move our physical relationship forward.

For now, though, we're content with simply pushing boundaries. A hand down the back of my shorts, squeezing lightly, my fingers wrapped around his erection in his tented boxers.

I marvel at how hard Flynn gets, and he marvels at my reaction when he simply kisses down my chest, sucks one nipple into his mouth, then moves to my other breast to do the same. "I love how that feels," I tell him over and over.

Still, these simple acts of foreplay won't be enough for long. Our bodies already demand more. And I know we'll succumb. You can't fight nature.

One morning when we're alone in the room and kissing furiously, Flynn rolls me on top of him.

Straddling him, I sit up, my eyes meeting his. "I love you," I blurt out, causing his lust-hooded grays to widen.

"What?"

"Don't look so shocked," I go on, smiling. "You have to know I love you, Flynn O'Neill."

He swallows hard, Adam's apple bobbing. It's not often I catch Flynn off-guard.

With his gaze softening, he reaches up to touch my cheek. "I love you, too, Jaynie. I've wanted to say it for so long now, but—"

I cut him off. Leaning down, I capture his lips with mine and shimmy my body lower. Flynn lets out a small moan when I push my core to where I feel him throbbing. Clearing my mind, I close my eyes and let my body take over. Soon, I am moving back and forth, simulating sex.

Breathing hard, Flynn lifts his hips and grinds up against me. "That feels so good," I tell him.

"Yeah?" His voice is rough, and it turns me on further.

I push down onto him and let out a soft mewl. "Fuck," I hear him murmur.

Flipping me over onto my back, he continues to thrust between my legs. "Is this all right?" he asks.

"Yes," I breathe out.

And it is. It so gloriously is. Only Flynn is in my mind.

Flynn places his head in the crook of my neck and kisses my shoulder. He trails a finger down my side, lingering at the band of my boy shorts. Still moving between my legs, he lifts his head, his eyes asking for permission to keep going.

I nod. "My heart is beating so fast," I whisper.

"Mine, too," he says. With two fingers hooked in the band of my shorts, he stills, "Tell me if it becomes too much, Jaynie."

"I will," I promise.

But the only reaction out of me is a breathy, "Oh, Flynn," when he slips his whole hand under the band of my boy shorts and moves lower than he ever has.

Gasping, I press the back of my head against the pillow. And when I feel his fingers gliding over my folds, and then lingering at my core with the promise of more, I start moving with him. "Don't stop, Flynn," I whisper.

He tugs my shorts down my legs. "I wasn't planning on stopping," he tells me.

And he doesn't.

Holding onto his strong shoulders, I squeeze at his flesh. I am aroused beyond belief. Flynn strokes me with a precision that leaves me wondering where he learned such things. I don't care, though. I'm just glad he knows what to do.

I feel a building pressure, and my whole body tenses in a way that tells me relief is at hand. Flynn then does something with his fingers that has me slapping my hand over my mouth to keep from screaming out.

This is ecstasy.

Or so I think, until I feel him move down my body and put his mouth on me.

That is indescribable.

And there in the dim morning light of the best summer morning of my life, Flynn gives me two back-to-back orgasms.

Chapter Nineteen

Flynn

Jaynie insists I take a shower before her. She tells me she needs time to recover. *Shit, hell yeah.* I'm a little smug, I admit it.

But though my ego has been stroked, I am mostly relieved Jaynie didn't freak out over how far we ventured. Things could have easily taken a turn for the worse. Recovery is tricky like that. I'd be lying if I didn't admit I was worried I'd do something to trigger some kind of panic attack.

Jaynie was okay, though. Better than okay, even. Who knows, maybe love *does* conquer all.

Speaking of love, it's left me in an uncomfortable position—I'm still hard and in need of release. That's okay. A few extra minutes spent in the shower will take care of things. I wasn't about to push Jaynie to do anything to me. Although I think she would have. I saw her staring at my dick—my erection obvious, even though I left my boxers on—and it wasn't in disgust.

Nevertheless, there's no need to race to the finish line. We'll get there in due time. The way I see it, we have forever ahead of us. I don't plan on ever leaving Jaynie.

Adjusting myself discreetly, I start down the hall. When I reach the bathroom, Mandy is coming out, and we almost crash into each other in the hall.

"Flynn," she admonishes. "Run me right over, why don't you."

I turn away swiftly so Mandy doesn't notice my, uh, condition. Thankfully, it's waning quickly.

"Jesus, don't you have somewhere to be?" I snap. "Like downstairs with the twins, eating breakfast."

"We should *all* be downstairs by now," she volleys back.

"Um, I'm running a little late."

"And Jaynie, where is she?"

"Running late, too."

Tapping her finger to her chin, she says, "Hmm, wonder why."

Mandy knows what goes on in the bedroom when she leaves. And she's not above giving me a hard time about it.

"Shut the hell up, Mandy," I say, but with a smile. Mandy may as well be my real sister; she harasses me like one would.

"Hey, I'm just teasing," she assures me. "You know that, right?"

"Yeah, I know."

She starts to walk away, tossing out over her shoulder, "Go get showered, Flynn."

I reply, "Yeah, It's probably later than we think. I guess I better make it quick, in case Allison's home."

Suddenly, Mandy stops in her tracks, like I've just reminded her of something. Spinning back around, she says, "Hold up a sec, Flynn."

Leaning against the bathroom doorframe, I wait for her to walk back over.

When she reaches me, she blows out a breath. "Hey, listen. I'm glad you and Jaynie found each other, really I am. You two are good for one another. I mean, look at Jaynie now compared to April. You've really brought her out of her shell."

I chuckle. If Mandy only knew the half of it. Maybe she does, because she then says, "Just be careful, okay?"

"What do you mean?"

"You and Jaynie are playing a dangerous game. If Mrs. Lowry—or worse yet, Allison—finds out what goes on in that bedroom every morning, there will be hell to pay."

Mrs. Lowry is not much of a factor since she's gone all the time. But Allison is definitely a concern. Everything Mandy is saying is true, but this is much more than what it looks like, and I want her to know it.

"I care about Jaynie," I blurt out. "We're in love."

Mandy smiles sadly. "If that's true, Flynn, then congratulations. But, remember, you'd be wise to keep that love a secret from both Lowry women."

"Yeah, especially Allison," I add sourly.

"Yes, *especially* Allison," Mandy agrees.

Mrs. Lowry's business trips continue into July. She must really be hitting up those future investors for loads of cash. *Whatever.* Allison remains in charge in her mother's absence. Lucky for us, she's still distant and distracted, focused solely on herself and her love life.

After her indecent proposal on the porch, she forgets about me again. *Thank God.*

Allison Lowry is as into her boyfriend as ever. She talks to him on her cell on the rare days she oversees our work in the barn. Every conversation is peppered with professions of love and devotion, in an especially loud voice. It's like she wants me to hear. Like I give a shit what she does or who she's banging. The only emotions her words conjure in me are feelings of pity for the poor dude she's dating.

Work days aren't too bad, all things considered, especially

when Allison takes off. Sure, the high quotas remain a bitch, but the atmosphere in the craft barn is easy and light without a Lowry woman peering over our shoulders. The continued better access to food makes a world of difference, too. We continue to have energy to spare. And when the work is done, the good times keep on rolling.

We become more inventive, organizing impromptu picnics up by the old barn, after downing meals of double-decker sandwiches. The twins, feeling fresh and sharp, search for new games to play. One late afternoon, we find an old rope in the barn.

"Let's play Tug of War," Cody yells.

Callie, mimicking Mandy, rolls her eyes. With her hands on her hips, she says, "Like that'll be fair."

I offer to be on Callie's side to even things up, but she wants to be on Mandy's team. And then Cody pitches a fit at the suggestion of being paired with Callie. "I have to play with her all the time," he gripes.

So it ends up with me and Cody against the three girls.

We boys win easily, and Jaynie throws me a mock-pout. "Callie was right," she says. "That was so far from fair it's not even funny."

"Yeah," Callie chimes in. "Flynn is stronger than all of us put together."

"Okay, okay." I throw up my hands. "Let's have a re-match."

The second time around, I instruct Cody not to pull so hard. "Let the girls win," I whisper.

Afterward, while the girls are celebrating their victory, Cody asks me, "Why we lose on purpose, Flynnie?"

I ruffle his new shorter hair. "Because sometimes holding back and letting someone else win is the true victory."

"What's that mean?"

"It means if you have the chance to make someone you love happy, you should go for it. The feeling you'll get in the end is way better than winning some stupid game."

Cody looks over at Jaynie; he knows she's the reason for the rematch. "You love Jaynie?" he asks. *Ahh, Cody is more perceptive than we give him credit for.*

Quietly, I say, "Yeah, little man. I sure do."

It's true. I fall more in love with Jaynie every day. And I want to touch her every second. But when I tell Jaynie about Mandy's warnings regarding our morning activities being discovered, we agree to put a stop to any in-house messing-around sessions. Taking a chance on Allison wandering upstairs one day and catching us in a compromising position is stupid.

So, from that point on, times spent in the house, and in the craft barn, are kept innocent. That doesn't mean I don't steal kisses when I can. But more intimate times are reserved for when Jaynie and I can sneak away to our secret spot in the woods.

One evening, up in those very woods, Jaynie is in a particularly playful mood.

"I can't wait to kiss you, Flynn O'Neill," she tells me as we enter our circle of pines.

I drop the blanket I'm holding in the center of the circle. "Why wait?" I say. "What's keeping you from kissing me right now?"

She stands on her tiptoes and whispers against my lips, "Good point."

Jaynie then kisses me under a red-streaked sky that's peeking through the high branches. Under a kaleidoscope of red and green, we become lost in each other, like we always do.

"God, you make me dizzy," Jaynie says when we finally stumble apart.

She feigns fainting, or maybe it's for real. In any case, I shake out the blanket so we can sit down. The blanket has become a necessity. Kissing on a bed of grass and soft pine needles was fine at first. But we recently discovered when clothes become disheveled—or removed completely—even the softest pine needle feels a little weird when it pokes you in a private place.

Speaking of private places, Jaynie and I have not yet had full-on sex. But we have come close a few times. She wants it to happen, same as I do, but there are concerns. One biggie is we have no protection. There's no fear of disease on either of our parts—we've been tested a dozen times in the system—but pregnancy is a definite worry.

The most pressing issue for holding back, though, has to do with Jaynie. Neither of us has any idea how she will react to actual intercourse. Foreplay is one thing, and not something the man who assaulted her ever bothered with. In that way, it's a blessing there's nothing we do that can trigger some latent memory. But the moment I enter her, who knows what will happen? Having a flashback is a real possibility. And, Jesus, the last thing I want is to cause Jaynie any more pain.

Tonight, however, all concerns are pushed to the background. Sex is far from our minds this evening. We kiss for a short while, and then find comfort in simply lying in each other's arms, watching the sky turn from fiery red to twilight blue.

I start to nod off just as Jaynie murmurs, "We should talk about the future, Flynn. Mandy leaves in a couple of weeks, and you and I turn eighteen this fall. We should have a plan in place."

I am half-asleep and not sure what she's talking about. There's no doubt in my mind we'll remain together. My assumption has always been we'll figure out all the details closer to when we actually go.

In my tired state, I forget that Jaynie is a girl. And girls like reassurances of how you feel about them and where the relationship is heading.

"What's to plan?" I off-handedly remark, yawning. I then try to pull Jaynie in closer to me, but she resists.

"What the hell, Flynn?"

"What?"

She sits up abruptly and stares down at me like I'm the biggest jerk on the planet. Shit, maybe I am. At least in this situation.

Sitting up next to her, I run my hands through my hair. "Okay, I'm an ass. I'm sorry, Jaynie, okay?"

Jaynie is too upset to hear my apology. Blinking back tears, she stares straight ahead in the darkness that has fallen.

After a full minute of deafening silence, she says, "I just thought you'd still want to be around me after we leave. But I understand if you don't. Who'd want a reminder of this place, anyway?"

"Whoa, hey, hold up there. Listen to me." I cup her face in my hands. "Of course I still want to be around you when we're out of here. How could you think any differently?" She shrugs, and I go on. "I love you, Jaynie Cumberland. You're my life, baby. Hell, without you I have no reason to be. You know this, right?"

"I know, Flynn," she whispers unconvincingly.

I wipe away a tear. "Are you sure you know? 'Cause I'm kind of getting a vibe that says otherwise right now."

She nods once. "I know, I swear I do. It's just… I guess I worry sometimes."

"Worry about what?"

"That you'll quit loving me."

Her eyes meet mine, and I see uncertainty clouding her greens. Knowing my stupid, off-hand remark has her questioning her lovability breaks my heart.

"Jaynie, Jaynie." I press my forehead to hers. "Nothing in this world could *ever* stop me from loving you. We're forever, you and me."

In a shaky voice, she tells me, "I need you so much, Flynn. I don't know how I'd make it without you. I swear I don't think I could."

"I need you, too," I reply. "But you're wrong about not making it without me. You could do it if you had to—"

She pulls away. "No, I couldn't."

I gather her back in my arms and assure her, "It's not going to happen, anyway. Don't even think about it. I think you're pretty much stuck with me now."

She sighs and rests her head on my shoulder. "Good. I want to be stuck with you."

After a long pause, I say, "I need to open up to you more. And you're right. We should have a solid plan for the future."

I then tell her about Mandy's contact in Lawrence. Not just how he'd help us if we had to get out of here fast, but how he can set us up with jobs. "Would you be up for that?" I ask when I'm done.

Nodding, she says, "I think we should definitely plan to go to Lawrence."

From that point on it's out there, spoken and set—our plan to start a real life together. World be damned, nothing better dare get in our way.

Chapter Twenty

Jaynie

*I*f there is one thing I know, it's that I need to move forward with Flynn in a physical way. He is sweet and patient with me, and I know he'd wait for months, but after our talk in the woods, and the possibility we may have a shot at a real life together, I want to prove to him—and myself—that I'm capable of being with someone in that most intimate way without having a meltdown.

I sigh. Not from fear or anxiety, but from the pain of knowing I can never really give Flynn a completely undamaged version of me. Still, the one I have to offer is a better version than before. I am healthy in so many ways, thanks in large part to Flynn.

Before we can move forward, though, we need to be responsible and nail down a birth control method. A baby would be disastrous at our age and under the circumstances. Problem is it's not like Flynn can bop on down to a store and buy what we need. Not that I'm able to, either. We really are prisoners on the mountaintop.

Lucky for us, there is someone who always seems prepared for any situation—Mandy. If anyone would have condoms, I bet it'd be her.

I find her in our bedroom and ask her if she can help.

"Yeah," she says. "I can hook you up with some. I still have a box from when I was with Josh."

"Awesome." I pump my fist.

Mandy goes to our closet, sits down, and digs around in the back. At last, she pulls a backpack out. I never noticed the thing before. It looks like it hasn't been touched since Mandy first placed it there, long before I ever arrived.

"Oh, shit," Mandy murmurs as she pulls a crushed box of Trojans from the bag. She pops open the lid. "There's only one left."

I sit down on the edge of my bed. "Damn. You and Josh were busy," I murmur.

"Hey." She twists toward me, brandishing the condom packet. "One is still better than none, right?"

"True."

She tosses the packet to me. I catch it and set it on the covers.

"Be sure to tell Flynn I said for him to make it last," Mandy says, laughing as she stows the backpack away.

"Oh, my God, Mandy, I am *not* telling him you said that."

"Yeah, forget it. We wouldn't want to exacerbate any performance issues he may have."

I'm quick to defend my man, even though Mandy isn't serious. "I'm sure Flynn is perfectly capable of performing under stress."

She raises a brow. "Let's hope so, right?"

I toss a pillow at her, and she bats it away. And then we both lose it. Mandy starts laughing so hard she has to stretch out on the floor, and I fall over sideways on the bed.

"Damn," I say once we've recovered and righted ourselves. "I'm going to miss you so much when you're gone, Mandy."

I feel her loss even as I say the words, and it hurts like crazy. I

Tomorrow's Lies

place my head in my hands. "You're not just my friend," I say. "You're the best girlfriend I've ever had."

"Hey, it'll be okay." She comes over and sits next to me on the bed. "We'll keep in touch."

"Yeah," I snort. "I know we say that, but just how is that supposed to happen?"

"After you and Flynn turn eighteen, you're free to leave this place. And that's only what? Three months from now for him, and four for you?" I nod, and she adds, "Flynn told me you two talked about Lawrence. He said you plan on meeting up with the guy I know. I'm certain he'll give you jobs at the sandwich shop."

My mood brightens. Mandy's contact is the key to my future with Flynn. "The guy's name is Bill, right?"

"Yes. Bill Delmont. And he's how we'll keep in touch. Once you're in Lawrence have him give you my number. You'll have a phone by then, I'm sure. I plan to buy one of those pay-as-you-go things. You and Flynn can get them, too. They're super cheap, sometimes even free."

I'm not too concerned with phones, not at this point, but I am curious as to what my new life with Flynn might be like. "Can you tell me more about Bill's place?" I ask.

"Well," Mandy begins. "Bill's sandwich shop is located in the heart of Lawrence. Not that it's a bustling city, but it is a cute little town. Anyway, his place is called Delmont Deli. I'm pretty sure there's an apartment above it, too. You and Flynn can maybe live there till you get on your feet."

I place my hand on Mandy's arm and give a squeeze. "Thank you," I whisper. "It really does sound like a promising start."

Smiling, she tells me, "It's the least I can do. I want us all to make it."

"Yeah,"—I nod—"me too."

"And besides," Mandy says, smiling mischievously. "Far be it from me to stand in the path of true love." She picks up the condom she threw to me earlier and slips it in my hand. "Or"—she raises a brow—"good sex."

"Ugh." I fall back on the bed, shaking my head.

"What's wrong?"

"I'm nervous," I admit. "I hope I can do it, Mandy. I don't want to have a breakdown when Flynn's inside me. How awful would that be?"

Mandy stretches out next to me. "Hey, you'll be fine, Jaynie. Look how far you've come from the first day you arrived."

"Yeah," I mumble, unconvinced.

"Oh, come on. This is Flynn we're talking about. You know he'll be gentle and patient. And if you can't do it, and you guys have to stop, it's not like he's going to make a big deal out of it. He'll understand, Jaynie."

"You're right, you're right. I know you're right."

"Just remember that Flynn loves you with all his heart. The first time he's with you isn't going to be about sex for him, no more than it will be about sex for you. The first time will be about one thing only—love."

I realize then she *is* right. I can do this. I can be fully intimate with Flynn because joining our bodies is the most natural thing in the world left for us to do to seal our love. After all, we already possess each other's hearts.

When I think back on it, maybe our souls were joined the day we met. There was a familiarity I felt with him from the start. In many ways, Flynn O'Neill is my soul mate.

Where he ends, I begin. And where I end is where he starts.

But being joined at all those undefined end points and start points is not what I want. I want Flynn *in* me, inside my body. I want him where there is no beginning and no end. I want him in a place where there is only us.

Chapter Twenty-One

Flynn

A week before Mandy is set to leave, she pulls me into the girls' bedroom.

"What's going on?" I want to know as I allow myself to be dragged past the door.

"I need to talk to you," she whispers conspiratorially. "Alone."

I glance out in the hall. "Jaynie is with the twins in the bathroom. I hardly think she can hear you."

With Mandy's imminent departure upon us, we decided it'd be prudent to have Jaynie take over the task of getting the twins ready for bed. And so far, it's gone smoothly.

"Just listen to me for a sec, all right?" Mandy smacks my shoulder to re-focus my wavering attention. "I need to be quick. I don't want Jaynie to know I'm talking with you."

"Okay, okay." When I start to move clothes off Jaynie's bed, so I can sit down, I'm poked in the hand with sharp scissor blades. "Ow."

Upon closer inspection, I discover the scissors are the same pair I nabbed from the craft barn a while back, for haircutting night.

"Hey," I say to Mandy, waving the scissors at her. "I thought you were supposed to put these things back in the barn."

"Give those to me." Mandy snatches the scissors from me and reaches around me to shove them under Jaynie's mattress. "I obviously kept them, genius."

"Why are you hiding them under Jaynie's bed?"

"Because I gave her the scissors this morning and told her to keep them handy for when Cody"—she narrows her eyes at me—"or *you* need a haircut."

I take a seat on the edge of the bed and shrug. "Yeah, it's not like they'll be missed. Allison never inventories anything, anymore."

"Allison has checked out," Mandy agrees.

"Hope it stays that way," I say.

Both Lowry women have been gone a lot lately, though I sense Allison's absences are more in desperation. Her boyfriend is slipping away. She cries after she talks with him on the phone, and she just has that frazzled demeanor of a girl who knows she's about to be scorned.

"Enough about annoying Allison," Mandy says. "Did Jaynie tell you about the condom I gave her?"

"Oh, hell no," I protest, hands out in front of me. "I am not talking about sex with you."

I start to stand, but Mandy places her hand on my chest to stop me. "Sit back down, Flynn," she says in her no-nonsense tone.

"Okay, okay." I do as I'm told.

"I'm trying to help you, okay?"

I can't imagine what possible "help" Mandy can offer, and I'm still not sure I like her meddling in my sex life, but what the hell.

Acquiescing, I say, "Go ahead," as I make a *let's-get-this-rolling* motion with my hand. "This should be interesting."

Mandy then informs me she has arranged for me and Jaynie to have the bedroom to ourselves all Sunday afternoon.

"Really?" I'm happy she interfered now. "I'm down with that."

"Figured you would be," she snarks. "Anyway, here's the plan. I'll take the kids up to the fields by the old barn. I have a bunch of ideas for games they can play. And you know how Cody and Callie lose track of time when they're having fun." She winks, and I roll my eyes. "In any case, I figure I can keep them occupied for a couple of hours."

"Sounds good to me," I reply, smiling.

But then I am suddenly struck with anxiety. "Shit, Mandy. I want this to be perfect for Jaynie. What if I fuck it up? What if I do, or say, something wrong?"

"Hey, look at me." Mandy grabs my chin when I remain panicked and distracted. "Perfect isn't what Jaynie needs. Can't you see what she wants, Flynn? The one thing she really needs?"

"What's that?" I'm curious to hear a woman's perspective.

She lets go of my chin, and tells me what I've actually known all along. "Jaynie wants you, Flynn. She needs *you*. Just be there for her. Let her know you'll stay by her side no matter what."

That, I can do.

Chapter Twenty-Two

Jaynie

Sunday arrives, and everything is set. Mandy takes the kids up to the old barn, as planned.

By the time I finish showering, I am both nervous and excited. After I dry off, I put on the white dress, the one Mandy gave me. It's Flynn's favorite outfit on me. With a swish of my palm, I wipe steam from the bathroom mirror. Green eyes stare back at me, hope and doubt warring within their depths.

"You can do it," I whisper to the uncertain girl in the reflection. "This is Flynn. This is love. You'll be okay."

I don't own any makeup, so there's not much to do in way of preparation. I simply tuck my damp auburn hair behind my ears, and smooth the cotton fabric of the dress over the gentle swell of my hips.

Flynn is waiting in the bedroom. I gave him the condom from Mandy earlier, so that part is in his hands now. It's funny that we've messed around several times and slept in the same bed almost every night. We've even shared our souls up at the cliff's edge, but here I am, hands shaking.

I just want to be good enough for Flynn. Oh, and I don't want to have a flashback.

When I walk into the bedroom, tentatively, like it's my first time entering an unfamiliar space, I find Flynn sitting on the edge of my bed, head in his hands.

Forgetting my reticence, I rush over and kneel down in front of him. "What's wrong?" I ask. "Are you having second thoughts?"

He lowers his hands from his face and places them on my shoulders. "No second thoughts," he assures me with a sweet smile, making him appear more handsome than ever. "I'm just hoping I don't mess this up."

"Oh, thank God," I breathe out. "I thought it was just me. I was thinking the same thing in the bathroom."

With his hand moving to my cheek, he says softly, "You look beautiful, Jaynie. And you're such a good person. You deserve for this day to be special."

I move up to the bed, and together we lay back on the covers. Nestling close to Flynn, I whisper, "I love you."

"I love you, too."

Nothing happens for a while. We are content lying together, legs intertwined. My head rests on his chest, and his arm is draped loosely around my shoulders. We don't even kiss, not yet, though there is something powerful building between us. Heat emanates through the thin material of Flynn's tee and the faded jeans he's wearing.

I feel my own skin growing warm, aching for his touch, longing for the hand that rests on my shoulder to run down my arm. Goosebumps rise at the mere thought. When I shift and let out a stuttered breath, Flynn does exactly what I wish for.

The floodgates open then, on both our parts. How long has this moment been building?

Our lips meet, desperate and insistent. Mouths open freely,

tongues dance, and bodies roll this way and that, making a mess of the covers. There are gasps and moans, from me, from him. And there is awkwardness and fun, too.

Flynn's tee gets stuck on his head when he tries to remove it in a seductive way. "A little help here," he says through the gray cotton.

We tug his shirt off him together, as a team, with me giggling and Flynn mumbling choice words. When his chest is bare, he rocks back on his heels and flicks open the top button of his jeans.

The giggling stops.

"Your body is stunning, Flynn." I say it often, but this time it's uttered with more meaning.

Reaching out, I trace the fine line of sandy brown disappearing under the band of his boxers.

He sucks in a sharp breath, and I ask, "Does that tickle?"

"It does a little more than tickle, Jaynie."

While I unzip his jeans, he undoes the hooks on the back of my dress. The spaghetti straps drop and the front gapes open, exposing my breasts since I've forgone a bra.

His eyes meet mine, and this becomes something serious.

Flynn rises to his knees and urges me to do the same. "I want to see you as I undress you," he says gently.

It's not going to be anything he hasn't seen before, especially up in the woods, but when he tugs the dress down, and the fabric falls to around my hips, I feel as if he is seeing me bared for him for the first time.

Tentatively, I reach forward and press my palm to his bare chest. "You're so strong," I whisper. I spread my fingers wide to feel the solid muscle beneath his warm skin. "But not just in this way. You're strong inside, Flynn."

"Because of you—"

"No." I shake my head. "That's sweet of you to say, but your strength is all your own. And it's so abundant, so overflowing. I feel lucky to stand beneath you and soak up whatever strength trickles down to me."

"Jaynie…"

My words move Flynn, but he moves me just by being him. He doesn't need words to inspire me.

I move closer to him, my lips grazing his. "Give me more, Flynn. Fill me up…with you."

We come together, skin pressed to skin, mouth devouring mouth. My dress is discarded, Flynn's clothes, too. We become two bodies, dancing a tango as old as time. Bare limbs brush over parts that are hard…and parts that are wet. We do things we've learned drive each other wild—stroking, licking, fingers exploring, and Flynn's mouth on me, making me come apart, again and again.

I am ready for him, and as he crawls up my body, I tell him what he already knows. "I want you."

He settles between my thighs, his hard length pressed to my core. This is it.

"Flynn," I whisper. "Please don't stop. No matter what happens. Keep going, okay?"

He leans across me, reaching for the wrapped condom by the bed. "Okay."

He sounds as nervous as I feel. I close my eyes. *Don't panic.*

When Flynn settles back between my legs, I feel him, wrapped, different. And up until this point, I've been fine. But the condom… ugh. The feel of it, the *smell* of it, it reminds me of Mrs. Giessen's son. He never did it to me without a condom, and now that's all I can think of.

"Stop, stop, stop," I cry. "Please, stop."

The panic I feel must come through in my tone. Flynn forgets about me telling him not to stop no matter what. Swiftly, he shifts his hips away from me. His torso remains covering me, though, and with a gentle hand to my cheek, he asks, "Do you want to stop completely?

We don't have to do this today."

"No, I want to try." I tap his hip, urging him to re-position and try again.

He does, and it's the same result.

"I think we need to ditch the condom," I say, sighing. "I know it's not the most responsible move, but the condom, the feel of the latex, the way it smells, it…it…reminds me of *him*."

Flynn peers down at me, uncertainty in his eyes. "We'll be taking a big risk, Jaynie. What if you get pregnant?"

"You could always pull out," I suggest.

He buries his face in the crook of my neck. "We both know that shit is unreliable." His words are muffled. He's torn.

I want to try, though, without the condom, so I say, "The chances of me getting pregnant are slim. This shouldn't be a dangerous time."

I pause for a beat. The only sound in the room is our breathing while Flynn contemplates.

Softly, I say, "I still want this, Flynn. I want *you*."

I watch as he lifts his head, his resolve crumbling before my eyes. "Okay." He nods.

He removes the condom and tosses it to the wastepaper basket on the floor.

And then he's back between my legs, brushing me bare. Already it's better. "Yes," I whisper as he kisses me.

I begin to move with him, his bare length gliding along my folds. "Fuck, that feels great," he grinds out.

"God, it does," I agree.

Flynn bare against me is indescribably good.

With our shifting and rocking, the tip of him slips inside. "Oh," I gasp.

He stills. "Are you okay?"

I nod, and he gives me a little more.

Grasping the sheet with one hand, and digging into Flynn's

Tomorrow's Lies

shoulder with the other, I say, "More."

A shallow thrust this time, then a deeper one. Two more and I feel overwhelmed, panting out a desperate, "Wait, wait, Flynn."

He starts to pull out completely, but I shift to keep him in place.

"I don't want you to stop," I whisper against his neck. "Just give me a minute to catch up."

Lowering his mouth to mine, he kisses me.

And kisses me…

And kisses me…

And then he is moving, fast. And I am moving with him, faster, wanting the friction. Flynn completes me in a way I never knew possible. It humbles me that an act I associated with repulsion and disgust is rewritten by Flynn. With every stroke, and accompanying kiss, and declaration of love, the damage written on my soul is erased and scribed anew to something beautiful.

Everything bad is turned good, and I am awed by the power of love.

Chapter Twenty-Three

Flynn

I fall asleep with Jaynie in my arms. I am spent, but contented. I could sleep for hours, but I only get what feels like minutes.

"Five more minutes," I mumble when Jaynie shakes me for a second time.

"We've been sleeping for a while, Flynn," she says. "We need to get up and be dressed before Mandy comes back with the kids."

She's right, so, albeit reluctantly, I get out of bed. I throw on the same clothes I was wearing earlier. Jaynie dresses next to me, but forgoes the white dress for jean shorts and a beige T-shirt. I watch as she carefully hangs the dress in the closet. When she turns around, I ask her how she feels.

"I'm good," she says.

"You sure?"

She nods, and then sighs. "What about you, Flynn? Are you okay with what we did? I mean the not-using-protection part."

Blowing out a breath, I tell her the truth. "I was really careful, and I think we should be okay, but I don't know, Jaynie. What we did was crazy-risky. We're going to have to think of something different for next time."

She doesn't disagree. "Maybe I can pretend to be sick and Allison will have to take me to town to see a doctor. I could ask for birth control, maybe something I don't have to take every day." She gives me a meaningful look because we both know the pill would be discovered.

"That might work," I say.

Before we can discuss it further, there's a frantic knock on the door.

"It's me." *Mandy and she sounds panicked.* "Can I come in?"

I race over to the door, and Mandy flies in so quickly she almost falls. Once she's righted herself, she looks me over, then does the same with Jaynie. "Good, you're both dressed."

"What's going on?" I ask. "Where are Cody and Callie?"

"They're downstairs." With a sour expression, she adds, "With Allison."

"Shit."

"Yeah, of all the days for her to make a Sunday afternoon appearance," Mandy scoffs.

I shake my head. "Unbelievable."

Sighing, Mandy tells us how Allison arrived with pizza for everyone. "But, dude," Mandy adds, "she is *so* not in a good mood. She keeps asking where you two are. Especially you, Flynn."

"Great," I mutter, sarcasm dripping.

"Why is she back to being so interested in Flynn?" Jaynie chimes in.

"Uh…" Mandy appears less than happy to be the bearer of bad news. "…I think that guy she was dating finally dumped her."

Jaynie's eyes widen. "Crap. We are so dead."

"Not necessarily," I interject. "Let's go downstairs and act normal."

Turning to Mandy, I ask, "What did you say we were doing?"

Unable to resist a laugh, she says, "I told her you two were putting away laundry."

The three of us glance around the room, which is a mess. There are clothes everywhere, mainly from the twins, but still, it sure doesn't look like any laundry was put away today.

"Don't worry," I say, more confidently than I feel. "She rarely comes up here."

"It doesn't matter if she comes up here or not," Jaynie says. "We still look guilty. I just hope she doesn't figure out what was happening, or there's going to be hell to pay."

With that thought in mind, we head downstairs to face our keeper's wrath.

Chapter Twenty-Four

Jaynie

Allison knows. I see it in her disdainful expression when Flynn and I reach the base of the stairs. She's out in the hall, waiting for us, the twins beside her.

Callie knows not to say a word, but Cody has no idea there's a secret to be kept.

"Flynnie, Flynnie." He runs up to Flynn and wraps his arms around his legs. "Why you no come out and play with us today?"

Callie winces, and Allison's eyes narrow. "Go to your rooms," she barks to the kids.

The twins pale as they scurry past us. They know when shit's about to go down.

"Where is Mandy?" Allison asks me.

"She's still up in the bedroom."

"Good." She peers past me and yells up to where the twins are paused on the second-floor landing. "Tell Mandy no one is to come down till tomorrow morning."

Little voices gasp, and then little feet keep little legs moving.

"Where were you two?" Allison hisses when the twins are out of sight.

"Um…" I am at a loss, until I remember our cover. "We were putting away laundry."

Accusing, ice-blue eyes scan Flynn in a licentious manner, and then snap to me. "Sure you were. Funny, but you don't look as if you were putting away laundry." Focusing on me, she says, "Jaynie, your skin is flushed. Why is that?"

She then has the nerve to reach out and press a manicured fingertip to where my pink-tinged skin peeks out under the *v* of my tee. "Hmmm," she muses, "my chest gets that same appearance, usually after I engage in something that *really* excites me."

I wince, and she thankfully stops touching me. Her eyes meet mine. "You've certainly come a long way in the touching department, haven't you?"

I shrug, and she says, "Even Flynn can touch you now, can't he?"

"Um—"

"I know he can," she interrupts. "I've seen him sneaking kisses with you in the barn." *Shit.* "I sure hope it hasn't gone further, for both your sakes. You do realize if you were to have sex it would be a severe violation of house rules?"

"We were putting away laundry," Flynn maintains. "There's no need for this interrogation."

Allison's finger returns to my chest. She smirks and curls her index finger so her pointed nail digs deep in my skin. "He had better be telling the truth, little slut."

"That's enough," Flynn interjects. He smacks Allison's hand away from me, and she spins to him, eyes blazing.

"You fucked her, didn't you? Little, innocent Jaynie," she mocks. "Bet you couldn't wait to shove your cock in her. Talk about a challenge, sticking it in the fucked-up girl who can't stand to be touched."

Allison's jealousy is ugly, raw and rancid as it seeps from her pores. I'm ready to bolt, but Flynn remains steadfast. He shakes his head and chuckles as if Allison has lost her mind.

"What is wrong with you?" he says in a light manner, an effort to placate her. "You know Sundays are for chores. Jaynie and I were cleaning up the room, making sure all the laundry was put away. It's hot up on the third floor, and Jaynie's overheated. That's why her skin is flushed."

Allison grits her teeth as she lets Flynn's words sink in. Still, she is not buying his story one bit.

Almost to the point of shaking—she's that enraged—she grinds out, "I've let you two get away with too much for too long. I allowed myself to be distracted by a guy who I meant nothing to." *I wonder, does she mean her boyfriend…or Flynn.* "It's clear to me now that there needs to be changes from here on out."

Here it comes—our punishment.

Flynn brushes his hand past mine. I know he'd like to hold my hand, give me comfort, but that would be the worst thing to do in front of Allison.

"What kind of changes?" Flynn asks.

Allison gathers her blonde mane and flips it over one shoulder. "First, the cameras go back on, starting tonight. Number two, no more periodic checking on the feeds. My mom's been lax with those cameras for months. Well, that stops tonight. I'm taking over, and I plan to start by adjusting the camera that's out of whack." I can almost hear Flynn's inward groan. "I'll be putting to use an app I downloaded a while ago. From today onward I plan to watch every movement in the upstairs hallway on my tablet."

She smiles victoriously, and my heart sinks.

Flynn appears as disgusted as I feel. I'll miss him in my bed at night, true, but more concerning is what will happen with Cody.

His nightmares are sure to resume once he's back in a room away from his twin. How will Flynn ever get him past those cameras if they're all positioned correctly? And, worse yet, the cameras are to be monitored by Allison, who clearly has an axe to grind? We are all doomed.

"Fine, whatever," Flynn says. He nudges my arm. "Come on, Jaynie."

"Where do you think you're going?" Allison steps into our path.

Flynn says, "We're going to go eat now. Mandy said you brought pizza home for everyone."

"Not for you two," Allison snaps.

We stare at her, incredulous. And still, she goes on. "Another change I'm making is there's no longer a free-for-all on the eats. Don't think I haven't noticed the amount of food you've been going through. I didn't care, not before, but now"—she stares directly at me—"everything has changed."

It obviously has, and not for the better.

"What about the twins?" Flynn and I ask simultaneously.

And then just Flynn addresses Allison. "Can we still give Cody and Callie extra food?"

"I'll think about it," Allison replies.

Flynn and I are then turned away and sent upstairs with no dinner. Flynn has no choice but to go to his own room, but he does give me a hug outside his door.

"I really want to kiss you right now," he whispers. "But anything more than this and God knows what the bitch will do next."

"You're right," I reply sadly. And then, clinging to him tightly, I say, "I want so badly for you to sleep with me tonight, especially after this afternoon."

If there was ever a night I needed to be held in Flynn's arms, it's tonight.

"What can we do?" he says, pained, his face buried in my hair.

"Nothing. We're trapped. Allison's on the war path now."

We part because we must, but it still hurts like hell. I head straight to my bed once I'm in my room. Mandy is busy tucking Callie in, and I ignore them. Not to be a bitch. I just can't talk to anyone right now.

Curling up on my mattress, I wrap sheets that smell like Flynn and me around my body. This afternoon feels like forever ago, even though only a couple of hours have passed.

"How could everything go from beautiful to ugly so quickly?" I mumble, bereft.

Mandy comes over and sits on the edge of my bed. "What happened downstairs?" she asks softly.

I turn to her, crying, and for the first time in ages, I allow someone other than Flynn to comfort me. Mandy lies down next to me and wraps her arms around me. I tell her everything—how I felt this afternoon with Flynn, how happy and optimistic life seemed, and then how Allison somehow *knew*…and promptly retaliated.

"She knew right away," I say to Mandy when I pull back. "She wasn't buying the laundry story for a second."

Mandy brushes hair away from my face, like I often see her doing with Cody and Callie. "She was bound to figure it out. It's so obvious Flynn loves you, Jaynie. She's just mad she can't have him, or at least have what you have with him."

"Yeah, but she has enough. She holds our lives in her hands. We're at her mercy."

"Maybe she'll lighten up in a few days." Mandy is trying to be optimistic. "If she gets back with her boyfriend, I bet she forgets all about today."

"I hope that happens," I reply. My instincts, though, tell me otherwise. This is not about to blow over in a day or two.

Suddenly, a little voice from across the room rings out. "Is Jaynie sad, Mandy?"

Mandy looks at me, and I nod. She lifts her head and says to

Callie, "Yeah, Jaynie is a little sad tonight, honey."

"Can I come over and sleep with her, too? Maybe she'll feel better with hugs from both of us."

I roll over and gesture for Callie to join us. We could move to Mandy's bigger bed, but this closeness feels right, like we're more united than ever.

Callie snuggles in between me and Mandy. It's a tight squeeze, but no one wants to move apart.

After a minute, Callie whispers, "Can I tell you a secret?"

"Sure," I reply. Just as Mandy says, "Yes, of course."

We smile at each other, but our smiles falter when Callie says, "I'm sad, too, guys."

"Why are you sad, sweetie?" Mandy asks.

"'Cause I miss Cody," Callie says.

We assure her he'll be okay and that Flynn will keep him safe.

"Yeah, but Flynn can't keep the nightmares away."

"He'll do his best, sweetheart," Mandy says.

"If you say so," Callie mutters, unconvinced.

Hours later I am awoken by blood-curdling screams from down the hall. Cody's nightmares have returned with a vengeance. Mandy is awake, as well. Her hand is on Callie's arm. Callie is staring up at the ceiling, crying and muttering her brother's name over and over again.

"That's it," I say. I sit up and toss the blanket aside.

"What are you doing?" Mandy asks as I climb over her and Callie.

"Going down the hall to get Cody."

When I start for the door, Mandy jumps up and catches me by the arm. "You can't do that," she says sternly. "If Allison is watching, or even if she's taping and looks at the footage later, things will get worse."

I look back at Callie, still on the bed, crying and shaking. Mandy is staring at her, too. And all the while, Cody's screams continue.

Tomorrow's Lies

"Fuck it," Mandy says, at last. "Let's go get Cody."

But when we open the door, Allison is there, standing in the hallway, arms crossed, blocking our way. "Going somewhere?" she says, her tone mocking.

I peer down the hall and notice the door to Flynn and Cody's room has a bar jammed across it, effectively locking them in. "You can't lock them in like that," I say, incredulous.

"I can do whatever I want," Allison snipes back.

Mandy tries to appeal to her. "This is insane, Allison. What if there's a fire? Or what about when they need to go to the bathroom?"

"It's only for tonight," Allison says, like that makes it okay. "You all need to be taught a lesson. I will *not* be disobeyed."

"Fuck you!" Mandy roars. She gets up in Allison's face, and I'm pretty sure she's about to lay her out.

I stop her, remembering all the times she talked sense into me. "Mandy, no, no, no." I pull at her arm, trying to get her to back off from the psycho bitch.

She drops back a step, averting her fiery eyes from a frightened Allison. But the damage is already done.

Once she's regained her paper-tiger courage, Allison jams a finger in Mandy's face. "I want you out of here now."

"What, tonight?" Mandy appears stunned.

"Yes, tonight. What do you think *now* means?" Allison points to our room and demands Mandy go pack up.

"She still has a few more days, Allison," I interject.

I am promptly told to shut up by Allison.

Mandy gives me a hug. "It's okay," she whispers.

"But it's dark outside, Mandy. And wasn't your social worker supposed to pick you up?"

Mandy whispers, "She probably wouldn't have shown anyway. I told you a long time ago that Mrs. Lowry pays our social workers to look the other way."

I know it's true. I haven't seen Saundra since April.

Mandy lets me go, but not before placing a hand on my cheek and saying, "Remember everything we talked about." Her eyes sear in to mine.

She means the escape plan, which has always been a last resort in case of complete collapse.

Well today, things began to crumble.

*B*ack in the room, all hell breaks loose. Callie screams and holds onto Mandy's leg as she readies to leave. "Don't go, don't go. I love you, Mandy. Take me with you."

"Hey." Mandy kneels down and wraps her arms around Callie. "You knew I was leaving. It's just a few days earlier than we thought."

"You can't go yet," Callie whimpers. "Cody and I were going to surprise you with a good-bye card we made. It's out in the barn."

"You can give it to me when we see each other again, okay?"

Mandy is trying so hard to be strong in order not to upset Callie any further, but she can't stop her own tears from falling.

"Don't go." Callie holds onto her more tightly.

Mandy gently pries Callie's arms away so she can stand. "I have to, baby. But I'll see you again soon. You remember that."

"I love you, Mandy," Callie cries out desperately.

Mandy drops to her knees again, gathering Callie to her once more. "I love you, honey." She kisses Callie, stands again to go. "Tell Cody I love him, too."

"I will."

Mandy gives me a hug, whispering, "Take care of my babies for me."

And then I am left crying, holding onto Callie, who keeps whispering over and over, "Mommy, please don't go."

Chapter Twenty-Five

Flynn

With Mandy gone life at the house becomes unbearable. It's like Allison pushed Mandy out so she could really bring down the hammer. Dinner is cut out completely, and the small lunches are resumed, at first, but then promptly halved.

Stealing additional nutrition bars at breakfast becomes imperative. I give most of mine to the twins, but spare a few for me and Jaynie.

I keep expecting Mrs. Lowry to come back and save the day. *Who would've ever imagined that, right?* But our foster "mother" spends more time away than ever. It's like she's found her own escape from Forsaken by taking business trip after business trip.

Conversely, Allison seeks no escape from anything. Not anymore. She gives up on trying to win back whoever she was dating in town. She even refrains from flirting with me. It's with hatred that she peers my way with her cold, dead eyes. She even lets her appearance go. Allison's once shiny, platinum hair becomes greasy and unkempt, her dark roots showing. She loses weight along with the rest of us, though her loss is a choice. And her new favorite clothes, worn daily, are jeans cut off at the knees and an old baggy tee which was once white, but is now gray. Most days she smells rank, but it's her attitude and actions that are beyond disgusting.

Allison doubles our quotas, and with one less person, we rarely meet the numbers. That becomes her justification to cut out dinner.

When Cody and Callie cry and wail that they're hungry, Allison pats them on their heads patronizingly and tells them with no emotion in her tone, "Work harder, then."

She then walks away.

The kids look to me and Jaynie with hope in their eyes. "We make numbers tomorrow, Flynnie?" Cody asks, desperate, starving.

"We'll try, little man." I ruffle his now-dull hair.

"I'm hungry," Callie whispers, leaning into Jaynie.

"I know, baby. Me, too."

And so it goes…

Times are desperate and our actions become desperate, as well. The lack of food, worse than ever before, leads to not thinking clearly, for me, and for Jaynie, too.

We take chances. We throw caution to the wind.

One night we run into each other outside the bathroom on the third floor. Jaynie is coming out and I am going in. I stop when I see her.

Wrapping my arms around her, I breathe her in. "God, I miss holding you at night."

"I miss you, too," she replies. "But, Flynn"—she glances up—"the cameras."

"Fuck the cameras," I say, and we hold each other for a good, long while.

There are no repercussions the next day, at least not beyond the ordinary food deprivations, so the next night I sneak down to the kitchen to see if I can raid the cabinets. Unfortunately, the door is padlocked.

"Fucking whore," I spit out, my stomach so empty it physically hurts.

"Who are you calling a whore?" a voice rings out.

I spin around to find Allison standing in the hall. "Jesus."

She leans back against the wall and propositions me. Not in a sexy way, just in a dull, why-the-hell-not manner.

"If you fuck me, Flynn," she says. "I'll give you some food." She's wearing a short robe. She unties the ribbon holding it shut and pink silk falls to the floor. "Just do me here. I don't care. You can do anything you want to me."

Her tone is flat, as are her eyes. I know she doesn't really want me. She's still playing her game. She'd love for me to be physical with her to stick it to Jaynie. Nice try, but that will never happen.

I step up to her, our bodies almost touching. There's a slight glimmer of life in her eyes when she thinks she might be getting some.

I extinguish that shit as soon as I lean forward and say, "I wouldn't fuck you even if it meant never eating again." She gasps, and I add, "That's right. I'd rather *die* than stick my cock in you."

She tries to smack me, but I catch her hand. "Fuck you," she hisses.

As I walk away, I hear her say, "You'll fucking pay for this, O'Neill."

Without turning around, I raise my middle finger and shove it high in the air. "That's the only fuck you'll ever get from me, so savor it."

This bitch will never beat me.

Chapter Twenty-Six

Jaynie

This level of hunger is like none I've ever experienced. Springtime, when we thought food was low, was a walk in the park. This is true starvation.

Hunger like this leaves you dizzy, in the early days. Then, the headaches arrive, a pounding, relentless variety of pain. Finally, you reach a point of no return. You feel empty in a way you've never known possible. A new breed of hunger gnaws at your gut, leading you to search for other ways to feel full.

For me, I look to Flynn.

One unusually balmy evening, the first day of September, Allison actually leaves the house. Before she goes, Flynn overhears her talking on her cell, telling someone she can stay wherever she's heading till midnight.

We are free of her, even if only for a few hours.

Flynn and I ask the twins if they want to go outside and play, like old times, but they tell us they're too tired and hungry.

"Can we just sleep?" Callie asks, crawling into bed.

Flynn and I watch as Cody joins her. "I'm hungry," he mutters as he closes his eyes, the dark circles under them almost black.

Flynn looks over at me. "You have anything stashed?"

We hide food where we can, especially for when the twins can't take it anymore. Unfortunately, I'm tapped out.

"No." I shake my head. "I had half a nutrition bar in a drawer, but I gave it to Callie this morning."

"Don't worry about it. I'll steal as many as I can next chance I get."

We both know that might not be for a while.

I look over at the twins, sleeping already. It's only six in the evening, not even dark, and these kids are dead to the world. I could kill Allison for what she's doing to them. Take it out on me and Flynn, I can live with that, but hurting Callie and Cody is beyond reprehensible.

On the nightstand, near my bed, lie the sharp metal scissors, the ones Flynn stole from the craft barn weeks ago. I entertain a hunger-induced fantasy of using them on Allison. I may do it, too, if pushed far enough, even if it's only to threaten her with bodily harm to give the twins some goddamn food.

The twins roll toward each other, their now-frail arms interlocking. Flynn and I share a sad smile.

"We'll have to separate them later," he says, sighing. "Get them into their own beds before Allison returns."

"I know. But even this little bit of time spent together is good for them."

"Yeah, guess so." Flynn sounds distracted and tired, and he leans on the wall closest to him for support.

I can't help but notice his high cheekbones have never been more pronounced. This weight loss is like nothing we've ever experienced. I'm wearing a short dress Mandy left behind. It's supposed to be form-fitting, but the floral fabric hangs on me. My ribs jut out sharply these days, and Flynn's body is nothing but tight muscle stretched over bone.

To me, he is still a god.

"Let's go up to our spot in the woods while the kids are sleeping," I say.

Flynn smiles thinly. "Okay, Jaynie."

I reach out to touch the little crescent-shaped scar on his cheek. "I don't want to go up there to talk, Flynn."

"Me neither."

Flynn knows this is what we need—a salve to lessen the pain. Nourishment, not for our empty stomachs, but for our souls.

When we reach the cliff's edge, we duck under the pines. The sun is setting, and it's already dark in the circle. We come together, urgent kisses, and hands roaming everywhere.

When we break apart, I stumble back. And then I unzip my dress.

Flynn breathes heavily, exertion taking its toll on his starved body. But neither of us can stop. This need transcends all others. Giving in to our urges promises to blunt our pain, and that is motivation enough to keep going.

Flynn lifts his shirt over his head, kicks off his jeans, and then his boxers. He's as ready for this as I am.

With a smile, I shimmy my dress up over my hips and peel my panties down my legs.

"Kick those damn things off and c'mere," Flynn says huskily.

I do as he asks, and when I step toward him, he wraps his arms around me and hoists me up. I tighten my legs around him as we become one. "Flynn," I sigh.

It's the first time we've had sex since the day our lives fell apart, and this experience is far different. This act of love is tinged with desperation, the sex quickly turning raw and rough.

We tumble to the ground, somehow never breaking apart. "Don't leave me," I cry out, meaning so much more than our bodies joined as one.

"Never," he rasps as he rolls on top of me.

The grass is soft, but pine needles stick to my sweaty back as Flynn drives into me, again and again. Peeling down the front of my unzipped dress, he rips open my bra. His mouth descends to a breast, and I reach down and grab his ass.

His muscles flex beneath my hand, and I urge, "Go faster."

He does. Flynn fucks me—and that's what this has become—into blissful oblivion. I know he feels it, too, our escape from hell.

When he comes, he's inside me. Neither of us cares. We remain connected, needing to experience each other's bliss in our now-barren world. Our love is the only good thing left to cherish.

"I love you, I love you," he says to me over and over again.

And me, I can do nothing but cry.

Flynn never leaves me, remaining inside me as he kisses away my tears. And when he's hard again and starts to move, I beg him, "Fill me again. Come inside me, and make me forget the hunger."

He does, and for the first time in weeks, I feel full.

Chapter Twenty-Seven

Flynn

As we approach the house at an almost run, I know it's late. The moon is high in the sky.

"It has to be after midnight," I say.

"I never meant to fall asleep," Jaynie replies, out of breath.

"Me neither."

We slow up and breathe a collective sigh of relief when we see Allison's car is not in the driveway.

"Thank God for small favors." Jaynie bends at her waist and places her hands on her knees.

There's no time for a break. I have to keep her going.

"Hurry," I urge, hand on her elbow. "We still need to get Cody back in my room."

"Damn, I forgot."

The next ten minutes are a blur—Jaynie and I racing into the house, running up the stairs, easing Cody out of the bed so as not to wake Callie, and then cradling him in my arms.

Tomorrow's Lies

"He's gotten so light," I lament.

Jaynie, by my side, whispers, "Just go, Flynn. Go."

When I turn around, something seems off. "We left the door open, right?"

Jaynie turns to the now half-closed door. "Shit, Allison is home."

"That's right," Allison's voice rings out. The door flies open and Allison is standing in the shadows, arms crossed.

Suddenly, all the night's exertion and underlying exhaustion catch up to me. I crumple to the floor with Cody in my arms. The kid's so out of it, he just mumbles something and falls back asleep.

"Flynn!" I hear Jaynie cry out.

I can barely keep my eyes open, but Allison's pink heels come into focus as she steps next to me. "What's going on in here?" she asks.

"It's my fault, Allison." Jaynie slumps down next to me. "I asked Flynn to bring Cody to the room for a little while."

I gaze up at an angry Allison. She's cleaned up for her night out. Even has on a matching shorts and tank outfit. Guess she was looking to reel in a new guy, or she's trying to lure back the old one. In any case, it's clear she was out fishing. Though from her miserable demeanor, I assume no one was biting.

I chuckle at my food analogy. Fuck, the hunger is screaming, ripping my stomach open from the inside out, like I swallowed razor blades.

"What are you laughing about?" Allison asks, her pointy pink shoe nudging me.

I can't shake the whole fishing imagery, and in a hunger-induced delirium, I look up and say to the bitch, "You are one rank piece of bait. Do you want to know why the fish weren't biting?"

Allison gapes at me, clearly confused by my outburst. Jaynie, meanwhile, shakes my shoulder. She's trying to rouse me back to some semblance of sanity. "Flynn," she hisses under her breath. "Stop it."

But I can't.

And suddenly, Allison gets it. "Do tell me, Flynn," she grinds out between clenched teeth. "Why, as you put it, were the fish not biting?"

I sit up, chuckling. Cody is still sleeping in my arms.

"It's simple, really," I say. "Despite your okay outer appearance, you are rotten to the core inside. Those *fish* smell you a mile away"—I scrunch up my nose in disgust—"and they know you're no good. They'd rather starve than take a bite of your rancid flesh."

"That's enough!"

I can't tell whether it's Allison speaking, or Jaynie. I've got nothing left in the tank and my body shuts down, leaving me no choice but to succumb to sleep.

As I fall to my side, Cody is wrenched from my arms.

And the last thing I hear is Jaynie and Callie screaming out, "No, no, no-o-o."

Chapter Twenty-Eight

Jaynie

After the heart-wrenching scene of Allison dragging Cody back to his own room, and then Flynn being made to wake up and follow, Callie begs me to sleep with her.

"I can't stand to be alone, Jaynie," Callie says, her tone and inflection far beyond her years. "That was too much."

"I know, honey," I tell her as we crawl into the same bed.

We're too restless to sleep, so we end up talking for a while.

"Where do you think Mandy is right now?" Callie asks.

Leaning my head against hers, I say, "Probably in Morgantown."

"With Josh, you think?"

"I hope so, sweetie."

Callie sighs contemplatively, reminding me of how far advanced she is. "I hope so, too," she says. "Mandy deserves to be happy."

"She does," I agree. "And so do you, sweetheart."

"I will be happy, Jaynie. When Cody and I get to go to live with Mandy and Josh, I'll be happy."

Drowsiness suddenly hits me like a hammer, and I murmur, "You'll all be a family soon enough."

"I can't wait." Callie yawns and snuggles in close to me. "I'm so tired, Jaynie," she whispers.

"Then go to sleep, baby girl. Tomorrow will be better."

My sleep is fitful, dreams morphing to nightmares. When I wake in the morning, I immediately sense something is wrong.

My bed feels too empty.

Jumping up, feet tangling in the covers, I stumble to the floor. "Callie? Callie?" I call out. "Where are you?"

As I untangle myself, I scan the room for Callie. She's not in our small bedroom, that's for sure.

"Oh, God, please, no. No, no, no." Callie is gone, and this is Allison's doing, I know it.

As I race to the door, Flynn swings it open from the other side. "Is Cody in here?" he asks. He sounds as frantic as I feel.

"No, Flynn. And Callie's gone, too."

"Fuck."

"This is not good."

Downstairs, we find Allison in the kitchen, guarding the nutrition bar box like her life depends on it.

When she hands one bar to Flynn, her sugary-sweet grin hiding the acid in her soul, he smacks it out of her hand.

"Ooh, testy today, aren't we?" she says.

"Knock off the shit," Flynn replies. "Where are the twins?"

Allison's expression turns cold, her true nature revealed. Fine, I'd rather see the real side of her than all her phony masks.

Slowly, enunciating each word for effect, she says, "The twins… Are…Gone."

"What?" I rasp.

"You heard me. They're gone, for good. I drove them to the group home in Clarksburg late last night. In fact, I just got back."

"What have you done?" Flynn's voice cracks.

Allison jumps up on the counter, swinging her sweat pant-covered legs, carefree as ever. "It was just too much," she says breezily. "Small children like that in my care. Without Mandy around, I wasn't even sure how to start their home-schooling."

"We could've done it," I say.

"You can barely stand," Allison snorts.

"Because you're starving us," I yell.

Allison ignores me. "Doesn't matter. It's too late now. I called my mom and told her she had a choice to make. Either the twins had to go…or I was going." Her hateful eyes move from me, to Flynn. "I'm sure you can guess her answer. Mom needs someone to run this freak show, now doesn't she?"

"You fucking cunt," Flynn snarls, shaking with rage.

He knows as well as I do that this is *our* punishment. Allison has taken away food, she's increased work quotas to unattainable goals, but none of those things diminish our love, or the bonds we've forged with each other. Her last weapon is to separate us, and then watch us break, one by one.

I place my hand on Flynn's forearm to keep him calm. "Flynn," I whisper. "Don't let her get to you. That's what she wants."

Essentially the same wisdom Mandy was always imparting. And I need for Flynn to listen and back down. Allison wants him to flip so she can revel in his pain, or send him away, too.

I watch as he slowly pulls himself together. I breathe a sigh of relief. I can't take losing him on top of the twins. I already feel numb and dead inside.

"Good," Flynn snaps. "Cody and Callie deserve a better home. Maybe now they can get some proper nutrition."

"I fed them," Allison whines, defensive.

"Barely," I interject.

"Go to the barn and get to work," she snaps. "I don't want to see either of you for the rest of the day."

And with that she shoves the box of nutrition bars at us—the whole box—and stomps away.

Flynn and I eat a bunch, famished as we are. But then we decide it'd be wise to squirrel some away. "Who knows when that bitch will feed us again," Flynn says.

"True."

We find hidey-holes in each of our rooms, and also out in the craft barn. While there, we stumble across the going-away card the twins made for Mandy, the one they never had a chance to give her.

"Look at this." Flynn says as he hands me an ivory sheet of folded cardstock.

With a heavy heart, I read the crooked messages scribed in pastel markers: *We love you. See you soon. We promise to be on our best behavior so we can come live with you. Don't forget us, Mandy. You're our mommy now.*

I start to fold the card so I can hide it in the pocket of my jeans. "What are you doing?" Flynn asks.

"Saving the card for when we see Mandy and the twins again." I stop what I'm doing when he turns away. "Flynn, look at me." He does. "We have to believe. It's all we have left. To make sense of these horrors, we have to trust Mandy will end up with the twins. And we have to believe we'll get out of here and our lives will go on, better than ever."

He looks unconvinced. "Okay, Jaynie, whatever you say."

"Flynn, you can't lose hope."

"Let's just start on today's projects, all right?"

I give up. There's no convincing him of anything right now.

Materials for the day's crafts are spread out on four work stations, saddening us further.

"She wasn't planning on sending the twins away," I say. "It was our punishment for sneaking out last night."

"No, Jaynie," Flynn corrects. "It was our punishment for falling in love."

Chapter Twenty-Nine

Flynn

With the twins gone and Mrs. Lowry still constantly away, Jaynie and I become Allison's prisoners completely. She watches us like a hawk, monitoring our work in the craft barn like never before.

Quotas remain high. The numbers are set for the work of three adults and two kids, but there are only two of us. Believe it or not, there are days we still meet the numbers.

"Fine," Allison says on those days. "I'll give you dinner."

Dinner, when doled out, consists of a single microwave meal each, the very small diet ones. Doesn't matter. Jaynie and I devour those things like they are gourmet feasts.

Our lives continue, and on the rare evening Allison leaves the house, Jaynie and I head up to our secret place by the cliff's edge, our only respite from hunger, sadness, and a gnawing sense of hopelessness.

The days grow shorter and cooler, but we welcome the night and the crispness in the air. Summer reminds us too much of the good times. Under the pines, we hold onto each other, our bodies pressed together, desperate in the darkness. When the losses we've endured get to be too much, we strip off our clothes, and all is forgotten. Losing ourselves with each other is all we have left. But our joining as one is not about sex. It's about love, a love that keeps us warm on cool fall nights.

One of those chilly nights, after sex that turned from hurried to sweet, Jaynie falls back on pine needles that have dried up and grass that has turned brown. I curl up next to her, the only good thing left in my life.

"Do you still want us to be together, Flynn?" Jaynie asks, her face buried in my chest. "Like, for sure, forever?"

I lean back so I can see her more clearly. She looks up, her face illuminated by the full moon in the sky.

"For sure, forever," I say, echoing her words back to her and smiling. When Jaynie still seems troubled, I add, "I love you, Jaynie. You believe me, right?"

"I do," she says. "And I love you, too. But things change. What if you get out in the world and meet other people—"

"Hey, stop right there. There's only you, Jaynie. *You* are who I want."

She bites her lower lip. "Okay, Flynn."

"That doesn't sound convincing," I say lightly. And then, more seriously, "What's bringing all this on, anyway?"

"I was just thinking." She sighs. "You turn eighteen next month. You can go if you want, be free of this place."

I'm aghast. "Are you serious? Even if Allison lets me go, which I kind of doubt at this point, I'd never leave you alone with her."

"I turn eighteen in November. I'd only be a month behind you."

"I'd never take a chance like that, Jaynie. Not with the way things have been lately."

Breathing what sounds like a sigh of relief, she says, "Good. I don't think I could stand it here without you, especially…well, now."

Something is up.

Placing my hands on either side of Jaynie's face, I ask, "What's really going on here, babe?"

Swallowing hard, she tells me, "I'm late, Flynn."

The earth stops spinning. Or maybe I *start* spinning. In any case, it sure feels like the world has tilted sideways. "Shit," I mutter.

Jaynie immediately begins to apologize, but I put a stop to that nonsense. "Hey, hey, don't say you're sorry. This is more my fault than yours. I haven't been pulling out—"

"I haven't wanted you to, Flynn."

There's a long pause. This is both our doing.

I flop down on my back, scrub my hand over my face. "Jesus, Jaynie, what are we going to do with a baby?"

She wraps her arms around me. "We'll figure it out. If Allison tries to keep us here, even after we turn eighteen"—she glances over at the cliff's edge, the sound of the water racing below us like a foreboding soundtrack in some movie—"we can always jump."

"Yeah, there is that."

Our long-ago devised plan is still an option, but then again, maybe not. Everything has changed. A dozen things could go wrong. Starting with Jaynie shouldn't make a jump like that in her condition. Though it will only become more dangerous if we wait. Would it be better to leave now? Having a baby wasn't part of the original plan, and I don't know what to do anymore.

Shit. Maybe we should wait till we're both eighteen. Two more months till November, I don't know if that's too far away. I do know Jaynie needs better nutrition. She's eating for two now. Unfortunately, she barely gets enough food for one in this hell hole.

Damn, I feel lost and uncertain, my thinking clouded by hunger. But in my foggy thoughts I know there is one thing I need to ensure—I want Jaynie to promise me just one thing.

Tomorrow's Lies

"If it comes down to a choice, Jaynie," I say, rousing her from the sleep she was falling into. "If it comes down to choosing between me and you, I want *you* to be the one to get away from this place."

"Okay," she mumbles, eyes barely opening.

"Promise," I press.

"I promise," she whispers. And then she is out.

God, please don't let her promise end up becoming another one of tomorrow's lies.

Chapter Thirty

Jaynie

October arrives, and still no period. I don't need a pregnancy test to confirm what Flynn and I both know. I am definitely with child.

There are days it seems surreal, actually *feeling* pregnant. Knowing there's a life growing inside of me fills me with renewed hope. My pregnancy wasn't planned, but it feels right. Maybe this is how all this was meant to play out. I think Flynn feels the same way. One indication is how he becomes fiercely protective of me. We have something to protect other than ourselves now, and we don't plan on failing like we did with the twins.

A couple of weeks into October, the most awful morning sickness kicks in. Most days, though, I have nothing to throw up. Allison begins to eye me suspiciously, especially when I continue to drop things I'm working on to race to the outhouse in the back of the barn.

And with increasing suspicion comes more contempt. I am berated again and again over the state of my crafts, all of which are constructed to specifications.

"No, not like that, you dumb bumpkin," Allison snaps one afternoon. "That branch is crooked."

It's a gorgeous October day, the antithesis of Allison's rotten mood. It also happens to be Flynn's eighteenth birthday. Allison hasn't mentioned it, so I don't think she knows. Just as well. Flynn and I are hoping to sneak off sometime this evening, even if it's just to one of our rooms. I have a nutrition bar I saved that I plan to share with him. It isn't cake and ice cream, but it will have to do.

"Are you listening to me?" Allison snaps, rousing me back to the here and now.

"Uh-huh." *Please, just go away.*

She twists a limb from the glittery black Halloween tree I'm working on, essentially ruining it. "See, this is no good," she says.

When I start to protest, she throws the curled twig in my face.

I look around for Flynn, but he's on the other side of the barn, preoccupied with cutting up wood for the next craft project.

"Maybe the tree wasn't *really* broken before," Allison sneers. "But it sure is ruined now."

"Because you ruined it," I retort.

I am too tired and hungry to put up with her shit. Besides, how much more can she do to us?

Flynn stops what he's doing and looks over. When he sees Allison hassling me, he rushes to my aid.

"What's going on here?" he says, placing a protective hand on my back when he arrives.

"Nothing that concerns you," Allison says.

"*Anything* concerning Jaynie concerns me," Flynn shoots back.

The look in his eyes dares her to defy him, and Allison is cowed… for now.

Before she turns to leave, she says to me, and only me, "We'll discuss this more later."

Later turns out to be that night.

Passing the kitchen on my way upstairs, I throw a longing glance at the padlocked door. There is no dinner tonight. Allison claimed we didn't make quota, even though Flynn and I counted and re-counted and were sure we had it.

But no, we were told we misunderstood the numbers. *Bullshit*. To make matters worse, Allison made Flynn stay in the barn to clean up.

Just for the hell of it, I step over to the kitchen door and try the padlock. Just a quick yank, but damn if that's not enough. The lock falls open.

"No way," I whisper. "The psycho bitch must not have checked to make sure it was fully clasped."

Her oversight is about to become my and Flynn's jackpot. I plan to grab bunches of nutrition bars—and whatever else is available—and sneak that shit upstairs before Allison shows up. Flynn can have a *real* birthday feast, instead of half a nutrition bar. But when I push open the kitchen door, I realize the unlocked door was nothing more than a trap. I groan, realizing I've been had.

Allison is waiting for me, perched up on the counter, expression smug.

"I knew you couldn't resist an opportunity to steal from me and my mom," she spits out, feigning outrage.

My mood from earlier persists. I can't take her shit, not today.

"If you didn't starve us, we wouldn't have to steal food."

She hops off the counter and takes a menacing step toward me. I stumble back, afraid not for myself, but for the baby.

"You little twat," she hisses. "You think I don't see what's going on? If you didn't get yourself knocked-up, you wouldn't be so goddamn hungry all the time."

I gasp. Though I suspected she knew, hearing her speak the words makes my pregnancy feel more real than ever. And in that moment I know I really, really want this baby. *Damn the circumstances.*

Placing a protective hand over my stomach, I rub the slight swell of flesh pushing out from between my jutting hips. Even starving, baby grows.

Allison's eyes widen. "Holy shit, you really are pregnant, aren't you? I took a guess, but wow, I never really thought…"

I am not discussing this with my worst enemy, so I spin around to leave. But before I am able to reach the doorway, the snarling bitch is on my ass.

Swinging me back around, roughly by the arm, Allison yells in my face, "Don't you ever turn your back on me!"

She then spits in my face.

With her saliva dripping down my cheek, I wrench my arm from her grasp. "Fuck you, Allison," I say.

She shoves me hard, and I am sent flying across the room, heading straight toward one of the granite countertops. I throw my hands up just in time to prevent the sharp edge from jamming into my belly.

Allison shoves me again, this time twice as hard. Jesus, she *wants* to ram me into the countertop. I twist my torso at the last second, and only my hipbone makes contact with the edge.

The impact still sends a sharp pain up my side, and I crumple to the floor. When I look up, Allison is staring down at me. She looks feral, eyes wide, hair a scraggly mess. Her hatred for me has never been more apparent as something akin to murder blooms in her eyes.

"Shit." I scramble to get out of her way.

Rising to my knees, slower than I intend—I am dizzy from the fall, or from lack of food, I'm not sure which—I catch a fleeting glimpse of a booted toe heading toward the one part of my body I have protected so well up until this point.

The kick lands hard, hard enough that I see stars. It's a direct hit to my abdomen.

I cry out and Allison's leg becomes a piston. She kicks me over and over again. All the while, I am trying to roll out of her line of fire.

"Stop it! Stop it!" I try to scream, but all that comes out is a raspy whisper.

Some of her kicks land and some are complete misses. She's in a rage, and I can't get around her. All I can do is curl up in a ball and pray for her to stop.

When she finally does quit kicking, she steps back, panting and sweaty. I glance up, blinking slowly. A blurry image of her face, hair stuck to her cheeks, burns in my retinas.

I close my eyes, unable to look at my tormentor, and she says. "Go away, Jaynie."

When I try to sit up, I know the damage she intended to inflict has been done. Behind the pain from the bruising on my abdomen, there is an all-too-familiar deep cramping.

When I choke back a sob, I'm told, "I said, get up and get the hell out of my face, you worthless slut."

Holding my middle like everything inside might fall out if I were to let go, I scramble to my feet and take off.

I am doubled over with pain by the time I reach the third floor, and I promptly stumble to the bathroom.

Blood, no. Bright red spots stain my panties, not unlike teardrops. There's no pouring gush, though, not like you see in the movies. This is more like spotting. I guess since it was so early on. "It was barely there," I whisper.

So, why does the loss feel so bottomless?

I lie to myself, for now. The truth is too painful to deal with. "It's my period starting. It was just late. It was probably going to start today, anyway. Getting kicked in the gut just hastened things along."

All my rationalizations and lies to myself don't change the truth—Allison has made me miscarry.

From that point on, everything I do is done in a daze. My actions are like snapshots blowing in the wind, images flittering away in the aftermath of a loss.

I wash up.

Tomorrow's Lies

I insert a tampon.
I walk down the hall to the bedroom.
I kick off my worn sneakers and watch them as they soar across the room, seemingly in slow motion.

That last one makes me laugh. And then it makes me cry.

No, no, no. I will not allow these emotions to cripple me. I've been there before—though for a different reason—and I refuse to go back. No more victim-Jaynie.

I take off my clothes, ignoring the purple and blue bruises blossoming on my belly like the world's ugliest flowers. Calmly, I swap out baggy jeans and a dingy tee for the white cotton dress that once belonged to Mandy. It's Flynn's favorite, and the best thing I own. The dress reminds me of happier times. And wasn't I planning on wearing it for Flynn's birthday anyway? Sure was.

See how well I'm doing?

When I tug my panties down my legs, so I can change into a fresh pair, my strong façade crumbles.

I unravel…

Clutching blood-tinged cotton in my hand, I throw back my head and scream as loud as I can. I go from zero to sixty, from no emotion to nothing but emotion. I embrace all I feel—denial, heartache, disbelief, anger. I put the first three on the backburner. The anger, I hold onto.

And, guess what? Anger ramps up to rage when you embrace it. A violence builds in me like nothing I've ever known, and soon I am vowing, "You are going to die for what you've done, Allison Lowry."

On the nightstand lie the scissors, the ones Mandy never returned to the craft barn. I snatch them up.

But then I freeze. There's a strand of black hair stuck in the blades. "Cody," I choke out.

Cody—sent away for no reason, another victim of Allison's rage, along with his sister.

I want to punch something. *Save it for Allison.*

Down the stairs, I flee, like I'm flying.

And then I'm standing at the kitchen door. Still unlocked. Good.

Allison's eyes bug out of her head when she sees me coming in. Crazy girl in white, dressed to kill.

She stares at the scissors clenched in my hand. I let her take it in, the scene before her, what it might mean. It's her turn to feel fear.

"Jaynie, what's with the scissors?" she asks, voice shaky. "You need to put them down before someone gets hurt."

"That would sort of defeat the purpose," I calmly reply.

"Jaynie, really. Think about this."

Allison steps back, but there's nowhere to go. She's trapped, just as I was.

"How does it feel?" I say.

"Don't be stupid. Let's be reasonable here."

"The time for reason has passed."

I think of a dozen other things to say to her: *You killed my baby. You murdered a part of Flynn, too. This is justice. You've had it coming for a long time. I will not be a victim again. I will go down fighting.*

In the end, I say nothing. I allow my actions to speak for me. It is not Jaynie Cumberland, teenage girl who fell in love in the wrong place at the wrong time, who goes after Allison. It is Jaynie Cumberland, victim no more.

Allison tries to jump out of the way, but I am faster. Jamming the cold, steel blades of the scissors into my tormentor's belly feels cathartic. It's wrong to exact vengeance like this, but I am no longer me. I am a woman robbed of a would-be future, a baby I'll never meet.

Allison crumples to the floor, eyelids fluttering. She passes out. Not dead. But she will be soon enough. The scissors remain stuck in her gut.

I stare down and slowly, very slowly, her crimson blood blooms around the blades.

I don't feel any better. I want to stab her again, make her hurt like I do. I kneel down next to her and reach for the scissors, readying to do exactly that.

But then, out of the blue, my plans are thwarted when I am yanked up to my feet. "What the hell?" I grind out.

I then fight like a wildcat against the person who has stopped me. And then I hear Flynn's soothing voice. "Shh, shh, Jaynie, it's just me."

I stop struggling, and he wraps his arms around me. "Calm down, sweetheart," he soothes. "You have to try to relax."

I start to cry. "She killed our baby, Flynn. She kicked me and kicked me, and now it's gone."

I then tell him everything, and Flynn comforts me, as only he can do. Afterward, he wets a towel and wipes the blood from my hands, soiling his own hands in the process, and essentially becoming my accomplice. Even our sins are now shared.

When he's done, his eyes fall to Allison. The scissors jut out of her belly as she slowly bleeds out on the floor.

"We have to get out of here," he says. "We need to keep you safe."

"Are we going up to the cliffs?" I ask.

"Yes, and you're going to have to jump."

"Jump, yes."

I know I can do it, since I already feel like I am falling.

Chapter Thirty-One

Flynn

"I'm taking the blame," I tell Jaynie as we run from the house.

"No," she retorts, breathless.

She's wearing the white dress she wore on one of our happiest days. How ironic she has it on this day, one of our saddest.

"I did it," she goes on. "I should suffer the consequences."

"We'll talk about it later," I say.

I'm only appeasing her to keep her going. What Jaynie doesn't know yet is that I'm not going with her. My intention is what it's always been—to keep her safe. Someone has to come back to call the police and take the blame for what happened. Otherwise, we'll both be fugitives, and the authorities *will* catch us. There's no choice but for Jaynie to flee to safety alone.

The idea was always for us to go together, and maybe we should have left ages ago. I see that now. With tragedy comes clarity.

I guess just having the option to go gave us a false sense of comfort. I don't know. We could have left the day the twins were

Tomorrow's Lies

taken away, but then—bam!—there was a baby to think of.

Now there's no more baby to worry about.

I should be relieved, but I feel nothing but sadness. I was sort of excited to have a baby with Jaynie. Maybe it was delusional of me to think so, but I kind of liked the idea of walking away from this place after we turned eighteen, already a family in the making.

But no, that would've been too easy. I guess I kind of always knew in my heart it would come down to this—running.

Jaynie stops to catch her breath when we reach the old barn up in the fields. Oh, for the days of playing Tag and Hide and Go Seek with the twins.

I place my hand on Jaynie's shoulder when she leans forward. "Are you going to be sick?"

"No. I just need a rest."

We can't rest, though, so I say as gently as I can, "I'm sorry, Jaynie. I know it's hard, but we have to keep going."

"Just one minute. Please, Flynn."

I nod. Since we're stopped this is as good of a time as any to tell Jaynie the "real" plan.

"Listen, babe." I take her hands in mine. "I'm going up to the cliff's edge with you, but I'm not jumping."

"What?"

"You heard me," I say. "You have to leave without me."

She begins to protest, but I share with her my fears, stressing that we'll never *both* get away. "I have to stay. At least for now, okay?"

I can tell she doesn't like it, but what other choice do we have? Everything I've said is true.

"How do you plan on calling the cops?" Jaynie wants to know. "It's not like we have cell phones. And there's no landline in the house."

"Allison has a phone. I'll dig around till I find it."

"What are you going to say?" she asks, stepping back. "Like, how do you plan to explain how Allison ended up stabbed?"

"I'll tell them it was self-defense."

She stares at me like I'm crazy. "Like you couldn't fight off Allison" She makes a scoffing sound. "Sorry, but I don't think they're going to buy it."

"I'm not planning on telling them I was defending myself, Jaynie. I'll tell them the truth, but with a twist. I'll say I walked in when Allison was kicking you and grabbed the scissors to protect you."

The thought of Allison attacking Jaynie makes my blood boil. I have to stay calm.

"Then I should stay," she says. "Corroborate your story. Only I'll say I got ahold of the scissors. My prints are all over them. "

"No way." I shake my head. "I'll go back and handle this. You know how corrupt this town is."

"Flynn, I don't know about this crazy plan."

"Jaynie, please. Don't fight me on this. You deserve a chance at a life."

"And you?" Her voice cracks. She's trying to stay strong, but I can see she's breaking.

"If I end up in prison, like my dad, so be it."

"Flynn! Don't say that. I swear I won't take another step if you don't promise me you'll be okay."

"I'll be okay," I say, hoping, but not knowing, if that's true.

"You'll explain things, make sure it's clear?"

"Yes."

"And then you'll come meet me in Lawrence?"

"Yes."

Our eyes meet. We both know this is a long shot, a mess of a plan. Still, it's the only option on the table.

Resigned that we are once again trapped, though this time by unforeseen circumstances, we head to the cliff.

Chapter Thirty-Two

Jaynie

"Jump," Flynn says.

I stare down at the swiftly moving river. "I can't, I can't," I cry.

"You have to, Jaynie."

From where we stand, on the edge of a cliff made of sandstone streaked with iron and copper, the water, black as night, scares me. Ink swirling in a bottomless well and I'm supposed to jump in?

I toss a glance back to the forest, and Flynn sighs. He knows what I'm thinking. "There's no going back, Jaynie," he says softly. "The only choice now is to move forward."

The cliff, the water, jumping in. He *is* right. Still… "I'm scared," I confess.

Flynn blows out a breath. "I know, sweetheart."

Soft, understanding, Flynn always gets me.

Regrets, the likes of which I've never known, wash over me, and I want nothing more than to turn back the hands of time and start this day over. The girl I was this morning, she is no more. That frightens me. Scarier still is who I may become if I leave Flynn. A lump forms in my throat at the thought.

"I changed my mind," I declare, shaking my head. "We shouldn't separate, Flynn." I tug on his arm, urging him to retreat with me as I take two steps away from the edge.

It's a move born of desperation, a last ditch attempt to pretend we're not in the situation we're in. But my delusion is short-lived. Flynn's expression tells me all I need to know. Going back, at least for me, is no longer an option.

"What if I never see you again?" I whisper.

"You'll see me soon enough." He doesn't sound so certain, and that scares the hell out of me.

"I'm out of here," I say.

When I start to walk away, Flynn grabs my arm. "Where do you plan to go, Jaynie?"

"With you, of course. Back to the house."

His grip tightens. "Uh, I don't think so."

He's right, but still, I try to slip away. My resistance is futile. One tug and Flynn has me snuggled in close to him. "Flynn…"

This is good, this is home, and I can't help but relax against him. I'd like to stay this way all night, my back pressed to Flynn's firm chest, my heart brimming full with his love.

Leaning down to whisper in my ear, Flynn gently nudges me back to reality when he says, "No changing the plan. You're leaving this place, today, now. This is me, Jaynie, making sure you're never in danger again."

And that's it for me. My walls crumble and I start to cry. "Please, no. Don't make me go. I don't think I'll make it without you."

Flynn's warm breaths, soft caresses on the back of my neck, send shivers down my spine, especially when he chants my name, like a prayer. "Jaynie, Jaynie." And then, "You're stronger than you think.

You can do anything you put your mind to."

I let out a derisive snort. "You believe in me *way* too much, Flynn."

"Nah, you don't believe in yourself enough. You never have, babe. You keep forgetting who you were when you first got here."

"I remember." *How could I forget?*

"Then you know how far you've come."

"Until tonight, Flynn. Tonight I screwed everything up." My voice cracks as I continue. "I failed myself. I couldn't hold it together, and I ended up failing *us*."

"Shh…" He walks me forward till we're back at the cliff's edge.

"The abyss," I murmur, looking down. *Still inky, still black, still scary as hell.* "You can't make me jump into that nothingness, Flynn."

"No, I can't make you. But you will jump."

I let out a scoffing noise, and press back into him.

His hands tightening at my waist, he says, "You want to know why I'm so sure you'll go?"

"Yes. Why?"

"Because, Jaynie." I feel his chin against my head as he nods to the water. "It's not 'nothingness' down there. That river is your way out."

I almost jump, right there and then, but panic overcomes me. I spin away from Flynn's grasp and come dangerously close to falling over the edge in the process. "Jaynie, Jesus," I hear Flynn say.

Shaken up, I move away from him, insisting the whole while, "I'm good, I'm good."

Yeah, right. I'm not anywhere near being okay.

As I back farther away from the cliff's edge, my heels digging into the soft earth, I try reasoning. With myself, with Flynn, I don't know. I guess with us both.

"I don't think I can go, Flynn. I really don't think I can."

He sighs, and I can tell he's gearing up to get me back to where I was. "Jaynie, come on."

Dirt cooled by the shortened days of fall squishes up between my toes, reminding me how rushed we were tonight. Suddenly, I have the most brilliant idea.

With a flourish of my hands, gesturing to my bare feet, I say as evenly as I can, "I forgot to put on my shoes before we left. I can't go without shoes, Flynn."

Flynn steps toward me, carefully, the way someone might approach a spooked animal.

"Shoes would just weigh you down, Jaynie. Better you left them behind. Swimming will actually be a whole lot easier this way."

I shake my head, the gravity of the situation we're in fully catching up to me. "I don't know, Flynn." I cover my face with my hands. "I don't know, I don't know. I don't know anything anymore."

But I do. The problem is I know too much. And that's what's killing me. This is the end—the end of my time with Flynn in this place, the end of easy smiles on warm summer days, the end of the family I cobbled together. But hardest of all to accept is this is the end of Flynn loving me. No one has ever loved me the way he has.

My heart breaks and I can almost see the shards of what's left of me falling away in the darkness.

"How can you let me go?" I sob.

Flynn yanks me to him, and I struggle to break free. But in the end, he wins. Holding me to him tightly, he buries his face against my neck.

Suddenly, I am angrier with him than I've ever been in the past. I try to shove him away—to no avail.

"How can you let *us* go?" I want to know, breathless and panting.

When he doesn't reply, I try to step back so he'll have no choice but to look me in the eye.

Flynn is far stronger, though, and easily holds me in place. "Please…just…stop," he whispers, voice cracking.

I stop struggling. This is hard on Flynn, too.

He squeezes my hip gently. "Be strong for both of us," he whispers. "The past is behind you. Your future is away from here." He finally lifts his head, eyes glistening with unshed tears as he nods to the river. "This is your chance to get away from all this bad."

But it's also me getting away from all that was good, I long to say. Instead, I simply ask, "What about you?"

"I told you before I'll be fine. I always am."

"I love you, Flynn."

A whir of wind kicks up and I fear my words are lost. Flynn hears me, as he always does. "I love you, too," he replies.

Sliding his hands up from my hips—carefully, so as to avoid the areas where I've been bruised—he murmurs wistfully, "You always look so beautiful in this dress."

"Even tonight?"

"Especially tonight."

Strong hands trail over white cotton worn to sheer in some spots. Those are the places I feel Flynn's warmth the best.

After a minute, he wraps his arms around me and we rock together. A slow back and forth, a final dance of sorts, one intended to soothe our broken souls.

Lips brushing over my ear, Flynn whispers, "Jaynie-bird. You'll always be my Jaynie-bird."

I smile. Flynn called me Jaynie-bird only once before. We were getting to know one another, and, ironically, we were standing in the same spot as we are now. I had told him if I had one wish it would be to fly away. *Away from this place, away from the pain.* Flynn promised me then that someday it would happen—I would fly away. But he was always supposed to go with me. This, this leaving without him was never an option, never a consideration. Not for me, at least. Doesn't he realize I can't do *this*—leave and possibly go live my life without him?

"I don't think I can live without you, Flynn," I confess, cramming all my fears into nine little words.

"You have to, baby, at least for a little while."

"No, Flynn. I don't like this one bit. What if things go wrong?"

"Just follow the original plan. Stop in the next town. Get yourself set up. Wait for me, okay? I'll be along when I can. You'll see. We'll be back together in no time."

"Yeah, that's the plan," I state flatly.

Disheartened doesn't even begin to cover the way I feel. Plans are great and all, but Flynn and I both know the truth. He may never make it out of here. Not with what occurred earlier tonight.

I choke back a sob, and he reminds me, "There's no other way, Jaynie. Not after—"

I press a finger to his lips. "Don't say it, Flynn. Don't say anything more."

He doesn't.

Eventually we join hands. Peering down at our solidarity, I am amazed that even in the black heart of a black night the bloodstains on our hands are still visible. Blood doesn't wash off so easily, and the night doesn't hide it so well. Maybe it shouldn't.

I shudder. No, I can't think about how those bloodstains led us here. So, instead, I focus on Flynn. Tall and strong, sandy brown hair as messy as ever, eyes as gray as the stormy day I met him.

"Jaynie," Flynn says when he sees me drifting off to a past we can no longer dwell on. "It's time to go. We can't stay here forever."

"I know."

"One of us *has* to make it out of here. If not, everything that happened earlier will have been in vain."

My heart constricts. "These things we've done and can't undo."

"Jaynie, don't."

I throw my arms around him and hold onto the love of my life one final time. I sob a good-bye I can't fully articulate, but he gets it. When we rock back on our heels, Flynn wraps a long strand of my hair around his hand. Raising the auburn tress to his nose, he takes a whiff and closes his eyes.

Smiling around a sniffle, I ask, "What in the world are you doing?"

"Breathing you in," he replies. "I'm making you a part of the air in my lungs."

He's also trying to lighten the mood to make this easier on me.

"There." He lets go of my hair. "I think you're in there pretty good now."

"Stop," I mutter.

Our eyes meet and smiles falter. We then literally fall into each other, sharing an embrace tinged with the desperation of knowing this will be our last night *ever* in this forest.

These woods have offered us refuge so many times in the past. This was a place to get away from all the bad down at the house. I'll miss these woods where Flynn and I shared so much. Naked and bare, in more ways than one, nestled in the bosom of the land, secrets were spilled like blood across the forest floor. We've loved and healed up here, away from prying eyes. Secrets remain safe here. We could share what we did tonight, and the forest would never tell a soul.

We say nothing, though. There will be no confessions, not on this night.

What was it my mother, whom I haven't seen in four years, used to say? *The times they are a-changin', Jaynie.*

A shiver runs through me, and Flynn leans back so he can see my face. "What are you thinking about?" he asks.

"I'm thinking again that maybe I should stay."

"No." His voice is firm now. He's tiring of this back-and-forth. "We agreed if it ever came down to only one of us getting out, it would be you. We agreed to save *you*, Jaynie."

"But we never imagined—"

"No, we didn't."

"So—

"Jaynie, *no*. No more stalling, no more putting off the inevitable."

Flynn moves farther away, giving himself more space. Still, it's not enough and he can't stop touching me.

Placing a calloused finger to my lips, he says, "We're out of time, babe."

I grab his hand and slide it up to my cheek. Memories of how Flynn's fingers feel pressed to other places on my body come to mind. And then I am reminded it's all about to end. "No," I whisper.

With care, Flynn lifts a strand of my hair and tucks it behind my ear.

My heart aches at the reminder of how I was first touched by him. It seems so long ago. "Flynn—"

"Jaynie, go. Please. Just leave."

I stare at him, taking him in one final time. Full lips, straight nose, the little crescent-shaped scar below one eye. I memorize it all. Placing my hands on his wide shoulders, I look up at a boy who became a man before my very eyes. Taller and stronger than the day I first met him, muscles more corded and defined, Flynn is formidable to someone like me. Next to him, I am a waif. And I am all too happy to break beneath him. I do so now, as I've done so many times before.

"I thought you were beautiful the day I met you," I confess. "But you're so much more than that." I tap his chest. "Your most beautiful places are in here." I choke back a sob. "You've helped me so much. Flynn. I was such a mess."

Tucking another strand of unruly hair behind my ear, he smiles sadly. "Quit thinking about the past. No more looking back, okay?"

"What if I don't make it, Flynn? I mean the fall, the water."

Tears form in his eyes. "You will," he whispers, like saying the words will make them come true.

I nod, because what else can I do? We don't think the fall will kill me, but you never know. In case we're wrong, I drink him in.

His cheekbones are too sharp from not getting enough to eat—*never enough food, never enough of anything*—and the fine sprinkling of freckles across his nose are barely visible now that he's practically a man.

"What are you doing, Jaynie?" he asks, smiling.

I lift my hand and trace his lips with tentative fingers. "I'm trying to memorize everything about you. I don't want to forget a single thing."

Flynn snorts, "Fuck that."

His lips crash into mine, and I realize this is what I've wanted all along, to get lost, to forget everything. Losing myself with Flynn is always easy, especially when his lips are on mine. Hell, he sure doesn't kiss like an eighteen-year-old guy. He kisses like a fully grown man, lips and tongue moving with a skill far beyond his years.

When he finally drops back, I grab hold of his shirt. "Promise me you'll be all right. Swear to me this will all turn out okay."

Tears flow down my cheeks unchecked, hot and burning. Not he, nor I, can stop them. Not tonight.

"I promise," he says.

"Swear to me we'll meet where we said we would, as soon as you can get away."

"I swear."

"Don't you dare go and forget about me, Flynn O'Neill."

"Like that would ever be possible," he says, chuckling. But then he, too, is choking back tears. "I promise you, Jaynie Cumberland, I will *never* forget about you. You are burned in my soul."

"Mine, too," I say.

"We'll meet, like we planned, as soon as things settle down. I promise you, a thousand times, okay?"

"Today's promises are nothing but tomorrow's lies. Isn't that what you once told me?"

He looks stunned. "I didn't mean for it to ever apply to us, Jaynie."

"But it could. We can't predict the future."

"Stop it."

His voice is a plea, and I back off.

"You'll find me, then?"

"Yes, of course."

"Say it again."

"Jaynie, enough."

Scrubbing his hands down his face, he tilts back his head and stares up at the starless night. His eyes are wet and glistening. Flynn is breaking right along with me. One last time, he tangles his hand in my hair, pulling and grasping, yanking me to him. This letting go is killing him, too.

"Nothing will *ever* keep me from you," he hisses, forehead pressed to mine.

"But what about what I've done?"

He steps back, eyes flashing. "Don't say it like that. It's what *we've* done, not just you."

"No, Flynn. I did it. It was all me."

Sighing, he says, "It doesn't matter. It was justice for what we lost."

Something squeezes my heart, making me choke out, "Oh, Flynn—"

"Don't think about it, Jaynie. Just go."

He turns me to the water. There is no going back, not this time.

I close my eyes.

Then I jump.

…And I am falling…

　…falling…

　　…falling…

　　　…falling…

Part Two

Chapter Thirty-Three

Flynn

I watch Jaynie fall. I watch her swim away, this girl who loves me, and who I love more than anything in the world. Gone, possibly forever, just like the baby I'll never meet.

My breath catches at the gravity of all that has happened, and at the same time, Jaynie gets caught up in the current. While she tries to swim away, every fiber of my being tells me to jump in after her.

And I almost do. But then she begins to swim with the current, strong strokes I wouldn't have expected from such a tiny, injured girl.

Jaynie's tenacity strengthens my resolve. I must remain strong, as well.

When she rounds a bend in the river and I can no longer see her, I turn away and run back to the house. Leaves, which died an early-autumn death, crunch beneath my sneakers, reminding me of how short life really is. That's why Jaynie deserves a good one, even if it's at my expense. I'm okay with what I'm about to do. From here on out my sole intent is to protect Jaynie.

I don't want the girl I love pulled into some court case. I told her differently, but I plan not to mention her to the authorities. I am taking the full blame. I'll act as if Jaynie had nothing to do with what went down. I'll say I got into a fight with Allison. I wrestled the scissors from her, and she ended up stabbed. The authorities will assume Jaynie took off—out of fear, or opportunity, it doesn't matter. She's close enough to eighteen they won't bother searching for her.

I *am* eighteen now, and I'll be tried as an adult. Probably end up in the same prison as my dad. Fuck, that's the last person I care to spend my days with. But there's no other choice before me, is there?

The house is dark as I approach, which is weird. I could've sworn we left lights on in the hall and definitely in the kitchen. Maybe Jaynie turned them off. Things were happening so quickly, it's hard to remember all the little details.

When I enter the house, I flip the light switch on in the hall and the area is bathed in an orangey glow, just like I remember it looking when we left.

Hmm, something seems off. I can't put my finger on what is bothering me, though. Maybe I'm uneasy because, after all, there's a probably-now-dead body in the house.

Heading to the kitchen, I expect to find Allison completely bled out. It's most likely a horrific mess. When I arrive, I close my eyes, and then flick the switch to the overhead light.

Am I ready for this?

No.

I open my eyes and am shocked, but not for the reason I expected. There's no massive amount of blood on the floor, there's no pair of scissors, and most disturbing of all, there's no body, dead or otherwise. "What the hell," I whisper.

You'd think nothing had gone down by the cleanliness of the room, certainly not a bloody attack.

As I scan the room for a body that seems to have disappeared into thin air, I realize what was bugging me out in the hall—Mrs. Lowry's high heels were lying askew in the corner.

Allison's mother is home, and has apparently cleaned up the body. "Shit."

I spin around to take off—it's not too late to catch up to Jaynie—but instead I run smack dab into Mrs. Lowry.

"Flynn," she says tightly. No phony smiles today. "I had a feeling you'd come back to the scene of the crime."

"I-I don't know what you're talking about," I stammer.

It's too late by the time I notice the hammer in her hand. She lifts and swings so quickly, I see nothing but a blurry arc of metal coming at me.

There's no time to react, and a sharp pain shoots through my head.

And then there is nothing.

Chapter Thirty-Four

Jaynie

Fighting the current is no good. You have to roll with it, succumb to the power of the water and let it guide your body.

I do exactly that and soon reach a state of peace. Or maybe the calm I feel is a side effect of freezing my ass off. The water is freaking cold in October. Not so bad as to bring on hypothermia—I don't think?—but icy enough that my hands and feet start to grow numb.

Relief engulfs me when I catch a glimpse of a break in the trees just a little farther down the river. "That must be the park." My lips are quivering, teeth chattering. *Oh, please, let it be the park.*

The break in the trees is indeed the park. Outlines of benches and trash containers dot the open area. I swim to the shore with renewed vigor. Freedom is mere yards away. I forget about the cold and thank the stars above, still hidden by cloud cover. I've successfully reached the town of Lawrence.

When I crawl up on the muddy riverbank, all the adrenaline that has kept me going since Flynn and I left the house drains out of me, along with what feels like ten gallons of water pouring from my sopping-wet dress.

After shaking out what I can, I crawl over to a wooden bench and rest my head on the worn seat. When I finally have the energy to stand, I wring out sections of the soaked cotton material sticking to my body. When I'm done with my dress, I move up to my dripping hair. *I wish I had a towel.*

Damp and shivering, I scan the area for the old oak tree so I can retrieve the key and unlock the locker Mandy has hopefully stowed warm clothes in. I spy one giant tree only, and it's nearby, right in the middle of the park.

There are signs all around the tree to not climb up in it, but I'm going to have to in order to reach the carved-out nook in the overhead branches. Summoning strength I didn't know I still had in me, I drag a park bench over to the base of the tree and climb from there.

The key is exactly where Mandy promised to stow it.

"Thank you, Mandy," I whisper as I stare down at the number 23 that is stamped on the plastic orange tab at the top of the key.

In locker number 23, I find a big backpack. Inside are clothes for me and Flynn.

Flynn...

Tears well up as I pull out a pair of guy's jeans that are Flynn's size. Re-folding them neatly, in the hopes he'll be along soon and will need them, I tuck the dark blue denim back in the bag.

What if he never makes it? My mind taunts. *What if he goes to jail for years and years because of something you did?*

I can't go there, or I'll fall apart. And I *must* keep it together to get through this. I concentrate on the clothes Mandy has thrown in the bag, the ones meant for me. There's an off-white long-sleeved tee, an oversized gray sweatshirt with a college name I've never heard of, a pair of blue jeans, socks, underwear, a bra, and an old pair of beat-up, navy Chucks.

I shrug out of my dress right there by the lockers. It's not like anyone is around to see me. It's a cool fall night and the hour is late. Besides, I have no excess energy to spare to search for a restroom, which would probably be locked this time of year.

After I've changed into my new clothes, I look around for a discarded plastic bag, the kind from a grocery store. I want to put my wet dress in something. With only two outfits to my name, it's kind of imperative I hold on to everything.

I eventually find a blue plastic bag that seems relatively clean. It's lying next to one of the trash bins. I stuff my dress inside, and then return the backpack with the clothes for Flynn to the locker. Before I leave the park, I place the key back in the nook of the oak tree.

I have to believe Flynn will find a way out of the mess we left behind. He'll be here soon, and then we can figure out this new life together.

Do you really think things will be so easily resolved? "Don't think about the alternative," I chastise myself.

Because if Flynn, who can wiggle his way out of most anything, can't make it, then how in the hell am I supposed to?

Chapter Thirty-Five

Flynn

I wake up in a hospital room, confused as hell. There's a pretty blonde nurse jotting down notes on a chart. "Where am I?" I ask her.

My voice is scratchy, no more than a hoarse whisper, but the nurse hears me. Her head jerks up, surprised. "You're awake," she says.

I look down at all the tubes in my arms, and then at the many monitors. "How long have I been out?"

"A couple of days."

"Jaynie… I have to go to Jaynie." I try to get up, but the room spins and shifts in all kinds of funny ways. I fall back on the bed. "Shit, maybe not quite yet."

The nurse rushes over to the bed, where she checks my tubes to make sure nothing has been dislodged.

"You need to stay put," she states firmly. "You suffered a fairly severe head injury and—"

"You don't understand," I interrupt. "There's somewhere I need to be. Someone,"—I struggle to put my thoughts into words since I'm still foggy—"someone I love is waiting for me. She needs me."

The nurse pats me on the arm and offers me a reassuring smile. "Mr. O'Neill, when all your tests come back with normal-range results, I'm sure you'll be discharged. But until then you need to stay calm and try to get some rest."

Events from before everything went black begin to come back to me.

When I remember how Allison's body was missing, I carefully ask, "What exactly happened to me? Things are really fuzzy. Was anyone else hurt?"

"You don't remember?" The nurse appears surprised.

I shake my head, which only make things spin again. "No," I mumble.

"You were brought in by…let's see here…" She scans the chart. "Oh, here it is. Mrs. Lowry came in with you and one other person, a woman in her early twenties. She was injured, as well, in the accident."

"Wait, what accident?"

I may have some blurred and mixed-up memories, but I know what Jaynie did to Allison.

The nurse seems not to know this, however, which could be a good thing. She continues to read the charts, reciting completely contradictory info to me.

"Oh, okay," she goes on. "It says here the woman who was injured along with you is Mrs. Lowry's daughter. Uh, hold on… Her name is Allison, and apparently she was helping you with a project in the craft barn when she tripped over something and fell onto a sharp object." *What?*

"It says here when you went over to help her, something heavy fell from a shelf and hit you in the head."

"It says that, huh?" I say.

Tomorrow's Lies

These are all lies in the chart, a clearly made-up tale. Seems Crafty Lo is craftier than I ever gave her credit for. No ambulance was called to the house and the police were not involved in any way. Mrs. Lowry drove me and Allison to the hospital. But why would Crafty Lo make up a bogus story? Why cover up what really happened? She has no reason to protect me, or Jaynie, so why would she?

A light rap on the door pulls me from my musings. "May I come in?" a cheery voice rings out.

A vivid memory of Mrs. Lowry wielding a hammer makes my monitors go crazy.

"Mr. O'Neill." The nurse hurries over to my bedside. "What in heaven's name has you so worked up?"

The door swings open, and Mrs. Lowry steps in the room. I can't react. If I blow the cover story she made up, I'll be implicating my own ass and possibly Jaynie's.

Mrs. Lowry's gaze falls on me, and I can't help but recoil.

Whatever Crafty Lo is up to, it can't be good.

The nurse relaxes when she sees it's only Mrs. Lowry who has come in the room. Of course. She *is* the town's savior, after all.

With an audience in place, Mrs. Lowry puts on her best phony face and rushes over to the bed.

"Oh, Flynn," she gushes. Fake tears fill icy-blue eyes that tell me I'd best play along. "I've been *so* worried about you. The entire time you were unconscious, I kept thinking how kind it was of you to come to my daughter's aid when she tripped in that dreadful barn. And then"—she waves her hand around at all the tubes and monitors—"for you to end up injured, as well. Such a sad turn of events for all involved."

Turning to the nurse, she adds, "I suppose what they say is true, huh?"

"What's that?" the nurse asks, brow furrowed.

Crafty Lo laughs, a high-pitched titter. "That no good deed goes unpunished. You've heard that one, yes?"

The nurse smiles tightly. She is clearly uncomfortable, but nods and agrees.

Typical Forsaken townsfolk behavior, no one daring to question anything Mrs. Lowry deems to be true. Her word may as well be gospel. If she claims something heavy "fell" on my head, then that's what happened. Forget what the wound itself may reveal. Same with Allison. Mrs. Lowry may as well have written up the charts herself.

Eyeing me with interest—probably wondering what I'm thinking—Crafty Lo asks the nurse if she can have a minute alone with me.

Mrs. Lowry naturally gets what she wants, and once the nurse is gone, she turns to me, the façade falling away with astonishing speed.

"You little fuck," she spits. "You're lucky I didn't kill you back at the house."

"Yeah? Why didn't you?" I ask.

She pulls up a chair and sits next to my bed. Adjusting her tweed skirt, she says, "Because that would have been too easy on you. What I have in mind for your future is much worse. And I'm going to enjoy every minute of it."

I feel sick. "What are you talking about?"

Her eyes drill into me, and it's evident where Allison gets her mean streak. "First, if you think I haven't pieced together what really happened, you are sadly mistaken. My daughter told me what she could recall, and I figured out the rest." She lowers her voice. "If you want that little tramp of yours to remain a free woman, as well as you yourself staying out of prison, you'll do exactly as I say."

I bristle at the mention of the girl I love. "Just leave Jaynie out of this, okay?"

"It's a little hard to do when she's the bitch who tried to kill my daughter."

"It was self-defense—"

Mrs. Lowry waves her hand in front of my face. "Don't lie to me, Flynn. What Jaynie did was no accident. And you helped her get away."

I start to interject that Jaynie had a reason, but what's the point? Mrs. Lowry doesn't care what her daughter did to drive Jaynie to attack her.

Mrs. Lowry continues, her every word another nail in my coffin. "If you want to keep Jaynie from being charged with attempted murder, you're going to do exactly what I ask of you. Otherwise, I'll recant my story. I'll tell the authorities you threatened me and made me lie. I'll tell them you were an accomplice to your girlfriend's crime."

"I don't care what happens to me," I mutter. And I don't, not really.

"That may be, but I know you care what happens to the girl you got pregnant."

I am stunned. She does know everything. "You know?"

"Yes, I know."

"Then you have to know why Jaynie—"

She cuts me off. "Stop right there. There's no excuse for Jaynie's actions. And"—she suppresses a bored yawn—"if you want to hear my honest opinion, I think my daughter did you both a favor."

I am going to throttle this bitch. And I do lunge at her, but she slides her chair back, the legs screeching as they scrape across the linoleum floor.

"Stop right there," Mrs. Lowry hisses. "If you hurt me, you and your slut both go down. Don't think I'm bluffing." Her eyes drill into me as she says, "I saved the scissors, you know. They're in a plastic bag, with your girlfriend's prints all over them."

I close my eyes and slump back in my bed, defeated. There's no way out. The bitch has me by the short hairs.

"What do you want, exactly?" I ask.

She leans in, confident now that she knows she's got me. "I want you to promise to never again see Jaynie. No seeking her out, no trying to contact her in any way. No going through back channels, like contacting Saundra or Mandy. And I want you to remain here in Forsaken. Not at my house, of course," she scoffs. "You're eighteen now so you can go get a job and find your own place to stay."

I say in a dead voice, "Okay." I wish she'd finished me off now.

"Sleep on the streets if you have to," she continues, reveling in the fact that I don't have a home. "I really don't care about that part. But remember"—she stabs a finger in my face—"I'll have people watching you all the time. This town loves me, and don't you forget it. If you so much as even *think* about Jaynie Cumberland, I will have you both arrested for what you did to my Allison."

With her words, I am condemned, trapped once again. Not by the law, or as punishment for the crimes I committed by helping Jaynie get away. No, I am shackled by a woman who always seems to end up holding all the cards. There's no way out of this one, not if I want to protect Jaynie. And I *will* protect her, even if it means breaking my promise to her.

"Do you agree to my terms?" Mrs. Lowry asks, like this is another one of her business deals. To her, I suppose it is.

The first crack in my heart fissures as I say, "Yes, I agree. I will stay in Forsaken. I will stay away from Jaynie."

"Good boy," I am told.

And with that, my fate is sealed.

Chapter Thirty-Six

Jaynie

The town of Lawrence is only a few minutes' walk from the park, and Delmont's Deli is easy to find. A cute storefront of red brick nestled between a thrift store and a bank on the main drag. The bank and thrift store are closed and consequently pitch-black. But there is a light on inside the deli, despite the fact it's now the middle of the night.

It takes a lot for me to muster up the courage to pound on the door. I've been secluded and isolated for so long that the thought of interacting with a stranger leaves my chest constricted. But I have to do this. Like Flynn said, all of this will have been for nothing if at least one of us doesn't make it.

Inside Delmont's Deli should be Mandy's friend, Bill. He doesn't know it yet, but he holds the key to my future.

I knock once more, this time more frantically. "You'll be okay," I assure myself.

I am so close to a breakdown, cold and exhausted and still wet.

Now that I've had time for the events of the night to sink in, I'm also terrified. *What if the police come? What if Flynn and I go to trial? What if I never see him again?*

"All right, all right, hold on a minute," a booming baritone calls out from inside the deli. Thankfully, the voice sounds more amused than aggravated. "No need to crash in the door. I'm coming."

I take a step back. My legs feel gummy, and I'm close to collapse. Damn, I need sleep.

Another light flickers on inside, this one closer to the entrance where I await salvation.

A young man with caramel skin, tall and with a slender build, twists a lock on the other side of the door. He looks at me through the plated glass and smiles kindly. I can't help but smile back.

"Are you Bill Delmont?" I blurt out the second the door is open.

"Yes," he says. "And you would be?"

The floodgates burst open. "I'm a friend of Mandy Sullivan. She was supposed to tell you about me. My name is Jaynie, Jaynie Cumberland."

Realization dawns on Bill Delmont's face. "Oh, yes, yes." He steps aside. "Come on in, Jaynie."

I walk into the deli and under the lights, I catch Bill frowning as he takes in my appearance. "Rough night?" he says with absolutely no humor in his tone.

"Yeah, you could say that." Gesturing to my disheveled clothes and still-not-dry hair, I add, "I kind of had to leave where I was staying in a hurry."

Bill doesn't press. "No need to explain," he says.

He appears not one bit surprised to have found a wayward girl at his place of business in the middle of the night. He's obviously seen worse, and I'm glad. I feel less self-conscious.

"Sometimes," he murmurs, "leaving in a hurry is better than not leaving at all."

Tomorrow's Lies

"You sure got that right," I reply.

He motions for me to follow him to the back of the deli. We pass a bunch of tables and some plushy chairs then stop at a counter in the back.

"Have a seat," he says, gesturing to a stool. I sit down at the counter, all too happy to get off my feet. Bill then goes on. "How about I whip up a couple of hot cocoas and grab a towel for your hair?" He takes in my too-thin build. "Maybe grab you some toast, too."

"Thanks, Mr. Delmont."

"Just call me Bill," he says.

"Okay, Bill."

Bill walks around the counter and steps through a doorway that appears to lead to a small office. I lean forward. There's a lamp on inside the back room area, illuminating a desk, a computer, and some file cabinets.

"I'll be back in a minute," he assures me before he disappears into the room.

Alone at the counter, I blow out a breath. I've never felt so relieved. Bill Delmont was expecting me. Mandy really came through, which is great. Bill won't be surprised when Flynn shows up next. This ordeal will be over soon enough, and Flynn and I can put it behind us and focus on our future.

Bill returns with two cups of hot cocoa in one hand, a plate of dry toast in the other, and a towel tossed over his shoulder. In the crook of his arm, he's carrying a fuzzy flannel blanket.

"I thought you might need something to keep you warm," he says as he sets the toast on the counter, hands me the blanket, and somehow manages to balance the steaming cups of cocoa so not a drop sloshes over.

Damn, Bill Delmont is as nice and helpful as Mandy promised.

Wrapping the blanket around myself, I ask about Mandy.

"She's doing great," Bill tells me. He sets my cocoa down in front of me, then drags a stool over from behind the counter so he can sit across from me. "She made it to Morgantown a couple of months ago."

"Did she find Josh?" I ask excitedly. I secretly hope so, since one of us deserves for something to have gone right.

Bill nods as he takes a sip of his cocoa. "Yeah, she sure did." He sets his cup down next to mine. "She and Josh are together now, got their own place not too long ago, too."

"No way, that is so great." I smile my first genuine smile of the night. "She can apply to foster the twins now."

The twins… My chest tightens. I'm afraid to ask the next question.

With my eyes on little bits of cocoa in my cup that didn't quite dissolve, I quietly inquire, "Do you happen to know what happened to Cody and Callie? Those are the twins. They were taken away from the house I was living in and thrown back in a group home. I just want to know they're safe…" I choke up, unable to go on.

Handing me a napkin to wipe away my tears, Bill says softly, "They're okay, Jaynie. The twins are safe. Mandy has been keeping up with them. Cody and Callie are living with a young couple right now. Nice people, good foster parents. Only thing is, Mandy doesn't think they want to adopt the twins." Bill blows out a breath. "Which is actually a good thing since she's still hoping to foster them. And, as you know I'm sure, Mandy and Josh are willing to adopt Cody and Callie. Mandy is gonna have an edge with knowing them so well. Plus, they get a say in the matter, and they want to be with her."

"So, you think it will work out?"

I dare to look up, and Bill nods reassuringly. "I do, Jaynie. I think it will."

I exhale a relieved breath. "It's what they've always wanted. Cody and Callie should be with Mandy."

We talk a while longer and the conversation soon turns to Bill's business. He tells me how he pulled himself out of a bad situation, got his life together, and applied for a small business loan for the sandwich shop.

"I never thought I'd get the money," he says. "But I think the loan officer saw something in me."

I look around at the warm and cozy atmosphere of the shop. It's hip and welcoming. A place you'd feel comfortable hanging out in after you finished your sandwich.

"Your place seems really great," I tell Bill. "The vibe is very… tranquil."

Bill laughs. "Just wait till you see how tranquil it is when it gets busy in here. You may change your mind."

We share a smile, and then he offers me a job.

I immediately reply, "Yes! I'll take it."

He laughs at my enthusiastic response.

I'm running on the caffeine in the cocoa and the thrill of talking with a new person I seem to get along with. But exhaustion is creeping back up on me. When I start yawning incessantly, Bill mentions a tiny apartment above the deli. "You can sleep up there, if you want."

"It's available?" I ask.

"Yes. Though I have to warn you it's not much. Just a bedroom and a small bath, there's not even a kitchen. I do, however, have a small fridge and microwave hooked up for whoever rents it."

"It sounds perfect," I say. "I don't need anything fancy."

He mustn't believe me because when he takes me upstairs to show me around the plain little room with a double bed, a wooden nightstand, and a closet in the corner, he says, "I'm sorry I can't offer you something better, Jaynie."

"Are you kidding?" Though spartanly decorated, the light blue room is tidy, cheery, and clean. "I love it. How much are you asking for rent?"

He thinks it over for a minute. "How's one hundred a month

sound?"

"That sounds like not enough, Bill." I look down at the shiny hardwood floor and white throw rug beside the blue quilt-covered bed.

"I don't want to take advantage," I say humbly. "You're already doing so much for me."

"Hey, look at me." I do, and he says, "I've been in your shoes, Jaynie. And I know sometimes a person needs a break to help them get started on living their life the way they want. I got my break from that loan officer. I don't know what he saw in me but whatever it was it made all the difference in the world. This is my turn to return the favor, pay it forward, if you will."

I sigh. "I don't know."

Bill motions around the room. "Look, this place is just a single room with a bath attached, nothing fancy. Plus, no one has stayed up here for a while. You'd actually be helping me out by saying yes to renting it."

Quietly, I thank him, and then I tell him, "Yes. I'll take it."

The first week in Lawrence is a whirlwind of activity, leaving me little time to think and dwell on all that has happened. The bruises on my body heal, but the wounds in my heart remain raw. I dig deep in my inner strength reserves and push my feelings to the background. I focus on setting myself up. I've been through too much to give up.

Bill gives me an advance on my first paycheck, and I go next door to the thrift store and buy more clothes. Afterward, I stop at a drugstore for various essentials.

And every day, with every customer who walks in the deli, I hold out hope that I'm going to look up and see Flynn smiling back at me.

That day never comes during week one.

At the beginning of my second week in Lawrence, I take a walk down to the riverbank to check on the locker. The backpack is still in place, untouched. Flynn's clothes are stuffed inside exactly the way I folded them. Items waiting for a sandy-haired boy to arrive to give them life, just like I wait for Flynn to come to Lawrence and give *me* life.

I keep a check on the newspapers, as well as scan news sites on Bill's computer in the back room office. I search for any kind of headline mentioning the Lowry house in Forsaken, any reports of crimes, any arrests.

Oddly, I find nothing. No news of a murder, no reports of injuries of any kind. *Strange.*

For as much as I hate Allison, I have to say I'm relieved she's not dead. I am not a murderer at heart. And I don't know if I could go through life knowing I'd killed someone. I'm thankful she's not dead for Flynn's sake, as well. No murder means he won't be charged as an accomplice.

So, why isn't Flynn here in Lawrence? Where could he be? What's holding him up?

With a lump in my throat, I begin to entertain the possibility that Flynn may have changed his mind. He may not be coming to Lawrence, like, ever. Maybe he never went back to the house. He could have jumped in the water later that night, but with a different destination in mind. Perhaps he swam to some other faraway place. Far away from me, miles from all the grief my actions rained down on him.

Time marches on, and the vibrant autumn leaves begin to turn brown. Dried up and dead, they fall from the trees, withered away, same as I feel. My initial enthusiasm to not give up on life wanes. My transformation occurs inside, though, and no one notices anything different about me.

I go through the motions, putting on a happy face for the customers and for Bill. No one need be burdened by this fresh, new round of grief. But every night when I'm alone in my little room, I come to grips with how empty my life has become. This sure isn't what I expected.

Curling up under the covers, I think of all I've lost—Flynn, the baby, Mandy, and the twins.

It always comes back to Flynn, though. The baby is gone, and Mandy and the twins are hanging in there, whereas Flynn's whereabouts remain a mystery.

The hole in my heart from not knowing if he's well—or even alive—grows until it becomes gaping.

What I end up feeling is something beyond sadness. This is the kind of deep-seated sorrow where you know your life has been severely altered and you will never be the same.

Chapter Thirty-Seven

Flynn

Crafty Lo comes to see me before I'm discharged from the hospital. She wants to make sure I intend to keep my promise.

Ha, like I have a choice in the matter.

Bitch brings me a bag of my clothes, plus some papers—my ID, birth certificate, copy of my diploma, shit like that. She tries to hand me some money, too. I tell her to stick it where the sun doesn't shine.

She ignores me and places the small wad of cash on a stand by the bed. She then hands me a pay-as-you-go phone.

"Why the fuck do I need a cell phone?" I say bitterly. "I'm supposed to be a ghost now, right?"

"Just shut up and take what you're given. It's the last thing you'll ever get from me."

With a resigned sigh, I take the money and the damn phone.

Later the same day, it's like the phone is burning a hole in the pocket of my jeans. Having a phone is wrought with irony, considering the situation I'm in. If I'd had a phone during my time with Jaynie, even if it'd had no service, I would've been using the damn thing all the time to take pictures of Jaynie. I'd have a thousand pictures now of the girl I will never see again. So, see, the phone can't stay with me.

I sell it on the street for twenty dollars. Twenty dollars, plus fifty from Mrs. Lowry means I won't starve while I search for a job. Speaking of which, I head to the local job center on the east end of town to see what's available.

There's a line out the door, guys standing around, smoking, yawning. Some look as desperate as I feel. I have an advantage, though. I'm young and strong, plus I have all my paperwork in order.

I leave the first day with a work order to come back the next morning at seven. Some local construction job, a Wal-Mart or some shit needs to be up by spring. The pay is low, but to someone who's worked the past two years for free, I have no complaints.

I don't have enough money to rent an apartment, even a shithole, so I search for a place to squat. Just someplace dry that provides shelter from the upcoming winter should be sufficient.

After a few hours' search, I stumble upon an unused warehouse that's next to a derelict apartment building. Both are on the edge of town, not far from the job center.

I break in the abandoned warehouse and discover a janitor's living quarters in the basement. It's nothing but a cement block room, with a cot and a toppled-over desk for furnishings, but that's enough for me. The toilet and sink around the corner seal the deal. I can do something with that.

The water service has been cut off for ages, but I tap into the neighboring apartment building's water supply and rig up the toilet so it will flush. I only divert a small amount so as not to arouse suspicion. I get to work on the sink, as well, using some old hosing I find lying around, and then I make a sort-of shower near the drain.

My makeshift living space is not the Ritz, but, hey, it's good enough for me.

Tomorrow's Lies

When I find a couple of old flashlights, I bop down to the local convenience store to stock up on batteries. I also purchase some food while I'm there.

Later that night, when I'm stretched out on the cot, freshly showered from my rigged-up system, I lie there and listen to the *plop-plop-plop* of water dripping down the drain. Finally, I allow myself to think of Jaynie.

There has to be a way we can be together again.

"Yeah, right," I mutter as I roll to my side, the cot creaking beneath me.

I have no doubt Mrs. Lowry is keeping close tabs on me already. I refuse to take any stupid chances and put Jaynie in jeopardy. Crafty Lo's threats are far from idle, and I have a feeling she'd get a special kind of joy from sending Jaynie to prison, thus separating us forever.

Still, as I nod off, I can't help but recall all the old, great love stories I used to hate reading about in English class when I was a kid. Now I understand them better and they don't seem so bad. I remember one theme always stood out—even in the direst of circumstances, love always found a way to prevail.

So why should my and Jaynie's story end any differently? But then, before I succumb to sleep, I remember life is not a novel.

Too bad for me.

Chapter Thirty-Eight

Jaynie

Forty-two days and still no Flynn... Forty-three days, forty-four.

I remain on autopilot. I work my job, eat a little, and sleep a lot. I buy a pay-as-you-go phone, but I can't bring myself to ask Bill for Mandy's number. It's not that I don't want to talk to her, because I desperately do. I miss my friend like crazy. I'm afraid, though. If I talk to her and tell her Flynn never made it to Lawrence, it'll make his being gone from my life all too real. And I just can't handle coming to terms with yet another loss. Not yet.

Bill invites me to a big Thanksgiving dinner he's preparing for the homeless people in town. I decline, choosing instead to stay upstairs in my rented room. Smiling for and chatting up customers at the deli is tough enough. I'm feeling more than a little tapped out in the social skills department these days.

I miss Flynn. I miss the family we once had, and I miss the family we could have been.

Standing at the counter in the deli the Friday after Thanksgiving, as I'm closing out the register for the day, something snaps.

I realize I cannot go on like this, dealing with all these problems alone. "I need people," I whisper to myself.

Bill is placing turkey sandwiches in the display case beside me. He stops what he's doing and looks over at me. "What was that, Jaynie? I didn't hear you."

I close the register drawer and wipe my hands on my regulation Delmont Deli apron.

"Oh, nothing," I reply. "But can I ask you a question?"

He smiles and says, "Sure. Ask away."

I clear my throat. This is a big step. This is me moving forward, possibly without Flynn. This is me accepting that I've maybe lost him from my life.

"Can I have Mandy's cell number?" I say.

"Of course you can." Bill watches me curiously as he adds, "Does this have something to do with Flynn?"

"No, not really," I mumble.

I'm surprised. Bill has never mentioned Flynn to me, and I've not said anything to him. I'm sure he knows about Flynn, though, from Mandy. Still, I suspect she never mentioned we were so deeply in love. Bill has probably long since figured that part out on his own. All he has to do is see the sorrow that never leaves my eyes to guess the reason why.

Crossing his arms across his chest, he says, "Jaynie, you should know before you talk to Mandy that she hasn't heard a word from Flynn."

"I figured as much," I say, which is true. "I still want to talk to her. We have a lot of catching up to do."

Bill then apologizes. "I wasn't trying to question your motives. I figured you'd want to talk to Mandy eventually. I just didn't want you getting your hopes up, is all."

It's weird to have a friend outside of the ones I had up at the

Lowry house. But it's in that moment I realize Bill is more than an employer and a landlord. He's also my friend, and he's looking out for me.

Softly, I say, "I appreciate that, Bill. Really, I do."

He nods. "Let me go grab my phone and get you Mandy's number."

An hour later, up in my bed, wrapped up in the same fuzzy blanket Bill gave me the night I arrived, I scroll to the newly entered number for Mandy and hit *call*.

Chapter Thirty-Nine

Flynn

I work, I sleep, and I eat. I don't bother making friends. My circle of friends—my *family*—is dispersed to God knows where. And I'm not ever allowed to contact them. *Fuck.*

I assume Jaynie is in Lawrence, making a new life for herself. How ironic that she's the one who jumped in the water, but it's me who is drowning, sinking in a life of nothingness.

I don't dare try to dig up any info on Jaynie, for fear of a reprisal from Mrs. Lowry. Eyes and ears are everywhere in Forsaken. People are waiting to report back, for money I'm sure. I can't research where the twins might be, and I definitely can't go find Mandy. I'm sure a maneuver like that would be reported back to Crafty Lo pronto. And she has those bloody scissors.

My throat constricts, and I mutter what I feel, "Fuck my life."

The next morning, for some unknown reason, I start up a conversation with the guy next to me. "Shit, it's colder than a witch's tit today," I say.

It's still dark, with sub-zero temperatures. There's a foot of snow on the ground and more on the way. I am waiting out in front of the job center, with the one guy as desperate as I am. I know from talking with him once or twice that his name is Crick. He's skinny as fuck and kind of squirrely-looking, but he seems like a decent-enough dude. Doesn't ask a lot of questions, which I like. Guess it's because Crick is dealing with his own demons. He's an ex-meth addict, I've heard, and he's trying to stay clean.

I assume he didn't hear my comment on the weather, seeing as he's still turned away, staring down the road. We're waiting for the rusty maroon van that picks up workers with no transportation, and then shuttles them to the construction site. Usually there are a few more of us standing around, but not today. No one wants to work in this shit, but some of us have to.

Crick turns to me, smiling a missing-tooth grin. He lights up a smoke and flicks the match down to the slushy snow on the salted sidewalk.

"You ain't just singing a song," he says, at last. I should have remembered from our few short convos that sometimes it takes him awhile to reply.

"Witch's tit, eh?" he continues. "You come up with that one on your own?"

Crick is a trip. I've noticed he likes to make up little sayings on his own. Usually they're messed up versions of existing ones. Guess he thinks I like to do the same.

I shake my head and laugh. "No. I'm not as creative as you. That one was something my dad used to say. But he didn't come up with it, either."

Crick gives me a good, solid once-over. He exhales a wispy plume of smoke. "Used to, huh? Your pops dead or something? That why you out on your own?"

"No, he's not dead." I look down and kick at a hunk of ice. "He's in prison."

Crick lets out a low whistle, but doesn't ask what happened to land him there. Not that I'd tell him. Though, maybe I would. Keeping shit bottled up inside is starting to wear on me. I have no one to talk with anymore. And I find the longer I go without, the more I crave human connection.

That's why when Crick offers me a cigarette, I take it.

"Thanks, man," I mumble from around the filter pressed between my lips.

I light up and, dropping my match next to his, I inhale deeply. The smoke burns my frozen lungs, but it makes me feel more alert right away.

When I start to cough, Crick says, "Hey, maybe I shouldn't have given you one. Don't wanna get you started on a bad habit."

"Nah," I assure him, taking another drag that doesn't make me choke. "I quit a while back, but I'm no newbie to this game."

"Still"—the cherry tip of his cigarette glows red as he inhales deeply, then exhales—"I hate to be the one pushing you back down the slide of death."

Laughing, I pat him on the back. "Don't worry, Crick. I don't have much to live for anyway. I did, once upon a time, but not anymore."

And with that, I take another drag.

Chapter Forty

Jaynie

"Hello?"

Hearing Mandy's voice all these months later brings me to tears. "Mandy," I choke out. "It's me, Jaynie."

"Jaynie! I was wondering when you'd get around to calling." Her voice is warm, not angry in the least.

"I'm sorry. I am so sorry." I try to explain, "I haven't been myself lately, Mandy. I'm in Lawrence now and… Wait, you know all this from Bill, right?"

"I do," she says softly. "And I know why you haven't been yourself lately. Flynn never showed up, did he?"

Of course Bill would have told her all this.

"Oh, Mandy, he hasn't, and I don't think he's going to." The tears start to flow. "I am so damn worried. Do you think he's okay?" I can't shut up now that I've started. "Maybe Flynn just moved on with his life, right? I'd rather it'd be something like that than some horrible alternative explanation. I'd die if something bad happened to him."

"Jaynie," Mandy says. "Calm down for a sec, okay?"

Mandy is as patient as always. That makes me happy and sad, all at the same time. But I do feel calmer just talking with her. "I wish you were here," I murmur.

"I'd give you a hug if I were," she replies.

I choke up again. "I miss you so much. I try not to think about it much—I'll go crazy, if I do—but I miss everyone like you wouldn't believe. We were a family, you know."

"I know, sweetie. I know."

She lets me cry it out, and I hear her sobbing once or twice herself. When we pull ourselves together, we talk. Oh, do we talk. I could stay on the phone all night with Mandy, and I just about do.

I tell her stuff she probably already knows—details about my job, and how much I love my little room above the deli. And she tells me about her and Josh and their new place. They went with subsidized housing, just like they planned, but they got lucky—they're in a house, not an apartment.

"It's tiny," Mandy says. "But even so, there are two bedrooms and a back yard."

"Cody and Callie will love that," I say. "Bill told me you're still planning on fostering them."

"The application is in," she replies proudly. "Though there won't be any word till we finish our parenting classes. Plus, there's a home inspection coming up. Gotta pass that, too."

"I'm sure you'll pass everything with flying colors. The twins need to be with you, Mandy. If there's one thing that makes sense in this world, it's that."

"From your mouth to God's ears," Mandy replies. And then, after a pause, "Damn, Jaynie, it feels good to share this stuff with you."

"It really does," I agree. "It's like old times."

"It is."

When the subject turns to Flynn again, Mandy says, "I'm not

going to ask what happened that night, Jaynie. But, I should tell you I've heard some things."

"What kind of things?" I cautiously inquire.

"Just some rumblings from people Josh and I know who've passed through Forsaken."

I can't even speak, and my throat closes when Mandy says gently, "Josh did hear something interesting the other day, but I can't verify anything. So, if I tell you, you have to promise you won't get all worked up."

"What is it?" I whisper.

"It's about Flynn."

"Mandy, please, I can't make any promises. Please, just tell me."

"Okay, okay." She takes a breath. "We're pretty sure Flynn is still in Forsaken."

Time stops. Flynn is alive. Everything in my world suddenly seems brighter. I'm beyond happy he's okay, but why isn't he here?

"God, Mandy, why would he stay in Forsaken?"

"I don't know, Jaynie."

"It doesn't make sense. What did Josh hear?"

"That Flynn works in construction. No one knows where he's living, but it's not up at Mrs. Lowry's place."

"Yeah," I mutter. "I wouldn't think so."

Mandy blows out a breath. "You need to know the other stuff we've heard, too."

"Okay." I can't stop my heart from racing.

"Jaynie, there are rumors of an accident up in the craft barn. Uh, rumors about the night you left. Word is Allison tripped and fell onto something sharp. She cut up her abdomen, pretty nasty stuff. And Flynn was supposedly hurt that night, too."

My heart switches from racing to pounding uncontrollably. "Flynn was never hurt."

Mandy doesn't ask how I would know that, or why I would think it. She just goes on. "He *was* hurt, Jaynie, along with Allison. He suffered a head injury"—*what??*—"and was in the hospital for a few days. Mrs. Lowry visited him a couple of times. She was there when he was discharged."

Oh my God, something must have happened to Flynn when he went back to the house.

I close my eyes. I never should have jumped. All this time and I had no idea Flynn was hurt. It had to have been Mrs. Lowry who hurt him. Allison was far too wounded to inflict damage on anyone. Crafty Lo must have come home early from her business trip. She would've found her daughter on the floor. And then, when Flynn went back…

This explains a lot. Maybe Flynn can't remember anything. "Do you think Flynn has amnesia?" I ask Mandy.

"I don't think so, sweetie. It sounds like he's fine."

"But, why doesn't he come to Lawrence? Why stay in a place he couldn't wait to get away from?"

"That's just it, Jaynie. I think Mrs. Lowry is holding something over him."

"Like the truth," I whisper.

It all comes together. "Oh, hell, we'll never be together. Mrs. Lowry will keep us apart forever."

"Um, maybe not," Mandy cryptically replies.

"Mandy?" I prompt when she falls silent. "If you know something you have to tell me."

"Okay." She clears her throat. "Word is, Mrs. Lowry is under some kind of investigation."

"No way. Finally."

"Right? It's about damn time, that's what I've been telling Josh. Anyway, she's not allowed to foster any kids until the findings come in."

"That's great news."

"It is," Mandy agrees.

We fall silent. I think of how much pain could have been avoided had this investigation commenced sooner, and I suspect Mandy is thinking the same thing.

"Hey," she says, at last. "I'll keep digging around for info on Flynn. We'll get to the bottom of this."

"Thank you, Mandy."

"I'll let you know the second I find out something more concrete."

"Hey," I say, "do you think in the meantime you could get a message to Flynn, a message from me?" My tone is hopeful. "Maybe it could be delivered through one of your or Josh's contacts?"

"I can't promise anything, Jaynie, but we sure can try. What's the message?"

"Tell Flynn I'll wait for him. Tell him no matter how long it takes, I will *be here*. I'll stay in Lawrence forever, if it means seeing him again."

Chapter Forty-One

Flynn

One day, on my way to the job center, some strange homeless dude tries to talk to me. He grabs my arm and tells me he has a message for me from someone I care about.

I wrench away from his grasp and walk on. "Yeah, right," I toss out over my shoulder.

The encounter haunts me for the rest of the day, though. What if the guy wasn't bullshitting?

On my way home from work, I look for him, but he's long gone. I don't see him in the days after, either. But I can't stop wondering what his message might've been.

Christmas comes and goes.

New Year's passes by, too.

January turns out to be colder than December, but that's fine with me. We're given a pay differential for working in the bitter weather. A lot of guys can't hang and end up quitting. I put up with the cold, work as hard as I can, and save money.

For what, I don't know. Maybe I'm still hoping there's a future down the road with Jaynie.

One freezing-cold morning, before heading to the job center to wait for a ride, I stop by a diner and buy two coffees to go—one for me and one for Crick. This has become our routine. I bring the coffees, and he brings the smokes.

I refuse to buy any cigarettes of my own. That way I can go on lying to myself that I haven't really started smoking again. I know Jaynie would be disappointed if she knew I'd thrown all those cig-free months away.

In the diner, someone has left a newspaper open on the counter. I pick it up. "Holy hell," I mumble as a headline midway down the page catches my eye.

Mrs. Lauren Lowry and Daughter Arrested on Suspicion of Embezzlement and Fraud.

"Excuse me, sir, would you like to purchase that newspaper with your coffees?" an annoyed waitress asks. She slides my two already-paid-for cups of java across the counter.

"It looks like someone left this one,"—I wave the paper around as I snatch up the coffees—"so let's just pretend it was mine, and I'll be on my way."

"Sure, whatever," she mutters, turning away.

Gotta love non-morning people, right? Hell, with the news story I'm scanning as I walk out the door—paper held up high in front of my face—I determine I pretty much love everyone right now.

Mrs. Lowry and Allison are about to go to jail for a long, long time. *How's that for karma?* All those business trips Mrs. Lowry took were apparently part of her scam. She was taking money from investors she'd conned, and then using it all on herself. Half those trips were lavish vacations. Crafty Lo soaking up sun on a beach, while we were all suffering. *Bitch.*

As for Allison, she was cashing checks from the state that were made out to her mom the whole time her mom was away. She is going down, too. *Yes!*

Happy in a way I've not known for a long time, I practically run to the job center so I can give Crick his drink before it gets cold.

"What's got you in such a good mood this morning?" he asks when I hand him his coffee with two creams and five sugars, smiling broadly.

"Oh, man, I never mentioned anything before, but there's this girl, this girl I love like nothing else—"

"Wait, you have a girlfriend?" Crick takes a sip of his coffee and shakes his head. "You kids nowadays, keeping everything all to yourself. It ain't good for you, you know. I'm telling you, you gotta learn to share."

"I'm sharing now," I reply, exasperated, but not really. "Would you shut it and listen for a minute?"

"Sure, sure." He waves his hand. "Go on."

Chuckling, I continue. "Anyway, this girl, her name is Jaynie. She's been waiting for me in another town. I couldn't even *think* about going to her before today—"

"Why?" Crick interrupts.

"Long story. But the good news is I found out something this morning that's giving me hope again. I think we may have a chance, after all."

"Good for you, kid. Love, especially young love, sure is something special." Crick holds up his coffee and winks. "Here's to you and your lady friend reuniting real soon."

I tap my paper cup to his. "I'll drink to that."

"Too bad we don't have some good whiskey," Crick laments. "We could make it a real toast, you know. Not to mention, it'd warm us up a bit."

Crick makes a show of shivering, but I assure him, "This is good enough."

"Yeah, guess it's gonna have to be."

I lean back against the wall of the job center, not a care in the world. I don't even mind when the cold frostiness from the brick exterior starts to seep through my worn coat and hoodie. Smiling, I flip open the paper and re-read the article detailing at least a dozen crimes against Crafty Lo and Allison.

I can tell Crick is reading the story over my shoulder. And sure enough, he asks, "You and your girl getting the go-ahead to be together got anything to do with that rich bitch on the mountaintop getting shut down?"

Looking over at him, I smile. "Maybe, Crick, maybe so."

He shrugs. "No matter what, kid, don't wait too long. You listen to old Crick now. I've got the knowledge." He taps his temple, and I chuckle. "You can't let a good love get away, especially since that shit only comes around a couple times in a lifetime."

Laughing, I say, "I think it's 'once in a lifetime,' man."

"Well, hell, that makes it even better. Don't let her go, kid."

"I don't intend to," I say. "I don't intend to, my friend."

Chapter Forty-Two

Jaynie

Mandy can't get my message to Flynn, but not for lack of trying. She and Josh enlist a homeless man from Morgantown. The guy is an old pal of Josh's. He's planning on doing some traveling, which includes passing through Forsaken.

Homeless guy tries, but Flynn blows him off. *Typical Flynn.*

I ask Mandy if Josh's friend can try again, but she informs me he's moved on.

"Damn," I say when we next chat on the phone. "There has to be another way."

"I don't know, Jaynie," Mandy replies. "Word is Flynn hangs out with one dude and one dude only. Otherwise, he keeps to himself on the construction site."

It's January, and I'm hanging inside the deli since it's much too cold to do anything outside. My shift is done for the day, and I'm munching on a second sandwich for lunch. It's nice, not starving. I'm in the back room, readying to log on to Bill's computer.

Deviated from our conversation for a sec, I say to Mandy, "Time to check the latest news in Forsaken."

"I'm sure there's nothing happening in that shitty town, same as always," Mandy replies. "I don't know why you even bother."

I don't share with her that I still worry about blowback from the night I attacked Allison. Under investigation or not, as long as Mrs. Lowry holds sway over Forsaken, I will continue to fear her. Flynn and I could go down at any time.

Returning to the subject of Flynn, I ask Mandy, "Does Josh know anyone else who could possibly get my message to that guy Flynn hangs out with?"

"Doubt it," Mandy says. "The guy is a real loner, like Flynn is now. Supposedly, he's some old ex-meth addict, half off his rocker. Not exactly Mr. Social, if you know what I mean."

"But Flynn likes him." I smile to myself. "I'm not surprised. Leave it to Flynn to befriend the one guy who has no friends."

I feel a swell of emotion. Flynn is still such a good guy. He hasn't lost hope in humanity, despite everything.

I finish my sandwich and continue scrolling through news stories. Mandy, meanwhile, suppresses a yawn.

"Tired?" I ask.

"Very."

Mandy has been working double and triple shifts to save money for when the twins arrive. Word is the couple they currently reside with plan to move to another state any day now. Cody and Callie would normally be thrown back in the system, but now they have a high likelihood of being placed with Josh and Mandy. In the state's eyes, a good placement is far preferable than sending the kids to a group home. And Mandy and Josh's place is better than good. They've completed all the necessary classes and recently passed the required home inspection. Everything is set.

Just as Mandy is telling me she's going to get off the phone so she can take a nap, I come across a news story that makes me say, "Wait, don't go yet."

"Why? What's wrong?"

"Nothing is wrong," I reply. "In fact, everything may have just turned totally right."

I can't believe what I am reading. But there it is, in black and white. "Mrs. Lowry and Allison were arrested last night, Mandy."

"*What?*"

I read the story out loud to her. She grabs her tablet, logs in, and together we go over the embezzlement charges, the fraud charges. Basically, all the things that promise to put our two least favorite people away for a long, long time.

"This is unbelievable," I say. "You mentioned Mrs. Lowry was under investigation, but this is way bigger."

"It sure is," Mandy agrees.

"You know what this means, then?"

"I sure do," she replies, her voice no longer the least bit sleepy-sounding. "If Mrs. Lowry was holding something over Flynn, it's over now."

"That's right," I agree, smiling ear-to-ear. "Flynn is free to come to Lawrence."

Chapter Forty-Three

Flynn

I am free to leave Forsaken. But that freedom feels surreal. The concept of true freedom is so overwhelming that I become shackled by indecision.

When should I leave? How will I get there? Can someone drive me to Lawrence? Is there a bus that goes in that direction?

Crick informs me there *is* a bus to Lawrence. It leaves every evening, and, ironically, stops smack dab in front of the park. That's right, the same park I was supposed to swim to months ago.

I go to the bus stop every day, but never quite get to the point of hopping on. Something holds me back, but I can't put my finger on what it could be. Mrs. Lowry divulging what she knows about that fateful night in October is no longer a concern. No one would believe her now, even if she did decide to tell. Her once-good name is mud these days, her reputation sullied beyond repair. She and Allison both pled guilty to reduced sentences, but they're still going to prison for a *very* long time.

So, yeah, they're not why I'm staying.

I guess I remain in Forsaken in the hopes of building my courage. I mean, shit, what if Jaynie has moved on with her life?

And there is this, my real worry. I still love Jaynie, but what if she's given up on me?

In the end, I decide *fuck it, she's still my girl and I can convince her to give me a second chance.*

The next day, I give my notice at the job center. "Just finish out this week," the lady at the center says.

"I can do that," I tell her.

On Friday night, with my last work week over, I head out to a local bar with Crick for a send-off drink. I'm underage, but no one questions me when I walk in with my friend. I know I look older than eighteen these days. Eating regularly has made me grow taller. Shit, I'm coming up on six-one now. And working construction has bulked me up. Muscles once long and lean are now bulging masses.

As Crick and I sit down at the bar, a burly bartender, who looks like a lumberjack, asks us what we want.

"Two drafts and couple shots of whiskey," Crick says. "Make it the good stuff, too, for the whiskey. Not that cheap garbage that'll give you the shits the next day."

Lumberjack-bartender laughs. "No problem."

When the drinks arrive, Crick takes a long pull from his beer, but I pretty much just stare down into mine.

"Listen up, kid," Crick says, setting his mug back down on the bar. "We gotta have a talk."

"Okay."

Crick lights up a cigarette, holds the box out to me. "You want one?"

I want one, but I decline. "No, I quit."

Crick shrugs and stuffs the box back into the pocket of his flannel jacket.

After taking a couple of quick drags, he squints over at me. "Your girl don't like you smokin', huh? That why you giving it up?"

Still staring down at my mug of untouched beer, I say, "Yeah, Jaynie doesn't like me smoking. She's the one who got me to quit the first time."

Exhaling, he says, "Must be a special lady."

"She is."

I finally take a drink of my beer. The shots, though, remain untouched on the bar, mine and Crick's both. It's like we're holding out, waiting for something worthwhile to drink to.

Crick reaches for a plastic ashtray, and as he's stubbing out his butt, he says, "So, can I ask you something, Flynn?"

"Sure."

"Why are you still in this shithole town? You could've left days ago."

"I'm leaving tomorrow," I say, defensive.

"So you say."

"I am, Crick, I am."

Peering over at me, he asks, "What's been keeping you here? Like, be straight with me. What's the real issue?"

"I don't know," I admit. "I guess I'm just worried."

"Yeah?" He lights another cigarette. "Worried about what?"

I'm suddenly thirsty, my throat parched as I confront my fears head-on. I down my beer in three seconds flat, and smacking the mug down on the bar, I signal the bartender for another. Dealing with this shit in my head, the crap holding me back, is going to require a little liquid courage.

Halfway through my second beer, I tell Crick the truth. "What if Jaynie's moved on, man? What if she found someone else, someone better? I mean, look at me." I gesture to my old jeans and flannel shirt, my beat-up winter coat hanging over the back of the chair. "It's not like I have a lot to offer her. I wouldn't even blame her if she didn't want me anymore."

Crick lights up what must be his fourth smoke, and shit, I almost ask him for one. But no, I need to stay strong. Just in case I'm wrong about Jaynie, and she does still want my sorry ass.

"Listen up, kid, and listen good." He flicks an ash to the tray and misses. "What you told me you had with this girl sounds like it was true love."

"It is." I sigh. "Or it was."

"So," Crick slurs. He's halfway to drunk, but he's been known to impart some of his best wisdom in this state. I listen closely as he says, "True love doesn't just up and die. True love stands the test of time, man. You better get on that bus tomorrow. Go find this Jaynie and make her yours again. Live your life, Flynn." His voice becomes more serious. "You've been given a second chance, and those don't come around too much. Take it from me, kid. Don't blow it."

I shake my head and chuckle. "Crick, I think that's the wisest shit I've ever heard you spout."

He holds up a shot, one of the ones we've yet to touch. "Well, I got one more. Here's to you and your girl, Flynn. May you find everlasting happiness."

I tap my shot to his. "I'll drink to that."

And then I do.

Chapter Forty-Four

Jaynie

a whole week passes, and still, no Flynn.

"Give him time, Jaynie," Mandy tells me. "He's a guy, and guys need to do things on their own schedule. Trust me, he'll be in Lawrence soon enough."

"I hope you're right," I reply, worried that Flynn has moved on.

I try not to bug Mandy too much, especially when she gets word from the state that the twins could be placed with her any day now. I'm as excited as she is when I hear *that* update.

"First thing I plan to do is figure out a way to come up and visit you guys," I tell her the day she gets the good news.

"Bill will bring you," she assures me.

And sure enough, Saturday morning, I am awoken by Bill's frantic knocking on my apartment door.

"Jaynie, Jaynie, it's me, Bill. Are you awake in there?"

I jump out of bed and open the door. "What's wrong?" I ask, half-asleep still.

Tomorrow's Lies

"Nothing is wrong, nothing at all." Bill smiles widely. "In fact, everything is good. Mandy called." I squeal, but he ignores me. "She's picking up Cody and Callie *this morning*."

"Holy hell, no way!" I start bouncing up and down on my toes.

"It's true," he says, chuckling at my enthusiasm. "If you're up for it, we can drive up to Morgantown and see them this afternoon."

"Really, Bill?"

"Yes, Jaynie, really."

I'm about to sprint out to the hall—I am *that* ready to roll—but then I glance down at my bummy sleep tee and PJ bottoms.

"Guess I should change, huh?" I say sheepishly.

Bill laughs. "Probably a good idea."

"Okay, give me a few minutes to shower and dress. I'll be quick." This is one of those times you wish you could snap your fingers and be ready instantly.

But, alas, Bill doesn't mind. "Take your time, Jaynie. The twins aren't going anywhere. They have a permanent home now, with Mandy and Josh."

"Yes, they do." I am so happy I could cry. "They sure do."

When I walk through the front door and into the modest living room at Mandy and Josh's place, two little bodies slam into me.

Overwhelmed and overjoyed, I drop to my knees and hold onto Callie and Cody like my life depends on it. Maybe it does. I certainly feel renewed by these two kids I love and haven't seen in what feels like forever.

"God, you even smell the same," I murmur into Callie's hair, then Cody's. I squeeze them tightly to me. "I don't think I can let you go."

"Then no let us go," Cody says.

"Okay, I won't."

We all squeeze together in a huddle of hugs.

"We missed you so much," Callie whispers.

"I missed you, too, babies."

"I not a baby," Cody declares as he leans back, breaking our snug little huddle.

"I know you're not a baby, sweetheart."

We break into peals of laughter, and oh, how I've missed these kids. "I love you both so much," I tell them.

I am told I'm loved back, and then the kids smother me in more hugs and kisses.

Slowly, one beat at a time, my heart begins to mend from all the sorrow of the past few months.

When we finally rock back on our heels, I peer at Cody and Callie with bleary eyes. At least my tears are happy ones this time.

Mandy is in the doorway of what looks like the kitchen. She motions for Bill to join her to give me some alone time with the twins.

"You've both grown so much," I say as Bill walks around us. "Look at you two." I brush back a lock of Cody's raven hair. "Your hair has grown again, and you're at least two inches taller."

"I grow a lot all over," he agrees.

Callie chimes in with, "I grew a lot, too, Jaynie."

And she has, but not as much as her brother. "You're both so big that you're lucky I recognized you," I tease.

"You'll always know us," Callie says. "Because you love us."

"Yeah," I sigh. "I sure do love you."

The twins look great. I'm glad they thrived with the couple they were with. They'll do even better with Mandy. It saddens me to think the twins weren't growing much at the Lowry house because they were so overworked and malnourished. The nightmare seems further away each day, but it's always there, directly below the surface. You don't walk away from what we went through unscathed.

Like Callie knows what I'm thinking, she asks, "How'd you get away?"

I could make up a tale, but the twins deserve the truth. "I ran."

Cody tilts his head and asks, "Flynnie run with you?"

"No, sweetie, he couldn't." *Crap, wrong thing to say.*

And sure enough, the next question out of Cody's mouth is, "Why he couldn't run with you?"

"Um…" I glance toward the kitchen in the hopes of garnering Mandy's attention. But her back is turned. I am on my own with this one.

"He kind of got out in a different way," I say.

Cody points to the closed front door. "Flynnie no with you, is he?"

"No, sweetheart, he's not."

His face falls. "He no want to come see me?"

"Oh, no, honey. It's nothing like that." I place my hands on his cheeks and wipe away the tears he sheds, tears that may as well be my own. "Flynn is busy working today," I fib, though I wonder if it's true. Flynn could be working at his job since he's obviously staying in Forsaken. And some construction jobs require Saturday laboring, right?

"Flynnie come another time and see me?" Cody presses.

His eyes meet mine, and I fear he'll see the truth. That Flynn may be making the choice to never see any of us ever again.

Thankfully, Mandy swoops in to save the day. "Hey, you guys, guess what Josh got for you?"

Two sets of matching curious eyes turn her way. "What?" Callie asks.

Mandy holds up an older-version PlayStation game. The twins don't know—or care—it's not the latest version. They're appreciative of any gift given.

"Ooh, fun. We play it now?" Cody wants to know.

A young man with wavy blond hair and a great smile walks in through the back door, which leads right into the living room on the opposite side from the front door area where I'm standing.

As he kicks off his heavy boots, Mandy introduces him to me and Bill. "Hey, guys, this is Josh."

Josh turns out to be as nice as Mandy described him. He heads upstairs with the kids to set up their new video game in their bedroom, and when he comes back down to the living room, he asks if anyone is hungry.

"I was setting up the grill when I was outside," he says, gesturing to the door he came in earlier. "I can cook up some burgers and dogs for everyone, if you want?"

"I could go for a burger," Bill says.

"Sounds great," I reply.

Bill offers to help Josh grill, and he accepts.

With the guys out in the back yard and the kids upstairs, Mandy and I have our first chance to talk alone.

"I'm so happy for you," I say to Mandy as we sit down on the sofa. "You did what you planned."

"Yeah, I did." She sighs, contented. "I can't believe it actually all worked out. Next step is adopting them."

"It'll happen," I say.

The twins trundle back down to the living room, looking sheepish, and Mandy wants to know, "Is everything okay?"

"Yeah," Callie replies. "It's just…we like the games and all, but can we go play outside?"

It's February, but a mild day. It's like the sun came out and the temperature warmed up just for Cody and Callie.

"Sure," Mandy replies, smiling. "Have at it."

As the kids head to the yard, I glance out the window above the sofa that offers a view of the back of the house. There's an old swing set in one corner, but it looks safe. The twins don't care either way, they run to it. While Cody and Callie take turns going down the slide, Bill and Josh turn to watch them. After a few seconds, their attention returns to the grill, where they talk and laugh and tend to the burgers and hot dogs smoking.

"This is so perfect," I say, turning back to Mandy.

She nudges me. "It is, but one thing is missing."

"What do you mean?"

"Next time you visit, I expect Flynn to be with you."

"Oh, Mandy." I place my head in my hands, stricken. "I don't know if that's ever going to happen. It's been over a week and I haven't heard a word from him. Maybe he's staying in Forsaken. Maybe he found another girl."

"Jaynie," she scolds. "Come on."

I peer over at her. "Seriously, Mandy, something is up."

"I don't think it's any of those things," she says. "Flynn just needed some time."

"I don't know, Mandy," I maintain.

But then I reconsider when she says, "Josh heard Flynn quit his job."

I perk up considerably. "He did?"

"Yep, and you know what that means."

"He's finally coming to Lawrence?"

"No, Flynn's not just coming to Lawrence, Jaynie." She points at me. "He's coming home to you."

Chapter Forty-Five

Flynn

I get off the bus in Lawrence, a duffel bag slung over one shoulder. That one bag holds everything to my name.

It's early evening, but dark already, as I trudge toward the park. For winter, the day's not too bad. Mild temperatures have melted the snow, but the ground remains frozen. Leftover fall leaves, ones that probably fell around the last time I saw Jaynie, crunch and crackle beneath my heavy work boots.

Suddenly, a cold breeze out of nowhere rattles the bare trees. I hitch my coat collar up around my jaw. The day may have been mild, but the night promises winter's return. My face feels cold since I shaved this morning for the first time in days. Not that I kept a heavy beard, but I was used to some scruff.

No worries, I want to look good for Jaynie. I bought some new jeans, and a new flannel shirt that I'm wearing fitted over a thermal. I stopped at splurging on a new hoodie and coat, though. I'd rather save the money to use on my new life with Jaynie.

Tomorrow's Lies

In the park, I search for the old oak. I locate it right away, shimmy up, and scoop the locker key from the carved out nook Mandy always talked about.

I try out the key, just to see what would've been waiting for me in the locker had I had a chance to follow Jaynie back in October. I discover the backpack is filled with clothes for me. I put it back for now. One bag is enough to lug around.

I'm stalling, I know it. My nerves are on end.

Taking a deep breath that allows the incoming cold air to clear my head, I finally start for the deli.

The whole while, my heart is racing like crazy. Now that I'm really here, I'm not sure what to say when I see Jaynie. *Hey, I finally made it* sounds lame. I guess I could start with the truth and hope she understands.

The deli is dark when I spot it from across the road. It's apparently closed for the day. Shit, it's a Saturday. You'd think it would be a big day for business. Maybe something came up. *Damn, I hope everything is okay.*

It's then I realize how disconnected I've become. I stopped living—like, really living—these past few months. I couldn't allow myself to think too much of Jaynie...or Mandy...or Cody and Callie. But that didn't mean I ever forgot about any one of them.

Crouching down in front of an old building directly across the street from the deli, I decide to wait it out. Where else do I have to go?

I lean back against the brick façade. I'll stay here all night if it means I'll get a chance to lay my eyes on Jaynie.

Hanging out like this makes me think of Crick. *Shit, I wish I had some cigarettes to pass the time.* But no, check that. Having none is for the best. I'm a non-smoker once again.

A few cars pass, but the town is small and not busy. I crouch down after awhile and doze off, and when I wake up I find it is freezing.

Just as I'm standing and zipping up the hoodie inside my coat, a car pulls up and parks in front of the deli.

"Fuck."

My nerves have me all over the place.

And then…I see Jaynie. Everything stops—time, space, the world we live in. I forget to breathe even, as she steps from the car. Auburn hair, long and flowing, and pale skin I know is so soft.

I want to run across the street, grab Jaynie up in my arms, and kiss her. And I almost do. But then I see Bill Delmont. Or rather, I see the man I assume must be Bill. He slips from the driver's side and proceeds to walk Jaynie the rest of the way to the deli.

The place is clearly closed, as established, and it's kind of late to be opening now. So, I guess Jaynie lives upstairs in the room Mandy told us about.

I watch the two of them as they walk to the entrance, not knowing what my next move should be. *Do I call out, get Jaynie's attention?*

Bill fumbles with the key and Jaynie laughs when he almost drops it.

I don't know… Jaynie seems so comfortable with this guy. *Shit.* Maybe she *has* moved on with her life?

What if he hugs her next? What if he kisses her?

If I see Bill Delmont kissing my Jaynie—nice guy or not—I may fucking lose it.

I know then I just need to leave.

Hunching my shoulders, I slip around the side of the building, out of sight.

And then I take off at a run.

Chapter Forty-Six

Jaynie

Before Bill leaves me at the deli door, he takes out his key and says, "See you tomorrow. You have opening shift, yeah?"

I nod. "Yeah."

I then remind him I have my own key, but he insists on unlocking the deli door.

He almost drops his key, and we laugh. "It's been too long of a day," he says, sighing.

"It has been," I reply. "But it was really great, seeing everyone again and meeting Josh, finally."

Something in my heart tugs. The day was amazing, spending time with Mandy and the twins. But I can't pretend that one very important person was missing—Flynn.

Dammit, where is he? There's no reason for him to continue to stay away, not now. He quit his job, right? I sure hope Mandy is right about this one.

Bill turns to go, and I catch the briefest flash of a guy across the street. Something registers familiar about him.

I blink, and he's gone.

My tired self takes a minute to process and review.

Definitely a guy.

Tall, with broad shoulders.

A guy bundled up in a worn tan coat and navy hoodie. *Wait.* Bundled in a worn tan coat… Oh my God, I know that coat. And I know that guy.

"It was Flynn," I murmur.

"Jaynie, are you okay?" Bill eyes me curiously.

I look at him. "Uh…"

Maybe Bill made Flynn run. Maybe Flynn misunderstood our friendly interaction.

I assure Bill everything is fine and pretend I'm heading inside the deli. Bill goes to his car, and then drives away.

The second Bill is out of sight, I race across the street. It must be close to eleven by now. The moon is high in the sky, all round and bright, illuminating the night.

"Flynn," I call out as I head around the corner to the side of the building.

No one is there. No Flynn, nothing.

Damn. If Flynn is running, there's no way I can catch him.

Which way would he go, anyway? To the left and to the right is a straightaway, running in both directions. I look each way, but there's no sign of Flynn on either side. That leaves one option—straight ahead, into the park.

Flynn must have run to the park. But he can't get too far, the river will stop him. Unless Flynn plans to swim away, he has nowhere to go.

I race over to the park and begin to thread my way toward the riverbank. I walk along a narrow trail that's surrounded by small trees and scraggly brush. The branches are bare, but wiry and tangled.

They poke at me like bony fingers, making me glad I have on a heavy wool coat.

When I reach the trail's end, I scan the banks of the river.

And then…

I see him, a shadow in the night. "Flynn," I call out to the shimmery silhouette down by the water.

A brisk wind drowns out my voice, and Flynn doesn't hear me or turn around. He remains still, his back facing me. He's filled out a lot since I last saw him months ago. And that's when it hits me—all the time that has passed, all the days and weeks and months without him. I've moved from depressed to functional, but there's always been this hole, an absence only Flynn can fill.

Choking back a sob, I run to him. As I near the boy I loved and lost, he doesn't hear my footfalls. Between the wind and the fast, choppy river current, I'm able to sneak right up on him.

When I'm a mere few feet away, I skid to a stop. "How fitting that we reunite by the water," I say.

Flynn spins around, and all the weeks and months condense down to one day, and then one minute, and then now. There is only now as our eyes meet. There is no more past and no future.

Flynn smiles at me. "Hey, Jaynie."

I smile back at him. "Hey, Flynn."

We come together, a crushing of bodies. My hands find purchase in his hair. His hands go to my face. Our lips meet, and it hurts, this reuniting. But it also feels so, so good.

Tears fall.

I remember this love. And the gaping hole in my heart, the one that healed a tiny bit today when I was with the twins, stitches back up completely.

When Flynn and I break from our kiss, he presses his forehead to mine. Breaths intermingle, wispy plumes, a testament to life in the dead, wintry air.

"You made it," I whisper.

"I would've been along sooner, but, uh, I guess you could say something got in the way."

"You mean some*one*," I correct.

"Yeah, someone… Someone we're free of now."

I step back, but Flynn's hands remain at my waist. It's like he can't let go of me now that he has me again.

"Flynn, I know Mrs. Lowry was holding that night over you. You don't have to explain any of that."

"Jaynie—"

I cut him off. "Seriously, Flynn, we can talk about it later." The last thing I want is to have our reunion tainted with talk of that evil wench. "Can you tell me one thing, though?"

"Anything, babe. You can ask me anything."

"Why'd you run off when you saw me out in front of the deli?"

"A misunderstanding." His hands tighten possessively on either side of my waist. "I thought maybe you'd moved on."

I lean in and brush my lips over his. "You know that's silly, right?"

He nods. "I do now."

I tell him what's in my heart. "It's *always* going to be you, Flynn O'Neill. Never anyone else. You came into my life for a reason. You healed me in the past, and you're healing me right now. You believe me, right?"

He shrugs.

"My life's been empty without you," I whisper. "I've been lost."

He lets out a choked laugh, or maybe it's a sob. "You don't even want to know what it's been like for me, living without you."

"Tell me," I say.

"I've been merely existing, Jaynie. One day blending into the next. The color in my world was gone without you in it. You were always the brightness, Jaynie. You made my world alive."

"I can make it alive again," I promise.

"You already have."

"So, you're staying?"

He smiles. "Wherever you are, Jaynie, that's where my home will always be."

I press my lips to his once more, salty and sweet. "Then let's go home, Flynn."

Chapter Forty-Seven

Flynn

Jaynie's room above the deli is small, but it's nice. Sure beats the abandoned warehouse basement I was living in for months.

What I told Jaynie down by the river was true. What I was doing in Forsaken wasn't living.

But now it feels like my life has begun anew.

I kick off my boots and shrug out of my coat and hoodie so Jaynie can place them over the back of a chair. When she takes off her own coat, I immediately notice she's no longer emaciated.

"You look good," I tell her as I scan over curves showcased by a tight brown sweater and jeans.

She slips off her winter boots and places them by the door. "Thank you, Flynn," she says shyly.

I walk over to her. Cupping her chin, I urge her to look up at me. When she complies, I say, "I've missed you so much."

Our eyes meet, lust and longing hanging in the air. But there is also hesitancy. This feels more real than down by the river. We're in a cozy, warm room, with a bed nearby. There's nothing to stop us from ripping off our clothes and ravaging one another.

Jaynie steps away. "Uh, this feels funny."

I don't lie. "It does."

She sits down on the edge of the bed. "Maybe we should just talk for a while."

I raise a brow. "Like, get re-acquainted."

She blows out a breath. "It's not that I don't know you, Flynn. But I have no idea what your life's been like the past few months. I feel like we shared so much all the time at Mrs. Lowry's. And then everything just…ended."

I step over to the bed. "I know, Jaynie." Gesturing to a spot next to her, I ask, "Is it okay if I sit down?"

"Yes." She shakes her head and laughs softly. "This is crazy. Just sit, Flynn."

I do. And we begin to talk in earnest. I tell her about my job, where I lived, and about Crick.

"He sounds a little out there," she says.

"He is kind of crazy, but in a good way." Sighing, I add, "He was my only friend. The one person I allowed myself to get close to."

"Do you think you'll ever see him again?"

Shrugging, I say, "I don't know. I have no plans to ever go back to Forsaken, I can tell you that much."

"Maybe he could come here to visit?"

I scrub my hand down my face. "Yeah, I don't know. Maybe, I guess. Though Crick is kind of a Forsaken-type of guy."

"Huh." She knows what I mean.

Jaynie scoots back on the bed and leans up against the pillows. She then indicates I should do the same.

As we both get more comfortable, she says quietly, "I don't think I can ever go back to that town."

"I agree. Too many bad memories."

Jaynie leans her head on my shoulder and says, "Let's not think about any of that right now."

There's so much to talk about, but I agree, for now, to talk about other things. The subject is changed, and Jaynie tells me of her visit to Mandy's place in Morgantown. Apparently, the twins are living with Mandy and Josh, as of this morning.

"Wow, that's amazing." To say I'm elated would be an understatement. "I always knew if anyone could make it happen, it'd be Mandy."

Jaynie touches her wooly-socked foot to mine. "Cody asked about you, Flynn."

"He did?" A lump forms in my throat as I finally admit to myself how very much I've missed the twins, especially Cody.

It takes me a minute to pull myself together. Even then all I can get out is a ragged, "Cody…"

"He wants to see you," Jaynie says.

"Shit, I'd drive up tomorrow, Jaynie, but there's one little problem. No car."

"Oh, and I forgot." She makes a face. "Not having a driver's license could be a problem, too."

"Actually, I got one of those."

She peers over at me, brow furrowed. "How'd that happen?"

I shrug. "I had to drive machinery and trucks at the site, so I got the hang of it pretty quickly. Then, the foreman took me over to the driver's license center one afternoon, had me take the test. He wanted me official so nothing could come back on him."

"Oh." She nods. "Well then, I bet we could borrow Bill's car for an afternoon."

"You think he'd really go for that?" I ask skeptically.

But Jaynie insists, "He's a really good guy, Flynn. I'm sure he wouldn't mind."

"Good. Then I guess it's a plan."

Tomorrow's Lies

Fuck, I can't wait to see Cody…and Callie…and Mandy. I sit there and smile, like a fool, for a good solid minute. But then I remember there's something else I need to address, something more practical.

"Hey," I say to Jaynie. "Not to overwhelm the guy with requests the first day I meet him, but do you think Bill is still up for giving me a job?"

Playfully, she nudges me with an elbow and says, "I think so. But, don't worry, even if he's hesitant, I'll put in a good word for you."

She's teasing, of course, but it gets us to laugh. We then spend the next few minutes joking around, like old times. We somehow end up in a tickle battle, or maybe I instigate one on purpose, just to remind Jaynie of the good times in our past. Oh, and it's a sneaky way to get close to her.

And as fate would have it, just like that special day so long ago, up in our secret spot, the day I first kissed Jaynie, she once again ends up pinned under me.

"Okay, okay," she cries out, tears rolling down her cheeks from laughing so hard. "I give up. You are, without question, the undisputed tickle champion."

"Not that this was ever about tickling," I say softly, my breaths coming faster and faster. "I was only looking for a way to get close to you."

"Flynn." She peers up at me, a tinge of sorrow in her green eyes. "You *are* close to me. You're in my soul. God," she sighs. "We've been through so much together."

We haven't talked at all about that night, or all that led up to it. I know she still feels the loss of our baby, even though it was only here with us for what felt like a minute. I think about what we lost from time to time, but I know it's not the same as it is for her.

"Do you want to talk about it?" I whisper.

"No," she says, shaking her head. "Not tonight. I think all I really want right now is for you to hold me."

We both know she means more.

I roll off her. As I slip out of my jeans, flannel shirt, and thermal, Jaynie watches me. After a minute, she tugs her brown sweater over her head and snaps off her bra. When her jeans join the pile of clothes building on the floor, I hook my fingers under the hem of my boxers and look at her, questioning.

She nods as she slips off her own underwear.

We turn off the lights and slip under the covers, both of us bare. I do take a second to grab a condom out of my duffel bag. This is a new start. There's no air of desperation hanging over us like there was in the past. We're going to do things right this time.

Wrapping up in each other's arms, it feels like old times. We begin right where we left off. All those nights in the third-floor bedroom, holding one another, hanging onto the anchors that kept us afloat. I supported Jaynie, while she kept me from drowning.

Tonight, however, we allow ourselves to drown, in each other. We become lost in our love, a love that is unquenchable. I lose myself in Jaynie for the first time in months. Our love was sidetracked for a while, but I will never again allow that to happen.

I make a silent promise to myself, and to her. It's a promise to never again fail her, no matter what the cost. From here on out, today's promises will never again become tomorrow's lies.

No, today's promises will always be kept.

Flynn and Jaynie learn to adjust to their new life in Lawrence, while Mandy and the twins do the same in Morgantown, when the story continues in Today's Promises (Promises #2) ~ 2016

About the Author

S.R. Grey is an Amazon Top 100 and Barnes & Noble #1 Bestselling author. She is the author of the popular Judge Me Not series, the new Promises series, the Inevitability duology, A Harbour Falls Mystery trilogy, and the Laid Bare series of novellas. Ms. Grey's works have appeared on multiple Amazon Bestseller lists, including Top 100 multiple times, as well as Barnes & Noble #1 in Bestselling Nook books.

Ms. Grey resides in Pennsylvania. When not writing, Ms. Grey can be found reading, traveling, running, or cheering for her hometown sports teams.

Author Website: srgrey.com/

S.R. Grey Facebook: http://www.facebook.com/pages/SR-Grey/361159217278943

Sign up for S.R. Grey's exclusive-content newsletter and never miss an update, cover reveal, or release:
mad.ly/signups/106801/join

Follow S.R. Grey on Twitter: twitter.com/AuthorSRGrey

Find blog posts on the S.R. Grey Goodreads Author page:
www.goodreads.com/author/show/6433082.S_R_Grey

Follow S.R. Grey on Instagram:
instagram.com/authorsrgrey#

Read the prologue of *I Stand Before You*, the award-winning first novel in S.R. Grey's bestselling Judge Me Not series.

I Stand Before You

Prologue

Chase

I lean my head back against the headrest, crank the passenger window down the rest of the way. The June night air rustles through my hair, reminding me I desperately need a trim. I run my fingers through the strands, chasing the path of the breeze.

My grandmother likes to lecture that I shouldn't have hair sticking out at odd angles, strands curling at the nape of my neck.

"You're such a handsome young man, Chase," Grandma Gartner said just this morning, *tsk*ing when I sat down for breakfast. "You look so much like your father did when he was your age. But, you know, *he* always kept *his* hair short and tidy." And then there was a pause, a long, dramatic sigh. She set down a plate of eggs—over easy—in front of me. "My poor Jack. God rest his soul." My grandmother crossed herself.

Her poor Jack, my father with the short and tidy hair—dead and gone.

I thought: *I am not my dad, Gram. He failed us, he gave up on us.* But the words never passed my lips. And they never will. Hearing them would only hurt my grandmother's feelings and she's too good to hear the angry thoughts poisoning my polluted mind. So I keep all that shit locked deep inside.

This morning was no different. I kept things light, said something like, "The girls like my hair like this, Gram. Got to keep the ladies happy, ya know."

Then I ducked and waited for the inevitable swat with the dish towel. But it never came. Instead, the lines in my grandmother's face deepened.

"You don't need to be concerning yourself with keeping ladies happy, young man. You're only twenty. Messing with women at your age will only lead to trouble."

I knew what she meant this morning, and I know it now too. She's worried I'll end up getting some girl pregnant. Then I'll be fucked, well and good. But I'm always careful, take the necessary precautions. Besides, it isn't my womanizing ways that's becoming a problem. If only. No, unfortunately, it's my ever-growing dependency on drugs—something my grandmother would never suspect—that has me worried these days.

These days... Yeah, right. More like these blurry, fucked-up segments of time.

Sighing, I roll the window up just enough to lean my head against the cool glass. *What am I going to do?* I silently ask myself.

What I really need to do is get the hell out of this tiny Ohio farm town I landed back in two years ago. I'm spinning my wheels here in Harmony Creek, hanging with a bad crowd. Problem is I have no plan, no money either. Drugs are my escape and have been for quite a while. My priorities are all fucked up. My life, it's upside down. Every day it seems like getting high—and staying that way—is my only goal. I want to stop—believe me I do—but I don't think I know how to anymore.

A lump forms in my throat at this thought, but I swallow it down. "Hey," I say to Tate, who is driving. "Let's get out of this town."

Tate Cody, my friend…and my partner in crime in everything wild and crazy these days—women, drugs, drinking, fighting—you name it, we do it. And if we're not doing it nowadays, chances are we've done it at least once over the past couple of years. We've yet to slow down; we live on the edge.

I sometimes wonder when we'll fall.

"What do you think we're doing, Chase, my man?"

I take in and process Tate's reply, while he lifts a bottle of cheap gin to his lips and hits the gas. And for this one long, tortuous drawn-out second, I can't make a distinction between what I asked Tate and what I was only thinking. I panic, assuming my partner in crime's response is to let me know it's finally happening, we're really falling.

But then Tate adds, "I'm getting us out of here as fast as I can," and I breathe a little easier. He just means we're leaving Harmony Creek. Not falling, after all. *Shit, I need to ease up on the drugs.*

I glance out the window, and though it's dark I can see we're heading east, nearing the state line. Soon we'll be out of Ohio completely, and in the neighboring state of Pennsylvania. That's where we're supposed to hook up with two girls tonight. They're from New Castle, and we're meeting at a lake across the state line.

I don't really care about all that, though. What I'd really rather do is keep on going. Hop on Interstate 80 and clock the miles to Jersey. Better yet, Tate and I could go farther. We could drive our asses straight into New York-fucking-City. Now that would be sweet.

So while Tate barrels down a back road the police rarely patrol— until you get into Pennsylvania, that is—I pretend we're leaving Harmony Creek for good. No looking back, no regrets, just flying the fuck out of this lame-ass small town.

And speaking of flying, I'm flying a bit now too, feeling fine, baby, fine. I close my eyes so I can savor the s-l-o-w creep of numbness that cocoons me like a warm and fuzzy blanket.

I feel nothing, yet I feel everything.

My skin tingles a little, but when I touch my hand to my face it feels detached, like these parts of my body belong to two different people, neither of them me. That thought makes me happy, escape is exactly what I crave.

Needless to say, I've smoked—a lot—and not just weed. But it's the pills I swallowed a while ago that are starting to wrap me up and spin me the fuck out.

A bottle hits the back of my hand and my eyes fly open. Shit, I forgot I am not alone in this car.

"Drink, fucker," Tate urges.

I take the gin, despite the fact I can barely see straight. *No* isn't part of my vocabulary when I'm like this. And, sadly, more often than not, this is exactly how I am. This is who I am becoming: Chase Gartner, burgeoning drug addict.

As per most nights, Tate and I stopped at Kyle's before embarking on *this* night's little adventure. Kyle Tanner supplies us with more drugs than we could ever hope for. And the quality is always top notch. Kyle takes a certain kind of pride in dealing only primo product. But you'd never guess such a thing if you saw the rundown shithole he lives in.

Our dealer resides on the *other* side of town, over by the closed-down glass factory, in a clapboard house he shares with his meth-addicted dad. Lately, going there has been a contradiction of emotions for me. I love and hate concurrently when Tate and I cross over the railroad tracks that mark the end of the safe neighborhoods of Harmony Creek. Then, I vacillate between love and hate as I watch the Sparkle Mart grocery store appear…then disappear. I lean a little more towards hate when we reach the run-down apartment building where the junkies hang out, where their emaciated bodies lean lazily against the dirty brick exterior.

I sure as fuck don't want to end up there, God, no. But maybe I'm powerless to stop my downward spiral. Lord knows, by the time we start down the long dirt road that leads to Kyle's place, I crave and I want. And love trumps hate by that point. Even the junkies seem less scary. So we go…and we go…and we keep going back.

Tate tells me the road to Kyle's house is the road to salvation. *Salvation, my ass.* I'd be more inclined to say Tate and I are traveling a path to hell. We're in the express lane to damnation, and one step closer to burning every time we travel down that fucking dirt road. I know it, he knows it, but do we ever do anything to stop? Do we try to crawl out of the hole we're wallowing in? No, never.

In fact, Tate wants us to delve in deeper—start selling. He says we'll make, at the minimum, enough money to help pay for the copious amounts of shit we ingest…snort…smoke. Yeah, we do it all, everything short of needles. I somehow know if I ever cross *that* line, there will be no going back.

But I'm considering the selling thing, albeit for a different reason than my friend. Tate hopes to eventually make enough cash to buy his own wheels. He hates borrowing the piece of shit we're currently in—his mom's old, rusted Ford Focus. I just want to make enough money to buy a ticket out of this place. The little bit I earn painting people's houses, picking up construction work here and there—it's not adding up fast enough for my liking.

Hell, I still live at my grandmother's farmhouse out on Cold Springs Lane. Granted, I recently fixed up the little apartment above the detached garage, moved from a bedroom in the main house to an area not too much larger. But that little apartment provides privacy, and that's what I need. I am no longer a teenager, like when I first moved back two years ago. That's why I want, more than anything, to just get the fuck out of here. I'm thinking the money I make selling will make escape a reality, not just some pipe dream. No pun intended.

I raise the bottle of gin to my lips and tip it back. Alcohol heats my throat. "I think I'm going to take Kyle up on his offer," I say after I swallow the burn, the resulting grimace distorting my voice. "I need the money and it's going to take forever to earn it legit."

"You're making the right decision, my friend," Tate replies as he reaches over to take back the bottle.

Whoa... My vision turns wonky. There are three overlapping filmy images of my friend, and then just two.

"It's all about the numbers, man," two filmy Tates tell me.

I tell myself I need to slow down, and then I say to Tate, "That it is." I squeeze my eyes shut to keep from swaying in my seat. "That it is," I repeat.

The irony is that I once had money. Well, my family did, enough that my parents had a trust fund set up for me. Not a big one, mind you, but enough that it would've allowed for me to go to a decent college, get set up in a new city, shit like that.

I have no idea what my future holds nowadays, but I know it's been tainted by my past.

Back when I was around eight my parents moved from this town out to Las Vegas. My dad, who'd been successfully building houses here for a while, started a similar construction business out in Nevada. The timing was right, the stars aligned. We caught magic in the early days of the housing boom. Everything was golden and money poured in. It was happy times. For a while.

During those good times, Mom got pregnant. She gave me a little brother named Will that I still love like crazy and miss every fucking day. We used to talk on the phone all the time, but now I'm lucky if I get a two-word text from my little bro. I suppose when you're eleven years old—and haven't seen your big brother in two years—memories become a little hazy.

That's another thing the extra money from selling drugs will help with: I'll have enough funds to fly out to Vegas to see Will. Or I can just buy him a ticket to come here. As it is my mom, Abby, barely makes enough to get by out there.

But, like I said before, it wasn't always that way. In the early years, my father's construction company grew and thrived, so much so that I once entertained dreams of taking over the business. I used to imagine following in my father's footsteps, as sons are apt to do.

One afternoon, when I was about thirteen, I told my dad I wanted to build homes, same as he did. I showed him some sketches, just some basic designs and floor plans I'd thrown together. My dad was impressed. And not the false kind of fawning parents often try to sell to their kids. No, my drawings truly floored Jack Gartner. I could tell he couldn't believe his eldest son possessed that kind of crazy talent. He told me I should aim high, the sky was the limit. My sketches were incredible, he said, especially for my age. I could be an architect if I wanted, design skyscrapers even.

I had no reason not to believe him.

When you're thirteen you think you can have it all. Life hasn't roughed you up so very much…yet. At least it hadn't for me. So I told my father I'd do both—I would design the skyscrapers, and then I'd build them. My buildings would sell like hotcakes, and I'd be as rich as Donald Trump. No, richer even.

"The sky's the limit," I said, echoing my father's words back to him.

Dad smiled and patted me on the back.

Jack Gartner wasn't patronizing me, he truly believed in my possibility. "You have talent, Chase," he said. "Just don't ever lose yourself. If you can stay true to your dream…to who you are…then you'll do more than fly. Someday you'll soar."

Yeah, right. I sure am soaring at the moment, but I have a feeling this isn't what Dad had in mind.

Tate tries to pass the bottle back to me, but my mood has

dampened. The pills, along with the memories, are doing a fucking number on my emotions. I'm sad one minute, reflective the next, mad at everything, contemplative over nothing. I guess I am officially fucked up.

I push the bottle away, harder than necessary, and clear liquid sloshes over the side. "Asshole," Tate mutters.

"Sorry," I say.

Do I really mean it? No, it's just a word, an empty string of letters. Empty, like me.

I tune Tate out. I am high as fuck and lost in my mind. We idle at a swinging red light hanging over an empty, dark stretch of road, and I sit waiting on an imaginary red light in my head, one on memory-fucking-lane.

When I blink, both lights turn green...

My dad started taking me to work the summer I showed him the drawings. I learned how to wire a home, how to put in plumbing, how to lay insulation. And that was just the beginning. I used to watch how my dad talked to the guys. He treated them with respect, and in turn they went the extra mile for him. It was all "Yes sir, Mr. Gartner," "Consider it done, Jack."

When I turned fourteen, my dad bought me a drafting table, a bunch of fancy software too. The kind real architects use, or so he said. I practiced all the time, got pretty damn good. I was building my wings, you see, preparing to fly.

Will was only five, but damn if that kid didn't love to sit around and watch me sketch. For him, I'd draw all kinds of ridiculous structures.

"Dwaw me a house, Chasey," he asked this one day.

I laughed while I tousled his blond hair. I remember the fine strands looked so light in the sunlit room. Hell, they were almost white. "All right, buddy, what kind do you want?"

"A house like a tweeeee," Will sing-song replied, green eyes innocent and wide as he focused on the sketch pad I'd picked up from my desk.

I readied a colored pencil and asked for clarification, "Okay, a tree house, right?"

"No-o-o." Will shook his little head vociferously. "A house that *is* a twee, Chasey."

"Aha, got it," I said.

And I did. I drew Will a tree house shaped exactly like a tree, big, sturdy, loaded down with bushy branches. The leaves I shaded in the color of my brother's eyes. I sketched a door at the base of the trunk, then drew a Will-sized truck and parked it under a low-lying branch. After I finished with some final shading, I held the drawing up for my brother to see.

Will's house looked like one of those tree houses in the commercials with the elves and the cookies, only this one I'd drawn was far better. There was a lot more detail, and I'd drawn the tree in 2-D. In among the branches and the leaves all the rooms were in cross-section, done up in varying shades of blue, Will's favorite color. I also made certain every last blue-shaded 2D-room overflowed with toys.

Will threw his arms around my neck and told me he loved his *twee house*. Then, he leaned back and told me he loved *me* even more.

He gave me a kiss on my cheek. That shit always touched my heart, choked me up a little. "I love you too, buddy," was about all I could say as I held on to a little boy who meant the world to me.

Things are never bad when love is abundant. I thought it would stay that way forever, I did. A home filled with love, a happy family, just a good and easy life.

Man, was I ever wrong.

Shortly after I turned seventeen my world began to crumble. The bottom fell out of the housing market. The wave everyone was riding touched the surf and crashed. My dad's business was one of the first to fail. He had overextended himself; all our assets were mortgaged. He made ridiculous deals, attempting to keep us afloat, but his efforts proved futile. We sunk faster than a stone.

I sold the fancy architect software on eBay, the drafting table too. I gave the money to my parents, but it was merely a drop in the bucket compared to what we owed. I watched my once-vibrant dad turn into a shadow of the man he once was. My mom, always so young-looking and pretty, developed dark circles under her eyes—from crying, worrying, not being able to sleep. She even tried her hand at the casinos, we were that fucking desperate. But everyone knows gambling is a loser's game. The house always wins in the end.

One night, my mom was at one of those casinos. It wasn't the first time she'd spent hours and hours away, trying to win back what we'd lost. She came out ahead a little here and there, but it was never enough, never enough.

Will had fallen asleep early that night, so my dad and I were more or less alone. He asked me if I was hungry. When I nodded slowly, reluctant to reveal just how ravenous I really was and cause my father any additional undue guilt, he sighed, picked up the phone, and ordered a bunch of Chinese take-out.

I swear I smelled that food before the delivery man even pulled up to the house. Beef Chow Mein, General Tso's chicken, Hot and Sour soup, and eggrolls, the first real meal I'd eaten in weeks. And even though my dad and I had to sit on the floor—our furniture had been repossessed days earlier—I savored every fucking bite.

Afterward, my dad said he had somewhere to go. There was something he had to do. Would I keep an eye on Will?

"Sure," I told him while shoving white take-out cartons with little metal handles— leftovers I'd saved for Will and Mom—into the fridge.

With my father gone, I had nothing to do. Our TVs were gone, the stereos too. Video games? Forget it. Those were among the first things to go. So, I wandered around the house barefoot, padding around on neglected hardwood floors. I trudged from one empty room to the next.

Then I took a minute to look in on Will.

My little brother slept on an air mattress in the middle of his now-barren room. The *twee house* sketch, the only thing left on his four stark walls, had fallen. It lay abandoned on the floor, close to Will's hand, close to where his little arm was dangling off the side of the mattress. To me, it looked as if my brother was subconsciously reaching for the drawing. Three years had passed since I'd drawn Will's tree house—and I'd sketched hundreds of other things for him since that sunny day—but that particular piece of made-with-love art was still my brother's favorite. I think to him it symbolized something more. He'd once said my sketch gave him hope. I guess it reminded him of when things were good.

I stepped into his dark room and picked up Will's hope. I kissed the top of his head and gently placed his *twee house* next to his sleeping form. I made my way back down to the living room, feeling solemn and too fucking worn for seventeen. Tears welled in my eyes, but I refused to let them fall. *Hell with that shit.* The paper bag that had held the Chinese food was still on the floor. Frustrated, I kicked it out of my way. A fortune cookie shot out and landed at my feet. I picked the projectile up, ripped the plastic covering off, and slid a tiny piece of paper from the confines of the cookie.

The fortune stayed in my hand, the cookie ended up in my mouth.

Truthfully, I was still hungry. Crunching away and savoring sugary goodness, I read the words on the little slip of paper I held between my fingers.

As I stand before you, judge me not.

It sounded a little hokey and I almost threw the fortune away. But there was something about those words that made me hesitate, something almost prescient. I ended up folding the little piece of paper in half and tucking it in to my pocket. Maybe I needed some symbol of hope just like my brother. I knew the things happening in my life would eventually define my future, and I guess I hoped no matter what occurred those things wouldn't ultimately define me.

My mom came back later that night, but my dad never did.

Jack Gartner had gotten on route 160, heading west to California. But he never made it out of Nevada. His car was found at the bottom of a ravine, below what the officers who came to our door to break the news termed *a treacherous curve*.

Killed on impact, we were told.

Did he lose control, or drive off the road on purpose? Maybe his plan all along had been to leave us and start a new life in California. That's what my mom believed at the time. Still does, in fact.

I, however, am not so sure. My father didn't pack a thing. Sixty dollars and a cancelled credit card, that's all he had on him. I think my dad just gave up. He quit on us, and that was the way he chose to end it. My mom can delude herself all she wants, but I know in my heart that I'm the one who's got it right.

Anyway, the bank took the house soon after my father's death. My mom sold off what little was left. For a while, we became nomads in the desert. We lived in the only big-ticket item that hadn't been repossessed, a white minivan. The Honda Odyssey was home… until Mom won enough money gambling to move us into a cheap apartment. Our new residence was a dump, but at least it had running water. And it was furnished. Kind of.

When we first stepped across the threshold and Mom caught me scowling at the rusty fixtures, the water-stained ceiling, the musty olive-green carpeting, she tried hard to convince me our new place had its good points.

"Like what?" I asked.

"It's close to The Strip. That'll be convenient."

"Convenient for who?" I sniped. "You?"

"Chase," she said pointedly, "it's better than living in a minivan."

She had a point there, so we moved in the next day. Will's first reaction was to run straight to one of the two back bedrooms and hang up his tattered *twee house* sketch. I followed him and watched as he stood on a soiled mattress on the floor—in a shoebox of a room we were going to have to share—and pinned hope on a wall.

After we were settled, time, as it does, marched on. Will and I attended school, while my mom—still fevered and sick with the gambling virus—spent her days in the casinos.

I turned eighteen that April. But no one really noticed. Well, Will did. Not much got by that kid.

He stuck a candle he found in the back of a drawer in the kitchen on a stale snack cake. He made me sit on the only kitchen chair that didn't rock when you shifted, and then he placed the snack cake on a card table we used as a kitchen table.

Will sang me the most beautiful off-key and from-the-heart rendition of "Happy Birthday" that I have ever heard, before or since. When he was done, I leaned forward to blow out the candle. Will stopped me and told me to make a wish first, so I did. And then I blew out the candle. Will clapped and cheered. He asked me what I wished for and I told him it was a secret. I didn't want to tell him I wished for him to be given a better life than what we were, at the time, living. My brother and I split the snack cake in two, dinner for the night, and ate in contemplative silence.

Summer arrived that year and I somehow managed to graduate. But—with my trust fund long gone—college was no longer on the table. With no real guidance, and a lot of pent-up frustration, my downward slide took hold. I was angry all the time, and ended up getting into too many fights to count. The places in Vegas where I'd started hanging were tough. Early on, I got my ass kicked…often.

But then something happened.

I learned how to use my strength, my quickness, *and* my anger.

I started to win. I had a real knack for fighting and rapidly turned into a badass nobody messed with. I earned street cred. All that really meant was guys started showing me respect and girls suddenly wanted to have sex with me. I happily obliged more than a few of the latter.

But all that shit meant nothing, I was empty inside. I had no one to talk to about the mixed-up emotions I didn't know how to deal with. Like, why was I so angry all the time? Why did I like to fight so much? Why did it feel so good to make someone else hurt?

But mostly I wondered why I missed my dad so much.

I missed talking to my father, seeing his face every day. I had relied on him, I still needed him. But he was gone. He took his own life. Why couldn't I just accept what had happened and forget him?

But I couldn't, and, worse yet, I longed for answers.

Every day, for a while, in my quest for enlightenment, I'd grab the bus outside our apartment and visit my father. Well, I'd visit his grave. At the head of where my father rested eternally, I'd sit under a big stone angel kneeling by his grave—thankful for the little bit of shade she offered under the hot, beating sun of the desert.

Sweaty and lost, I'd ask her if she could tell me why my dad wasn't still alive. Why had God allowed Dad to take himself away? Why did my father choose to leave me? Why would he leave Mom and Will too? Was our love not enough for him? Did he regret his decision when he realized there was no going back?

Of course, the stone angel had no answers, and one day I just quit going. No more sitting in the shadow of the angel, no more hot and beating sun. No more asking questions that could never be answered.

My trips to the cemetery were over, but that didn't mean I wanted to forget that *someone*—even though he'd left—had once believed in me. Despite everything, I still loved my father and part of me yearned to be just like him.

So, July of that year, I had his angel's likeness—the stone one at his grave—inked in profile on the middle of my upper back, between my shoulder blades.

I shift in the passenger seat now.

I can almost feel her back there, watching over me, like my dad's angel watches over him. And like his angel, mine is kneeling. The edges of her heavy robe lie in a puddle of fabric around her. Her wings are folded against her back. Her hair is long, obscuring the side of her face. And her head is bowed. In supplication or in shame, I haven't decided which. But if she's been watching the shit I've been doing these past two years, it's probably in shame.

After the angel tat healed, Mom hit for more money. I successfully talked her into paying for another tattoo, guilted her into it really. In any case, I ended up with big, intricately detailed wings inked up and over my shoulder blades. The top feathers curve onto my shoulders, while the wings dip down the sides of my back, effectively framing the angel.

But the angel and the wings weren't enough. I wanted something more to remember my father, something to remind me always of that final night, when it was just him and me, eating Chinese food on the floor of an empty home, a last supper shared.

I kept coming back to the cookie, the fortune inside, the hope it symbolized.

As I stand before you, judge me not.

Words printed on a piece of paper, but really they were so much more. So I had those words inked—in concise and script letters—around my left bicep.

My tats were but temporal attempts to heal my soul, as my heart remained an open wound. There was no solace to be had at home. In fact, things were getting worse. I started to drink and do drugs to ease the pain and fill the void. I hated what had happened to our family. Seeing Will transformed from an energetic little boy to a sullen nine-year-old left me sad and frustrated. And watching my mother try to heal her fractured heart with gambling—and eventually men—just pissed me the fuck off.

But at least Mom wasn't indulging in one-night stands like I'd been doing. Nope, Abby actually went out on dates. Still, her attempt at dating led to a revolving door of boyfriends. Some lasted a week or two, some a little longer, but the one common denominator they all shared was that not a single one liked me.

Mom told me to try harder, give these guys a chance for her sake. I laughed and told Abby her men could blow me. "Chase, don't be crude," was her response.

By the end of the summer Mom hooked up with what turned out to be steady boyfriend number three. I was no fool; I immediately sensed my days were numbered. I would've had to have been blind not to see the writing on the wall, a wall I didn't realize I was hurtling toward. But it wasn't just Abby's lame new boyfriend disliking me that was a problem. There was something else, something she'd never admit to. There was no escaping it though, not really.

I saw Abby's problem every day when I looked in the mirror.

Standing in a cramped and steam-filled bathroom, hot water running, can of shave cream poised in hand, I couldn't deny the truth in front of me. I'd swipe at the misted mirror with my free hand, leaving it streaky, but mostly clear. And it wasn't me I saw in the reflection, it was my father. That's how much I looked like Jack Gartner, even at eighteen. And *that* was my mother's real problem.

Shit. Even thinking about it now—two years later—fucks with my head.

I glance over at Tate. He's quiet, taking long pulls from the bottle. I shift in my seat and wind up the window the rest of the way. Time to assess my bleary reflection, time to compare it to what it was, time to compare it to the man who made me…I sometimes do this just to fuck with myself.

When I take in my reflection, I laugh. Hell, the resemblance is still uncanny. And just like when I used to stare at the steamed-up mirror in the bathroom, it's my dad's eyes staring back at me now. But these pale blues are all mine. Yeah, *his* whites were never shot with red like mine.

Still, even with the bloodshot eyes, similarities far outweigh differences. Though it's not *short and tidy*—like Grandma Gartner would like it to be—my hair is the exact same shade as her son's once was, light brown. Jack also blessed me with his straight nose, his square jaw, and his defined cheekbones. Everyone used to say my dad was good-looking, I guess I am too. Girls seem to think so, that's for sure. And my mother sure was smitten with my dad.

Abby used to lean across the front seat of the sporty car my dad bought for himself during the good times. Will and I would be in the back, rolling our eyes at each other. My mom would kiss my dad, making him swerve a little as he drove. She'd tell him he was gorgeous, and that she loved him. Dad would laugh and tell Abby he loved her even more. He'd say his love for her burned hotter than the Vegas sun above us. My mom loved that shit. Will and I, however, would groan in disgust and make gagging noises.

Shit, I feel like gagging now. Not because of the memory, but at how closely I still resemble my dead father. I turn away from my reflection. I can't bear to endure this self-inflicted torture any longer. No wonder I was fucking sent away. Too bad I couldn't disappear completely just as easily right now. Guess, in a way, that's why I live my life the way I do, filling it with drugs…sex…violence.

Back then my very presence in my mom's life must have been a constant reminder of all she had lost. When you're striving to move on, you don't need an anchor to the past. She could move forward with Will, he was just a kid. Besides, he looked like her, not like my father. But I was eighteen, an adult, and far too much my father's son for everyone's comfort. I guess it was just too difficult for Mom to look at me—see *him*—and be reminded of all she'd once had.

So the day steady boyfriend number three, a guy named Gary, told her she could move in with him, I kind of fucking knew the invitation wouldn't be extended to me.

Sure enough, on a blistering hot afternoon, my mom sent Will out to ride his bike and told me we had to talk. She sat me down on the ratty couch in our shitty apartment. I felt like a condemned man waiting to hear his fate, and all the while the noisy air conditioning unit in the window behind me kept blowing gusts of lukewarm air across the back of my neck.

Not that it mattered. I barely noticed. I was mostly numb. In preparation for this "talk," I'd done a couple of lines of coke in my room. Of course, I hadn't brought that shit out until after Will had left. One thing I stuck to was that I never let my little brother see me taking part in any of my newfound vices.

Anyway, that day in the living room, I couldn't sit still. Fidgeting, fidgeting, tapping my foot. Mom took no notice, she was almost as bad. Pacing back and forth in front of me, smoking a cigarette, a new habit she'd just acquired. Gary smoked, so she'd picked up the habit too. *Pathetic*, I remember thinking.

My mother appeared so edgy and wired I almost asked her if she was dabbling in drugs, like me, or if what she had to say was really just that fucking bad. She started speaking before I ever got the chance.

"You're not a kid anymore, Chase," she began, still pacing, ashes peppering the olive-green carpeting.

She took a drag, crinkled her brow, and leaned over to stub her cigarette out in a plastic ashtray on a low table.

"You have to get started on doing something, somewhere, kid," she said as she spun to face me.

She stood right in front of me, and though my head was down I watched her every move. She blew out a breath and I watched her dark blonde bangs lift up off her forehead. A few strands stuck to her skin. Mom was starting to sweat.

"So, Grandma Gartner called the other day," she continued, her words deliberate, pointed, like a knife. "She said she's got lots of room in that old farmhouse back in Ohio. And she sure could use some company."

I looked up at her in disbelief. This woman who'd given me life tried to smile, but she could not. She knew damn well she was spewing pure bullshit. She just wanted rid of me.

"Just spit it out," I ground through clenched teeth, my voice far from even.

"Okay, of course, honey." She looked everywhere but at me. "Uh, so, Gram thinks moving back to Harmony Creek might do you some good, get you out of Vegas, give you a chance to start over, and—"

"Mom, I'm only eighteen. Start over?" I blew out a quick breath. "I haven't even had a chance to get started *here*."

Her expression grew stern. "Chase, don't act like I don't know the things you do behind my back." I tried to protest, but she shushed me. "I know you use drugs. I know you bring girls back when Will's not around. That shit isn't going to fly once we move in with Gary. He won't stand for it, Chase. He has standards—"

I snorted, "The fuck he does—"

"I'm not going to argue with you about it," she said, her voice tired and cracking.

When she reached for her pack of cigarettes, I noticed her hands were shaking. "Honey, I just think Grandma Gartner's is the best place for you right now, okay?"

I picked at a hole in my jeans. "Do I have a choice?" I asked, defeated, and, truthfully, feeling like I'd just been set adrift.

She shook her head no.

I'd known it was coming, but her words still flayed me up the middle and pierced my already damaged heart. I was shocked that my heart could continue beating, since it felt all smashed to hell. But beat it did. In fact, my heart pumped faster and faster, like it was going to burst right out of my fucking chest. Whether my reaction was from cocaine…or despair…I couldn't quite figure.

With my heart pounding like a sped-up death knell, I tried to push some words out of my cotton-dry mouth. "Mom…" I croaked, my voice catching.

I just couldn't finish.

Verbal communication failed me, so I tried to meet her eyes, speak to her soul. Was this really what she wanted? Send her eldest son away? Give up on me? Just like Dad did with all of us.

I searched and searched, but my mother had no answers in her big green eyes, no more than the stone angel had at my father's grave.

Abby took in a stuttered breath and turned away. She swiped at a tear. "It's for the best, Chase," she mumbled.

And then she left me sitting there, all alone, warm air blowing across the back of my neck.

I went back to my room and cut up three more lines.

That was nearly two years ago and here I am. Mom is still in Las Vegas with Will, on steady boyfriend number six, last I heard. She's still chasing the elusive jackpot too, hoping to recapture the life she once knew.

Good luck with that, I think bitterly. *Jackpot, my ass.* If anyone needs to hit a fucking jackpot, it's me.

Suddenly, drug-induced visions of flashing pots of gold swim lazily into my head, along with some break-dancing leprechauns, and I can't help but chuckle.

Tate looks over. He must think my mood has improved, 'cause he starts talking all excitedly about how much money we're going to make from our new business venture with Kyle. I listen to his voice, not really hearing any words, but then the cell buzzes and I am alert, very alert.

Tate tosses it my way. "That there would be the ladies," he says—

all smooth like—as I catch the cell with one hand. Even impaired, my coordination is impeccable.

"Ladies, my ass." I roll my eyes.

Tate laughs, knowing as well as I do that the two girls we're meeting up with tonight are no ladies. They're looking for the same thing we are, but therein lies the beauty.

"What's it say?" he asks, nodding to the cell.

The text is kind of blurry, but, then again, everything is. I blink a few times and my vision clears. When I read it out loud, I mimic a high-pitched girl's voice, just to be an ass. "Crystal and I are almost at the lake. Come prepared. Tammy. Laugh out loud, winking smiley face."

"Dude-e-e." Tate shoots me a knowing sidelong glance. "You know what *come prepared* means, right? You got that covered, yeah?"

As reckless as I am—and that's pretty fucking reckless—I always make sure I wrap my shit up. Better safe than sorry. But as I feel around in the pockets of my jeans I realize I've left the condoms at home. "Fuck," I mutter.

The blue *Welcome to Pennsylvania* sign looms ahead, our headlights flashing off the reflective letters.

Tate asks, "What?"

I rake my fingers through my hair. "I forgot the goddamn things at home."

"Not a problem. We'll just stop at the convenience store across the state line."

"Bad idea," I counter. "Cops are always hanging out in there. You think they won't notice how fucked up we are?"

"How fucked up *you* are," Tate corrects, laughing. "I didn't smoke nearly as much as you."

"You smoked plenty," I mumble under my breath.

But Tate is right, I smoked more. And Tate smoked only weed. Plus, my friend didn't see the pills Kyle slipped me before we left.

Still, I nod to the almost-empty bottle. "You pretty much drank that whole thing, dickhead. You'll never pass a field sobriety test."

"Yeah, but I don't plan on taking one, my friend. And, I hide it better than you." He shrugs. "Trust me, I got it covered. Just wait in the car. It'll only take a sec."

Tate's always confident like this. He can talk anyone into just about anything. I always tell him he's a natural-born salesman. Maybe if we ever get our shit together he can do something legit using his smooth ways. It's cool, it's Tate's thing, and it helps make him popular. He's an okay-looking guy—brown hair, brown eyes, kind of skinny—but it's his smooth talk that gets him in with the girls. They eat that shit up.

We cross the state line, turn into the convenience store. No cop cars. "See, we're good," Tate says, still as confident as ever.

I flip up my black hoodie hood and slouch down in my seat. "Just be quick," I mumble.

Tate hesitates, and I know something is up. "What the fuck are you waiting for?" I ask.

He begins his sentence with "Don't be pissed—" and I cut him off right away, hoping I won't have to kick my good friend's skinny ass. It would be a damn shame really, since Tate wouldn't stand a chance against the likes of me. I am way bigger and far stronger, and the rage within me has no match.

"What?" I spit out, clenching my jaw.

Tate ignores my attitude; he's used to it. "I kind of need you to hold on to something while I go in there. Just in case."

"Just in case of what?"

I am running out of patience. I scrub my hand down my face, wary to hear what Tate the salesman is up to now.

He smirks, and I tell him to knock that shit off, save it for the "ladies."

"Okay, okay." He raises his hands in mock surrender. "I may have kind of asked Kyle to give us a little something to get our entrepreneurial gig started."

"Us?" I say, feeling the anger rise up. "You didn't even know I was going to sell with you until about ten minutes ago."

"What can I say, man." Tate places his hand over his heart. "I had faith."

"Whatever."

I try to stay pissed, because what he did was really out of line, but my anger fades fast. High as I am, these strong emotions are too fucking slippery to hold on to for very long.

Tate hands me a plastic packet filled with little pills, a rainbow of color. "Jesus." I know all too well exactly what this shit is. "X? You're fucking higher than I thought. We're supposed to start small, bitch. Move a little bud, see how it goes."

Tate shrugs. "We'll make more money this way. Like, I know we can sell to the girls tonight. Hell, I bet we can talk them into buying *our* hits."

He's laughing at his own ingenuity, but I ignore him. I'm too busy trying to count the pills in the packet. But being in the condition I am in, it's a bit of a challenge.

"How much is this anyway?" I ask, giving up on figuring it out for myself.

"Twenty hits," he tells me, and then he has the balls to throw another packet in my lap. "Make that forty…maybe a little more."

"You're fucking crazy. If we get caught, Tate, this isn't possession. This is possession with intent to sell."

"That's why I'm leaving the shit here with you."

"Oh, that's real fucking cool." Back to being pissed, even my high can't calm me now. I whip one of the packets back at Tate. "I am so not getting caught with forty hits of Ecstasy, asshole."

"Calm down, man." He gingerly picks up the packet I've just thrown and holds it out for me to take back. "If a cop shows up just hit the road."

"What about you?" I ask as I grudgingly accept the X.

Tate grins. "Don't worry about me. You know I can play it cool. Just swing by after the heat's gone, and we'll be back in business."

"The heat? What is this, the seventies?" I ask, laughing, but Tate's already out the door.

I tuck the two packets of Ecstasy into the back pocket of my jeans and think nothing more of it. Until a few short minutes later when a state cop pulls into the lot. Then, I panic.

I start climbing over the console to get the fuck out of there, but, suddenly, with every fiber of my being, I know I've just made the dumbest mistake of my life. That, however, doesn't stop me from slipping down into the driver's seat, throwing the car into reverse. I hit the gas, peel out of the parking lot, and leave a cloud of gravel and dust in my wake.

I've got the Focus up to eighty, music playing…loud, loud, fucking blaring. Maybe I can outrun this cocksucker? I'm tapping my hands on the steering wheel along with the beat, flying so fast it's amazing I don't lose control and crash.

But I don't, I stay steady.

I even make it a good five miles down the road before a cop heading my way—backup, I'm sure—screeches to a wide arced stop in front of me. His patrol car blocks the entire road, so I have no choice but to hit the brakes and squeal to a halt.

My car ends up parallel to the cop car, both of us straddling the lanes, engines idling like we're in some fucking action movie. The air reeks of burning rubber, and smoke billows around us. The speakers beat out a song from 50 Cent that is frankly ironic at this point.

When all the smoke clears, the sign for the lake is right smack dab in front of me. I can't help but laugh. The shit situation I'm in, and all I can think of is that Crystal and Tammy are out there, waiting, for two boys who are never going to show.

Two more cops—including the one from the store—pull up

behind me. I pitch the door open, tumble from the seat. I hit the warm pavement and try to stand. Someone yells, "Hold it right there, hands on your head."

I hear guns being drawn, cocked. This isn't a movie, I know they're loaded. I squint to try to see what's happening, but all the flashing lights leave me blinded. Before I can think another drug-muddled thought, someone tackles me from behind. My face smacks right into the yellow center line, but I don't feel a fucking thing.

Whoever tackles me yanks down my hood, frisks me, and comes up with my wallet. Oh, and the forty hits of X, of course.

It's all ambient noise from that point on, but I do hear, "Chase Gartner, you're under arrest."

I have no idea that, despite the altered state I'm in, these will be the last coherent words I will remember for a very long time.

****

The time following has no sense of structure. Days, weeks, they all blend together. I'm in jail, facing a long, long list of charges. But it's the X that has me fucked.

Bond is set high. I call my mom, but all she does is cry. Like, these horrible wailing sobs that do nothing but make my head ache more than ever. She keeps apologizing for not having the money and swears she'll help me when she can. I hang up. I won't be holding my breath. The past has taught me not to put too much stock into Abby's flimsy promises. Mirages in the desert are what they are—get too close and they disappear.

My grandmother wants to mortgage the farmhouse, all the property around it. We're talking a good fifty-five acres. It'd be enough to make bail, but I tell her *no way*. She's done enough for me already, and look at how I've repaid her. I don't deserve her money… or her love.

So I'm on my own. And not thinking very clearly. Once all the illegal shit is out of my system, I find myself in a constant state of agitation. I can't sleep, I barely eat. I sweat bullets even when it feels like I'm freezing.

Eventually all that passes, but then all I want to do is fight. Like beat heads in. It's worse than when I was back in Vegas; I feel so much more fucking rage. I sit around clenching my fists, hoping for a chance to kick some poor unsuspecting soul's ass.

Finally, my wish is granted.

They throw a cellmate in with me and my ass is on him like an animal, beating the hell out of this never-saw-me-coming sap. But then two guards see what I'm doing, pull me off the bloodied and broken man, and promptly return the favor.

Another blur of pain.

This one, though, I welcome. The medical staff gives me plenty of drugs, legal ones this time. And still more before I am put before the judge.

Even in the sedated fog I float around in, I quickly learn the law… and some new math.

MDMA, Ecstasy—X, as I like to call it—is a schedule I narcotic, and carries as stiff a penalty as heroin if you're caught dealing, which they naturally assume I was. Casual users don't tote around forty-plus hits of Ecstasy, but dealers do.

I say nothing one way or the other to dispel their myth, I rat no one out. I just stay quiet and accept my fate.

My math lesson continues…

Ten pills are equal to one gram, and I've been caught with over forty pills. Forty pills equal four grams, which is more than enough to be charged with possession with intent to sell. But I already knew that part, right?

My lesson isn't over though. It's only just beginning.

I learn in Pennsylvania, the state in which I've been apprehended, four grams can easily earn you a prison sentence. This is especially true when you don't have enough money to hire a good attorney. Add to that, your public defender isn't getting paid enough to care. Not that you're doing much to help the overworked, underpaid man do his job. And, oh yeah, don't forget that one prior arrest for fighting last fall. It didn't seem like much at the time, but it sure haunts your ass now.

Are you keeping up?

Some final math…

Four grams buys you a six-year sentence at a state correctional institute when you have no resources, and, really, no heart to fight it.

Twenty years of age feels like ninety when your freedom is stripped away.

It takes one hundred and forty-three steps to walk down a long, noisy corridor to reach cell block seventy-two.

And when they turn the key, you hear one life—the only one you've ever known up until now—ending.

"It's all about the numbers, man," as Tate would say.

It sure is, my friend. It sure is.

Printed in Great Britain
by Amazon.co.uk, Ltd.,
Marston Gate.